Dan Fesperman

The Small Boat of Great Sorrows

Dan Fesperman is a journalist for *The Baltimore Sun* and
served in its Berlin bureau, covering Bosnia-Herzegovina,
Croatia, and Serbia during their civil conflicts. He won the
John Creasey Memorial Dagger Award for *Lie in the Dark*.
His latest novel, *The Warlord's Son* is available from Alfred
A. Knopf. A graduate of the University of North Carolina
at Chapel Hill, he grew up in Charlotte, North Carolina,
and now lives with his family in Baltimore, Maryland.

ALSO BY DAN FESPERMAN

Lie in the Dark

The Warlord's Son

The Small Boat
of Great Sorrows

A NOVEL

Dan Fesperman

Vintage Crime/Black Lizard
Vintage Books
A Division of Random House, Inc.
New York

For Emma and Will,
the chairmen of the board

Awesome symbols, the Crescent and the Cross;
their kingdoms are the realms of graveyards.
Following them down the bloody river,
sailing in the small boat of great sorrows,
we must honor the one or the other.

From the Serbian epic poem
The Mountain Wreath
PETAR PETROVIC NJEGOS, 1847

The Small Boat of
Great Sorrows

Prologue

Eastern Bosnia

When they came to arrest the general he was polishing his boots, an orderly man to the very end. At least that's what the soldiers would tell the debriefers and reporters, having found the boots on the bed with a blackened rag, the smell of polish still strong in the air.

Earlier that morning it had rained, and when the soldiers first assembled in the trees some two hours before dawn the general was asleep. Lulled by the wet drumbeat on his bunker roof, he dreamed of marching, watching a nocturnal parade pass before him—his men, their men, everybody's men, it seemed, the dead and the wounded among them. They wore bedclothes, he realized with a start, and their feet stirred clouds of dust that coated their skins in chalky gray. He wanted to look away but couldn't, hypnotized by the tramping feet, row after row of everyone he had ever commanded or fought.

Then the rain on his rooftop slackened. The sleepwalking legions faded. And when the tinny alarm on his watch sounded a few minutes later, at 5 a.m., the general awakened with the taste of dust sticky in his mouth. He climbed from the bed craving water, drinking straight from the tap, as if he were bivouacked in the field, crouching at some farmer's spigot.

The gray light of the mirror revealed a drawn face with bags beneath the eyes, deep creases framing loose jowls. Stubble everywhere. With luck it would be a full beard within a week, though he couldn't say for sure, never having grown one. He had a high, jutting forehead, peaking with a thick shock of gray in need of a trim, brushed straight back and smelling of the pomade that forever scented his pillow. But the most striking feature was his gray-blue eyes, as clear and cool as stones in a stream, eyes that could convey either rage or resolve without a word being spoken. "Command eyes," one colonel had called them, and they had watched dozens of offensives come and go before the guns had fallen silent nearly three years ago. It was only later, in the calm of peacetime, that people in other places had decided that his army had exceeded the rules—rules made in their lands, where no one knew the fears and histories that ruled his. And somewhere, he knew, in some room with maps and charts and file drawers stuffed more richly with information than any order of battle, others were still fighting his war. They were still assessing his movements and commands, clucking and shaking their heads, exercising a calm reason that one never had time for in the midst of battle.

He remembered the heat of those five days that were now the subject of such scrutiny, the hardness of the roads on soles worn thin by four years on the move. Cicadas roared in the spiky underbrush while his men forded the thickets of scrub and low trees, calling out to one another, and to the enemy, too. The town in the eastern valley, so long a problem, had finally fallen, months of stalemate bursting like a worn belt in a tired engine, and during the first night thousands of the panicked foe had broken through to the forest, becoming a long, sinuous column in the darkness. By morning they were running, a herd cut loose with only fear to drive it, and his army joined the chase as if it were a hunt, the rattle of gunfire nonstop.

The cleverness of his men had astonished him, a rustic ingenuity blooming in the elation of pursuit. Some donned blue helmets—the trademark of the UN "peacekeepers"—luring the skulkers from the trees by shouting through loudspeakers, pledging protection, food, water, a bed to sleep in. Others drove hospital trucks slowly down country lanes past patches of woods, beckoning the wounded out of hiding. We will heal you. We will save you. Give yourselves up and end the struggle. It worked more often than he would have believed.

The roads were dry. There was nowhere to fill your canteen, and the dust was so heavy that by nightfall of the third day he and his men were coated, ghostly in its whiteness. Too weary to wash, they slept where they halted and swallowed dust in their sleep, and by morning it was the taste of death itself, so they rinsed and scoured with shots of brandy, passing bottles down the line. They grew giddy with the flush of alcohol and the promise of another easy chase; more fighting that would help bring this war to a close. Destroy a hundred of their sons and you saved a hundred of your own. It was an old formula, closed to debate. With any luck they would shut down the bastards for a generation. So they moved back onto the roads and into the trees, clipping their ammunition into place, a sound to get your blood going.

Late in the final day a messenger arrived with new orders, and the general took fifty of his best men to an empty factory six miles to the rear. The torn innards of its machinery sat rusting on high grass out front, and the big building echoed with voices, a hollow sound leaking from high windows. Hundreds of the enemy were inside, stragglers and quitters, men and boys, eyes lit by fear and exhaustion. The general strolled indoors, and the stench nearly gagged him, all the sweat and shit and grime mixed with the factory smells of metal and machine oil. The noise was unbearable, too, like the keening of newborn calves. A cordon of his troops stood on one side of the walls next to large sliding doors while an officer in a black beret walked the general to the opposite end. They climbed a catwalk raised on a steel frame, draped with pulleys and chains, and as the general rose into view the crowd's noise seemed to rise with him, a swell of echoes appealing incoherently for his mercy.

"Listen to them, General Andric," the officer in the beret shouted above the din. "They must think you're the lord high executioner."

The general looked the officer over, scanning the pockmarked face. The man stank of brandy, and a belt of ammunition was draped across his torso like a sash, a risky stunt done only for style. The raked beret was smudged brown across one side. Popovic, his name was. Branko Popovic. A freelance, accountable to no one. The man did know how to fight, after a fashion. He could secure a village, clean it out, and keep moving, and you knew that nothing from that quarter would ever threaten your flanks again. But his methods were, at best, unorthodox, and the general kept his distance when he could, although lately that had become difficult. To his way of thinking, their fortunes had become far too enmeshed.

The crowd quieted after a minute or so, the men jostling as they sat or squatted on the oily floor, spent from five days in the heat. Sunburned faces turned toward him as if he were about to deliver a speech, and he looked into the eyes of a few, seeing sons and fathers, the rough hands of plowmen and hay balers, the flab of shopkeepers. Boys who needed scolding and a firm hand.

For a moment he wavered, and Popovic must have sensed it, for the man was suddenly bobbing at his side, gun at the ready. Colonel Popovic, it was, though God knows where the rank had come from. There was nothing about either the man or his unit that said "regular army." The deep scars of acne and the croaking voice. Two days earlier the general had seen him in a burning village with a column of laughing men, their arms full of stereos, televisions, bottles of whiskey. Some hauled bulging sacks across their backs like Father Christmas, cheeks powdered by the unceasing dust.

"Take them now, sir, and we'll never have to fight them again," Popovic urged. "Let us finish it, sir."

The general wanted to laugh at all of the "sirs," as if suddenly Popovic considered himself a real soldier, and this was their usual way of fighting. For the slightest moment the man's insolence was more distasteful than the thought of the rabble at his feet. But the orders were clear, so he nodded without turning, not giving the man the satisfaction of verbal acknowledgment.

The men below must have been watching for a sign, because they began standing, eyes rolling, panic taking hold. Fathers clutched at their boys, and the wailing resumed. The younger men shoved, going nowhere in the crush of bodies. Then an officer shouted, Popovic perhaps, and the shooting began, close and rapid, with no place for the bullets to go but into the meat and the filthy clothes, the shrieking roar and clatter of all that death locked beneath the low metal roof.

Most of the general's memory of the moment had gone fuzzy. All that remained sharp was the image of a single face—some farmer or laborer who happened to stand out from the crowd for a split second, his mouth opened as if gasping for breath, then overflowing suddenly with blood, chin covered in red, a gargle of anguish. Everything else was unclear, a miasma of sound and stench. But his memory of the dust remained sharp, and he still tasted it every morning as clearly as if he'd swallowed a spoonful each night before bed.

The general ducked beneath the faucet for another drink. Then he rechecked his watch—5:08. Timing was important. He mustn't be late, of course. That would be the end. But acting too early might be fatal as well. He strolled to the high window, the one he always kept open no matter the season, anything to rid the room of the damp concrete smell of a prison. The sky was clearing, moonlight beaming through the tall, slender pines like searchlights. Nothing stirred but a cow, slumped low against a dim bank of underbrush. Even his sentries were quiet, their usual bee buzz of conversation stilled for a change, although he could smell their cigarette smoke, could hear the chirp of a lighter.

He gazed at the stars, seeking omens in the deepness of the sky. There was no light from any of the houses in the valley, yet he sensed their presence, the red rooftops that climbed the gentle slope like a tile footpath. He inhaled deeply, smelling turned earth, the resinous bite of the pines.

At times like these the general found it easy to imagine the hills were enchanted, a place where mere farmers and peasants slipped their skins by night to become ogres and knights, gliding into the trees to joust and thrust in secret, writing new chapters in the lore of the forbidden. There were treasures in these fields and forests, for those who knew where to look—old bundles in oilcloth, dormant beneath cabbages and pumpkins, or concealed in the darkness of stables. So much that was buried, not just in his valley but in all of them—plots and secrets just beyond reach of memory. Wait long enough, perhaps, and the moonlight would lay everything bare, melting the cover as if it were snow, at least until morning, when all would again be concealed in the white light of dawn.

But a soldier would grow old and die waiting for the moonlight to do his work. And old soldiers didn't die, he mused, nor did they just fade away, as the arrogant American had so famously said. They simply grew slow and fat awaiting the judgment of history, listening alone for the knock of the verdict upon their bunker doors.

Not him, the general thought, as sure of himself as ever. Not him.

CHAPTER ONE

November 1998

Down in the mud of central Berlin you never knew what you might find. Last week it had been an American bomb, as long and fat as a giant bratwurst. A poor fellow from Poland poked it with a shovel and the whole thing went up. Five more fatalities for the casualty lists of World War II, courtesy of a B-17 that hadn't flown for half a century.

Then there was the corpse, or the skeleton, rather, that rose from the ground on the yellow teeth of a backhoe. Probably nobody famous. Just a Russian from 1945 who never made it home, judging by the buttons, the boots, and the rusty helmet. Two efficient men in sport coats and ties hauled him away in a black plastic bag.

Barbed wire turned up, too, on this landscape of accidental archaeology, but that was of a more recent vintage, left by the East Germans in the path of their long and formidable wall. And sometimes when Vlado Petric trudged through the ooze, he pondered all the German shepherds that had patrolled this narrow strip of land, day after day, year after year. Plenty of their leftover shit mixed in the mire, he supposed, and for all those reasons he spent ten minutes at the end of each workday cleaning the waffled soles of his boots with a screwdriver, prying loose the mud. It was the richest sediment of twentieth-century misery the world had to offer, and he had no wish to track it home. He'd tramped enough to his doorstep already, nearly five years earlier, as one of the hundreds of thousands of Bosnians who'd escaped their own war for some quieter venue across Europe's sagging theme park of history.

So, when Vlado and Tomas Petrowski mounted backhoes Monday morning to dig into the muck of Potsdamer Platz, they knew there was always a chance they would unearth some history, even though they were construction workers, not archaeologists. They were the merest of drones, in fact, two among thousands on a landscape that Berlin's boosters were billing as the world's largest construction site. Not since Albert Speer unrolled his blueprints for Hitler had the city witnessed such architectural hubris, and tourists with nothing better to do could pay a few deutsche marks to climb the stairs of a red building on stilts at the heart of it all. Indoors there were photos, maps, and charts to see. But the real attraction was out in the elements atop a switchback of corrugated metal stairs. It was a high viewing platform where you could stand in the wind and rain to marvel at it all, to watch the city be transformed from the inside out, as if an alien spaceship had uprooted a massive highrise shard of downtown Dallas, and dropped it onto the belly of Europe.

If you stood there that Monday morning with a set of binoculars, you might have picked out Vlado and Tomas as they went to work, marching toward their backhoes, almost emulating a goose step as they picked their way through the slurping ooze, yellow hard hats bobbing. They were a few hundred yards from the green edge of the Tiergarten, Tomas a short and stubby Pole with the golden hair and beard of a Viking, Vlado of medium build and measured expression, clipped dark hair above deep-set brown eyes, a face that strived mightily to give away nothing. Each wore jeans and a flannel shirt bought from the battered metal stalls of outdoor markets on a gray Saturday morning, and each knew how lucky he was to be working for twelve D-marks an hour, with all the right papers and documents to make it legal.

Neither spoke the other's language, but both spoke enough German to grunt and nod their way through a day on the job. Their task was simple enough. Other men drove stakes and markers into the ground, then Vlado and Tomas dug trenches and holes between them, generally working straight through until lunch. At noon they carried brown bags to benches in some damp birch glade of the Tiergarten, as calm and green as an Alpine meadow, then ate their sandwiches and apples, watching rucksacked legions of young Germans glide past on bicycles.

But this morning, if you'd been patient with your binoculars up there on the viewing platform, you might have noticed an interruption in their routine, shortly before ten, when they shut down their engines and dismounted.

Tomas had found something.

The jagged mouth of his backhoe had struck a slab of buried concrete, and out here that meant you'd made a discovery. The rules were clear on what to do next, and both were careful about knowing the rules.

"Who's going to tell them?" Vlado asked in his halting German.

Tomas shrugged. Somewhere in the warren of trailers where the supervisors sat was a keeper of old maps who could put a name to what they'd found. And somewhere in a ministry nearby, in a room with rolled yellowed charts bearing faded swastikas, there was an authority on this subterranean history, an expert in naming and classifying every hibernation chamber where men in gray had once hunkered down for defeat. He was always the one who decided how to proceed, and so far his decisions had never varied: Rebury it and keep building.

"Maybe it is not something to report," Tomas said, knowing as the words left his mouth that he was wrong.

Vlado's answer seemed to take them both by surprise. "I think maybe you're right. Let's make sure it's worth reporting. Let's investigate."

A half century earlier such disobedience would have earned each of them a bullet in the head. Now, labor rules being what they were, the consequences would scarcely exceed a tongue-lashing as long as everyone's immigration papers were in order. Few Germans would work for these wages anymore, no matter how high the unemployment rate, which is why thousands of Poles, Irishmen, Scotsmen, Russians, and others streamed every morning to this grand amphitheater of mud. Bodies had become too valuable to spare on this front line, especially with companies like Sony and Daimler waiting eagerly to move in.

So, Vlado and Tomas climbed aboard their machines and went back to work, grinning as they heaved and shoved at the earth to expose more of the slab, fighting down a panicky sense that they might be stopped at any moment. Within an hour they uncovered the top of a door. An hour later they reached the bottom, and by

1 p.m., having forgotten about lunch altogether, they'd completed a sloping trench that would let them reach it on foot. It was then, with stomachs growling, that they finally shut down their engines and dismounted again, sweating in the cold, stunned by the sudden silence.

They glanced around to make sure no one was watching, then descended the mud passage and pushed against a heavy steel door—once, twice, then a third time, ready to give up until it began groaning open against the concrete floor. Leaning with their shoulders, they pushed it further ajar, the air issuing from it like the stale breath of a tomb. Then, breathing rapidly, they stepped into the damp chill of May 1945.

Vlado flicked his cigarette lighter to reveal a mural on the opposite wall, as bright and fresh as if it had been painted the day before. The flickering light played across the faces of rugged SS men, dapper in pressed uniforms, standing watch over blond wives and blue-eyed children, a sunny tableau of Aryan comfort for this gray day in November.

Vlado and Tomas might well have spoken, but their new language tended to fail them at moments like this, as if they'd misplaced the manual for some particularly unwieldy tool. But both knew they'd gone far enough, and Tomas strode off to fetch the foreman. Vlado waited in silence, wondering what sort of ghosts might yet lurk in a place where the concrete walls still smelled wet and new after half a century underground.

He took a deep breath, then, flicking his lighter again, walked across the floor into a second room, where he found a row of low iron beds with thin mattresses. Steel lockers lined the opposite wall, but Vlado's eyes were drawn to a yellow-and-black inscription on the door, a lightning-bolt insignia of the SS. Above the door were German words in Gothic script. It took a second for him to translate: THERE ARE MANY PEOPLE, BUT FEW GOOD MEN.

Vlado stepped slowly, as if there might be someone asleep just around the corner. None of the noise from above could make its way down here, and he felt a weight on his chest, a change in air pressure, or perhaps it was all in his head. His flannel shirt was damp with sweat, cooling against his skin.

There was one last room, and he stepped inside. It was emptied of furniture, with a mural on the wall, only this one was a map, a meticulous paint job of the Nazi empire at its zenith. Germany lay at the center in red, her spidery borders encompassing Austria and Czechoslovakia and half of Poland. Beyond it, slanting red stripes covered captured lands—Hungary, Scandinavia, Belgium, and the Netherlands, as well as much of France, the Soviet Union, and the Balkans. He found his own land, the old name "Jugoslavia," and, to the upper left, "Kroatien," for the puppet fascist statelet of wartime Croatia, its borders encompassing most of what was now Bosnia. His home city merited a black pinprick, and he touched the careful lettering for "Sarajevo," the concrete chilly, its surface just bumpy enough that he could imagine the mountains themselves were beneath his fingertips. How odd to feel a stab of homesickness from this map of conquest, yet, if he closed his eyes, he knew he would see old women in kerchiefs and long *dimije* skirts scuffing down dirt lanes, bent men in wool caps seated atop mule carts piled with hay, wheels creaking. For the most part Vlado had been raised a city boy, but farms and villages were always only a valley away, and they were the places that called to him now. Strange, he knew, especially down here in this well of captive darkness. Enough to make him feel like a homesick old peasant who'd never been five miles beyond the milking shed.

The sound of a voice made him jump. A column of chattering men was approaching the door down the slope of the muddy trench, and he retraced his steps to the bunker entrance just in time to see a foreman in a hard hat squeezing through the opening, looking hurried and embarrassed, chattering rapidly in German, loud voice going hollow as he entered. Accompanying him was a tall, balding man in a suit, shod in Italian loafers caked with mud. Tomas was behind them, looking scolded, saying nothing. The second man unrolled a blueprint in the beam of the foreman's flashlight, everyone's breath misting in the ancient air. The man needed merely a glance before he found what he was looking for. He poked at an upper corner of the map while shaking his head slowly as if disappointed in them all.

"Ja," the construction boss said. "Hier." And from their expressions Vlado gathered this was a well-known place.

"Der Fahrerbunker," the man in the suit mumbled.

"*Führer*bunker?" said the foreman, eyebrows raised in panic. He looked ready to flee.

"Nein, du blöder Idiot! *Fahrer.*"

Drivers, in other words. Chauffeurs. This had been the home for the SS men who drove around the generals and the chiefs of staff. But with nowhere left to drive in the springtime rubble of 1945 they had mostly stayed here, awaiting the end. Vlado had heard of the place. It had been unearthed a few years ago and resealed, lest it become a shrine for neo-Nazis. This was not the sort of tourist attraction the locals wanted in the heart of the new Berlin.

"Bury it," the man announced in German, rolling up his blue-print with a disdainful flourish. "And next time," he said, eyes aimed straight at Vlado, "come to me before you go this far. We already knew of this place. There was no need for all this."

They plodded back to the surface in single file, Vlado reluctantly. He had wanted to stay a while longer, not just to poke among the relics but to get a handle on the climate, the atmosphere. Such readings seemed important when you had recently lived through two years of a siege, with death dropping from the sky like cinders from a chimney. He and his neighbors had somehow made it through, subsisting on the world's handouts of bread and beans—two winters without heat, two years without electricity or running water or glass for your windows, coffee for your breakfast, salt for your food, soap for your bath, candles for your darkness. Two years without a wife and child to keep you company. And down there in the bunker he had suddenly seemed very close again to the feel of those lonely nights, to the mood of a city where even a funeral became an invitation to gunfire from snipers who might have once called to you by name.

Surviving that qualified him as something of an expert on man-made disaster, he felt, and what better place to take comparative readings than in that damp hidey-hole. Check the barometric pressure, the relative humidity. Collect the motes of dust. How could you possibly draw such air into your lungs and not be changed in some small way, and who knew where that might lead?

Or maybe this was just the wishful thinking of a man who, for all his joy and relief in escaping a war and rejoining his family, ached to return home, or, at the very least, ached for change. Four years, ten months, and counting in this land of flat horizons, doing work that numbed him to the bone. The mountains of home had begun to seem like something out of a dusty old atlas, a fairy tale of a place, with all its crabbed problems snagged in the creases of the hills.

But as the foreman departed, Vlado felt a giddy sense that perhaps change was in the works at last, that a day already so different from all the others would only become more so.

Within an hour they had regraded the mud into a neat, level surface above the bunker. Then other workers poured a layer of new concrete, the foundation of yet another high-rise. Vlado and Tomas watched in chastened silence as they belatedly ate their sandwiches, marking the location by other points of reference, mapping it in their heads for posterity. No matter what rose here, they'd always know what lay underneath, like a dormant cell of some once virulent plague.

So this is what becomes of the ruins of war, Vlado mused, staring at the wet concrete, and he wondered if his home in Sarajevo had already been torn down and rebuilt in his absence. Or his favorite café. The house where he'd grown up. His office? That would be fine, considering the way so many people in it had ultimately betrayed him. Then he thought of friends, some of them dead, and of a woman he had barely met yet whom he felt he knew quite well. And as he sat on a curb to clean his boots in the gathering dusk, he took extra care in removing the day's mud. Then he brushed off his hands and walked a half mile to the long stone platform of the Unter den Linden S-Bahn station. He boarded a rattling commuter train for a forty-minute ride to the eastern reaches of the city, out to where, if you kept walking, the plains would take you all the way to the forests of Russia.

By the time he reached his stop it was dark, and it took a brisk twenty-minute stroll to reach a tall, gray high-rise where he rode an elevator to the eleventh floor. He opened a door at the end of the corridor to find an American in a suit waiting for him on the living room couch.

CHAPTER TWO

"He has been here for an hour," Jasmina whispered quickly as Vlado shut the door behind him. "I've made coffee twice. I ran out of things to say twenty minutes ago."

She was flushed, wiping her hands briskly on a dish towel. Their daughter, Sonja, was nowhere to be seen. Across the room on the couch, the American visitor put down a German magazine and looked toward them expectantly.

"Did he say what he wants?" Vlado whispered. "Who he's with?"

"Nothing but small talk. Family and jobs and the lousy German weather. Said he's here on business and left it at that."

The man's gray suit said government, but nothing else did. He was all elbows and knees, folded into place like a jack-in-the-box, and on closer inspection even his uniform wasn't what it had seemed. The suit was wrinkled, the shoes were scuffed, the tie was knotted with the slapdash skill of a groom late for his wedding. His face was impassive, probably as intended. But the eyes gave him away—an expressive gleaming brown, lively and eager. If he had a tail, it would be wagging, and Vlado wondered why. And why an American?

The authorities, both national and international, had long since lost interest in Vlado following his sudden arrival nearly five years ago. He had shown up unannounced at an American military base in Frankfurt on a cargo plane from Sarajevo, spilling from a wooden crate like the misloaded parcel he was. As a homicide detective who had smuggled himself out of a sealed war zone with a sheaf of incriminating documents, he had been something of a sensation at first. Not the sort that made headlines—just the opposite, in fact, for the results of his work had been an embarrassment for more than a few international agencies. So, he had attracted various men in gray from miles around, fretting over what secrets might have been blown, who might have been compromised, whose credibility might need to be rebuilt.

Just about everyone had wanted to hear the story he'd unearthed, a tale of theft, smuggling, murder, and corruption that might have been impossible to believe if not for the packet of evidence in his satchel.

He'd been debriefed by everyone who seemed to count in this part of the world—the UN, NATO, the Council of Europe, Interpol, and half the embassies in Germany. Protocol demanded that the Germans go first. Then came a tag team of Americans and French, arguing loudly over who had precedence. Next came the British, the most polite but somehow the most frightening, with the cool clipped manner of executioners. The parade seemed as if it would never end, and everyone spoke the careful language of damage control.

Some played it friendly, offering cigarettes and jokes. A short, jolly American talked Yugoslav basketball for a while, biting off half his questions with inappropriate giggles, lunging forward every time he came to a key point. Vlado, who knew a thing or two about interrogation, figured the man was probably proud of his style. The ones who weren't good at it usually were.

The French and Germans were icy, unyielding, seeming to frown at his every word. An intense chain-smoking German named Rolf kept asking about another German named Karl, who, judging from the line of questioning, must have been a Balkan smuggler of some success. Pleading ignorance of Karl only earned a raised eyebrow from Rolf, followed by an unconvinced smirk and a slow release of cigarette smoke.

The whole thing lasted four days, hours on end in a small, windowless room under a cool blaze of fluorescent light. Mornings brought lukewarm coffee in chipped mugs that left sticky rings on white Formica. Cold lunches arrived on a wobbly cart. Then more questions, followed by a bland, overcooked dinner and a night of poor sleep in a steel-frame bed down the hall. A guard outside the door turned the pages of newspapers throughout the night while Vlado tossed in his sleep, trapped in dreams of long walks through ravening crowds, awakening exhausted and sweating to the knocking of a radiator before the whole business started again. He could only guess what the fallout had been back in Sarajevo—a few less bureaucrats to worry about, perhaps, but probably little else.

In the end, the Germans deemed him unsuitable for repatriation—too many enemies on both sides, especially in the middle of a war, when it would have been too easy for someone to kill him. Besides, it turned out he had a family already living in Berlin. They'd been there for two years, in fact, a wife and daughter who were evacuated during the first month of the war. So the authorities did the easy and humane thing by letting him stay, and sent him packing to Berlin with a train ticket, a residence visa, and a work permit. Later he would discover just how rare and valuable such documents were when the Germans began sending home every Bosnian refugee they could find.

But for all their care with paperwork, the authorities never bothered to inform his family that he was on his way, or even that he had escaped. For all Jasmina and Sonja knew, Vlado was still back in their besieged apartment, biding his time until his next monthly phone call to Berlin, still braving the bombs and the bullets. Which is why when he showed up on their doorstep on the eleventh floor, fresh off the train, he'd been something of a shock, making for an awkward moment or two.

Since then the international authorities had forgotten him. There hadn't been a single visit, letter, or phone call, either to thank him or to let him know what had occurred in his wake. It was as if he'd been dropped into one of the holes at Potsdamer Platz.

Until now.

The American opened his mouth to speak.

"Herr Petric?" he said.

"Vlado Petric. Yes. And please, speak English. Mine is a little out of practice, but it is still better than my German, Mr. . . . ."

"Pine. Calvin Pine."

Pine stood, tall and bony, reminding Vlado of the big construction cranes that loomed above him at work, like praying mantises in search of a meal. Being an American, Pine smiled and held out his right hand for a firm shake. The only people who grinned more in this part of the world were Japanese tourists. But the smile at least had a glimmer of mischief at the corners, a boyishness that made it hard for Vlado to feel put upon. His light brown hair was as stiff as broom straw, with various sectors in revolt. And when he spoke, at least he kept his voice down, unlike the noisy Americans you saw rattling down Unter den Linden in bright clothes and running shoes, shooting videos of everything that moved, griping about exchange rates and whatever they'd just paid for lunch.

Vlado wished he'd had time to clean up, wished he'd shaved that morning, wished he hadn't just stepped from a huge, muddy hole in the ground. He wondered what sort of impression he must be making.

"You're from the embassy?" he asked.

"Actually, no. From The Hague. The war crimes tribunal. I'm an investigator."

Vlado knew of only one matter, a single name, that could have brought the tribunal to his door, and it had nothing to do with his work back in Sarajevo, where the criminals he'd dealt with were smugglers and black marketers, commonplace murderers intent on money, not ethnic slaughter. All he knew of the tribunal he'd learned from a Bosnian in Berlin, someone whose name he didn't wish to utter just now—someone, it now appeared, who had gotten him into deep trouble. If that was why Pine had come, this would be an unpleasant evening indeed, for Jasmina as well as himself.

"Why do you need to speak to me?" Vlado asked, knowing he must already sound like a suspect. Probably looked like one, too, reaching for his cigarettes and staring at his feet.

Pine seemed to note the change. He paused briefly before plowing ahead. "Because we need your help. We've got a job we think you might be interested in."

The answer was a pleasant surprise. Vlado glanced toward Jasmina, as if she might offer a hint of what came next, but she only shrugged. "I'll make more coffee," she said. "And Vlado, why don't you ask our guest to sit. You've both been standing for the past five minutes. You look like gunfighters in an American Western."

Vlado translated her remark for Pine, who grinned and folded himself back onto the couch. He had that American way of informal amiability, the salesman's knack for banter, for easing into his surroundings. As they sat, Vlado saw Sonja peeping around a corner.

"This is my daughter, Mr. Pine," Vlado said. "Sonja, who I haven't even said hello to yet."

He coaxed her out with a smile, but she wasn't yet ready to forgive Pine, who had taken her usual spot on the couch. It was where she and her father always sat at this hour to read, and she held a storybook in her right hand.

"We'll do that later," Vlado whispered, switching to his native tongue. "Go on now. I'll come and get you."

She turned, casting a parting glance of cool appraisal toward the couch.

"She's nine?" Pine asked.

"Just turned it."

Pine had learned that either from Jasmina or from a file, and Vlado wondered uneasily what other information he'd dug up.

"Oh, and one bit of housekeeping," Pine said. "Before we continue, I have to ask that you keep the details of our meeting entirely confidential, no matter what you might decide to do. For reasons of operational security."

So here it comes, Vlado thought, worried again.

"I suppose I can agree to that."

"Good. In that case, how would you like to go back to work? Real work, I mean. Police work, like you used to do. A temporary job only, I'm afraid. But it could lead to something permanent, if you decided that's what you wanted."

Vlado tried not to show his relief, lighting a cigarette then offering one to Pine, knowing the American would probably refuse.

"No thanks. Don't smoke."

"Investigative work? I hadn't heard you were short of help at the tribunal. And it's not like I could just pull up and move to The Hague, if that's what you're saying. But what exactly are you saying?"

"You wouldn't be working at The Hague. You'd be going back to Bosnia. Only for a few weeks, at the most. Then, later, for good. If you wanted." Pine glanced toward Jasmina in the kitchen. "Which you'd have plenty of time to think about, of course. And we'd help with resettlement. Housing. Plus a regular job, doing what you did before. Investigations. In a jurisdiction that would actually be glad to have you."

"But not working for the tribunal. That part would only be temporary, as you said."

"Yes. A one-time job, I'm afraid."

This got stranger by the minute. Vlado wondered which police jurisdiction in Bosnia would actually be glad to have him, or if such a place existed. Pine wore a little smile, as if sharing an inside joke about the way that Vlado had left things in Sarajevo. There was no sound from the kitchen, but Vlado sensed Jasmina's presence just beyond the doorway. She'd be listening with her mouth set firmly and her hands still, wondering what was about to happen to the little world they'd made in Berlin, which, on balance, was comfortable enough. Safe enough, too. If there would be a problem in taking this assignment, Jasmina would be the reason. Like many Bosnian women strewn across Europe by the war she had somehow blossomed on the barren soil of abandonment, spreading shallow but hardy roots in an unwelcoming land. Vlado had seen it happen in plenty of these families, the women picking up confidence while the menfolk, suddenly adrift, wandered and drank, sliding off toward melancholy and dreams of home.

"Maybe we're not too eager to go back," Vlado said for her benefit. "And maybe you'd better tell me a little more about this one-time job."

Jasmina had moved to the kitchen door, wearing an expression that let Pine know she wished he'd never come. Vlado, however, was transformed. The sagging man of ten minutes ago was now edging forward in his chair.

"Of course you'd always be free to stay here, once our work was done," Pine said, perhaps playing to his audience in the kitchen. "The Germans have assured us of that. And either way you'd be well compensated. If you took the assignment."

Vlado blew a cloud of smoke toward the ceiling. These past few years he had tried to think as little as possible about his old line of work. Burning your bridges and nearly getting yourself killed can have that effect. But it wasn't hard to recall the buzz of putting together an investigation, peeling away the wrappings until you found the prize at the center or, sometimes, found nothing at all. Guessing and arguing with colleagues as you went, like scientists waiting for the smoke to clear in a beaker. That sort of business seemed a long way from here, another distant land with its own hills and valleys, and he'd pretty much given up hope of returning.

He sighed, already sensing the weight of a decision. If his life was about to pivot, he hoped he had the energy for it, the resolve, and he recalled his sense of premonition from earlier in the day, down in the bunker. Walk through a door into 1945 and this is where you came out—into a room where a tall American arrived bearing gifts, offering to usher you back through another door you hadn't entered in years.

"Maybe you had better tell me about this assignment."

Pine looked awkwardly around the room. "I'm afraid your wife will have to leave first. Some of this isn't supposed to go beyond you and me. Not for now, anyway."

"It's all right," Jasmina said briskly, striding past with a tight smile. "I'll go read to Sonja."

They waited until they heard the door of the girl's room snick shut. Sonja, who'd been eavesdropping from the hallway, complained noisily at the injustice of it all. Vlado and Pine looked back at each other, leaning forward with forearms propped on knees, a hint of conspiracy in the air.

"There's a suspect we want to bring in," Pine said, almost in a whisper. "Have wanted to for some time. A Serb general, Andric. Heard of him?"

"Yes. From the massacre at Srebrenica. His name comes up around here now and then. All their names do, if you talk to the widows. And going after him would only make more widows. He's protected. It would be suicide."

"Which is why we're letting the French army do it. He's in their sector and they've promised to take care of it. He'll be their first arrest, but at least they'll be starting off with a bang. After two years of letting him drink coffee right under their noses, of course."

"That's a pretty big deal if you get Andric."

"It won't be easy. Especially when the French like to think Belgrade still has a soft spot for them. The timing's tricky, too. Bad time to go stirring up Serbs, with Kosovo ready to blow sky-high next-door. But that's where we come in. We provide the consolation prize. A suspect from the other side—a Croat from the American sector—

to help balance the scales a little. Unofficially, of course. That way the Serbs don't feel so singled out, which helps keep the French happy, diplomatically speaking. And if the French stay happy, maybe they'll go after more suspects for us, further down the road. But our part of the deal looks a whole lot easier than theirs, 'cause our man's been out of action for fifty-five years."

Vlado knew right away where that kind of math led. "A suspect from the Second World War?"

"Yes. From Jasenovac. Heard of it?"

"I should think so."

It was like asking a German if he'd heard of Auschwitz. In the Balkans, Jasenovac was the darkest stain of the Second World War, perhaps of any war. It was a concentration camp where, depending on whose history you were reading, anywhere from 20,000 to 600,000 people had died—Jews, Gypsies, and Muslims, for starters, plus a few thousand political dissidents and assorted others from Hitler's roster of "undesirables." But the great majority of the victims had been Serbs, killed not by the Germans but by their local collaborators, the ultranationalist Ustasha, a faction of Croatians ruled by puppet dictator Ante Pavelic. All of which explained why the death toll was still a matter of debate. In that war the Croats had been the reigning villains. In the latest one, the Serbs were the ones with the bloodiest hands. And in both conflicts, bitter ethnic arguments had at times masqueraded as scholarly debate over body counts and degrees of cruelty. Depending on your ethnic vantage point, Jasenovac was either the great blot of Croatian guilt or the overblown lie of Serbian propaganda. The outside world had pretty much settled on the former version.

But if the death toll remained in doubt, there was nothing ambiguous about methodology. The killings at Jasenovac had been brutal and blunt, a crude Balkan antidote to German industrial precision. The locals had done things their way, using bludgeons, knives, axes, and pistols, often employing an inordinate amount of time. It was a genocide of gouging relish that had shocked even the Nazis, whose officers had huffily written Berlin to complain about the barbarity. Not that their letters did any good. Hitler seemed to like the idea of an ally willing to show some initiative. Besides, even the local Catholic church had tacitly endorsed aspects of the project, with the priests and bishops of Zagreb lining up in support of the new regime.

"Of course I've heard of it," Vlado said. "My mother's Catholic. She was more interested in religion than nationalism, so she was always ready to admit that Jasenovac was something horrible. Her parents were a different story. Her father put me on his knee to tell me all about the lies of the Serbs before I even knew what a Serb was. He'd point to Orthodox priests in their beards and black frocks as if they were vampires who'd just stepped out of a tomb. I used to have nightmares about them snatching me in my sleep. But mostly it sounded like a lot of old people getting too worked up over things that didn't matter anymore. Then the shells started falling in '92, and I realized maybe I should have paid closer attention."

"You and everyone else with any sanity. Well, the fellow we're after can tell you all you'd ever want to know about Jasenovac. Ran a guard unit there, right in the thick of things. There's an interesting file on him back at The Hague. You'll be reading it soon enough, I hope."

"I'd be more interested in finding out how he managed to avoid being caught after the war."

"That's not a bad tale, either. Up through Austria and into Italy. Hid out at farms and monasteries awhile. Then a DP camp, a big holding pen for displaced persons, before he ended up in Rome. Stayed in Italy more than fifteen years, with a lot of help from some church people, a bunch of Croatian priests who ran a little operation on the Tiber. Ever heard of the ratline? Laundered Western money paying for forged documents and freighter rides to Argentina. Seems that the Brits and we were already more worried about Stalin than a few leftover Nazis. We figure he made his way back to Yugoslavia in 1961. Living under a new name and doing okay for himself. These days he's a pretty successful businessman. Gas stations. Beer and liquor. And still pretty active. Lately he's been winning economic-development grants from the European Union. Brokers stolen cars on the side."

"Then why do you need me?" Vlado asked. "This one sounds solved. Sounds like what you need is an armed escort. A bodyguard. You've got a name for it in the States, I'm sure."

"A marshal, you mean, or a process server. Yeah, we could use a few thousand of those. It's generally not our job to pick these guys up anyway. Ever. Then again, we're not really supposed to be handling cases from the Second World War, either. I guess you might say all of it's a little unorthodox, or even off the books. SFOR is who normally picks up our suspects—the peacekeeping forces—but they usually say no thanks whenever we ask. They like to keep things quiet, not stir them up. But this guy's in his seventies, off in a backwater. His security's decent, and he's pretty careful, but if our plan works, using force shouldn't even be an issue. And that's where you come in."

"Meaning?"

"You'd be working undercover. Posing as an expat Bosnian who's just returned, which will be true enough. You'd carry in the bait. Lure him out in the open where we can pick him up with as little fuss as possible. Preferably at his favorite café. That way he comes along nice and quiet so nobody gets hurt, as we like to say."

"Why an expat? Why not a real local? Buy off somebody from his village who he'd really trust." Vlado realized he might be talking his way out of the job, but the strategy didn't add up. "In fact, I'd say you've got a few million locals to choose from without flying me anywhere, or a few thousand, even if you're just talking about policemen. One of the local constables would probably do it for a few cartons of cigarettes."

"The local constable is one of his top cigarette distributors."

"Which I should have guessed," Vlado said with a smile. "You can tell I've been away from home too long."

"Look," Pine said, "let's just say we have our reasons. Good ones. Some of which we can't get into right now because of security considerations." It was a line that immediately put Vlado on his guard. But Pine quickly moved on. "Another reason is the bait. It has to come from an outsider, but one with some local connections, and you're the perfect match."

"What's the bait?"

"A demining concession. Mine removal. He's been wanting a piece of the action for a while."

"Doesn't sound like the most desirable work in the world."

"You'd be surprised. It's lucrative business. Everybody and his brother wants a piece of it. Warlords, crime lords, mayors, police chiefs."

"Which covers at least two people in every municipality."

"You got it. But in this fellow's case, he's always stayed out of local politics, unless you count the bribes and the vote fixing for some of his buddies."

"Forgive my ignorance, but how much money can you make digging up a few hundred mines? Or even a few thousand?"

"More than you'd guess. There are millions floating around. Some of it's UN money. Some is from the EU. The rest, from various international do-gooders. Think of Princess Di. This was her pet cause. That made it glamorous, so now you've got donations from all over, well-meaning people handing it out wherever someone will take it. And if you're the top local contractor for your area, you can usually pocket about half the grant for yourself, then pay the rest to a bunch of poor dumb farm boys who'll work for cigarettes and a few D-marks. They dig 'em out the old way, with sticks and crowbars. Hand tools. Every week or so somebody gets blown to pieces, but so what. The boss has his cut, and the locals have a little hard currency and a big funeral with two lambs on a spit. And guess who gets to keep some of the unexploded mines if nobody's paying close enough attention to your demolition program?"

"Ah. Lots of money, and free weaponry, too."

"Which is why the UN has been wary about giving our man a piece of the action. But you'll be arriving as his guardian angel, the new EU representative for demining operations in his region, with a slick new business card that will knock his socks off. He'll figure that since you're Bosnian, he might finally get an even break, because you'll know how to do business the way he likes."

"With payoffs and kickbacks, you mean."

"Something like that. But you'll learn everything you need to know in debriefings at The Hague."

"What's his name, this suspect?"

"Sorry. Still classified. Everyone and his brother knows we're after General Andric because his indictment's four years old. This indictment's sealed. We don't want to risk tipping him off and having our little bargain fall apart at the last minute. But he's no one you've heard of, that I can guarantee."

"A location, then?"

"A small town in central Bosnia. Sorry. That's as specific as I can get for now."

"And you, Mr. Pine. You're an investigator yourself?"

"A lawyer, to be exact. I'm what the prosecutor's office calls a legal officer, working with a team of about a dozen investigators, plus a military-intelligence guy. I do some interrogations, a little fieldwork, then usually I'm cocounsel when cases hit the courtroom, the one who can connect all the dots. But if you look at the last line of my job description, which my boss did just the other day, there's also something about 'undertaking such special assignments as may be required.'"

"Which makes it sound like you'd rather not be here."

"Let's just say I already had plenty on my plate involving the here and now without spending a few weeks on World War Two. And let's just say this could all get kind of tricky if something gets screwed up. Which is why you really can't be talking about this."

"What did you do before the tribunal? Your job back in the States."

"I was an assistant U.S. attorney. Drug cases mostly. Part of a DEA task force for a while. Mostly young American thugs, with the occasional South American and Nigerian for good measure. Sort of like working on an assembly line. Which is why I volunteered to come over here. A little like you, I guess. Another reclamation project a long way from home."

But did Vlado wish to be reclaimed, especially if it meant going back to police work in a country where the economy had gone to hell and half the population was still nursing a grudge? It was the sort of work that tended to turn honesty into a game, a series of bargaining sessions between integrity and expedience. If you weren't careful, you soon found yourself slapping backs and buying rounds with all the wrong people.

Nor was he yet convinced this invitation didn't have at least something to do with what he'd gotten involved with here, a role that made him feel guiltier by the minute. So much for his reputation as the clean cop. He'd have to check a few things for himself before he could say yes. He would also listen to what Jasmina had to say. They could wait until later to decide on whether to move back, because that would be the tough part, the part with the arguments and the tears, no matter who prevailed.

His gut told him that he wanted the assignment, and if spending a few weeks back in Bosnia cost him his construction job at Potsdamer Platz, well, there would be other holes in the mud to dig, in other parts of town that led to other regions of the past.

Pine stayed for dinner. It went without saying unless Vlado and Jasmina wanted to violate every law of Balkan hospitality. They talked shop for a while, swapping tales of old colleagues and cases, stories full of humor and language that had to be edited for Sonja's ears. Vlado cleared the dishes while Jasmina put Sonja to bed. The girl had stared sullenly at Pine throughout the meal.

Vlado and Pine were relaxed, both sensing that, even without an official answer yet in hand, their immediate futures were decided, and that it was time to begin getting used to each other's company. Vlado uncorked the obligatory bottle of slivovitz—plum brandy—and the drinks flowed as they spoke of families, friends, and others they remembered on the distant landscapes of home.

Pine said his father was an *advokat*, a lawyer working in a small town in the American South.

Vlado's had been a foreman in a machine shop. Metalworking. Could do anything with tools. Made the equipment sing but never said much himself. He'd let his work do the talking.

"Still alive?" Pine asked.

"No. He died fifteen years ago."

"And your mother?"

"Two years later."

"Did your father fight in the war? World War Two, I mean."

"As much as most people did, I guess. It was that or hide in a root cellar. He was with some volunteers, although it never came to much. There really wasn't much fighting where he grew up, so it was lots of digging trenches and guard duty. Some marching through the woods at night and lots of time being hungry. There wasn't much room for a Muslim in that war, which is one reason he seemed to be one of the few who didn't try to make it something more noble than it was. When I was a boy I used to resent that, especially after hearing other fathers brag about what heroes they'd been. Now I realize it was a virtue. It was the lying that got everyone in trouble in the end."

"Well, good for him, then." Pine raised his glass. "He was from Sarajevo, too?"

"Farther south and west. Podborje. Small village in the hills toward the coast. Rattlesnake country. After the war he couldn't find work, so he moved to Sarajevo. They lived in a small valley a few miles from the city until I was about six. From then on we were in the middle of town."

"Brothers and sisters? Uncles and aunts?"

"I was an only child. They got a late start. Either that or I was all they could stand. Some uncles and aunts in Sarajevo, mostly on my mother's side. A few in little places out in the country. We'd visit a few times a year, weddings and funerals. Most of my father's people had died by then. I only remember one uncle, down on a farm with goats that were always trying to eat my sleeves. He and my aunt lived like hermits, so we only saw them once or twice. My father and he would drink brandy all night out in the back. It was about the only way you could get my father talking."

That was an understatement, Vlado thought, recalling his father's brooding silences. Like a bird on its perch, seeing things below that others didn't but never bothering to share what they were. His mother had always been the talker of the family.

"Family always seems to make such a difference in your country," Pine said. "Families and where you grew up. I'm always amazed. You'll meet people from the tiniest villages who got uprooted in the fighting, maybe had to move twenty miles down the valley, but you'd think they'd had to move to another country, the way they talk. Their village was all that mattered. Hell, if you're from a small town in America, the first thing you want to do is get out. Staying is a slow death. I think that's one reason we don't understand half of what's gone on in Bosnia. We had the Civil War, and we drove out a few million Indians along the way, and we've got race and crime and poverty. But history is pretty much, well, history. People are too worried about their jobs and their sports teams and whatever's on cable that night to be shooting each other over something that happened fifty years ago, much less six hundred."

"That's because you didn't grow up listening to everybody older than you gripe about the last war. Telling you not to believe all that crap about peace and brotherhood because someday those people over in the next house would try to do it to you again. In some places it was the same whether you were a Serb or a Muslim or a Croat. So I guess the mistrust never really went away, and once the fighting started, boom. No more peace and brotherhood."

"We've got plenty of old farts griping at the dinner table, too. But I thought part of growing up was to not believe a word your parents tell you. In America nobody listens to the old farts except other old farts. What happened to you guys?"

By now Pine was drunk. But Vlado, tipsy himself, realized the man had made a pretty good point.

"I guess we all bought into the whole 'wisdom of the elders' business a little too much. Even I did. And look where it got us."

"But you weren't out there hunting down Serbs during the war, so you couldn't have been too poisoned. What was the wisdom of the elders in your house?"

Another good question. Vlado shrugged, thinking it over. "My father couldn't have cared less about politics," he said, "so maybe that's why I didn't care much, either. It was little things, mostly, that he passed along. The way he lived. His work habits. Being trusted, relied upon. Showing that even when times got difficult, you could bend without having to break."

"But none of the small-mindedness, then. None of the village mentality he must have grown up with."

"Again, just little things. Old stories about his cousins or aunts. Traditions on holidays. The best way to butcher a lamb for a wedding feast. Best way to mend a broken universal joint. Things you did with your hands. Some fathers passed on their beliefs, their hatreds and passions. Mine gave me his way of looking at life. And a toolbox."

"A toolbox?"

"It's the main thing he left me when he died. That and some old photos."

Pine had nothing to say to that. He rubbed his face, slouching toward the table. "I've had too much to drink."

Vlado grinned. "Maybe a little."

"Guess we drove Jasmina off to bed."

Vlado's smile broadened. "Now we're the ones acting like old farts from the village. Drinking late after the womenfolk go to bed. This is when we're supposed to get out a deck of cards, or start an argument and push the table over."

But Jasmina wasn't sleeping. Vlado looked down the hall and saw the crease of light below their door. It made him remember something that had been knocking around in the back of his mind throughout the evening. Before the night was over, he'd have to deal with it, face-to-face. Pine spoke up from across the table, breaking his reverie.

"Well, give America another six hundred years and maybe we'll be burning each other's houses. Of course, by then everybody will have unlimited channels on his cable system. So nobody will have time to start a war."

They clinked glasses over that one, laughing.

"Maybe all Bosnia needs is a little collective memory loss," Pine said. "A lot of us at the tribunal figure it's the only real solution. A little electroshock therapy for everybody and your troubles are over."

Pine laughed again. Vlado wanted to. But there was something vaguely troubling in the thought of all those Americans and Europeans in their trim Dutch apartments, laughing over cocktails at his country's recurring genocidal folly. Making sport of all the raw country people with their quaint ignorance, as remote to most modern Europeans as the dough-faced peasants of a Brueghel painting.

Vlado pulled deeply on his cigarette, then blew a cloud toward Pine. If the man could get used to Balkan history, then he could get used to Balkan smoke. Then he leaned across the table, lowering his voice. "Look, this job you're asking me to take. I'll tell you right now, I'll probably take it. Jasmina won't want to move. She hates the work around here, but she likes the peace, the stability, so that's something we'll have to decide later. But I still have to wonder what the hell I'm getting into. The way I see it, you want my 'local expertise' to help you go after an old man who I've never heard of from a war I never knew in a town I've maybe never seen. And I'll tell you now, I've never done any undercover work. I'm not sure how convincing I'll be posing as some kind of broker for demining concessions. So tell me, then. What part of the picture am I missing? Why me?"

Pine smiled, squinting into the tobacco smoke. Vlado saw him reel slightly, perhaps from the exhaustion of the long train journey, the heavy meal, and five shots of brandy. Then Pine straightened in his chair, as if realizing he'd lowered his guard. He was a careful one when he had to be, Vlado observed. Maybe that was part of his training as a lawyer.

"Good questions, all of them. But you'll have to save the tough ones for my boss. You'll meet him later this week. Just say yes and you'll know soon enough. Suffice it for now that, based on your file, you're what he likes to call 'the last honest cop in Bosnia.'"

It was good for another laugh, and Vlado poured a final shot. Pine's answer should have sounded an alarm bell, he knew, but Vlado had his own means of answering the questions still troubling him, never mind the lateness of the hour.

For the moment, however, his overriding urge was to pack his bags, to sit before a pile of case notes, to begin the sort of work he had done before. If pressed, he might even have hopped into a car this very moment to drive south for eighteen hours, where he would ride across the border and climb into the green hills, his ears popping and the windows down, feeling the cool air of the beeches, the poplars, and the pines against his face. He was ready to go home, the sooner the better.

They said their good-byes at the door a few minutes later, Jasmina joining them, her arms folded.

When the elevator doors opened on the ground floor, Pine strolled to a pay phone outside.

All in all, he thought, it had been a productive evening, even if it had taken him a while to warm up to the man. He'd read Vlado's file on the long train ride from Amsterdam and had been suitably impressed. Vlado's evaluations from his years as a detective had been particularly striking; he was bright, inquisitive, independent to a fault, which didn't bother Pine because the same sort of words always showed up in his own evaluations. Even better, the man had stayed off the bottle, no small feat when you were an exile working a low-paying job well below your talents.

Nonetheless, Pine's first impression in the flesh had been jarring. Vlado looked like one of those young tobacco farmers from back home in Lasser County, the kind his father had always evicted for some landlord, or sued for their last penny on behalf of the power company. They struck the pose of the rough and ready but were actually naïve, always believing better times were ahead, until awakening one morning to find themselves old and poor, realizing too late that hard work alone wouldn't save you.

But Pine had been wrong before when he applied American standards over here, so he reappraised, shifting into his European gear—after more than five years abroad he was pretty good at it—and he now discerned a face that was classic Balkan, features cut close to the bone, with the dark searching eyes and cropped black hair you saw everywhere down there. Vlado, he surmised, would be slow to smile, slow to trust. There was also something vaguely Germanic in the man, a stolid sense of order, of everything in its proper place. Or maybe he'd drawn that conclusion from the apartment—simple but well-kept furniture with clean lines. No clutter. Floors and walls spotless. Shoes in a neat row by the door.

But it was another, darker part of Vlado's file that had brought Pine halfway across Europe, a piece of grim trivia that made the man oddly perfect for the job at hand. The time for those revelations would come later, and Pine didn't wish to be the one who delivered them. For now, it was time to call the boss, and he dropped a few D-marks into the coin slot.

It was nearly midnight. Spratt would be asleep, but to hell with him because this had been his idea. Besides, he'd wanted to know.

"Hello?" said a sleepy voice with a flattened Australian accent.

"It's Pine. The deed is done."

That seemed to rouse him. "Good work. So he's come aboard?"

"Not officially. Has to talk it over with his wife. But rest assured, he's hooked."

"And our secret weapon. Still a secret?"

"Not by my choosing."

"Understood. But don't worry."

"I'll let you tell him that."

A muffled chuckle. "I'll be happy to when the time comes. Don't worry, the wound won't be mortal. Now get some sleep, Pine. And let me get some sleep. You sound drunk, by the way. Hope you're not driving."

"On our budget? Mass transit all the way. And it's a forty-minute S-Bahn ride to my cheap hotel."

"Then don't miss your stop. And make sure to bring Mr. Petric back to The Hague with you. An awful lot of people are eager to meet him."

CHAPTER THREE

If Pine had stayed on the phone much longer, he might have bumped into Vlado, who soon headed out of the building on his own midnight errand.

Vlado and Jasmina looked at each other the moment Pine shut the door. They were exhausted, not just from the lateness of the hour but from the weight of the questions now facing them. Should Vlado take the assignment? If so, what came next? They were too weary to discuss it but too stirred up to sleep, and for Vlado there was a more pressing matter to deal with.

He grabbed his jacket and headed for the door.

"Where are you going?" Jasmina asked.

It wasn't something he could tell her, not now. Maybe never. Not her or Pine or anyone else.

"There's something I need to find out before I can give him an answer." He came up with the closest thing to an explanation he could offer. "It's . . . a law enforcement matter."

"At twelve o'clock? In Berlin?" Jasmina frowned, incredulous.

"It's related to the war. Some people from home. You'll just have to trust me. It's their affair, not mine. I just have to make sure it's been dealt with before I can say anything to Pine. Please, that's all I can tell you. But it won't take long."

"You're running to catch up with him, aren't you. To catch Pine before he changes his mind."

"Don't be crazy. I wouldn't do that without talking about it with you first."

She considered that a second, seemed to accept it.

"How long will you be?" she asked.

"No more than an hour. Probably less."

He hoped it was true.

She sighed, still skeptical. "But you are going to take it, aren't you? This job."

"Maybe. I don't know. Probably. If you think you and Sonja can handle it."

"The better question is how we'll handle it if you don't. You'll be in a black mood for the rest of your life. What I'm more worried about is what comes next, when this is over and you want to move back."

"Maybe I won't feel that way. Maybe it's still as bad down there as everyone says. Just knowing I can visit awhile is good enough for now."

She shook her head, smiling.

"One walk in the mountains is all it will take. One of your old paths."

"Until I see a mine on one of my old paths."

"Sure. Then you'll run right back to your trusty backhoe. Let's see, what would Vlado rather do for the next twenty years? Dig holes in the mud or go around asking people nosy questions, and for a better salary, too? I'm sure you'll need a lot of time to decide that. Especially since you already love it here so much. The food you're always raving about. The sunny weather."

Vlado grinned. "Don't forget the beautiful flat countryside."

She smiled back. "And I hate it, too," she said. "Some of it. Being a stranger all the time. Not understanding half of what people are saying no matter how hard I try. The stares we get from all the people who wish we'd just go home. If it were just the two of us, I'd go back tomorrow." She nodded toward the hallway. "It's Sonja I worry about. She's spent all but two years of her life here. This is where she learned to speak, to make friends, to read and write. This is her home. She's a German, Vlado, a Berliner, whether you and the Germans want to admit it or not. She likes bratwurst and *döner kebap* and those little chocolate eggs with toys in the middle. She hums the tune to 'Liebe Sandmann' every morning at breakfast—excuse me, every *Morgen am Frühstück*, or however you're supposed to say it. She probably even likes the idea of schools and playgrounds that haven't been blown up or burned to the ground. And, okay, even if half the people on the U-Bahn give her a dirty look when she sits down, at least most of them wouldn't kill her if she wandered into their neighborhoods without permission, which is more than you can say about our lovely country."

"I know. All that's true. And we'll talk about it more later. After I'm done. When we've slept on it."

He pulled her closer, and she whispered in his ear. "It's also nice not worrying about you every day. Even if you do hate the job. At least I always know you're coming home."

"You wouldn't say that if you knew where I'd been this morning," he said. "Ghosts and old Nazis, down under the ground. It's been a strange day."

And it was only about to get stranger, he feared.

Vlado walked briskly from the building. The U-Bahn stopped running in less than an hour, but his destination was only a few blocks away. The man's name was Haris, and Vlado's stomach still did a back flip recalling the first time he'd heard it. He'd noticed the man's presence almost the moment he returned to his family five years ago.

He'd knocked twice, feeling more like a postman with a package to sign than a husband and father. Jasmina opened the door and gasped, then smiled, nearly collapsing, while the warm air of the apartment poured into the hallway. Sonja looked up from the floor just as you'd expect a skeptical four-year-old to do when a stranger was on her doorstep. She sat before a menagerie of toy zebras and lions on a carpeted plain, gathering them to her with a frown, then gasping when her mother actually embraced the stranger, sobbing and pulling him into their home.

To her, Daddy had become a voice on the phone that called once a month from a place called Sarajevo, a private radio show broadcasting only for her, a novelty that had grown old over time. This man stepping into the house was something else altogether.

It was only a few minutes before Vlado noticed the sports magazine on the table, the one in his native tongue with the names of football stars he had once cheered for. Not long after that he found two beers in the refrigerator. Jasmina hated the stuff. Once she recovered from her initial surprise, she dashed about tidying, almost imperceptibly snapping up the magazine as she collected assorted clutter, her cheeks rosy, and not just from the excitement, he supposed. She headed first to the bedroom, carrying Vlado's suitcase to the closet and quickly stuffing some items into a plastic bag as he peered down the hall from the couch, where he sat exhausted, overwhelmed by the idea that the last two years had finally come to an end. His war really was over. The idea of another man having been here shouldn't have surprised him, he supposed, and for the moment he was too dazed and weary to feel angry or even hurt. He had been sealed away for so long, with no prospect of escape, and suddenly here he was, watching his daughter eye him from the kitchen door. He knew from his own experience that lonely people in unfamiliar places either made friends or went crazy, and sometimes friends become something more. Beyond that, he was too drained by the interrogation, the long trip back to his family. And it was less than a week since he had left Sarajevo. The emotions of the years under fire still clung to him like wet clothing.

Jasmina never once mentioned anyone, or offered another hint, although there were times when she seemed to hesitate, to hold back in conversation, whether in reluctance to hurt him or in sorrow for some loss, he couldn't say, and wasn't sure he wanted to know.

Fortunately they had Sonja to distract them. She warmed to Vlado quickly, some old bond taking hold, as if she had encoded his smell, his voice, the way he felt when you snuggled up to him with a book, asking to be read to, and within a week she had latched on and wasn't letting go. He developed an afternoon routine of reading her a storybook in German. It was good practice for both of them, although it was a toss-up as to who was doing the teaching. He proceeded down the pages like a man on stilts while she gently corrected his pronunciation, her little hand darting to the page while she deftly enunciated the throat-clearing sounds. Her Bosnian—if that's what they called his language now, Serbo-Croatian having become a contradiction in terms—faded more by the day. He and Jasmina used it around the house, but breaking into their native tongue began to seem like shuttling to another era on a tram that had become creaky and outmoded.

Their marriage felt that way for a while, too. They'd lost their feel for each other's rhythms, their comfortable give-and-take with its catchphrases and gestures. It was like relearning a language, but with each day more words came back to them.

Vlado never wanted to ask about any man, though he was tempted to broach the subject with Sonja. It would have been so easy to inquire about "Mommy's friends." But in trying to form the words, he'd feel the policeman in him coming out, interrogating his daughter, so he'd push the thought away. Besides, Jasmina showed no signs that anything had continued. No lengthy unexplained absences, no furtive moments on the phone—and yes, he listened for them, with an attentiveness that made him ashamed. The only clues she offered were those moments of emptiness, when she would gaze into corners where there was nothing to see. Whose face was still over there, he wondered?

After a few months it had all surfaced anyway, while Jasmina was out shopping. Sonja was playing on the floor with a small plush giraffe, with orange yarn for its mane.

"That's a nice toy," Vlado said from the couch, just making conversation.

"Haris gave it to me," she answered, and at first it didn't register. He figured Haris for a playmate, some generous boy from the *Spielplatz*.

"When he brought Mommy the smell-good."

Now she had his attention.

"The smell-good?"

"Yes."

"Show me," he said, dropping slowly to the floor, sidling up to his daughter like a conspirator, but keeping his voice light. "Show me Mommy's smell-good."

"You knowwww." She crinkled her nose with a smile, shaming his ignorance.

"No. I don't know." He smiled back. "Bring it to me."

And like a good little informant she hustled off down the hallway with the wobbly walk of a four-year-old. He watched through the open door as she raised herself on tiptoes in their bedroom, rummaging in the top drawer of Jasmina's dresser.

"Here it is," she said sweetly, approaching with the prize in her outstretched hand. "The smell-good. See?"

It was a bottle of Chanel.

Vlado unscrewed the cap, sniffing. Jasmina hadn't worn this since he'd been home, but the bottle had been used. He held it to the light, feeling the coolness of the glass, admiring the amber color. Even the bootleg versions of such items fetched quite a price in the streets. On their income something like this would be a real sacrifice. He pulled Sonja to him in a tight hug, blinking back tears at the corners of his eyes.

"Isn't it nice?" she said, her voiced muffled against his shirt.

He summoned another smile. "Yes, sweetie. It's very nice."

So now he had a name. Haris. He mentally flipped through a catalog of faces from their building, from the bar, the wurst stand, the market, trying to remember a Haris. There was the Bosnian Cultural Center in Kreuzberg, a place where his countrymen sometimes met, celebrated holidays, held weddings. But the only Haris there was an old man, soup on his shirtfront, always muttering about his lost sons and the crimes of the Serbs.

The front door opened with a jolt, and Jasmina, soaking wet, stood clutching two cloth bags overflowing with groceries. She stared at the bottle of perfume in his hand, then at Sonja, who was back on the floor with her giraffe, oblivious to the sudden charge in the air.

The color rose in Vlado's cheeks, and he gently set the bottle on a table by the couch. Jasmina walked to the kitchen without a word, not bothering to remove her shoes, trailing wet footprints across the carpet. He heard keys clattering on the counter, the opening click of the refrigerator, then a bustle of slamming cabinet doors, clanking bottles, rustling bags. He wanted to be angry but felt only coldness, a dull, deep pain.

He looked again at the bottle. Now was his chance to return it to the drawer, any drawer. The move would save face for both of them, buying time, a gesture to build on. Then they could talk about it later. But instead he switched on the television and returned to the couch, leaving the bottle in full view, an open accusation. Exhibit A for the prosecution.

They waited until after dinner, when Sonja was asleep. Then Jasmina made tea for herself and opened a beer for him, bringing it in a glass. That seemed a first step toward accommodation, and he seized the opening, speaking slowly.

"Sonja told me about someone named Haris."

Jasmina folded her legs beneath her at the opposite end of the couch, the mug steaming in her hands.

"Haris," she said, pausing, "is a friend. Or was a friend. A friend and, sometimes . . ." She faltered, looking into Vlado's eyes with an expression of care and concern. "Sometimes something more. A companion. More for warmth against the loneliness than anything. The days without you just went on and on. Between calls I would think you were dead. I'd be sure of it sometimes, knowing that no one would even find you in the apartment for days, and that even when they did, no one would know who to reach, or how. And it was on one of those days that I first met Haris."

He didn't need to hear more. He only needed to hear the man was gone, finished in her life. Otherwise the conversation would veer toward the stalemate they'd often reached since his return. Both seemed intent on proving to the other that they'd suffered the most during their two years apart. And it was true that neither could fully appreciate what the other had endured. He'd never known the fierceness of life alone in an unwelcoming place with nothing but your child and your wits for company, swept along in a cold stream of indecipherable babble and officials who always wanted to see your documents, papers and more papers. She, on the other hand, could never fathom the fear and exhaustion of two years inside a claustrophobic little war, where shells and bullets were part of the weather, in a stale atmosphere that stank of backed-up plumbing, burning garbage, and death.

But the mention of the man's name—hearing *Haris* pass from her lips—seemed to prod Vlado out of his accustomed trench, and she out of hers, and from that day on neither was quite as insistent about documenting their two years apart. Gradually, those discussions faded, and with them the name of Haris.

It was not the last time Vlado would hear the name, however, and he regretted that all the more now that the American, Pine, had arrived on his doorstep.

He had met Haris more than four years following his return—a mere month ago—in a place called Noski's. It was a bar, one of the few where a Bosnian could hang out and not worry about being beaten within an inch of his life by the neighborhood pack of young toughs. Vlado went there sometimes to read outdated newspapers and magazines from Zagreb and even from Belgrade piled at the end of the bar. Sometimes there was a fairly recent copy of the Sarajevo daily, *Oslobodjenje*. The manager, an old barman from Prijedor, never seemed to mind that Vlado seldom bought a drink. He knew most of his customers couldn't afford it, and the few who could more than made up for the others by drinking themselves to oblivion, day after day.

Vlado was sitting at his customary roost when a voice hailed him from behind.

"You're Vlado."

He turned to see a thin, grizzled man in jeans and a scuffed black leather jacket, hair unkempt, eyes that would have been a nice calming blue if they hadn't been bloodshot. But they were eyes that wouldn't let you look away, and Vlado knew exactly who this must be.

"And you're Haris."

The man nodded. "I'll buy you a drink. Then I'll tell you a story."

He sat down at the next stool, smelling of whiskey. But he seemed sober enough, neither swaying nor slurring his words.

"I don't want a drink," Vlado said. "And I definitely don't want a story."

"It's a story for a policeman, and you're the only one I know. And, okay, it's a story for a husband, too. A husband who only wants to read his newspaper and go home to his wife and daughter." He turned to the bartender. "One beer, please. And a whiskey." Then, turning back to Vlado, "Just hear me this once. That's all I ask."

Those eyes again, pleading from some far and distant hill in the man's past.

"Okay. Just this once."

Haris waited for his whiskey, then began.

"I came here with my sister in late '92. My sister Saliha. From Bijeljina. We grew up there. Went to school there, got jobs, made friends. Most of our friends were Serbs. When the war started, I knew we would all be fine, because everyone knew us. No one would let anything happen."

He took a long swallow of the whiskey, wincing, then wiping his mouth with a sleeve before he continued.

"Saliha was raped in the first month of the war. Five times by a group of men in a room where they kept her for two days. I was put in the concentration camp at Keraterm. They loaded fifty of us on a bus and put us behind a fence. Nothing to eat for four days while they took us out, two at a time, beat us around the head, chained us to trucks. A few of us they shot. Me they just beat. Legs and face. Left us behind the wire for five weeks until one day a commander drives up and sets us loose. All the ones who hadn't died, anyway. But they took our papers, our money, then put us on trucks and drove us up to the front lines, where they dumped us out and told us never to come back.

"Snipers shot two of us while we were walking to the other side, stumbling across the lines. Another one stepped on a mine. The UN was there and everything, but there was nothing they could do. I think someone filed a protest later."

He sipped the whiskey again, gestured toward the foaming mug of beer. "Please. You will need to drink if you're going to hear all this." He put a crumpled bill on the bar for the first round.

"I found my sister three weeks later in a school gym where she was sleeping on the floor. The place was full of refugees. Hundreds. Whole families on towels and blankets, laundry hanging between the basketball hoops.

"Lice, bad food, every smell you can imagine. That was life in the gym. My sister wouldn't talk to anyone. Just lay there all day on a cot, eyes open. I slept on the floor next to her for a week. Then on the eighth day she finally stands up and decides to take a walk outside. It is snowing and she is barefoot, but she just keeps walking while I follow her, afraid to say a word. Two blocks and she stops and looks down at her feet and begins to cry. I carry her back, and on the way she tells me what had happened, whispers it into my ear like a child telling her father she's done something bad. She knew the men, three of them anyway. Knew their faces and names. One taught our nephew in school. One grew up on the farm next to our uncle's. I used to play football with him at school. The other guy was from the village, a baker." He paused, shaking his head. "Five months later we came here. This was late '92. And for a year she was pretty much the same, not going anywhere, just lying around the apartment, watching TV.

"Then one day it was sunny and warm, a spring morning after some rain, so I took her for a walk, almost had to push her out the door and carry her down the steps. But she started looking around. We stopped to sit on a bench awhile, across from a bus stop. Then we decided to catch a bus, to go for a ride. We crossed the street and she looked at the crowd, seven or eight people waiting for the bus. And that's when she saw him, one of the men, not one of the three she knew but their leader, the main one, the one who had the scar and wore a black beret, leaning into her face with brandy on his breath, sweating onto her for twenty minutes. She tried to scream, tried to tell me who it was, but nothing came out of her mouth until the bus had gone and the man was on it. She told me his name was Popovic, and I'd seen him, too.

"So the next day I go to the bus stop again, waiting for him. Nine hours I'm there. Then the next day, and then the day after that. I decide I will go every day until he comes back, like it's my job, because I didn't have a real job anyway. Just construction work without papers, tearing out old walls and plaster, and half the time we didn't get paid. So I kept going to the same corner. And that is how I met Jasmina."

Hearing him say her name was a jolt. But Vlado kept quiet, waiting for Haris to continue. He'd stopped for another swallow of whiskey.

"She'd seen me, I guess, seen me on that corner day after day, like someone obsessed. And I *was* obsessed. Crazy and dirty. Same coat, rain or shine. Same little water bottle tucked under my arm with a newspaper.

"She came up to me one day, curious more than anything, and asked who I was looking for. After days of being ignored by almost everyone in Berlin it seemed like some kind of revelation, like I'd been invisible to everyone but her. And when you're feeling like I was, so focused on something that you can't see anything else, when someone actually notices what you're up to, it seems like magic. Like they have powers no one else has. So we talked. And I relaxed a little. I felt almost normal for those few minutes before her bus came. And the next day we talked again, and I still hadn't told her why I was there, or who I was after. But she told me she was waiting on someone, too. I think that morning I might even have shaved. Changed my shirt. Wiped off my coat. I don't really remember now. But on the fifth day she brought me an apple. I must have looked pretty pale. And in a few more days I stopped going there altogether. So we would meet instead in other places, more normal places, and we became friends."

That was all Vlado cared to hear on the subject. He started to speak, but Haris raised his hand.

"Please. Another beer. I pay, you listen. I am through with the part about your wife, but I had to tell you that much, so you would know."

The bartender put down another round, Haris another crumpled bill.

"Later I heard more about this man, Popovic. It wasn't the name he used here, and people who knew him said he had gone back, back to Bosnia and the fighting. He had his own unit, his own men with their own black uniforms and a nickname. Popi's Lions. But by then I had a life again. I was working in old buildings. Painting, or stripping out insulation. Paid in cash at the end of every day, or sometimes not paid. My sister didn't care. She stayed at home, quieter than ever, the TV on. After seeing Popovic that time she wouldn't leave the house again. But I kept working. And, yes, sometimes I saw Jasmina."

It was the only time Haris came close to raising his voice, a brief note of defiance.

"Then, in early '94, the person she'd been waiting for came home. And for me, that was the end of Jasmina. She called me—only once— and said good-bye, said good luck. And for a while it seemed that was the end of life. So I kept trying to find jobs. Made a little more money. And forgot about women, and even forgot about this Popovic. Until three weeks ago, when I saw him again. I'd heard about him some, like lots of people. Someone had told me that in the last year of the war he'd been at Srebrenica when the city fell, leading his unit again, helping round up men and boys. Looting, killing, doing whatever it is he did. Other people said later he must have gone to Belgrade, or even to Kosovo.

"But now it was peacetime and there he was near the same bus stop as before, this time walking across the street toward the U-Bahn. He was in a hurry. Before I'd always worried I might not recognize him if I saw him again, that his face might have gone out of my head for good, just to torment me, but even after more than four years I knew him right away, and knew that he hadn't seen me watching him. So I followed him, got on the U-Bahn a car behind his. Watched him through the windows and got off at the same stop. A long ride, a couple of changes. Then half an hour of walking and he's on the Ku'damm. And by now I'm looking out of place, I'm sure, a grimy Bosnian on this nice street of shops and theaters. The West Berliners with all their money and bored expressions, and I'm half a block behind him, trying not to lose him.

"He goes into the KaDeWe, the big department store, and for a few minutes I couldn't see him. I thought I'd start crying right there in the store if I lost him after all that. Then I saw his head across the counters, heading toward an escalator. He went to the café, upstairs at the top of the store, all those plants under a glass roof. He sat down. He was waiting for someone, so I went to another table. I had to buy something, or they would have kicked me out. I took five marks out of my pocket for a coffee, and it drains me for the rest of the week."

Vlado couldn't help but think of the bottle of Chanel, which must have drained him for a good month.

"I watch him eat his schnitzel, his pastry, his Coke, and his coffee. He spends what must be twenty marks just having a snack, and he keeps looking at his watch until finally a woman comes and sits down with him. Nice-looking. Probably a Bosnian, but I couldn't be sure because I couldn't hear what they were saying. But she was done up. A nice dress and black stockings. Lipstick. Very nice, and she was his. She belonged to the rapist, the killer. Gave him a little kiss, then they talked for a while, a lot of smiling with his little smirk. And later she said good-bye. I think she must have worked there. Then he walked back, same way he'd come. Same U-Bahn stations. Same stop at the end, and now I'm excited. Because now I know he's going home.

"He walks into a house. A building like yours. And I was almost in a panic because I didn't know what to do about the elevator. If I get on it with him he will recognize me, I am almost sure, or will see something in my eyes and know I'm crazy enough to kill him. I felt like I was about to lose him after all of this. And then, my lucky day. Movers are using one elevator. Loading some big piece of furniture. The other one is broken. Kaput. So he took the stairs, and I stayed one flight back, tiptoeing so I don't make noise. I heard the door open at the fourth floor, and I ran up behind as it shut. I look down the hall in time to see a door closing behind him, and I get the number and check the name on the door and the mailbox. It was fake, of course, because I knew his real name. I had heard it many times, had even read it in the newspapers.

"So, then. What to do next? First I tell my friend Huso, because he was from Srebrenica. He'd run through the woods for four days, trying to get away from there. And he had seen this man Popovic with the crowds of Chetniks, putting people onto buses, calling men and boys out of the woods. Both his brothers went, but he kept running. He made it to Tuzla, but they never did. They got on the buses. No one ever saw them again.

"Huso says all we need to do is tell the police. He says we tell them, then they tell the war crimes tribunal, then someone will come and arrest him. So we did that, the very next day. We waited two hours at the police station, and you would have thought we were thieves the way they acted. Like we were dirty and they just wanted to put us in jail or send us home, all the way back to Bosnia. But finally they took our information. They said they'd make a phone call."

"And then?" Vlado asked. By now the policeman in him was hooked. He swallowed some beer, not taking his eyes off Haris.

"And then, nothing. Two weeks go by and I check on him every day, just to make sure he is still here. Every day he goes to see the same woman, but in different places. Sometimes he spends the night with her. Sometimes she comes back with him. He wears the same nice clothes and spends his marks like they mean nothing at all. But no one has come to arrest him or take him away. And Huso and I, we've started to think that no one ever will."

Haris paused, as if reluctant to continue. He asked for another whiskey, then looked straight at Vlado.

"So now you want me to do something about it," Vlado said. "Because I used to be a policeman."

"Because you know how these things are done. Making arrests. Bringing people to justice. You've been a part of that."

But it wasn't the policeman in Vlado who answered. It was the husband, suddenly and irrationally angry that this man who'd taken comfort from his wife wanted comfort from him as well.

The policeman in him would have said, "Let matters take their course. Report him again if you want to feel better. Make yourself a nuisance if you have to, or telephone The Hague directly, and definitely offer yourself as a witness, but otherwise stay out of the matter. You'll only be asking for trouble."

The husband in him shouldered such practicalities aside.

"If the police were going to do something, they would have done it by now. Someone like Popovic must not rate too high on their list. The Germans are more worried about Asians selling tax-free cigarettes, or Turks dealing heroin. All they want from Bosnians is an exit visa and a quick wave good-bye. The only way to get them interested in someone like Popovic is to bring him to their doorstep. If you and Huso want something done about Popovic, you'll have to do it yourself."

Having said that, Vlado immediately felt ashamed, even a little nervous, like a kid who has lit the fuse of a huge firework and now must throw it, not knowing where it might land. He flashed on an absurd scene of Haris and Huso tying up Popovic with about a hundred feet of rope, squirming like a team of comedians, then dumping the man at a police station with a gag in his mouth and a note penned to his shirt, scribbled in ungrammatical Bosnian. But Haris was still staring at him, as if awaiting further instructions.

Vlado obliged, unable to resist the temptation to coax the flame a little further along the fuse.

"Look, if Popovic is living here as another person, under another name, then who do you think would miss the real Popovic? No one. They would miss this other man. But the other man doesn't exist, except as fake papers and passports. Which the authorities would discover as soon as they searched his house or looked into his background. Assuming they even bothered."

He sipped the beer, the foam cold on his lips. "And if you've heard nothing from the tribunal, how much does that say about their interest? Sounds like you and Huso are the only two worried about it. It's possible he hasn't even been indicted, and if that's the case now, who knows, it might never happen."

"But Huso saw him, saw what he was doing in Srebrenica. My sister saw him, too. There must be plenty of witnesses who've mentioned his name."

"Maybe investigators have never talked to any of them. And are you sure that's what you want to put your sister through? Have her up in the dock, answering questions from some attorney for Popovic, who'll keep telling her how much she wanted it, how much she'd been asking for it. He'll ask her what kind of dresses she wore, what kind of perfume she used, how many men she'd slept with. Is that what you want?"

Haris had no answer. He just bolted down another swallow and set his glass heavily on the table, nodding once, a look of resolve in his eyes, and for a moment Vlado wanted to take it all back, to tell him, "Take it easy. I'll make some calls. Let me handle this."

But the moment passed, and Haris stood, laying a last crumpled bill on the bar.

It wasn't long before Haris took his advice. Four nights later the phone rang. Luckily Vlado was the one who answered.

"It's Haris."

The anger rose up in Vlado almost immediately, but Jasmina and Sonja were in the next room, so he didn't shout.

"I don't want to hear any more about your problems," he muttered. "I want you out of our lives."

"Then come downstairs, and you'll have your wish. I promise. Huso and I are down here."

Hearing that both of them were there suggested some foolhardy plan in motion.

"What have you done?" Vlado said tersely.

"Just come. There isn't much time."

He found them standing in a dimly lit corner of the entrance, by a pay phone next to the mailboxes, trying not to attract attention and therefore doing exactly that, a sweating and nervous-looking pair who stank of effort and exhaustion, their eyes glazed with a barely contained wildness and more than a little drink.

"Outside," Haris whispered. "Follow us."

They walked to a far corner of the parking lot, which backed onto a small grove of trees. Both streetlights in that corner were burned out. Broken glass crunched underfoot. Their car was the only one within a twenty-yard radius, and Vlado almost laughed to see it was a brown Yugo, like the punch line to some elaborate and clumsy joke—two bumbling expats and their expat excuse for a car.

They stopped by the rear of the car, a nervous huddle, Haris looking at Huso, who fumbled for the keys. Vlado felt his stomach sink as the trunk lid clicked open, swinging up into the darkness with a high creak. A man, presumably Popovic, was curled into place, hands bound behind his back. Vlado desperately hoped he was still alive, but the mouth was open, not gagged, and the smell boiling up out of the cramped dark space was of blood, blood gone cold and stiff on clothing and skin.

"He's dead," Haris said.

Huso looked back at Vlado. It was the first time Vlado had met him. Broad flat face and a squat body, and the brown frightened eyes of a dog that has just chewed the morning paper. What did they want? For him to arrest them? This was hopeless, and he sagged with the enormity of what they had done, of what *he* had done. Headlight beams crossed them briefly as another car swerved into the opposite end of the lot.

"For God's sake, shut it," Vlado said. He was dealing with idiots. Why was he dealing with them at all? How had he ended up out in this lot with these two men and this body?

"I want to tell you how it happened," Haris said. "We didn't want to kill him. And now we don't know what to do."

"Get in the car," Vlado said. "Tell me while you drive. But don't just stand here attracting attention. If a policeman were to pull in now, this is the first part of the lot he'd check. C'mon. Get in."

They obeyed, tame and tired. Huso sat at the wheel cranking the whining engine, the works tooled in some far corner of home, years ago, before the war—back when owning a Yugo wasn't such a bad thing, and living in a mountain village was a poor but tranquil pursuit. You were forgotten and so was your country. But now their problems were scattered everywhere, a diaspora of feud and vengeance. They had brought the war to the *Spielplatz* and the wurst stand, little Bosnias everywhere.

"Head for a busier street," Vlado said from the backseat, the cop taking control. "And don't speed, don't do anything that will get you pulled over."

Huso was rigid at the wheel, the posture of a student driver afraid to do anything other than what the teacher tells him.

"How the hell did it happen?"

Haris turned from the front passenger's seat.

"We followed him home this afternoon. He'd gone back to the KaDeWe. Back to see that woman. On his way back he stopped in a park for a walk. He went up in some bushes to take a leak, and Huso grabbed him. Huso had a knife."

"Where's the knife?"

Haris got a blank look. Huso shook his head.

"I'm not sure." Haris said. "Maybe in the trunk. I don't know."

It was how amateurs always screwed up. Some major detail left unattended to. Vlado had seen all the signs before in his work. Now here he was driving along with a pair of such fools, inextricably linked to them. All three of them could end up behind bars. Why was he even along for the ride, speaking with them, conspiring? With every moment he dug himself deeper, but there was no turning back.

"We got on either side of him and told him to come with us," Haris said. "Huso showed him the knife, but we told him it was about money. That if he came with us and just heard our offer, we could all make a lot of money."

That, at least, had been smart. If Popovic had known he was dealing with two fellows bent on revenge, he would have bolted for sure.

"He wasn't happy, but he came with us. You could tell he was trying to figure the odds. I think he thought the knife was something he could deal with. So we walked to the car. Huso had borrowed one, and it was only a block away. Huso kept the knife under his jacket."

"So this isn't even Huso's car?"

"No."

"What's he lying on back there? A blanket? Anything?"

"There's a big sheet of plastic."

Sometimes amateurs got it right, too, in spite of themselves. He wondered how much blood they had on their clothes. He remembered how grimy they'd seemed in the dim light of the apartment building. Not a good sign.

"Keep going. Then what?"

"We drove out to a construction site. A new shopping center where Huso has been doing some work, some painting. We pulled around the back. Huso got the knife out and told him to turn around. I tied his wrists. We told him we were going to take him to our stash of drugs."

Vlado was amazed Popovic had gone along with it. Either too stupid or too greedy. Maybe both. Or perhaps he'd merely been frightened. People used to giving orders rarely knew how to act when receiving them. But once he'd let them tie his hands, he was a dead man.

"We weren't going to kill him," Huso said from the front. "All we wanted was a confession. Then we were going to turn him in to the police."

"A confession?"

"Of all he'd done," Haris said. "I was going to take a statement."

He reached beneath the seat and pulled out a spiral notebook with two pens slid into the loops of the binding. As if he were a cop doing the report. Haris really had thought they were going to take care of it themselves, the stupid bastard. Mostly because a real cop had been careless enough to tell him they could.

"Go on," Vlado said, his voice barely a whisper.

"He laughed at us. He said, 'This is all you want? Some confession? No business to do, just some crap about the war?' So Huso hit him. Hit him across the face and asked about his brothers. I told him he'd raped my sister. He just got quiet, wouldn't say anything. I think he was beginning to get a little scared, but he wasn't going to admit it, wasn't going to say anything, either. So we told him we were taking him to the police, that we knew his real name and that they would arrest him."

"And he told you to go ahead."

"Yes. How did you know?"

"Why wouldn't he? The police wouldn't know what to make of him, other than some Bosnian with bad papers. They'd deport him and he'd be away from both of you, and he'd know better than to ever come back to Berlin. I just can't believe he was stupid enough to dare you. Or to laugh."

"We decided he was right," Haris said. "Or I did. I told Huso we couldn't take him in. We began arguing in the car. That's when Popovic knocked open the door latch with his knee. He got out and ran, up toward the street. We caught him and tackled him, dragged him back to the car. Pushed him up against one of the back walls of the building. Then he spit. Spit in Huso's face. Said, 'Fuck your brothers, they deserved to die.' And that's when Huso stabbed him. He stabbed him once, then he couldn't stop."

Haris paused. Huso sighed deeply in the driver's seat, as if recalling some distant unpleasantness.

"It was over fast. Like killing an animal. All the thrashing and the breathing, the air and the blood coming out of him, the knife going in and out with that sound, like stabbing a sandbag."

"Then you put him in the trunk."

"And came to see you. We didn't know what to do next. Where to take him. What to do with his body."

Vlado took his bearings. They were on a four-lane road heading east, out of the city, the buildings growing sparser.

"Keep going," he said. "I know a place. Somewhere I did some work when I first got here. Another mile or so, then go north. I'll tell you when."

It was too late to back out now. Too late to do anything but keep driving and do the best with what they had. The man in the trunk was dead, and he'd always be in the back of Vlado's mind as a casualty he'd inflicted, his first. It would be something to hide from his wife and daughter and anyone else he ever met. There would always be this man's body riding behind him.

It took another twenty minutes to reach the site. Vlado had unloaded old pipes there, the innards of some building he'd helped gut during his first month in Berlin, before the construction job had opened up. The lot was closed, just as it had been then, with broken padlocks on all the fences, which made it an ideal place for illegal dumping. There was an old waste lagoon in the back, sludge and chemicals and abandoned grocery carts jutting from the ooze.

They looped some of Huso's rope through cinder blocks and a discarded section of heavy iron scaffolding. Then they tied everything to Popovic, knotting the rope around his chest. It took all three of them to heave the body and all the weight over the lip of the lagoon. He sank slowly into the dark, bubbling mess. For a moment they stood, wiping their hands on their pants, staring at the spot as if the body might bob back to the surface at any moment. Then, without saying a word, they climbed into the car.

No one spoke on the way back, and Vlado hadn't mentioned a word of it to anyone in the few weeks since then. But now, with Pine waiting for an answer, Vlado had to see Haris one last time. Had to ask him if anyone had come poking around with questions, or if anyone had ever responded to his initial report to the police. He especially wanted to know if Haris had ever heard from anyone at the tribunal. For all Vlado knew, this assignment might yet have something to do with Popovic. Or maybe that was just the convoluted thinking of a guilty conscience.

Vlado had learned earlier where Haris lived, and now he took the elevator to the sixth floor, the building quiet at this hour. It was a carbon copy of his own, one of those gray slabs the East Germans had built in their haste to replace the wreckage of World War II. Vlado knocked, not looking forward to the moment of confrontation, worried about what he'd learn. And even with everything that had happened, he still wasn't used to the idea of speaking with someone who'd slept with his wife. He knocked a second time, worried no one was home. But finally there was a scraping sound, and the door opened narrowly against a security chain. A woman's drawn, thin face stared back at him, her body stooped before its time. This would be Saliha, Haris's sister.

"I've come to see Haris," he said. "Tell him it's Vlado. Vlado Petric."

His name seemed to flip a switch, and a smile flickered slowly to life, although it was hard to recall any smile more mirthless.

"Then I know why you must be here," she said, not budging from the door. "What do you want with him?"

"To speak with him. Only a minute or two. Is he home?"

"Yes, he is home." That glint in her eyes again. "Home in Bosnia. He and Huso both. They should have come and killed you instead, but Haris said no, he'd had enough of killing. So they went back a few days ago. And now I am here by myself, alone, because I won't go back. He has deserted me, thanks to what you made him do."

"Well," he said, feeling a need to redeem himself, to excuse his visit at this late hour. "I just wanted to make sure that he was safely out of things. To make sure the authorities hadn't caught up to him. But I suppose they haven't."

"There was one," she said, with a questioning look that slowly turned to a smile as she watched Vlado's alarmed reaction.

"One?"

"One man. Only three days ago. The day after Haris left. He came looking for him." She paused. "He asked about Popovic, too. The devil himself."

"Who was he, this man? Where was he from?"

"He didn't say."

"The war crimes tribunal?"

"He didn't say. I told you."

By now her smile was full. She probably hadn't enjoyed anything this much in ages.

"Was he German? In a uniform?"

"No. Not in a uniform. And not German. Not Bosnian either. A foreigner."

"American?"

"I don't know. He spoke our language. A few words of it, anyway, and not like a German would. But he spoke it. Enough to tell me he wanted to see Haris. To ask him about Popovic."

"What else did he say?"

"Nothing. When I told him Haris was gone, he left."

"Was he tall? Short? Fat? Thin? Old or young?"

"About your age, but maybe not. It was dark. Taller than you, but maybe only a little. And he wore a big coat, so I can't say if he was thin."

So it might be Pine and it might not be. Vlado had no idea if Pine spoke any Bosnian. He must have picked up a little if he'd been traveling there for five years.

"What else did he want to know?"

"If Haris was coming back. Where he could find him. If I'd seen Popovic."

"And?"

"I told him I knew nothing about any of that. I said that Haris had gone back because he was homesick. That he had been in love but that his girlfriend's husband had returned." Her smile widened. "But that was all, and he didn't ask any more."

"Did he leave his name, give you a contact number? A business card, maybe?"

"None of that. He just left. And I haven't seen him since."

And I hope to God I haven't, either, Vlado thought as she shut the door, the dead bolt sliding with a great heavy click.

CHAPTER FOUR

In the gray light of morning, Vlado's fears seemed unfounded. He awakened in a swelter of dry heat. The apartment building's furnaces had run full throttle through the night, and the air smelled of baking metal. Vlado sat up in bed, mouth dry, eyelids glued, hair poking stiffly in all directions. Jasmina's side of the bed was empty, with the sheets thrown back. He got up to crank open a window. Cool air flowed in like a balm, pooling around his bare feet, though it tweaked his nose with the smell of burning coal. The sun was up, and he knew by the light that he was already at least an hour late for work. Jasmina stepped into the doorway.

"I decided to let you sleep," she said. "You'll need your strength for the trip."

So it would be that easy. He met her at the foot of the bed, sliding his arms around her waist, pulling her closer. Her hair smelled like shampoo, her breath like coffee.

"Just promise me two things," she said. He nodded, chin brushing the top of her head. "That you won't do anything stupid. And by that I mean dangerous, or anything as dangerous as it was for you before, in Sarajevo."

"Okay. That should be easy enough."

"That's what you always say. And what makes it worse, I think you really believe it."

"Relax. He did his last fighting before we were even born. He's an old man."

"And a war criminal. People who learn to kill when they're young don't forget just because they're going senile. It's like learning to swim, or ride a bike. It's part of their muscle memory."

Vlado laughed. It was her typical alarmist attitude. "Fair enough. I promise not to turn my back on him, especially when he's just had his prune juice. So what's the second promise?"

Jasmina shook her head but moved on. "That you won't make up your mind about moving before we talk." She looked up, straight into his eyes. "Don't get swept off your feet by the hills and a few old friends. By a few glasses of *rakija* or a few bites of *cevapi*. Give us a chance to talk it out rationally, thinking of everything. While you're here, not there."

He nodded again. "Okay. I promise."

She smiled, shaking her head lightly. "Sure you do. I can already see it in your eyes. All that eagerness to go back." Her eyes shone. "I wish I could, too. I woke up in the middle of the night, just aching to be home. I wanted to look out the window this morning and see everything I used to see, then take Sonja around her old city to meet her new playmates, and be able to talk to her without feeling like we were speaking some special language that only the three of us know, like it's some family code. That's the way she thinks of it, you know. Like it's our private tongue, nothing to do with anybody's country or anyone but us."

"I know. She told me. She heard a boy on the U-Bahn speaking Bosnian one morning and said, 'Listen, Daddy. He's talking *our* language.' She didn't like it. I guess she figured the boy had broken into our house and stolen all the words."

"Hi, Daddy." Now Sonja was at the door, clutching her *Sandmann* doll with his peaked red cap and his wisp of a beard. His confident little girl who rode the subway with the bored authority of an old commuter, knowing all the tricks for handling crowds and grabbing the best seats. Knew the best stands for wurst and *döner kebap*, too. It was true. She was a little German, comfortable here. He beckoned to her, and they all climbed into bed for half an hour, chatty and cozy, with the draft from the window coiling atop them like a cool velvet snake. Down in his chest he felt the excitement of the journey building.

Jasmina looked in his eyes, seeing the faraway fires, and said, "Go. Get up and call him before he leaves or changes his mind."

Vlado stepped barefoot across the floor to telephone Pine from the kitchen, suddenly needing reassurance that the night before had even existed, all those hours now mixed in a swirl of ghosts—spirits from the dank bunker, dreams of Haris and the body in the trunk. Just the thought of that was a dead weight sinking through the lightness of the morning. He wondered how long it would haunt him. Forever, perhaps. He had a fleeting vision of Haris's sister from only eight hours ago—could that be possible?—her doorstep still darkened by the shadow of whoever had visited a few days ago.

But if Pine knew about any of those events, he wasn't saying so this morning. And his voice on the phone seemed real enough, bubbling with excitement when Vlado accepted the job. Within an hour he was back at Vlado's door, holding a train ticket, again wearing his puppy-dog face and talking a mile a minute. He handed over a small stuffed envelope.

"Maps and directions," he said. "Nothing in here you'll have to eat or burn afterward. But remember, don't speak about the details with anyone before you leave. I'll be heading back to The Hague in an hour. You'll follow later this morning. I know that's short notice, but it's six hours by train, which will barely leave us enough time to get you up to speed before leaving for Bosnia tomorrow."

"Tomorrow?"

"Yes. It's moving fast, I know. But they put this together in a hurry. Apparently there isn't a big window for action, especially on the Serb general, Andric. He's the French army's problem, not ours. But their operation impacts our timing, and they seem to be worried he'll head off to Kosovo soon. A lot of reports on troop buildups, so you never know. Sorry I can't book you a flight, but that's our budget. I'd hate to tell you how many trips into the field I've canceled or cut short. That's what happens when your bean counters are across the ocean and your crime scene's a thousand miles away.

"You'll arrive late afternoon. Take the number seven tram to Churchillplein. You're staying at the Hotel Dorint. It's right next-door to the tribunal, so just walk on over when you've checked in. Security will be expecting you. Then we can get started with the backgrounders. And I'm sure Contreras will want to meet you."

"Contreras?"

"The new head man at the tribunal, although his official title is chief prosecutor. Took over last month. A judge from Peru. Made his name putting drug lords in jail. Survived two car bombings and got his house burned out. Big hero down there. After dealing with the Shining Path, he figures Bosnians are little lambs, so he can't understand why we don't just go out and haul everybody in. NATO's already sick of hearing from him. They figure he's threatening to upset the status quo just as things are coming to a boil in Kosovo."

"What does Kosovo have to do with us? If they start bombing, I mean. Do we cancel?"

"If a war starts there, we'll be the last things on anyone's mind, so we just keep going like nothing happened. It might complicate the Andric case, though. With the French as cozy as they are with the Serbs, maybe they won't still feel like cooperating if the Americans are bombing Belgrade. But we're supposed to act like that doesn't matter, like there's no connection at all. Either way, our guy will still be in business, and we'll have an offer he can't refuse. Contreras is a full-speed-ahead kind of guy, so far anyway. He's also as political as they come. Always seems to have a few diplomatic types over at the office, touring them around. So we're a little on edge these days, wondering who'll be the first to screw up under his 'new aggressiveness' mandate."

"Like us, you mean."

"Only if we find some way to become an embarrassment. But you need to be ready to roll as soon as you arrive. If our man is going to do business with us, we'll know pretty soon."

"And if he decides not to?"

"Then we go to Plan B."

"Which is?"

"Classified." He smiled, patting Vlado's shoulder, then reached into his pocket for a business card. Pine's name and title were embossed above a blue UN globe and the tribunal's long official title.

"My phone number, just in case. Plus the address of the tribunal. If you end up on the wrong tram, just hail a cab and show him this. Most of the cabbies speak English. Don't try any Bosnian on them. The Dutch aren't too thrilled with refugees these days. Even less than the Germans, in their own repressed little way."

He held out his hand for a shake. "Welcome aboard, Vlado. It's a strong team we've got. Definitely the underdogs, but we play hard."

All this American slang was going to take some getting used to, but Vlado took Pine's hand firmly—"sealing the deal," he did know that one—while searching Pine's beaming face. The man's enthusiasm was infectious.

"It should be fun," Pine said before throttling back a notch, his smile turning almost sheepish. "Or interesting, anyway. Oh, and hang on to your receipts if you ever want to get reimbursed. Contreras is just as tight with the dollar as his predecessors."

Vlado smiled. Some things about police work were the same no matter who you worked for.

The train was the perfect decompression chamber for traveling from one life to another. By the time they'd crawled through Berlin into the pines of the countryside, Vlado felt as if old circuits were springing to life after years of idleness. He bought a Coke and a bag of chips from a vendor pushing a cart down the rocking corridor, then dozed for half an hour, awakening refreshed and thinking of his family. Jasmina had been excited for him, and a little jealous. It was Sonja who'd remained dead set against the whole thing, tugging at his coat as he stepped out the door. The memory cooled his elation. It was still too easy to recall the emptiness of his two years alone, the time and energy he'd spent mending fences. Now he was bolting off on his own again, leaving them behind for who knew how many days, even weeks. But when it was over they'd have new possibilities. Easy, he warned himself. Don't start making up your mind. Just enjoy the adventure.

He stood to stretch in the corridor, swaying with the motion of the train as the bleached November landscape passed at 120 miles per hour. He wondered for a moment what Tomas must be up to about now, piloting the backhoe through the clay and rubble.

In the afternoon they crossed the border into the Netherlands, and the view gradually changed. Canals separated fields, with boats seemingly parked in the middle of nowhere until you realized that the water led everywhere. There were even a few windmills. Vlado stood at the window, elbows propped against the glass. Phalanxes of schoolkids on bicycles waited at rail crossings, headed home. Rainwater pooled in low spots and creases. That plus the canals left the impression of a countryside afloat like an earthen raft, which the slightest shift might send sliding beneath the waves.

· · ·

The Hague was a typical European act of concealment—a medieval village wrapped inside centuries of construction. You could chart the rapid pace of recent development in the chockablock outermost suburbs, and even toward the center a new section built of steel and glass loomed above old parks and canals.

But the aging heart of the city still hunched together on narrow cobbled lanes of low brick buildings. Statues of grave old Dutchmen stared from manicured parks. Orderly columns of black bicycles dominated the traffic. The air carried the damp, briny touch of the North Sea, with a raw cold that crept into your skin as if prepared to linger until spring.

A brief tram ride took Vlado to tribunal headquarters, a curving four-story building of steel and glass that looked like the insurance office it had once been. Out front a collection of abstract sculptures sprawled from a concrete pond, hulks of metal like wreckage dropped from a helicopter.

Vlado spotted his first Bosnian while security men scanned his trousers with a metal detector. It was a woman, bustling past as she spoke his native tongue to a guard, who answered in kind. The guards directed Vlado to the second-floor canteen to wait for Pine. Men and women sat at small tables behind a low partition, hunched over coffee cups and full ashtrays, voices buzzing in English, Bosnian, German, French. Being foreign was just part of the scenery here, not something to hide. A man strolled by with the dark hair and narrow-set eyes that could only come from home, and Vlado was tempted to hail him with a familiar greeting. Then Pine burst through a nearby set of doors, walking at double time.

"Welcome to the big cop shop," he said. "Trip go okay?"

"Sure. Everything was fine."

"Hope you're rested and ready to work. Let's go upstairs, and I'll start introducing you."

They rode to the third floor, strolling down blue-carpeted hallways to a partitioned cluster of cubicles where several men sat at desks, each of them on the telephone.

"This is my team of investigators," Pine said. "A little crowded as you can see, about a dozen in all when everybody's here. Let's see if Benny's got a minute. Hey, you'd probably like some coffee, wouldn't you?"

"That would be great."

"I'll run downstairs. Take your coat off and get comfortable. Looks like everybody's on the phone now, anyway. Don't worry, none of them bite."

Vlado draped his overcoat across a seat at the closest desk. Three of the nearby cubicles were occupied. A man with a buzz cut and a stylish shirt in electric blue spoke what sounded like Italian as he scribbled in a small notebook. Opposite him was a spidery bald fellow who loomed well above his desktop, dark brown skin drawn tight around a narrow head, giving his forehead the hardened look of a coffee bean. He spoke a language Vlado couldn't place, like the sound of running water, then he slipped suddenly into English without missing a beat.

Closest to Vlado was the one Pine had called Benny, the noisiest in the bunch. He was an American, much shorter than Pine, belly spilling over his belt, tie askew. He leaned back in his chair while talking on the phone, feet propped on a messy desk. A torn newspaper photo of Madonna was tacked in a corner of his partition, next to a bumper sticker in Cyrillic lettering that said FUCK SFOR. The back of the chair groaned as the man shifted. The phone cord was twisted and knotted in a dozen places, and he'd jammed his left foot against his phone to keep it from sliding off the desk. He was muttering, nodding quickly, and seemed to be growing impatient with whoever was at the other end. The man glanced toward Vlado, rolling his eyes. Then the show began.

"Yeah," he said. "Yeah, I know. But it's because he's a criminal, okay?" His accent was heavy. Vlado had seen enough American movies to place it somewhere near New York. "I said, 'A criminal,'" shouting now, then a mutter—"Christ, these phones"—followed by another shout: "A goddamn *war* criminal, okay? Why else would we wanna bring him in? You've heard of us down there, right?" Glancing at Vlado, again rolling his eyes.

Squad-room humor. Break out the cigarettes and the naughty calendars. This, too, felt like a sort of home to Vlado, and a warm flush of energy surged through him.

He leaned forward for a closer look at this fellow while pulling a cigarette pack from his pocket. Benny saw it and swiveled in his chair, leaning toward Vlado, who braced for a wagging finger or a shake of a head. But the man only rolled closer, chair wheels squealing. As if by magic, he produced a lighter, raising it toward Vlado as he leaned from the groaning chair. The lighter chirped and Vlado bent toward him, inhaling, nearly brushing the man's fingers with his own as his breath pulled the flame into the cigarette.

An absurd vision of the scene sprang to Vlado's mind, a twisted parody of Michelangelo's *Creation of Adam*—outstretched hands meeting in midair—and the thought made him laugh, dragon smoke bursting from his nostrils as the New Yorker receded, grinning as if he understood and approved.

"I'm Benny," he whispered, cupping a hand over the mouthpiece. "Welcome to the zoo."

Then he resumed his verbal assault. "Yeah, yeah. Yeahhhh. Well, if that's the case, then you tell your boss . . ." A pause, then he shook his head impatiently. "Then you tell your captain, you tell him we're not just a bunch of scared-shitless bureaucrats rolling over at the first sign of more paperwork, or every time some local warlord waves a gun at us, and that we're coming after this little shit down in your sector whether you're with us or not."

By now sweat was beading on Benny's forehead, reminding Vlado of condensation on an overworked refrigerator, which seemed appropriate enough because, for all his bluster, Benny struck him as a cool customer, someone who'd be imperturbable in the field. Vlado would love to see how he dealt with stubborn checkpoints, or paper-stamping officials who tried to slow him down.

Pinned on Benny's desk under his right elbow was a thick document with a bright blue cover. The boldfaced word **INDICTMENT** printed at the top. He folded open a page as Vlado scooted closer for a look, able to read a paragraph at the bottom:

The accused, often assisted by camp guards, usually shot detainees at close range in the head or back. Often, the accused and camp guards forced the detainees who were to be shot to put their heads on a metal grate that drained into the Sava River, so that there would be minimal cleanup after the shootings. The accused and guards then ordered other detainees to move the bodies to one of two disposal areas where the bodies were piled until they were later loaded onto trucks and taken to mass graves.

Benny saw Vlado looking and slid more papers his way, with a quick nod that said "Get a load of this."

WHEREABOUTS was the heading. It was a list of indicted suspects not yet in custody, a sort of scorecard put together by some group calling itself Balkan Watch. There were six pages in all, covering about forty men. Vlado read the first one:

CESIC, Nenad. Crimes against humanity, murder, rape. Frequents the Club Markala restaurant in Zvornik. Lives at home, works for local reserve police. Shares red Honda motorbike with cousin, also under indictment. Both often seen riding through town.

He flipped to another page:

GOJKO, Dragan. Crimes against humanity, torture. In June 1998 was working as a police trainer in school in Prijedor. Owns the Express bar, where Momcilo Zaric (also indicted, see below) often drinks.

He found Zaric a few paragraphs later.

Crimes against humanity, murder, rape. Nicknamed "Juka." Drinks *rakija* every morning around 10 o'clock at Krsma bar. Can be seen in town driving blue VW Golf. Passes local International Police headquarters every day on his way home.

Vlado glanced at Benny to make sure he wasn't watching, then scanned the pages until he found the entry he sought. Just reading the name made his pulse quicken.

POPOVIC, Branko. Genocide, crimes against humanity, torture. Commander "Popi's Lions" paramilitary unit. Believed in Kosovo. Often seen at bar of Hotel Grand, or driving black Toyota Land Cruiser. May live in military barracks in Pristina, but also has home in Belgrade. Frequently travels in Europe. Confirmed sightings since January '98 in Zurich, Augsburg. Unconfirmed sightings in Vienna, Berlin.

The Berlin reference made him flinch. But there was nothing more. No mention of witnesses, addresses, or a possible disappearance. He checked the date on the front. The report was two weeks old, and who knew how old the sightings were? Whoever had visited Haris's apartment had done so since this report had been updated.

Benny was raising his voice again, seemingly working himself toward the finale.

"You wanna be at his house? Then be at his fuckin' house. You wanna sit on your ass at a checkpoint and listen for gunshots? Then you do that. 'Cause we're coming, SFOR or no SFOR, and all the military industrial ass draggin' in the world ain't gonna stop us, okay? . . . I said, Okay?" Pause. "Hello?" He squeezed his eyes shut, then roared, "Christ! These fuckin' phones! How these people ever gonna have a country if they don't have decent phones? Man!" He slammed down the receiver, shaking his head. "Five minutes of prime reaming-out wasted. I think I even had the guy on the verge of ordering up an operation for us. Or at least thinking about it." He sighed. "Either way, I feel a helluva lot better than I did five minutes ago."

Then he looked up with an exasperated grin that said he'd loved every minute. "Benny Hampton," he said. "You must be Pine's Bosnian. Not that I'm supposed to know or anything. But, hey, I *am* team leader, so I guess I ought to be able to find out a few things around here. Although if Spratt hears about that last conversation, I may not be team leader much longer."

By then Pine had returned, throwing his jacket on the back of a chair and placing two steaming cups of coffee on the desk.

"Benny, Benny, Benny," Pine said with some affection, the accent sounding mild after two minutes of hearing the New Yorker. "How many times do you have to be told? SFOR is our friend. Just like IFOR was our friend, and UNPROFOR before them."

"Yeah, the army of a thousand names," Benny muttered. "Give 'em another year and they'll change it again. They oughtta call 'em WHAT-FOR, then maybe somebody'll figure they've been doin' nothin' all along. Sitting around all day watching our suspects have a beer."

Vlado knew the acronyms well. During the war the troops wore blue helmets and drove white armored vehicles, working for UNPROFOR, the UN Protection Force. After the peace agreement they painted their helmets and vehicles green and were joined by twenty-four thousand better-armed Americans, renaming themselves IFOR, the Implementation Force, which in a year or so shrunk by a few thousand soldiers and became SFOR, the Stabilization Force.

"You know how it goes, Benny," Pine said. "We're just not a vital part of the mission statement. Oh, and Vlado, sorry, but no smokes up here. This is World Health Organization territory, not the Balkans. You'll have to snuff it out or take it to the canteen."

"Fuckin' SFOR," Benny was still muttering. "Fuckin' NATO. Biggest and baddest army in Bosnia and they can't even get it up to roust a hungover old Serb in his pajamas. The guy hasn't had a bodyguard for two years and he's still listed as 'at large.' He must pass through a couple of their checkpoints a day, and all they do is wave."

"Then you go roust him, Benny."

"Hey, I aim to. That's what I was telling them I'm gonna do. He probably knew I was bluffing, but with this new mandate from Contreras, who knows? Maybe I'll even get the chance. Can't be any worse than goin' into some project in the Bronx. I'll handcuff him and drag him halfway to Budapest if they let me."

"Which they won't. Contreras talks a good game, but he's no more likely to run a cowboy operation than the others. If he starts a firefight where SFOR's got to ride to the rescue, they'll never lift a finger for us again."

"Lotta difference that would make."

"But never mind that, Benny. Say hello to Vlado Petric. Vlado, meet Benny Hampton, who thinks he's still banging heads back in Brooklyn."

"The Bronx, for Chrissakes. Yeah, we sorta met, but this makes it official."

Vlado grasped his outstretched hand. It was hot and springy, like a warm ball of dough.

"So you're the guy who pissed off half of Sarajevo on your way out the door. And you let this backwoods yahoo Pine talk you into going back?"

"Thanks for making my life easier, Benny."

"Well, if you need help while you're down there, give me a shout on the cell phone. I'll be in the field for the next week or so, if you end up anywhere near Vitez."

"That's Benny's little way of trying to find out what we're up to and where we're going. But we'll keep your offer in mind, Benny."

Pine steered Vlado toward his own office, in an opposite corner.

"Yeah, yeah," Benny called after them. "Get out the secret decoder ring and I'll just move on. What are you guys up to anyway that even the team leader can't know? I've been hearing all week that something hinky was in the works."

"Hinky?" Vlado asked.

"Screwball," Benny clarified. "Something that's not quite right. For one thing, I hear even the French are involved. Those lovely guys who let Mr. Karadzic get away last year."

"Is that true?" Vlado asked, amazed to hear that one of the biggest suspects of all, the wartime president of the Bosnian Serbs, had even come close to capture.

"Maybe," Pine said, glaring at Benny. "But we're really not supposed to talk about it, are we?"

"But we will anyway, now that you're one of us," Benny muttered. "There was a raid planned, but it never came off 'cause some French major tipped Karadzic. Late summer of '97, and talk about the shit hitting the fan."

"*May* have tipped him off," Pine said. "And there *may* have been a raid planned."

"The French were supposed to court-martial the major. Instead they posted him to a desk in Paris. Not bad, huh? And now I hear you guys are actually going to work with them. Can't wait to see how that turns out."

"Loose lips sink ships, Benny."

"Tell that to the French major. Sounds like his ship made it home okay."

Pine shot Benny another look that said he'd been talking out of school long enough.

"The file you need to see is on my desk," Pine said, steering Vlado toward his door. "Go ahead and use my office awhile. We won't be here long enough to get you a desk of your own. Suspect's name is still confidential as far as anyone else is concerned."

He glanced significantly at Benny, who grinned and offered a parting shot. "Don't worry, Pine. I get the message. Good to meet you, Vlado. If we don't have time for a cold one before you hit the road, maybe we'll meet up in-country."

Vlado stepped through the door. Like Benny's desk, Pine's was a jumble of files and papers. Pine had a window, with a view of tram tracks and a narrow brick street. Posted next to the window was a bright blue calendar with pictures of smiling young men above a basketball schedule for the University of North Carolina. The grinning players faced directly across the room to an opposite wall, where a row of unsmiling men from Bosnia stared back in black and white. It was a wanted poster of five suspects, enough to form their own basketball team. Pine noticed Vlado looking at it.

"My biggest case," he said. "Massacre in the Lasva Valley in April '93. Two in custody, three at large. But for the moment"—he opened a manila folder on the desktop, revealing a few single-spaced sheets—"here's our man. This is just the summary. There will be more to read later. Army-intelligence files, old diplomatic cables. Some of it's still beyond even my security clearance for the moment. But this will get you started." He checked his watch. "You've probably got half an hour."

Vlado eased into Pine's chair and relaxed. Reading case files used to be drudgery. Now it seemed like a privilege. He'd never much cared for paperwork, as if anyone did, but he had always enjoyed spreading the facts before him late at night as an investigation unfolded, watching characters and plots take shape by the light of a single lamp in an empty office, looking for patterns and anomalies, feeling the excitement of moving toward a solution while the city around him slept.

He took the sheet of paper in his hands and eased back into his past as if he were seated at his old desk, up on the fourth floor, a brown glass building on the south bank of the Miljacka River, a cup of Husayn's terrible coffee steaming at the ready. He looked up, glancing at Pine's calendars and notepads, as if to reassure himself he hadn't really slipped through some time warp. Then, smiling to himself, a little giddy, he began reading, happily back at work.

CHAPTER FIVE

The suspect's name was Pero Matek, and his recent history sounded all too familiar. He was your garden-variety wartime thug and profiteer, quick to recognize opportunity amid war and chaos. Vlado had seen them by the dozen in Sarajevo during the siege, so he already viewed this one with weary distaste.

It was the man's earlier history that fascinated him. Vlado, like most of his generation, had been taught only broad-brush treatments of World War II, set pieces of Titoist heroism and selfless sacrifice by the People and the Partisans, a united front of Communist rebels battling Nazis and a few scattered traitors, mostly local fascists and royalists, the Ustasha and the Chetniks. If the recent war had taught him anything, it was that the truth was usually a lot more complicated.

Matek was born Pero Rudec in a remote section of Herzegovina in March 1923. That would make him seventy-five. He grew up on a farm, attended public schools, and at age sixteen enrolled in a military academy training officers for the federal army.

Matek was a Croat, and during his teens he joined the nationalist Ustasha movement, the tinhorn fascists who eventually threw in their lot with the Nazis. Hitler was their ticket to statehood, and at age eighteen Matek was among the thousands of cheering people in Zagreb on April 10, 1941, to welcome the declaration of Croatian independence under puppet dictator Ante Pavelic. By then Matek had joined Croatia's Home Defense Army, and he was soon promoted to lieutenant during action in early 1942 in the Kosarev Mountains, a brutal campaign of killing and burning in northern Bosnia, notorious for its forced conversions of thousands of Muslims and Orthodox Christian Serbs to Catholicism. On a few occasions, Serbs who remained unconvinced had been burned alive in their churches.

In the spring of 1942 Matek was wounded in the right shoulder, putting him out of commission for a month and resulting in a transfer to lighter duty at Jasenovac, the infamous concentration-camp complex on the Sava River. There he commanded a squadron of guards who distinguished themselves, if that was the word for it, as particularly brutal and efficient, not only in their duties at the camp but in raids on nearby towns and villages, looting and killing and rounding up the usual suspects. In 1945 he was promoted to major. His trail became murky in April, the last month of the war.

One report said he'd headed north with several thousand other fleeing soldiers and civilians, a group that suffered heavy losses to ambushes and outright massacres by Partisans and Soviet troops. Other reports placed him in a convoy of trucks that left Zagreb with weapons and certain "assets of the State." This version branched into three further trails, like a legend that has grown and become embroidered in years of retelling. One variation had him and a pair of others making it safely to Wolfsberg, Austria, with their cargo, sheltering in a monastery before being taken into custody by the British. The second said they abandoned their vehicles at a mountain pass near the Austrian town of Liezen. The third said Matek had been one of the few to survive a Partisan ambush near the Slovenian town of Maribor.

Whatever the case, after four months on the run he ended up in Austria, where the British sent him to a displaced-persons camp in Italy near the town of Fermo. With him were some twenty thousand other temporarily stateless people, mostly from Croatia, Bulgaria, and Hungary. The DP camps were way stations for the millions of Europe's homeless, people who'd been shoved aside by armies or freed from concentration camps, and the living conditions were notoriously bad. The camps were also popular hiding places for war criminals, officers and administrators who shed their uniforms and identities to try to blend with the masses.

The risk of this strategy was that you might be lost and forgotten for months at a time, susceptible to disease and malnutrition. Or someone might recognize you, or discover something among your papers that would give you away, unless you had friends who could come up with new documents or a way out.

Matek apparently had such help, although it was slow in arriving. He spent nine months at Fermo before being released to Rome, into the custody of the Pontifical Relief Commission for Refugees. In Rome he took a job in the offices of the Confraternita di San Girolamo degli Illirici, where a Croatian brotherhood of Franciscan priests ran efforts to assist their wandering countrymen, with a headquarters on the right bank of the Tiber, only a mile or so from the walls of the Vatican.

The priests there were anti-Tito, anti-Communist, anti-anyone who might want to dig up old secrets about their friends. They secured a new set of identity papers for the newly named Matek, who shed his old name of Rudec.

He stayed in Italy until 1961, a few years after Pope Pius XII died. Afterward, it seems, many of the more questionable Croatian émigrés began to wear out their welcome. Matek repatriated to Yugoslavia under his new name. He apparently made it across the border without incident, resettling in the central Bosnian town of Travnik, quite a distance from where he'd grown up, and well away from anywhere he'd served during the war. And that's where he remained, having done well for himself in the interim. There was no reference to how his true identity had suddenly surfaced after all these years, but apparently his neighbors were still none the wiser.

The recent war had afforded him unprecedented opportunities for expansion of his various enterprises, and he now owned a string of gasoline stations and had managed to win several UN and EU reconstruction grants—some $200,000 worth to date—with some of it actually going toward the rebuilding of homes. A Norwegian grant intended to help rebuild a local soft-drink distributorship had somehow been diverted to help rebuild a local beer-and-liquor distributorship—the largest in the region, in fact, owned by Mr. Pero Matek. And practically none of a year-old World Bank economic-development loan of $100,000 to stimulate local employment had yet been spent on its intended purpose. World Bank officials were now convinced that the borrower would default. Too much overhead and red tape, it seemed. Too many unrealistic expectations. Though the borrower was doing all he could, of course.

Vlado shook his head at the waste and folly. He was nearly as out-
raged by Matek's recent behavior as he was by the man's past. Otherwise you might chalk him up as another bent old man playing
chess and trying to forget, wanting to be left alone with his grand-
children. This one had never married, never raised a family, and had
stayed up to his elbows in the rough work of making money from
hardship and corruption. And now Vlado was going to meet him,
was going to dangle before him the carrot that he apparently craved
most—entrée into the lucrative business of demining.

Vlado flipped to the last page, an update from only a week ago.
Matek seemed to be in excellent health, based on the account of a
World Bank official who'd paid him a call to inquire uneasily about
the state of the grant. It now seemed he was Internet-ready, if
still a bit rough around the edges in his countrified manner, offering great quantities of charred meat and strong drink. Glass after
glass of *rakija*. His security people seemed to have made quite an
impression—several men with large guns, a guardhouse at the gated
entrance—and he was seldom seen in Travnik without a bodyguard,
unless he was meeting women. One woman in particular, the wife of
the mayor from a neighboring village, seemed to have drawn most
of his recent attentions.

Vlado stretched, checking his watch. The half hour had come and
gone, and through the glass he saw Pine with Benny, in deep discussion. He put the report back in its folder, leaving it on Pine's desktop
and opening the office door.

Benny saw him first, looking up with that glint of mischief that
Vlado had already decided he liked.

"So, ready to join up?" he asked.

Before Vlado could answer, a commanding voice interrupted
from another direction.

"Pay no attention to him. He'll have you believing we're nothing
but a bunch of misfits. Welcome aboard, Vlado. I'm Phillip Spratt,
head of investigations."

Another hand to shake, as Vlado tried to puzzle out the
accent.

"From Australia," Spratt said without prompting. "Volunteered.
Like pretty much everyone in the building. Fifty-six countries and
most every wart and flaw of their legal systems, all under one roof.

And, yes, I know the rest of you have heard this little speech, but Vlado hasn't."

Spratt had a wide face that looked hard enough to cause mortal injury if you were to run up against it, a grooved oaken forehead beneath a widow's peak of coppery bristle. Pine, only half joking, had told Vlado that the only reliable indicator of the man's mood was the patch of skin beneath his ears—tiny thermometers where the color rose whenever he was building to a boil. For the moment they seemed to be at midlevel red. The crowd around him had gone silent.

"Has Pine given you the grand tour yet?" Spratt asked.

"Haven't had time," Pine answered.

"You should take a look at our courtrooms while you're here. Quite impressive."

"And both of them look like the bridge of the starship fucking *Enterprise*," Benny piped up, "only with wood paneling."

Everyone laughed uneasily. Benny seemed to be the only one who could get away with such an interruption. But before Spratt could respond, another voice rang out, a sharp fluting sound like the most reckless sort of music. Vlado spotted the rising flush below Spratt's ears and correctly surmised that the big boss must have arrived.

"Ah, there you are, Mr. Petric. Freshly arrived, I trust. I'm Hector Contreras, the chief prosecutor. Almost as new to this place as you."

Vlado's immediate impression was that Contreras was a gentleman of means, yet also a gossip and an intriguer. He would have been hard-pressed to say exactly why. There was something of the rake in the man's glance, which came at you from an angle, a slight tilt of the head, as if he'd been looking at something to your left and swiveled his eyes just in time to catch you red-handed. He couldn't have been dressed any snappier, in a tailored navy suit with lapels and pockets cut like racing stripes, set off by a red handkerchief peeping from the front pocket. He wore a small mustache—a gigolo's mustache seemed the only way to describe it, again, for reasons Vlado couldn't name. By now a few others had drifted over from their desks for the show, and ten faces were turned toward Vlado, awaiting his response. Hardly what he was used to at the construction site.

He blushed, then blurted a muffled "Honored, sir," feeling self-conscious, as if his English had suddenly stiffened into the worst sort of Balkan caricature.

Contreras responded with quick grace and warmth. "The honor is mine. A good man in a tight spot, and incorruptible into the bargain. That's what I've heard so far, and I'm only expecting to hear more of the same. You'll be coming to dinner tonight, of course?"

"Of course." Vlado tried to hide his surprise. Pine looked shocked. Then Spratt, whose ears had gone tomato red, spoke up.

"Sir, I was just about to invite them. I only got word myself in the past hour."

Vlado saw Benny smirking.

"No matter," Contreras said. "All's well now, and I trust I'll see the three of you at seven for cocktails. Drinks will be an open affair, with assorted members of the diplomatic community, the sort of people we have to keep happy if we're to pay the light bill. Then we'll shoo them away and shut the doors for the need-to-know crowd, everything off the record. Sort of a combination debriefing and get-acquainted session. I decided it would be just the right atmosphere for kicking off, well, such a grand event."

"Grand event, huh?" said Benny, who apparently would cut in on anyone's conversation. "Tell us more."

Contreras beamed his rake's smile while Spratt glared at Benny. "All will become clear soon enough. It will be part of the new order around here, and down there as well. But for the moment, I'm sure the rest of you know enough to say nothing of these matters outside this building. Understood?"

There was a round of small nods and muttered assents.

"Very well."

Contreras turned on his heels and strolled away, in the manner of a particularly flamboyant butler. It was no surprise he'd been a judge, for he obviously enjoyed performance. Vlado could easily imagine him playing to a jury or a press gallery.

The investigators straggled back to their desks, but Pine was in a panic. "Did you bring a suit?" he asked Vlado.

Vlado shook his head. "I thought we'd be traveling light."

"You figured right, but we'd better get you one." He scanned the room for possible donors, then checked his watch. "C'mon. We'll hop a tram into town. We'll expense-account it. Contreras can put it on his goddamn party budget. Got a white shirt?"

"One."

"One's enough. Let's roll."

They headed for the heart of town. Every seat was taken, so they held the overhead straps, swaying with the turns and bumps while Vlado stooped to look out the windows. It was charming, in its way, this toy-town layout of bricks and bicycles. There were cheese shops brimming with red waxen wheels the size of bus tires, greengrocers with taut bright awnings, and the curtains of every home were thrown open boldly to the evening, lamplight pooling on the sidewalks out front. But the sense of order was almost unnerving— every brick in place, all those black bicycles wheeling in sync. Most of the faces in the street seemed as humorous as the glowering statues in the park, seeming to disapprove of all they beheld. He wondered how Pine fit in here, a sprawling American with his unruly hair.

They reached their stop, walking a few blocks to a men's shop where Pine said he sometimes bought shirts. Pine employed his halting Dutch to explain their shortage of time, and a high-strung clerk quickly measured Vlado while fretting that this was no way to buy such a fine suit. He laid out a few choices on a counter while Pine thumbed through a rack of ties.

"I better get you up to speed on what to expect at this cocktail hour," Pine said. "Haven't seen the guest list, but it will probably be a minefield. Here, this tie ought to do."

It was a bold red with gold paisley. Vlado frowned.

"Trust me. Go with red. Power color. Half the people there will want to pigeonhole your politics within the first five minutes, and the ones who disagree will try to eat you alive. How much have you been keeping up with the state of play back home?"

"In Bosnia?"

"Not Germany, that's for sure."

"A little. Sounds like it hasn't changed much since I left. Same parties with the same stupid views."

"I was talking more about the people really running the show. The high representative's office. The EU. NATO. All the NGOs and internationals. You know?"

Vlado didn't.

"I'll give you the short version. At the top you've got the high representative. Mostly a Euro perspective and bureaucratic as hell. He's supposedly just overseeing things, letting the national governments and parties do their stuff. But his people control a lot of hard currency and tell the NGOs and aid agencies what they can and can't do, so who's really the boss now? Here, try the blue one." He'd grabbed a dark blue suit from the rack, tossing it onto the other three. Vlado saw the old salesman blanching at the brisk treatment of his merchandise but biting his tongue. Guilders were guilders.

"Then there's SFOR. Benny's feelings are pretty representative on that topic, but they're still the biggest army. The international police force is around, too. Powerless. Might as well not be there.

"Then you've got local police, your old employers, but with three separate ethnic breakdowns, and with the civil side and the Interior Ministry side, the old MUP people who will still lock you up for your politics if you're not careful."

Vlado glanced up, shaking out his sleeves. This one would do. He nodded to the clerk while Pine continued.

"Somewhere at the margins of all this you've got the private investors, all trying to make a buck while looking as altruistic as possible, and yes, I know I'm going fast. Here's a tie you can live with. Red and boring, perfect. Strap it on. What's that one cost, sir, sixty guilders?"

The salesman nodded without a word, not wanting to interrupt the flow of commerce.

"Nationality matters, too. The French don't trust the Americans, the Americans don't trust the French, and any Yank will run like hell at the slightest whiff of *anyone* from Iran, Afghanistan, or Morocco, the old suppliers of the mujahedeen forces who technically aren't supposed to be there anymore, even if everyone knows the holy warriors never went away completely. The Scans are pretty much everywhere, doing good and keeping quiet in the usual Scan way. All the Germans want is to get in and out without having any soldiers caught painting swastikas, which has already happened, so too bad for them. The French want to give the Serbs an even break but without upsetting the balance next-door in Kosovo. The Brits want to make it look like they're independent from the Americans, only with-out pissing off the Americans."

"And the Americans?"

"Oh, the Americans ask very little. We only want the greatest amount of influence for the least amount of money and aggravation. Anything complicated is the high representative's problem, and the lower you go down that food chain the more likely you'll find one of their people hanging out with local bureaucrats, the kind who always have their hands in somebody else's pockets. So things get murky. Sometimes even dangerous. Three people dead behind a gas station and you don't know why. Then a week later ownership papers change hands on a dozen local storefronts. And one of the new own-ers is somebody like our guy Matek. Throw in a few dozen leftover warlords with various cuts of the black market, plus some rabble-rousers who didn't get quite enough of the war, then overlay that with the usual thieves and drug barons, including a few radical Mus-lims and some interlopers from the Albanian heroin trade, and that pretty well sums up the state of play. Homesick yet?"

"Sounds like business as usual in the Balkans."

"Pretty much."

Vlado pulled his own trousers back on. The shopkeeper had pinned the new pair and handed them to a tailor in the back, where you could hear the thrum of a sewing machine. A few minutes later the tailor, pins in his mouth, hustled the suit back up front, where the dizzied clerk waited to be rewarded with a tribunal credit card.

"Okay," Pine said. "We're cutting it kind of close. Better catch our tram. You can change at the hotel, and I'll swing by and get you at quarter to seven."

"That should give me just enough time to check in with Jasmina."

"Which reminds me," Pine said, suddenly looking sheepish. "No outside calls. They've put a stop order on the phone in your room. Operational security. Which I know must sound pretty lame with all the blabbing you've already heard. But no calls home till we're done." Then, in a softer tone: "I really am sorry."

Vlado felt a flush of anger. The last thing he wanted to do was make Jasmina worry. "You might have told me earlier. Jasmina will assume the worst."

"Spratt told me not to, until now. I can have one of the secretaries call. She'll tell Jasmina everything's okay but that she won't hear from you for a while."

"What else haven't you told me?"

Pine frowned. "Not much. But by late tomorrow you'll know everything."

Vlado, holding the new clothes across his arm like a valet, knew that this should set off alarms. He'd heard these kinds of assurances before. Nothing good ever came of them. But he felt powerless to protest.

"Look, I'm not happy with this part of it, either," Pine said. "If it were up to me, I'd have outlined the whole thing for you back in Berlin. You'll just have to trust me."

Vlado had taken that kind of advice before, too. The last time it had nearly gotten him killed.

CHAPTER SIX

Contreras had found himself a big brick home on the edge of a park, the grandest residence to date of any of the chief prosecutors, and he liked to show it off. This would be Pine's third visit. The first two were for staff cocktail parties, where the investigators and prosecutors turned themselves into genteel drunks, padding about on Oriental rugs while immigrant waiters replenished their drinks. No one seemed to know quite how to react to these events with their crystal glasses and bottomless booze, but with every sip they uneasily hoped the tribunal wasn't footing the bill. The smart money said the Peruvian embassy was paying the freight, gratified to have their man in such a high-profile position. But some believed it was Contreras himself.

The story on Contreras was that he'd married into a rich family, a wealth that not only bought him into the Peruvian judiciary but also kept him living in grand style. The tale had assumed enough heft and substance to keep the staff drinking without guilt. But for most of them the novelty had worn off.

Vlado would rather have spent the evening locked in a room with files and briefing papers, reading more about their suspect. Instead he was strolling up a brick walkway in his new suit, smelling the resin of the tall pines in the raw November evening.

The red-and-white flag of Peru was hanging out front, as if this were a consular home and Contreras its resident poo-bah. A waiter opened the door, bowing slightly and gesturing toward a large room to the side where Vlado glimpsed white tablecloths and silver platters. Already there was a buzz of conversation, the tinkle of ice cubes in glasses. Brushed and bald heads gathered beneath the shimmer of a grand chandelier.

Vlado felt calm enough, considering. He gave a final tug at the knot of his tie. The suit did wonders for the general impression he made, it seemed. Already people reacted as if his IQ was forty points higher than when he wore the mud and denim of Berlin.

"If anyone asks who you are, say 'staff' unless I introduce you," Pine muttered. "Try to stay close by. And if the waters get too deep, just smile a lot and laugh at their jokes."

Vlado doubted one could get into much trouble here. The scene struck him more as an overly stuffy reception, something that an archbishop might put on, or some government official who'd just been promoted beyond his capabilities.

A deep voice came at them from behind.

"Calvin, you're starting to look bored at these things already." Pine tensed, and Vlado turned to see Spratt, who seemed just as stiff as he had in the office. Unwinding didn't seem to be part of the man's repertoire. "So, all squared away for tomorrow?"

"More or less," Pine said. "A little more time to prepare Vlado might have been nice."

"I suspect he'll do fine. And you'll have more time to bring him up to speed once you're in Sarajevo."

Vlado thought he saw an odd look pass between them, and he wondered what it was all about. Having missed lunch, he grabbed a handful of peanuts from a nearby bowl. A waiter swooped in to pour wine; Spratt waited for him to depart, then glanced around for eavesdroppers and lowered his voice.

"Now, if the French will just hold up their end with Andric," Spratt continued, "we'll be in business. You boys can do your bit and be back in a matter of days."

"So, you really think it will be that easy?" Pine asked.

"The way we've got it sketched it would seem to be a foolproof operation."

"I just hope we're not underestimating the old man."

"Not as long as we get him away from the bodyguards. Which is where you come in, Vlado. That's what makes you indispensable. I'm more worried about rounding up all our witnesses on Andric. We're still holding out for Popovic as the star, but apparently nobody has seen the man in more than a month."

Vlado nearly choked on a peanut at the mention of Popovic. He half expected Spratt and Pine to turn toward him to spring the trap, demanding an explanation. But if this exchange was for his benefit, they were disguising it well.

"I thought they'd tracked him down," Pine said. "Lounging at the Grand Hotel in Pristina."

"You're thinking of some other thug. No trace of Popovic. He could be anywhere. Vienna. Kosovo." A brief pause. "Berlin. Belgrade. You might want to ask LeBlanc, our friend from France." Spratt gestured toward a far corner. "Apparently he's been making some noise about it."

Vlado tried to see whom Spratt was referring to, but there were six or seven people where he'd pointed.

"He's apparently the one who helped link these two cases together," Spratt said, "he and Harkness."

"Who's Harkness?" Vlado asked.

"A meddlesome blowhard," Pine said. "Paul Harkness. Officially he's the State Department's special liaison to the tribunal. Used to be posted to the embassy in Belgrade, then to Sarajevo. But damned if I know what he really does other than stick his nose into everybody else's business."

"Now don't be too nasty about Paul," Spratt said in a scolding tone. "He's done a lot for us down there. And none of this would be happening if it weren't for him."

"Which should tell us something about the whole operation."

"How'd he get interested in Matek?" Vlado asked.

Spratt looked toward Pine, as if to ask how much Vlado knew. "I can't say with any authority," he offered hesitantly, "but apparently one of them turned up something in an old file, he or LeBlanc. That's his counterpart from France. An unlikely alliance, I must say. Those two have spent the past five years trying to tear each other's liver out, and now they're getting along like Ginger Rogers and Fred Astaire."

"More like Jekyll and Hyde," Pine said. "Now if you could only tell which was which."

"Apt enough. But it's the jurisdictional problem that worries me more than any of the personalities. We've got no business going after some old Ustasha. We're only authorized for crimes committed since '91."

"So our part of this operation is illegal?" Vlado asked.

Pine smiled ruefully while Spratt rattled the ice in his drink. His ears were red again. "Technically . . ." He said the word with evident distaste. "No. But for *official* purposes, all you're doing is arranging a meeting with Matek for interrogation of a potential witness. Then, while he happens to be under our control, a unit of SFOR troops will take him into custody on behalf of the Croatians, who are supposedly putting together an indictment as we speak."

"And unofficially?"

Spratt grimaced, so Pine picked up the thread. "We're rounding him up, plain and simple. Jurisdiction be damned."

"But if it works," Spratt said, "Contreras will be the toast of the town, and our international sponsors will be happy as clams."

"So here's to Hector Contreras, then," Pine said, raising his glass. "The founder of the feast."

"He's an Ebenezer Scrooge?" Vlado asked.

Spratt looked up with a glint of astonishment. "Looks like you've got a sharp one, Calvin," he said, sounding like the headmaster speaking to the hall proctor. "It's not every Bosnian who'd have nailed that reference."

"I took a lot of English in school," Vlado said, nettled by the condescension. "I guess if I want to stay in character, I should say 'God bless us every one,' and let Pine carry me on his shoulders."

"Sorry," Spratt said, rattling his ice again. "Running low here. Better get another."

Vlado watched him head for the bar in the corner. "Sounds like a popular case we're on," he said to Pine.

"Well, anything that puts Andric in the bag can't be all bad. Who knows, maybe you'll even learn a little of your history."

"Nobody ever said much about the war growing up. Just the heroic stuff."

"Not even that cranky old uncle you mentioned?"

"Yes," he said. "Uncle Tomislav. Off in the middle of nowhere. Big dry hills where nothing grew but goats and rattlesnakes. I must have been ten or eleven the last time we went. I slept in a back room upstairs while my uncle and father sat in the back garden all night, playing cards and drinking brandy. I woke up in the middle of the night and they were shouting, going back and forth like drunken debaters. And my sense of it was that they were arguing about the war. Nothing specific, just a lot of old grudges about who started it, who did what, all the things no one ever talked about. It was probably the only time I ever heard my father talking politics, so I went to the window to watch. They were panting like bulls, mad as hell. Kind of funny, but a little scary, too. My aunt and my mother had to come out in their robes and pull them off to bed. The next morning we left without even having coffee, which is about as rude as running off with the silver." He looked up at Pine. "And what about your family? What's your father like?"

"Oh." Pine snorted, smiling. "Atticus Finch. That's what he always looked like anyway. Or dressed like. Another literary reference for you."

"Atticus? A Roman name?"

"I guess you read mostly Brit lit. Atticus Finch is from *To Kill a Mockingbird*. Hero lawyer of the South. He was for civil rights before civil rights was cool. And every morning my dad went off to work looking just like him. Linen suits and seersucker. A wardrobe made for mopping your brow on the courthouse steps, right next to the statue to Our Confederate Dead."

"So your father was a crusader?"

Pine shook his head. "Not exactly. I doubt any of his clients ever ran from a lynch mob, although to their credit I guess none of them ever led one. They'd have been on their porches a few blocks away, sipping drinks and wondering what the ruckus was. Doctors, bankers, real estate developers." He swirled his wine, a faraway look in his eyes. "Jaycee glad-handers wanting to dispose of one little problem or another. A wife past her prime or a tenant behind on his rent. The kinds of things you didn't want people talking about at the country club. And with my father you got discretion with a capital *D*. For a nice hourly fee, of course. I guess that's why he could never stomach the idea of his son slumming with thugs and gumshoes. On a government salary, no less."

Vlado wondered at the tone of disappointment. It all sounded perfectly respectable to him. But now Pine's expression was transforming from disappointment to worry, and Vlado turned to see a woman approaching from across the room, a grim look on her face, striding purposefully in her high heels. She drew up close to Pine, then, seeming to have just noticed Vlado, turned to accommodate them both.

"Hello, Calvin."

"Janet."

"So, guess who drew the short straw on helping the Croatians prosecute Matek?"

"You?"

"Don't sound so disappointed."

"It's not that. It's just, well . . ."

Vlado watched their body language with interest. The woman had eased a foot closer, as if challenging Pine's right to his spot on the floor. Pine leaned away but without moving his feet, making him look stiff and off balance. They made an interesting pair. It occurred to Vlado that if you were to breed them, you might produce a new species of wading bird, a little tottery on long, thin legs and bony frames. Or perhaps the woman was just uncomfortable in high heels. She had large hazel eyes and light brown hair that swept around an oval face. Her small, prim mouth seemed to barely move when she spoke, as if she was used to imparting secrets.

But for the moment she was zeroed in on Pine. When she moved, her hair nearly brushed against his face, and Vlado could have sworn Pine flinched, ever so slightly, while holding his wineglass before him in a defensive position.

"Well, look on the bright side," she said. "It probably means they never found out. Otherwise, they never would have paired us on anything this sensitive."

Vlado cleared his throat, as much to remind them of his presence as to pierce the bubble of their conversation. She turned without missing a beat.

"You must be the Bosnian. Vlado, is it?"

Somehow he didn't mind it from her, maybe because her offhandedness seemed directed more at Pine than at him. Or perhaps it was the trace of irony in her tone, as if she was saying she knew exactly what it was like trying to prove yourself to this crowd.

"Yes. Vlado Petric. And you are?"

"She's Janet Ecker," Pine said. "An attorney on loan from the

NSA. That's the National Security Agency. Code breakers and official snoops, basically, so she's usually the one who gets to handle information when it starts to get touchy."

"Which is probably why they put me on Matek," she said. "To make sure nothing too sensitive is handed over to the Croatians. Or the French. They've got me working overtime with the black marker."

"And you two are friends of some sort?"

Pine winced, but a smile flickered briefly on Ecker's face, as if sharing in Vlado's minor insurrection. Vlado wondered how much she'd had to drink.

"You could say that," she said. "Just don't say it around the office. And if you were going to be here for long, I wouldn't say it around you. You see, Calvin spent months looking for a good Dutch girl but settled for an American. Until he got something going down in your part of the world. Doing his part for better diplomatic relations."

Pine reddened. Vlado considered sauntering off for another drink, but Ecker mercifully changed course. "So, what do you make of his file?" she asked Vlado. "Matek's, I mean."

It was pleasing to suddenly be treated as an equal, even if only as part of her fencing with Pine. "I haven't seen much. Just the summary. But he seems like standard-issue Ustasha."

"So far we've only gotten the sanitized stuff," Pine said.

"If I have my way, you'll be entitled to as much as you want," Ecker said. "It's amazing stuff."

"That's what Spratt said the other day."

"Spratt doesn't know the half of it. And without some of my connections I'm not sure I would."

"Meaning what?"

"Meaning there's been some strange information management going on. Someone trying to keep too many stray pieces from adding up to anything beyond the specific charges. There are a lot of old State Department cables and CIC reports that make interesting reading. But some of it has been deemed a little too interesting."

"CIC?" Vlado asked.

"Army Counterintelligence Corps. From the U.S. of A., which doesn't come out of this looking too good, even though most of this stuff is fifty years old."

"What could be so embarrassing, after all that time?" Vlado asked.

"Details, mostly. And names. James Angleton for one. Dead now, but once quite a wheel at the CIA. The ultimate cold warrior. And just after the war he and plenty of others were ready to make nice with an awful lot of Nazis. Nothing new about that, but the conventional wisdom was always that we only helped a few actual war criminals escape. Klaus Barbie, one or two rocket scientists. This stuff makes you wonder. And that's before you even read about the so-called missing assets. At the worst it looks like Matek might have helped loot the State Bank of Croatia as the war was winding down. Beyond that I'd better keep my mouth shut."

"Maybe we should get you another drink and find out more," Pine said, seeming to regret his words the moment he spoke them.

"That's his idea of a little joke," Ecker said to Vlado. "A drink or two always worked pretty well for him where I was concerned. In fact, maybe that's all it was."

"That's not what I meant."

"Pleasure meeting you," she said, again turning abruptly toward Vlado. "I think I'll go for a refill." She strolled away as briskly as she'd arrived.

"Sorry about that," Pine said after an awkward pause.

"No problem."

"Big mistake on my part."

"She doesn't look like a big mistake."

"Not in that way. I mean, I was kind of a jerk about the whole thing. Fortunately for both of us nobody found out."

"These things happen."

"Yeah. But if anybody asks . . ."

"Don't worry."

"Thanks. Trouble is, she's very good, so I still like working with her. And she's a Balkan linguist on top of everything, so nothing gets lost in translation." Pine scanned the room, perhaps looking for Janet. Seemingly satisfied that the coast was clear, he said, "Excuse me, but I could use something a little stiffer than wine. Interested?"

"No thanks. But please."

Pine headed for the bar, leaving Vlado momentarily isolated in the growing sea of people, the volume of conversation rising to a roar. He felt a tap on his shoulder and turned to see a pale, composed face with shimmering brown eyes.

"You must be Monsieur Petric," the man said.

"And you must be Monsieur LeBlanc."

"So Pine has already warned you about me."

"Afraid so."

LeBlanc was trim and alert, eyes always moving. In conversation he was prone to making little touches here and there, the clever hands darting and quick. In manner of dress he carried off the small flourishes that only Frenchmen seem able to manage, and for the moment, even though he wore a dark suit like every other man, he somehow looked a cut above them all. His skin was of a pallor that said he wasn't outdoors much, but Vlado knew looks could be deceiving. So many of these supposed diplomatic types who'd come to his country during the war had fancied themselves men of action, and that was also the case with LeBlanc, who had been fond of following close in the wake of major offensives by both sides, driving nothing more imposing than a blue Renault while shells burst within a few hundred yards. He eschewed the field jackets favored by so many photographers and aid workers, dressing for war as if he might suddenly be invited to Paris for lunch.

"I have great respect for Monsieur Pine," LeBlanc said. "One of the few who isn't so partisan, to risk a Yugoslav pun. And in the interest of equal treatment, I hope he at least warned you about Monsieur Harkness, of the American State Department."

"He did."

"So, tell me, then. How many people have you met tonight who claim to understand your country? Quite a few, I'd think. All it takes for an American is about a week and he thinks he's got the answer to six hundred years of Balkan problems." LeBlanc heaved with a light laugh. Vlado couldn't help but join in.

"An Englishman's worse," LeBlanc continued. "He reads a few books and thinks he has it worked out, but at least he usually has the good grace to keep it to himself. None of this hanging on your shoulder with a drink in his hand to confide his secret knowledge in your ear, waiting on your approval. Always remember, there's nothing an American craves more than approval."

"And you say that from how much time in America?"

"Touché. But I am sorry to disappoint you. I was posted to Washington for five years in the eighties. And you'll find that need among all of them. Pine as well. Forgive an American for the sins of his country, and he'll be your friend for life. But I guess I should be glad for their usual bluster and ignorance. It's the ones like Harkness that can create difficulties. He actually knows the Balkans. Lives it and breathes it. Knowledge like his turns the comic element into something dangerous."

"I thought you were partners on this?"

"Oh, we are. Willing partners. Perhaps I just can't help being suspicious now that we finally agree on something. But the more important question for the moment is what do you know of us? What do you know of America, for instance?"

"Music, mostly. Rock 'n' roll. We listened to all we could in high school. Led Zep, Talking Heads. And books. Hemingway, Fitzgerald."

"And what did those songs and stories tell you about Americans?" Vlado wondered. The songs had mostly meant a good time, offering someplace to dream about. But that seemed too shallow an answer for LeBlanc, and he realized he'd let himself be intimidated. "It told me about their generosity, I guess. And optimism."

"When you've got that much to spread around, it's not so much generous as indiscriminate. Everyone gets a little something if you hang around Americans long enough. Just don't mistake it for trust. But enough of that. Your escort has returned. Cheers." He tipped his glass of red wine toward Vlado's.

"Cheers."

Pine arrived with a bourbon in hand, looking perturbed that he'd left Vlado at the mercy of Guy LeBlanc.

"Hello, Guy. Hope he hasn't been interrogating you too much, Vlado."

"He did most of the talking, actually."

"About what?"

"Americans."

Pine chuckled, with LeBlanc joining in, not seeming the least embarrassed.

"It's one of his favorite subjects."

"But the important thing, Monsieur Petric," LeBlanc cut in, "is that soon you will be headed home at last. And no doubt a few surprises will be in store." Pine cast LeBlanc a tight-lipped glance. "In seeing what has become of your country, I mean. A lot happens in five years."

"Most of the damage was done by the time I left. I doubt I'll be too shocked."

"I was referring more to the psychological sense. It is a conquered nation, Monsieur Petric, run by dollars and deutsche marks. I hope you will not be too disillusioned."

A waiter glided up with more wine.

"Monsieur seems to have had enough already," Pine said, not smiling. LeBlanc laughed lightly and nodded for a refill.

"Surely you aren't suggesting that a Frenchman cannot hold his wine? Don't worry, Calvin, your secrets are safe with me."

Once again, a small alarm sounded in the back of Vlado's mind, and it was only about to get louder.

"As long as the subject is secrets," Pine said, "what's the latest on Popovic? We haven't heard a word in weeks, and you're supposedly the man with the plan."

Now even LeBlanc's smile faded. Vlado gripped his wineglass tightly.

"No need to worry. He is still, as you Americans like to say, our ace in the hole."

He was in a hole, all right, Vlado thought, stifling a sudden urge to come clean.

"Just as long as you decide to play him someday," Pine said.

LeBlanc turned toward Vlado. "It has been a pleasure, Monsieur Petric. And only the first of many meetings, I hope."

"My pleasure as well."

They watched him stroll away.

"Kind of a prick, isn't he?" Pine said. "But for some reason I like him anyway. Not that I'd trust him as far as you could throw him."

"I don't think he trusts you, either."

Pine laughed. "Which I guess you wouldn't be telling me if you didn't trust me a little. Or maybe you're just too tired to care."

It was a curious thing to say, Vlado thought, and he tried to get a read on Pine's expression. It seemed almost wistful. Vlado sipped his drink and felt his face flush as the alcohol worked deeper into his system. He told himself to slow down. The weight of the day was settling into his legs, and there was still plenty to do, plus an early departure in the morning. In little more than twelve hours they would be landing in Sarajevo. He would be home. Home with uncertain company and a strange job to do, but home nonetheless.

"Christ," Pine said. "Now Harkness is heading this way."

"The one in the little bow tie?"

"Yes. Likes to think he's virtually British after all his years abroad. Says things like 'chap' and 'old boy.' 'Petrol' instead of 'gasoline.' When he's in tweeds you'd think he'd just been shooting birds on a country estate. He's no dandy, though. He'll walk right into a firefight in eight-inch boots, like the Great White Hunter on safari."

Vlado watched the man approach. He would guess that the man was in his late forties, a little older than LeBlanc. His cheeks were red, and he tilted his nose into the air as if he were the most perspicacious of bloodhounds.

"Hello, Calvin. Good to see you, old boy."

"Hello, Paul. Meet Vlado Petric."

"Yes, the last honest man in the Balkans. How does it feel?"

"Like you're having a little fun with me."

"Well parried. But merely my hyperbolic way of opening with a compliment."

By now Vlado was feeling a burst of spark and spite, having been under inspection for nearly an hour. "At least you haven't given me the ancient-hatreds lecture about what's gone wrong in my country," he said.

"Oh, ancient hatreds is quite passé these days, old boy. Now it's all economic opportunism and the wrath of Milosevic. We Americans like to personalize our conflicts. Makes it easier to sell them to the vox populi. Stalin. Saddam. Slobodan. They all have a certain ring to them, don't you think? And if old Slobo is ever in the dock, I'm sure we'll come up with a new one. We're gradually making the transition from Marx to Mohammad, which makes Bosnia all the more interesting, seeing as how we've thrown in our lot with the Muslims."

He had a good laugh at himself, going red in the face, then said, "You'll have to get used to a more rustic sense of humor if you'll be hanging around Pine much. North Carolina boy. Surprised you can even understand him through the accent."

"What Mr. Harkness is trying to say is that I'm not Ivy League. I'm public school, just not in the British sense."

"Easy, Calvin. LeBlanc must have gotten things off on the wrong foot."

Someone across the room began banging a fork against a glass. It was Contreras, resplendent in a dark suit with a red boutonniere, beaming at his audience.

"If our dinner guests will please begin retiring to the dining room. And may I wish the rest of you a very pleasant evening."

The milling crowd split like an amoeba, one part shuffling toward their coats, the rest pulling slowly toward an opening of two sliding doors to another chandeliered room, longer and narrower, with floor-to-ceiling windows looking onto a garden gone dim in the night. As Vlado began scanning the table for his place card, a voice whispered into his ear from behind. It was Harkness, still hovering.

"I'd like a moment with you later, if you get a chance. It's about a mutual friend of ours." His breath reeked of gin. "No need for Calvin to listen in, if it's all the same to you. Enjoy your dinner."

The remarks unsettled Vlado, and it was a relief to finally tuck himself into a chair, where no one could buttonhole him for further conversation. He'd spent the past hour being reminded of what it was about his old job that he hadn't missed. The office politics and maneuvering. Trying to say the right things while pondering the deeper meaning of offhand comments. Two days ago he'd only had to worry about getting his German right while ordering a wurst and fries. Now he was answering to lawyers and diplomats. He checked his flanks—the head of operations to his right, a prosecutor he hadn't met to his left. The only person who could ambush him from the rear would be a waiter.

The meal was excellent—roast lamb with potatoes, salad, and string beans—although Vlado seemed to be the only one eating with relish. The others seemed bored with such fare, but they hadn't been living on a ditchdigger's salary. But for all the billing as a working meal, the dinner was largely ceremonial, filled more with toasts than with operational detail. The names Andric and Matek weren't mentioned once, although the subject of "the mission at hand" came up repeatedly.

Every time Vlado looked around it seemed that either LeBlanc, Harkness, or Ecker was staring toward him, although only Ecker would break into a smile when Vlado returned the gaze. Pine, Vlado noticed, seemed always to be staring toward LeBlanc, Harkness, or Ecker. A curious bunch, to say the least.

Contreras concluded his evening's duties with a ponderous speech, flowery boilerplate about the common enemies of hatred and intolerance. It was his closing line that got everyone's attention, when he remarked on "what a pleasure it was to know that the genesis of our current mission had been the diplomatic corridors of Paris and Washington."

Tribunal lawyers looked down or shuffled their feet in apparent embarrassment, but Contreras either didn't notice or didn't care.

The evening's final toast was to Pine and Vlado. Janet Ecker proposed it. Her words seemed appropriate enough as long as you ignored the line about Pine's "great rapport with the Bosnian people."

As the gathering emptied into the raw night air, Vlado emerged into the darkness with the relief of a student who has completed his finals. A poke here, a prod there, but overall not so bad. Then a cloud of gin materialized at his left shoulder, and the voice of Harkness rumbled up out of the gloom like a premonition.

"Tell me, old boy. Something I've wanted to ask you all evening." His tone was pitched low, conspiratorial. "How does a clever fellow who's reduced to digging ditches end up mixing in the business of a shady operator like Branko Popovic?"

Vlado was thankful for the darkness, because the shock surely must have shown in his face. He didn't know what to say, and Harkness plowed on.

"Perfectly understandable if you're not up to discussing this just now. But he's a friend of mine, you know. Or, more to the point, a valuable source. So give him a message when you get a chance." He then seemed to hesitate. "Or do you even understand a word of what I'm talking about?" Harkness was now facing him, studying him carefully. His right hand grasped Vlado's forearm with a squeeze that seemed to tighten by the second. They'd reached the end of the sidewalk, and others were walking past, hailing cabs and stepping into limousines.

"I'm not sure I understand any of it," Vlado said in a low voice, surprised at the steadiness with which he could lie.

"Just as well," Harkness said, his expression unreadable. "But if you happen to be lying, or worse, if you happen to be working for the man, then you can count on seeing me again, soon, and in more places than you'd like."

With a final squeeze, Harkness fell away, releasing himself into the current of the crowd. Vlado realized that the man had never said what his message was for Popovic, once he seemed to have second thoughts. Vlado looked around for Pine, needing a familiar face. Suddenly he wondered if going back home was such a good idea. Peace treaty or not, he'd just been reminded that it was still a dangerous place, a landscape of mines, of grief, and of well-hidden interests.

CHAPTER SEVEN

Pine and Vlado watched Europe float distantly beneath them out the window of the jet. Even from the air the land seemed gridded and plotted, the countries backed up against one another like too many children in the same bedroom. Except now they'd all grown old, harboring their fears and grudges in the same, stale space.

A question from Vlado broke the silence.

"Tell me about this operation. How does this compare to your others?"

"How do you mean?"

"In organization, preparation." He paused. "It's just that this one seems sort of . . ."

"Half-assed?"

"Yes. Half-assed." Vlado smiled. Even he could sense how funny the words sounded in his careful accent.

"That's because it is. I'd never heard of Matek until last Tuesday. I'd never heard of you until the day before I came to Berlin. Spratt called me and said go get this guy, we need him."

"Which I still don't understand."

"Oh, it all makes a certain sense, I guess, when you consider that for our first couple years all we had was one Serb in the dock and two waiting. If you can't do better than that, you might as well not be in business. Lately the pace has picked up, but it's still not exactly what you'd call an overload on the courtroom side. So, we'll take whatever we can get, especially when it's somebody as big as Andric, no matter who puts the deal together or how they offer it up."

Meaning Harkness and LeBlanc, Vlado supposed, which reminded him uneasily of Harkness's parting remarks the night before.

"And you think their motives are strictly diplomatic. Tit for tat. Keep both sides of the fight happy while still showing that the West means business."

"Something like that. But with guys like them you never really know."

"What do you mean, 'guys like them'?"

"You met them. What did you think? Did you get a sense that maybe they operate on other agendas they never tell us about?"

"To say the least."

He wanted to say more but was too worried about where it might lead. The last thing he wanted was another discussion of Popovic.

"Then there you go. They've got their agendas, for whatever reason, and we have ours. And this time, at least, our interests coincide. So if we have to rush things a little bit more than we'd like—the half-assed part of it—then at least we're getting what we wanted. Or that's what Contreras would argue."

"You wouldn't?"

"Hard to say. I'm leery of ever letting the political side get involved. Whether it's a federal drug investigation or sending in a hundred French troops to arrest Andric."

"That's how many they're using?"

Pine turned in his seat, glancing around to make sure no one was listening.

"So I've heard. He's out in the woods, near some cow town in the east. And if hauling in some old fart that the U.S. helped repatriate is what it takes to get the French to flush out Andric, so be it. The more you stay focused on that, the better you'll feel about what we're doing."

Pine spoke that part with true conviction. He did seem to believe in the tribunal's mission. It had been true for just about everyone Vlado had met in The Hague.

"You like this job, don't you?"

"Beats what I was doing before."

"A federal prosecutor?"

"Assistant U.S. attorney for the district of Maryland. Narcotics, mostly. Sometimes it seemed like we were locking up half the high schools of Baltimore."

"Baltimore. I know Baltimore. *Homicide.* The TV show. You can see it in Sarajevo. Dubbed, of course."

Pine laughed. He liked the idea of Bosnians getting their first look at Baltimore in a TV show about murder.

"Maybe they should film a show in Sarajevo," Pine said. "Call it *Genocide.*"

Now it was Vlado's turn to laugh. "So what made you want to quit to come over here?"

Pine shrugged. "Burnout. Office politics. A few other things not worth mentioning. Maybe I was just looking for a better class of criminal—a little more adult, a little more conscious of what he was doing. Seemed like a good way to get back my sense of mission."

"Kind of a strange cure for burnout, isn't it? Investigating genocide to make yourself feel better about the world?"

Pine smiled. "When you put it that way. But I've learned a lot. I mean, look at this." He nodded toward the window. "Europeans don't realize how small and cramped everything looks to an American. Even in the middle of the Alps you can't go more than a mile or two without running into a *Gasthaus* and a busload of Japanese tourists. No wonder the Germans like vacations in Texas. All that wide open space."

But Vlado had to wonder about the trade-off Pine had made. The way he saw it, evil here was just like evil there. Only the motives changed. In America they killed you for your money, your car, maybe the way you looked. Over here, for the sound of your name, the church your father went to, the sins of your grandfather. And sometimes, in both places, they killed simply because they had nothing better to do, nothing but the grim boredom of a hopeless, hardened life in the middle of nowhere. So they were easily swept up in moments of collective passion, neighbors rising in common cause against a single household or an entire village. The call to arms could be seductive. Once a war was in progress, few bothered to ask who'd started it, or why.

An hour later their flight crossed out of the snowy Alps, approaching Bosnian airspace.

"Not much longer now," Pine said, and Vlado leaned across for a better look. "Christ, what am I thinking. Let's switch. You haven't seen home in what, five years?"

They shifted awkwardly, crushing against the forward seats. Vlado settled in and gazed down at Bosnia's mountains. Some were dusted with snow, but mostly the scenery was gray, the forests leafless. Tiny streams of smoke poured from chimneys into valleys scattered with red-tile rooftops. Within half an hour the plane began its descent. They approached Sarajevo from the northwest, the suburbs of Ilidza zooming below, looking considerably better than he'd last seen them.

Most of the houses were patched. People were in the streets. A glint of sunlight flashed from the river, reminding him of the cold water that he could still taste from his last day in the city. As the plane descended lower, they seemed to enter a huge bowl, sheltered by the hills, a comforting feeling he hadn't experienced in far too long. The wheels bounced, the pilot throttled back, and they taxied to the small airport that had once been fortified by high walls of sandbags. Now it looked like any other terminal of Eastern Europe.

Pine had arranged for a white European Union car to be awaiting them at the airport as part of their cover. A woman at the airline counter had the keys, and they found the sedan parked out front, next to where UN sentries used to be posted in case of sniper fire.

Vlado had an odd feeling almost from the moment Pine opened the trunk to stow their bags. It didn't take long to figure out why. This was the first time he'd been in a car since the night with Haris and Huso. It was as if he'd expected to see Popovic's body curled in the dark space below, still locked in his fetal embrace with death. It must have shown on his face.

"Don't look so stunned," Pine joked. "You really are home. It's not a mirage."

"Yes," Vlado said, forcing a smile. "I guess it just hasn't hit me yet." He slid into the front seat, taking in the surroundings, but for the first few blocks it was as if Popovic were still riding behind him with their luggage, awaiting disposal.

Gradually the sights of the city stole back his attention. Vlado was dismayed to see so much that was still destroyed or abandoned. Some buildings were missing altogether, the rubble pushed aside by bulldozers. Others had been patched here and there. But the trams were running and the shops were full. The city was alive again, and the blank expressions of people in the streets suggested they'd even grown a bit bored with peacetime. Or maybe they were still worn out. He'd understand that, too.

They arrived at the bright yellow façade of the Holiday Inn, camped on the main boulevard that had once been known as Sniper Alley. It was odd to be back at this building that had marked so many important times in his life. It had been a proud place during the Olympic Games in '84, with its disco and its restaurants and its high atrium lobby draped with plants, a shining wonder from the West. But now it wore its scars openly, still defiantly facing the river where the siege lines had stared back from a mere three hundred yards. Shell holes had been patched and repaired. And now the place again had uninterrupted heat, water, electricity, and phone service, with real windows instead of the sheets of plastic that had been taped over the shattered frames during the fighting.

Yet the lobby still smelled faintly of leaks and dampness, mildew and smoke, an enduring desolation that clung like rot. Or perhaps that, too, was Vlado's imagination. The place had been cleared of all the journalists who'd stayed here during the war. They'd moved on to more active venues, and most guests now seemed to be business-people. The man behind him spoke German on a cell phone. Two Japanese stood by the elevators, next to an American.

Pine and he checked in to adjoining rooms. After unpacking, Pine dropped by. He looked ready to launch a discussion of the job ahead, then seemed to think better of it and said, "You could probably use a walk first, before we begin. Get reacquainted with the place. I wouldn't mind a little break, either. And there's someone I want to meet."

"Ah. Your friend. The one Janet is so jealous of."

Pine reddened. "Why don't we meet back here in an hour and a half. Then we'll get down to business."

Vlado was surprised at how soon he felt at home in the streets, although every corner confronted him with a rush of powerful mem-ories, some from well before the war but most of them from the siege. Places where he'd seen bodies in the streets. Alleys once piled with crumpled cars as a barrier against sniper fire. Some of the steel-and-glass towers that had been burned out and shelled still stood empty, but no one paid them the slightest attention. New trees sprouted near the stumps of old ones that had been chopped down for fire-wood.

But sunlight washed the streets, and everyone seemed to be out. And after a few minutes of working the stiffness out of his stride, Vlado felt a joy he hadn't experienced in years. He again had the freedom to simply walk without a care or worry in this place he knew so well. No one was looking down from the hills at him through the scope of a gun, and everyone spoke his language. He gazed up at the hills, which again seemed beautiful and benign, dusted by a snowfall that, down in the city, had been shoveled to the curb in great sooty piles.

He listened to passing snatches of conversation.

"Come here, they've got one now," said a man by a shopwindow.

"Mommy, I'm hungry, can we get just one?"

"That idiot, he wouldn't know his ass from a hole in the ground!"

He considered stopping by their old apartment, although he figured by now it must have been parceled out, confiscated, given to some refugee family or a returnee whose own home had been destroyed. If it was standing at all. He wondered how much might remain of their furniture, or his clothes. And what had become of the little lead soldiers that he'd painted by candlelight? In his sudden departure he'd left behind stacks of old bills, family records. There were some photos he wouldn't mind having back. But maybe he wasn't up to shouldering all those memories right now. For the moment, just being back was enough.

The cold was raw and moist, and he shoved his hands deep in his pockets. But, as in the hotel, a faint ghost of the wartime smells remained—a hint of garbage being burned, the stench of clogged systems and pipes. Looking through the windows of stores and cafés, he noticed that the same sort of clientele that had held sway during the war seemed to be dominant still—men in shiny leather jackets with cell phones in hand, women in fine clothes who wore plenty of jewelry, the same hard-currency crowd of mobsters and hangers-on, in other words.

A block later a familiar voice called out his name. It was Marko, an engineer. He'd lived in a remote suburb, so Vlado had hardly seen him once the siege had begun, but here he was, all in one piece, even if his smile seemed fixed, a trifle programmed.

"Where have you been?" Marko exclaimed. "It's been years."

"Berlin. We live there now. I'm just here for a visit. I don't think I've seen you since '93. Glad to see you made it. Are you working again?"

"Oh, sometimes. Contract jobs that never last. Restoring the water system. The electrical grid. But lately not so much. We lost Dario, you know. During the war. He was killed by a sniper."

"No. I hadn't heard. I'm sorry."

"Yes. In late '94, just when things were getting quiet. He was up on a hill on his bicycle and, well . . ." Marko flicked away his cigarette.

"I was gone by then."

"So were a lot of other people." Marko shrugged. "After the war we finally gave him a proper burial. Before he was not in a good place. So we moved him last spring. The flowers were out, and it was all very pretty. Your family, they're all well? Sonja must be growing up by now. I don't think she was even walking the last time I saw her."

"Walking and reading, too. In German. She's nine. Speaks the language better than we do. We might end up back here, though. Who knows. Everything is sort of up in the air."

Marko smiled. "I am surprised to see you here at all, really. I'd heard maybe you weren't so welcome anymore. It spoke well for you. A lot of crooks in the government."

It was nice to know that was the word around town, that the judgment on the streets was positive. It mattered to Vlado more than he would have expected.

"True enough. But I'm not a policeman anymore. I'm working for some internationals now. Nobody important."

"Oh, and you can't talk about it. Even better. And more impressive, too. Maybe you can clean this place up."

"It's not like that," Vlado said, realizing he was sounding too mysterious for his own good. "Just some aid work. No big deal. But are there still a lot of rackets going?"

"Same as during the war. You just don't notice them as much because they can't carry their guns around now. They lost their cover when the fighting stopped. Now you can only tell them by their cell phones, and even that's getting harder, 'cause now it seems like everyone's got a phone."

"But the place looks good. Or a whole lot better, anyway."

Marko shrugged. "I guess. Maybe I haven't noticed because the changes have come so gradually. Or because I never go into any of the new stores. Versace. Benneton. There's even a McDonald's coming. But who can afford it? If you don't have mob money, or work for the internationals, then you probably don't have any hard currency. And it's the internationals who run everything."

"So I've heard."

"It's better that way, believe me. Our own people would only fuck it up and start another war. The new parliament couldn't even agree on a flag, or a license plate. It's still an international call to Banja Luka, just because a bunch of Serb idiots think they're still a part of Serbia. Still, do we really need fourteen thousand foreigners here?"

"That many?"

"And maybe more. They're the only ones paying real wages, but even then you're usually just an interpreter or a driver. Not much call for engineers. The outside contractors usually bring their own. But what about you? An aid agency, you said?"

Vlado remembered his cover and figured he better start using it. But he wondered, too, if Marko was fishing for a job. Already hustling him at some level, not that he would have blamed him. In that way the war was still on.

"The European Union," he said sheepishly. "A few grants and programs I'm involved with. Mostly with demining."

"No need to be ashamed," Marko said with a laugh. "It's not like you have a choice. Impressive, in fact. And you think your family might be coming back?"

"I don't know. We'll see."

Marko nodded. "I understand. Believe me, if my family was in Germany, I'd stay until the Germans kicked me out. Well, good to see you. But bring them for a visit, at least."

Poor Marko, Vlado thought. And suddenly it didn't seem so bad to be "stuck" in Berlin. Maybe things would feel different out in the countryside.

A block later he contemplated stopping for coffee. He had some D-marks and a little local currency in his pocket, courtesy of the tribunal, and felt like treating himself before heading back to meet

Pine. There was a new café nearby, and he gazed through the big windows, checking the scene. He noticed a familiar face.

It excited him more than he would have wished. It was Amira Hodzic. Without her he never would have escaped Sarajevo, would probably be buried somewhere out in the soccer field with all the other casualties, listed as a sniper victim but actually done in by the mob. Her role hadn't involved much risk, but she'd provided him with shelter just long enough so he could plot his final escape, having been pursued halfway across the city. Amira and her two small children had tended to him as if he were a member of the family, though he'd barely known them. She had been a prostitute then, forced into the work by hardship. With her husband dead on some battlefront far to the east, she and her children had been herded into the city along with tens of thousands of others from the surrounding valleys.

Vlado had turned to her when he had nowhere else to go, and the way he remembered it now it seemed he had sought her out as much for her warmth and spirit as for the knowledge that she would be a safe harbor. And now there she was, speaking with someone at her table, keenly interested. From the look of her clothes and makeup, she was one of the lucky ones.

Then, seeming to receive his signal through the glass, she suddenly looked his way, reacting first with astonishment, then with a slow but wide smile and a glint in her eyes that almost looked like tears.

Now he had no choice but to go say hello, a thought more pleasing than he cared to admit. As he entered, her companion turned, and for a fleeting moment of panic he was sure it was Calvin Pine.

But no, it was some other foreigner. A European, perhaps an American. The man rose in greeting as Amira spoke a few hasty words of introduction in her English, then he stood by the table as if he didn't know quite what to say, seeming as flustered as Vlado. But he had the composure to realize that this reunion deserved a few moments of privacy, or as much as you could muster in a crowded café. His name was Henrik, and he graciously pulled an empty chair from another table. "Here. Join us. Vlado, was it?" The accent was German. "I'll get a waitress, or else you might be waiting an hour. The service is notoriously slow." And he left them.

Vlado was impressed with the way Henrik handled the moment, keeping things more comfortable than they might have been. But why should it be awkward at all, when nothing had happened between him and Amira?

He remembered the warmth of her apartment, heated by a wood-stove, in a high-rise that had otherwise been as cold as a slab of granite. He recalled the faces of her two young children peeping from around a corner as he'd bathed and toweled, then as he'd eaten an orange, his first fresh fruit in months.

Amira, too, was standing now. She reached for Vlado across the table, but with a certain reserve, and not just due to her friend Henrik, he sensed.

Vlado settled into the chair, not sure where to begin. "How did you two—"

"I'm an interpreter," Amira replied. "For the Red Cross. And sometimes, when they don't need me, for other people. I once did some work for Henrik. He's an assistant to the high representative. It seems the only people I work for anymore are foreigners. So, still whoring, as you can see."

She smiled but Vlado grimaced, coloring slightly, looking down at the table. She reached over, touching his hand. "Please, don't be embarrassed. It's just the way I feel sometimes."

Vlado hoped for Henrik's sake she was referring to her job, not to her romance. She reddened, as if realizing how the remark might be taken.

"I'm only speaking of my work, of course. You sell your speaking to the rest of the world, and it's all they want. Not your ideas or any thoughts on whether they're doing things right. Henrik was the only one who ever asked about any of that. The only one. Everyone else just wants a mouthpiece, although lately they've started to let me do a little more. I guess they've decided I'm not going to crash their computers if I sign on now and then. And it's a living, with lots of hard currency, which is more than you can say for almost everybody else."

Vlado wondered at the undertone of bitterness from one who was doing so well.

"And you?" she said. "You are living here again?"

He shook his head.

"Just visiting. A small assignment for the war crimes tribunal." He caught his mistake too late, realizing he should have said the European Union. So much for his cover story, at least with Amira.

"Nice to hear you're still fighting for the right side," she said. "But I never thought I'd see you in Sarajevo again. So many memories from that time when you left."

Now he was sure of it. There *were* tears in her eyes. Something was troubling her, and Vlado couldn't place it. "Amira, what's wrong?"

She paused, reaching into her purse for a tissue. She dabbed her eyes, then checked her face in a compact, touching her cheeks lightly and turning her head, seeing that her makeup was in place before looking back at Vlado.

"Do you remember my children?"

"Yes. Your daughter, Mirza. She must be what, nine by now?"

"Ten."

"And your son. What was his name?"

She lowered her face, speaking into her plate. "Hamid." She looked around quickly, almost furtively, but Henrik was still across the room, leaning into a doorway in the back, no help from the kitchen in sight. Had she not told Henrik about her children? Vlado found that unimaginable. But perhaps that was the sort of thing that would scare a man off.

"The day after you left my house, the authorities came," she said. "As you'd said they might. They were looking for you. Your partner had remembered me coming into the office to answer questions. He knew I was one of the whores from the French barracks, and they got my name from one of the others. So they came for me. You must have been on the plane by then, but I didn't know, so I told them nothing. They didn't believe that, of course. They thought I was your lover. They wanted to know what you'd been doing, what you'd been saying, where you'd gone. Fortunately I'd already given the things you left to a neighbor for safekeeping, so they didn't find them. But they did find your dirty clothes, the ones I'd washed. Some colleague of yours recognized them.

"So they took me away for more questions, for more time to let me think about what might happen to me if I didn't cooperate. I asked them to let me call a neighbor to take care of Hamid and Mirza, but they wouldn't. They said they'd take care of them."

She looked around again. Still no Henrik. Vlado had a bad feeling about where this was headed. "I hope they didn't mistreat you too badly," he said. "Or the children."

"Not really. They kept me overnight, but nothing much actually happened. Just a lot of the same questions over and over. I think by then they must have realized you'd gotten away and they were start-ing to panic, were starting to worry more about saving their own skins than about me. So they let me go in the morning. They'd taken the children to the orphanage, the one near Kosevo Hospital, so I walked there to pick them up. It was a terrible place. Pickpockets and thieves, children running everywhere in the halls. Dirty. Loud. They'd been separated, to the boys' side and the girls' side. Both of them were terrified. They thought I'd abandoned them, that they'd never see me again. But I calmed them down soon enough."

At that, Vlado began to breathe easier.

"I'm glad they were okay."

Then a fat tear rolled down her cheek, and he realized she wasn't finished.

"Two nights later Hamid began coughing, and by the next morning he couldn't stop. I boiled water to make steam. I went and found a doctor. I asked my neighbors, but no one could help, and Hamid couldn't stop coughing. I wanted to take him to the hospital, but it was too full, and there weren't enough doctors. They told me to keep him at home. The next day he got a fever. He was like a little kettle, hot to the touch, and sputtering with his cough. There had been whooping cough and scarlet fever in the orphanage, a miracle that Mirza didn't catch them. I heard later that five of the boys there died. I think it was especially bad on the boys' side, and Hamid had caught them both. And in four days he was dead. Lying there in his own bed, not breathing. I had fallen asleep in a chair next to him and didn't even know when it happened. I had bought every medicine I could get my hands on with my whore's money. But he was dead. I knew as soon as I woke up and saw his face. The strangest part was that I had just had the most beautiful dream, and my first thought coming out of it was how thankful I was that I had finally been able to sleep, and all that time he'd been dead. I carried him downstairs, across town, all the way to the morgue, the whole place stinking with all the bodies from the war. All the shooting we had come through, the shell fire that I'd worried about every day whenever they were outside. Then my son is killed by a cough and a fever."

She wiped her face with the tissue, then snapped it inside her purse. There were no more tears. Vlado was horrified, claustrophobic. He looked around for Henrik but saw no rescue in sight.

"Oh my God," he whispered. "My God. I am so sorry. I am so . . ."

"Responsible?" She looked up at him, face rigid, and he teetered on the edge of the moment, knowing that was how he felt but desperately hoping she felt otherwise. "No," she said finally. "You're not responsible. It is all of those other people. The ones who were after you, the ones who started the war. The ones who were supposed to take care of us. The UN. All of them. And it was luck, too, of course. The same luck that used to decide if you would be shot or not when you walked across town. But I didn't always think this way. Just be glad you didn't come back a few years ago. I probably would have killed you." She fished a lighter from her purse and lit a cigarette, inhaling deeply.

Vlado didn't know what to say. He felt like he was in free fall. But Amira seemed to recover quickly. After all, she'd had nearly five years to think this over.

"I shouldn't smoke," she said. "But I have to have one right now. Henrik hates cigarettes. Unusual for a German, don't you think?" She offered Vlado a grim smile, biting her lower lip, placing her hand for just a moment atop his on the table, squeezing lightly then withdrawing. She wore some other face now. One last brush at her cheeks for any trace of tears, then a hasty rummage through her purse for the compact.

"And so now I have this. A real job. A man. A good man. Henrik is sweet. And he doesn't know what I used to do to make a living, so I hope that you won't tell him."

"Of course. And you still have . . ." Vlado almost couldn't say the name. "Mirza?"

"Yes," Amira said, showing her old self for a moment. "And most of the time that's enough. It's only because of Mirza that I kept going at all. But I did stop trying to get us out of the city on any aid convoys. My whoring suffered, too, sad to say." She laughed briefly.

A woman at the next table who had overheard her remark frowned and ostentatiously shook her head.

"Stupid cow," Amira muttered. "Her lover is a cigarette smuggler. So she should know all about whoring." She paused. "I think having Henrik is even better for Mirza than for me. Sometimes I think Mirza gets tired of me. I spent all my time for a while hovering over her. For years, if she sniffled or coughed even once, I put her straight to bed."

Amira looked out the window of the café, as if gazing at something in the distance. "Even now there are mornings when I wake up and the first thing I think of is Hamid. And then I remember right away that he is dead. Hamid is dead. I have to say it out loud to stop thinking it. The days that start like that are my busiest, my most efficient, because I never want to stop for even a second. Grief as a job skill. They ought to teach it in training." She stubbed out her cigarette. "It would be a nice slogan for the government, just like one of Tito's. 'Peace, brotherhood, and sorrow, for a better tomorrow.'"

Henrik's voice piped up from out of nowhere. "Success at last." He carried a china cup of steaming coffee, placing it with a rattle in front of Vlado.

"Finding a waitress was one thing. Finding one who would actually help was something else altogether."

Amira looked up at Henrik with a smile that, while warm enough, came from some other place than where she'd just been traveling, and Vlado was chilled by the transformation, though he wasn't sure if it was on her behalf or Henrik's. Perhaps both. Somehow Vlado doubted she'd told the man about Hamid. She seemed to confirm this suspicion with a quick glance, a look that sealed a tacit understanding. Henrik restarted the conversation, and a few moments later Vlado stood up to leave. He was due to meet Pine back at the hotel in fifteen minutes.

"You will phone me again before you leave?" Amira asked. Vlado couldn't think of a decent answer, other than to say, "Yes, I'll try."

"Then take one of my cards." She fished one from her handbag, then scribbled her home number across the bottom. As she gave him the card she clasped his hand, briefly but tightly, and once again he thought he saw the beginnings of tears. "You're working for the right people," she said, voice lowered. "Put a few of those bastards away for me, will you?"

Vlado nodded, glad he didn't have to tell her about the suspect from 1945, although he supposed that Matek had played his own role in lighting the fire that had consumed them.

He took a roundabout way back to the hotel, completing his circuit of the city with a stroll through the old Turkish Town, with its low tile rooftops and thatched masonry. Passing the faces in the streets, he wondered how anyone who'd survived the war could ever move beyond it as long as they stayed here. Say what he would about Berlin, it at least gave him some distance from the grief. He thought of Hamid and his heart sank, and he wondered uneasily who else might have been destroyed in his wake. He remembered the boy's face watching him from around the corner of a door, staring with widened eyes while Vlado had stood in a tentative embrace—his first and only—with Hamid's mother. Vlado's stomach knotted, and he stopped to lean against a signpost that was still tattooed with slugs from sniper fire. He wanted to vomit but couldn't. Then the wave of nausea passed and he walked on, face covered in sweat. How long could one survive in this sea of loss, he wondered, without drowning?

CHAPTER EIGHT

W hen Vlado reached the hotel a few minutes later, Pine was waiting outside his door, arms folded, smiling tightly, a file folder in one hand. He followed Vlado into the room, tossing the folder onto the bed and shutting the door.

"One last thing you need to see before we get started," he said. His voice sounded strange, quieter, a hint of strain in it. "It won't be easy reading, I'm afraid. I would have let you see it sooner, but, well, orders from upstairs."

Vlado sank gently onto the bed. His earlier excitement at being home was gone, replaced first by grief over Amira's story and now by rising apprehension. He knew all too well what he was about to read. So here came the revelation he'd been dreading, the name of Popovic catching up to him at last. But what Vlado still couldn't figure was how it all tied in to the case. Or perhaps there was no case at all, and everything had been an elaborate pretense to lure him here on some other, more dangerous chore, with Popovic as leverage.

"Tell me," Vlado said, gesturing toward the folder. "Once I've read it, are you going to arrest me? Or hold some sort of charges over my head?"

Pine squinted, genuinely puzzled. "Arrest you? I think the better question is whether you'll arrest me. For withholding evidence. More likely you'll just want to punch me out. And if you do, you'll find me in the hotel bar."

Pine shut the door behind him, leaving Vlado more confused than ever. He opened the folder, still expecting to see some sort of report on his own recent whereabouts. But when he began to read, his first reaction was puzzlement, followed by relief.

The name at the top was ISKRIC, JOSIP.

It meant nothing to him. He wasn't sure he'd ever even met an Iskric. Perhaps one in school growing up, but nothing more familiar than that. And from the dates it seemed clear this was another tale from World War II. Iskric had been born in 1922, a year before Matek but in the same remote corner of the country. Vlado skimmed the lines below, looking for something to jump out at him, something to solve the mystery Pine had suddenly dropped in his lap, but there was nothing extraordinary. It seemed to be a mirror image of Matek's dossier: officer-academy education in the Yugoslav Army. Joined Ustasha movement. Disciplined by army for nationalist activities. Joined Croatian Home Defense Army after declaration of Ustasha dictatorship. Served in the same unit as Matek. Involved in Kosarev Mountains offensive in early 1942. Twice decorated for bravery. Reassigned to Jasenovac concentration camp, May 1942. Promoted to lieutenant. Placed in charge of guard squadrons. That would have made Iskric Matek's equal. Hometown boys still in tandem. Vlado kept reading.

Fled Croatia April 1945. Captured by British forces in Wolfsberg, Austria, along with two others. Interned at Fermo DP camp, Italy, released June 1946 into custody of Pontifical Relief Commission. Yes, it was the same track, with only a few minor variations. Perhaps Iskric was a potential witness, and maybe they were going to pick him up as well, an extra bit of work that Pine had waited until now to spring on him. In fact, maybe there were even more suspects he didn't yet know about, and they were destined to be here for weeks instead of days. The thought was troubling but not insurmountable.

From 1946, Iskric's career continued to track Matek's. The two must have worked together in Rome. They even repatriated the same year, 1961. But by then Josip Iskric, like Matek, had a new identity.

His new name was Enver Petric.

Vlado stared in disbelief. Then he recalled Pine's sheepish attitude from a moment ago, and now he knew why. He calculated the man's age. It fit. He continued reading, dazed, knowing exactly what would come next. Enver Petric had relocated to Klanac, a village south of Sarajevo. He'd married the following year, and in 1963 his wife had given birth to their only child, a son, Vladimir. Nickname Vlado.

Vlado could have filled in the rest but kept reading anyway, in numb fascination. Moved family to Sarajevo in 1968. Employed by a machine shop, promoted to foreman in 1974. Died 1983, survived by wife and son. Son graduated Sarajevo University 1984. At outbreak of hostilities in spring 1992 was employed as an inspector detective with municipal police force, assigned to homicides. Wife and child evacuated to Berlin, where he joined them in early 1994 following investigation of local corruption.

Vlado closed the folder, still shocked. He needed to stand, to pace, to wail like an animal, but all he could do for the moment was stare at the folder, and at the name typed so neatly at the top: JOSIP ISKRIC.

So this was what happened when you didn't come back home on your own terms, he thought, temples throbbing. You learned of the death of a friend's son, and your role in it. Then you learned of your father's genocidal past. And what did that make him, other than the blundering son of a murderer, a man whose accidents killed children, as well as a man who helped killers hide and bury their victims.

He felt haunted by a strange sense that his personal history had suddenly been altered as punishment for his own recent crimes, as if Pine were some cosmic messenger who would now disappear into the ether, along with the assignment and the entire tribunal. Stepping into that old bunker in Berlin had made him slip into some uncharted place where old scores are settled and justice is absolute.

The radiator below the window kicked into action with a hiss of steam, and he jumped, startled. He reopened the folder, touching the papers as if they might somehow be proven fakes, a forgery. The cop in him cried out for details, facts, witnesses. He drew his right hand across the ribbed bedspread and looked to the window, into a blue sky where the sun shone and gray hills rose in the distance.

Everything was real, all right. So much for his worries about Popovic. This was the great secret they'd held out on him, their means of leverage in trying to lure Matek into the open. Hire the son of the man's old comrade, then throw in a demining concession for good measure. If that was even really part of the operation. Maybe all they had was Vlado, the family tie. They'd found his name in some file and thanked their lucky stars that he was so available, this outcast in Berlin who so desperately wanted to go home. And a cop into the bargain.

Then he remembered his conversation with Pine, only two days ago. Vlado had spoken glibly of his father's basic goodness and honesty while Pine did nothing but nod, the smiling American, letting him rattle on like a fool. And with that thought his panic simmered quickly to a boiling anger—at Pine, the tribunal, anyone who might be handy.

Breathing rapidly, he stood, volcanic, wanting to smash a wall, slam a face. He would burst down the stairs two at a time, find Pine in the hotel bar, and fall on him like a predator. Ram the man's head onto the table until the teeth of his smile rattled to the floor. Men in suits staring openmouthed while he glowered above the fallen man, catching his breath, as their cell phones rang.

But he took only one step toward the door, then stopped, turning, compelled instead by some deeper, nameless emotion that he knew he couldn't fight. He stepped toward the window, gazing out at the blushing horizon and the mountains he knew so well. Out there was his father, buried, beyond reach and accountable to no one, speechless against these monstrous charges.

Vlado raised his right fist high, like a hammer, then cried out, a gurgling roar that ended with a pounding blow high on the tinted brown glass. There was a dull crunch as the entire room seemed to shake, and suddenly the window was crosshatched by a thousand tiny cracks, radiating like a map grid from the point of impact. Just like the war, he thought, staring with odd fascination, when every window was smashed and gone, covered by sheets of plastic. And for an eerie instant of déjà vu he was transported back into the siege, alone in a single room, cut off from wife and child with nothing but shell fire for company.

The detonation of his anger complete, the implosion now began. How could he have let his father fool him all those years? Shouldn't there have been a sign, some telling moment? He thought of every cutthroat or killer he'd ever arrested, and the smug certainty with which he'd always approached them, fancying at times that he could actually see the guilt glinting in their eyes. He thought he'd even detected that quality in Haris. Yet for the guiltiest one of all he'd missed everything.

He groped for a memory of his father, the calm man who'd always seemed so rational. Vlado remembered visiting the workshop as a boy, accompanying his father on the daily walk home for dinner. Sparks flying from a grinder, the hum of the motors and the whirling leather belts. The agonized noises and the smell of hot oil, yet his father a tranquil and solid presence, intent on his work. You saw it in the way others approached him, deferred to him, and you sensed his quiet pride. Those moments had spoken to Vlado far more than his father ever had, and they had remained as his final judgment on the man's basic values and common sense. Good with his hands, everyone had said. But now that phrase was twisted into something terrible.

Vlado sat on the bed, spent, watching the horizon darken through the cracked glass. He felt as if he'd just run ten miles. So he lay on his back, folding his hands across his stomach, laid out for viewing. Then he shut his eyes. They were dry, yet as strained as if he'd sobbed all afternoon. Listening to the everyday sounds of the traffic from the streets below, he felt a bereft numbness descending like a heavy blanket, and he eased himself into a troubled antechamber of sleep, seeking whatever refuge was available.

Then he dreamed. Nothing coherent at first. Just faces and sites from his past. Friends he hasn't seen in years, making their way through the city. And now he is in the crowd with them, walking purposefully. They are trooping toward a soccer game, one he must have actually seen long ago, because he already knows the score, hoarding it from the others. He knows the outcome of each play even as it unfolds. The field is emerald green, a thrilling surface onto which red and green uniforms pour, the players taking their places, excitement high in his throat as he shouts. The ball pings from foot to head with the springy tap of leather, the crowd rising so that for a moment he can't see the field, nothing before his eyes but a wool overcoat and someone's hat, the smell of their cigarettes and cheap beer. He is a child now, too short to see over anyone, and his friends are gone, but strong and able hands take hold under his armpits from behind, lifting, thrusting him into the sunlight. It is his father, he knows, although he cannot see the face, doesn't want to look. He lands easily atop the big shoulders, staring down now at all the hats and bald heads afloat on this sea of excitement.

"Look, Vlado. Look!"

It is his father's voice, years younger than he last remembers it, excited, calling his attention back to the game. "We are going to win!"

Vlado turns his eyes to the field and sees a hundred or more people in kerchiefs and dark rags, long coats, flat caps. It is an army of peasants, all facing the far end of the stadium. Shepherding the rabble are helmeted soldiers in creased gray uniforms, men carrying long rifles with bayonets that gleam in the sunlight. And down at the front, ordering them hurriedly, hands moving briskly, is Vlado's father, whose face is now plainly visible. He looks impatient, shouting commands that Vlado can't hear above the din of the crowd.

The people move toward the goal at the far end, herding toward the white posts and yellow netting, where now the head of the procession is descending into the earth, into a great brown opening of turned soil, marked at the edges with crosses and crescents, and even from his perch in the stands Vlado feels the chill and dampness of that opening, as if the earth were exhaling from deep below the surface.

A thumping noise begins, the beating of a drum, steady and insistent, and a voice calls his name.

"Vlado. Vlado, are you in there? Vlado?"

Vlado rolled over on the bed, blinking in the darkness of the hotel room. It was Pine, pounding on the door.

"I'm okay," he croaked in reply. "I was asleep."

He stepped sluggishly to his feet, feeling as if he'd been asleep for hours, then opening the door to a face creased with concern, even alarm.

"Sorry," Pine said, speaking fast, running his words together. "I was worried that you . . . that you, might have left or something. I thought maybe, I don't know. I also came to apologize. I've been trying to figure out for the last three days exactly what I would say to you when this moment came. The best I could come up with was that I was only following orders, which told me all I needed to know about what I've been a party to."

"Don't waste your breath," Vlado said, coming more fully awake.

"Fair enough."

"And don't try to explain yourself."

Pine nodded, saying nothing.

"I can't do this, you know. Not after the way it was handled."

Pine nodded again, biting his lip, still standing awkwardly in the open doorway, Vlado blocking his way. "Okay. I guess I figured that might happen. Okay." He paused, as if waiting for Vlado to say more, or to at least step aside. When neither happened he continued, if only to fill the silence. "I'll see if there's a flight back to Berlin tomorrow. I won't try to talk you out of it. You'll be paid for the last two days, of course." Vlado scowled. "But do one thing for me, will you? Or do it for yourself."

Vlado said nothing but nodded, as if granting permission to speak.

"Try and think about how you're going to feel about all of this in a week. It's horrible, especially to learn it like this. But it can't be undone, and I just want you to think about whether or not you might feel differently later. Because if you change your mind, well . . . by then, the whole operation will be over. It will be too late."

"You'll go after him anyway, you mean. This man, Matek. This . . . *friend* of my father's."

"We've got no choice. I'll just pose as the demining guy myself. I've already got the fake business cards, just in case this happened."

"Your 'classified' Plan B," Vlado said with derision. It wouldn't work, and they both knew it. Not with someone as wise to schemes and ruses as Matek. Deception was how he made a living.

So let it fail, Vlado thought. Let the old bastard keep being an old bastard a while longer. In a few years he'd be dead anyway.

"What about Andric?" he asked. "They'll carry out the raid anyway, right?"

"I guess. Assuming I can grease the skids at this end."

Vlado sighed. Already he could see what was coming. The arrangement would fall apart, Andric would remain free, and he'd have played a role. Living up to his father's good name.

And what of Matek, for that matter. The man would die on his own terms. Worse, he would die with his secrets, which Vlado now wanted to know more than anything. Telling the tribunal to go to hell would be throwing away his only chance to find out more about what had really happened, and why.

Then why not keep working, he asked himself, not as a good soldier or even as an opportunist seeking resettlement and a new job, but as a son seeking vital leads into his past. Once Matek was captured, Vlado would participate in the debriefing whether the others liked it or not. Pine would probably let him, if only out of guilt. If his questions annoyed the others, they could fire him. Tomorrow would mark the end of his short career with the tribunal anyway. And for the moment he didn't wish to consider bringing his family back to Bosnia. The information in the file had changed everything. He didn't want his daughter growing up anywhere in the path of his father's bootprints.

He turned toward Pine, angrily resigned to the inevitability. "You already know what I'm going to do, don't you?"

"No, I don't. Tell me."

"When were we supposed to make contact with Matek?"

Pine frowned, looking away. "They just changed that part, as it happens. Tonight, they say now. The French were getting antsy, so they've moved up the Andric raid a day. They want us to adjust our schedule accordingly."

"So whenever I'm ready, in other words."

Pine nodded grimly. "That's about the size of it."

"I want a drink first."

"No problem. Have two. As many as you want, long as you can still say the man's name. We'll go down to the bar."

"No," Vlado said, now deciding on a different approach. "No drinks. Just the phone call. Let's do it now. Then I'll have the drink, but not with you. By myself."

"Look, if you want to—"

"Just give me the phone number, okay? Then tell me what I need to say. Then leave me alone. I'll tell you when it's over."

"Whatever you say," Pine said, holding out his hands as if pleading for calm. "It's your show."

It certainly was, Vlado thought mordantly. A macabre cabaret from his father's past, and he was about to take the stage. Lights, please. Then the script. Let the entertainment begin.

CHAPTER NINE

Pero Matek loved the Internet, loved the whole idea that you could sit in a dump like Travnik and still command a world of contacts and information. At moments like this it always made him smile to look around his office. In recent years he'd taken particular pains to portray himself to outsiders as a provincial king on his rustic throne, barely schooled and barely presentable, a backwoods potentate who could be kept happy with a pat on the head and a generous cut of the action.

So, when UN people and aid delegations came calling he always gave them the best show possible, from the décor to the drinks to his pose as an unpolished rube who simply aimed to please. The charade began with the herd of goats wandering the grounds, animals that almost invariably crowded around the cars of guests as they parked, trying to chew anything that moved, bleating and pawing at the scuffed grass as the visitors stepped daintily through the droppings. Once inside, the visitors stepped onto a brown linoleum floor in the entrance hall, with fluorescent tubes popping overhead. Then it was down the hall to his office, to be seated on bulky brown couches left over from Communist times. The windows were draped heavily with awful patterned curtains in orange and brown, and the wall-to-wall carpeting was threadbare and burned by cigarettes.

The real show, however, was Matek himself, seated behind a varnished desk the size of a battleship. He was invariably clad in an oversized brown double-knit jacket. His trousers featured busy patterns chosen to clash with the ones on his open-collar shirts, where chest hairs proclaimed his enduring virility, a signal to remind them that along with the oafish charm came sterner stuff—this was his turf, his rough-and-tumble topography, where a false step could leave you wandering in God knows what sort of valley or village. The highlight of Matek's ensemble, however, was his hair, still a lush full head of it, a salt-and-pepper shock styled in the pompadour wave customary among self-made Balkan lords.

His office was in the back room of a farmhouse on a few acres of sloping land, cleared of everything but a few plum trees on a grassy scatter of slate and granite. The goats did the mowing. His compound—he always loved to hear the reports describe it as such— sat at the end of a twisting gravel road, halfway up the mountains that towered above the town of Travnik like a six-thousand-foot iron gate, shutting the north side of the valley tight. The view from his upstairs bedroom encompassed not only the glittering Lasva River far below but also long stretches of the main highway into town, as well as the road leading to his property. He liked seeing visitors before they saw him. Most of his enemies would never have the initiative, much less the stamina, to approach on foot through the trees. And while the internationals might not know it, his local reputation was that of someone who never let anyone take him by surprise, either in a business deal or in some more rudimentary form of confrontation. Those who tried tended to disappear.

Even at seventy-five, Matek had kept most of his vitality, and he liked to show that off, too. He looked remarkably well for his age, still trim except for the slight poke of his belly, his face creased but not crinkled, and he was still handy with the women when necessary, which in his case was about once per week. At least one or two were always hovering nearby on trips to his favorite café, and they weren't averse to a few moments with him later in more private quarters, so long as there was time first for a few shots from his bottle. He wasn't so vain that he discounted the power of wealth in this equation, or of the bottle in steeling their resolve. He considered his bankroll merely another mark of his manhood, of his ability to beat the competition.

Not counting his bodyguards, Matek lived alone. Long ago he had briefly tried marriage but hadn't found it to his liking, and nowadays the occasional mistress suited him fine. No womanly clutter around the house. No voice at his shoulder telling him what to do and when to do it. He believed that was why the laugh lines around his eyes had remained jolly, not careworn. And he was still quick with a noisy joke or a belly laugh, his brown eyes still prone to twinkle at a good comeback or a savored memory. All of which came in handy when it was time to play the garrulous host for the outsiders who came grinding up the mountain with their money and their contracts. He found that meeting their expectations left them resigned to a certain level of waste, slippage, and overruns, and even some manner of fraud, but not in the sense that some accountant might understand it in Brussels or New York. And so, when they inevitably returned six months later with their bar graphs and flow charts, there was always an atmosphere of the parent-teacher conference, a sighing inevitability that they'd known all along this would be part of the bargain. So, instead of yanking the rug they would merely tug and whisk at its corners, letting him know they could still see his few signs of progress. And by then, of course, they'd taken note of his firm grasp on local needs and conditions, and the ways his enforcement could turn severe, even brutal, if necessary. So they tended to tread lightly, even in admonishment, and would gasp through their sips of his fiery home brew, a round of shots inevitably served on a Turkish tray of hammered brass, the glasses smudged just so.

The great joke of this was that what Pero Matek really would have preferred was a calm sip or two of a Chianti Classico in shining crystal stemware. But those bottles were kept locked in the cellar, with humidity and temperature controls. Kept out of sight just like his Dell desktop computer with its twenty-one-inch Sony monitor.

On the rare occasions when company could be coaxed to stay for dinner he would order up a big mixed grill just to set their teeth on edge and their stomachs into a roll—quivering Balkan meat fests of lamb, veal, and sausage, piled atop platters oozing with grease and char. Load their plates like troughs and watch them grin woodenly, knowing they'd compare notes later in their Range Rovers and Mercedes SLs, laughing at the hopeless rube. Perhaps his most important visitor ever, an assistant from the high representative's office, had later called him "Pero the Barbarian," and when Matek received the report from one of his secretarial spies he laughed about it for days, spreading the nickname through the village as if it were a promotional pamphlet, cementing his reputation for putting a not-so-fine edge on things. One American investor who'd nosed about the valley for a week, an Oklahoman with tall boots and a big voice, had compared him to an Ozark moonshiner, albeit one who could be leashed and trained as long as he got his ration of skim.

So he let them believe he was trainable, and housebroken, and kept getting his share, time after time, from just about any financier or do-gooder with currency to burn.

The irony of this dynamic was that it had begun to make him legitimate, even in the eyes of some of the more naïve locals. The back-channel thuggery of his wartime markets was slowly turning into a well-documented realm of signed contracts and foundation grants. His participation in the stolen-car operation, regrettably, had been a necessary casualty of the transformation. Too much law enforcement attention had begun to zero in, so he had quietly transferred control to a few obliging lesser rivals, who were thrilled at their sudden windfall of rolling stock from Germany and Switzerland via Poland and Ukraine, only to be dismayed when it all came apart a few weeks later with a well-informed bust of their open-air distribution market. By the time they suspected Matek's role in the matter several were in jail, others were dead, and the car market was gone. It would be back, of course, an option that would always be available if Matek ever needed it. But for now the international spigot was running full-blast, and he was content to paddle in the lucrative broth of Europe's alphabet soup, the NGOs and EU subagencies that ran this country in a manner befitting the Hapsburgs and Ottomans.

In the case of his other illegal operations, why sell bootleg gasoline in wine bottles and plastic milk cartons when you could run six INA stations, supplied straight from Zagreb at subsidy prices? Why keep selling booze in back alleys when your distributorship in spirits and beer was now the largest in five surrounding municipalities? It had been so ever since the previous spring, when his biggest competitor drove across an antitank mine. Never mind that the man's neighbors still wondered why he'd been driving off-road in that particular patch of woods. Out hunting, perhaps, for that was his hobby, although no one ever found out who might have invited him. And never mind that the property in question had supposedly been cleared of mines, or that it was owned by Pero Matek, although the deed had percolated through so many proxies and riders and silent partners that you could spend weeks poring over papers at the municipality's hopeless little archives and not make heads or tails of it.

Not that Matek ever worried about establishing his provenance, if need be. All the original documents were filed neatly in his safe, the hulking one in the corner of his office, behind the cabinet with the Dell, where Matek now sat hammering at the keyboard with his farmer's hands, the pockety-pock rhythm putting him in a fine mood, as soothing as the ringing of a cash register must be for a village shopkeeper. This was the noise of commerce today, he thought to himself. "Even for a barbarian," he muttered aloud, breaking into a laugh. You could check commodity prices and shipping rates, then plug them in to your budgets and your cost schedules. Type in a few serial numbers, plus a password or two, and your orders were updated, the status flashing at you from six different locations. Send an e-mail to Emilio in Trieste, a duplicate to Francisco in Madrid, a confirmation with a bonus porn photo attachment, just for fun, to a supplier in Bulgaria he knew only as Christo.

All of them were people he had never met because, frankly, it was still a risk to travel abroad and perhaps always would be. It was his one great regret in life. Crossing the border would probably never be a sure thing, considering what they'd done with his papers and his passports all those years ago. He had others, of course, two different sets that were best kept out of sight, and neither carried his old name, his real name. There was no safe or strongbox yet built secure enough for that knowledge, so he kept it only in his head, well toward the back lest it show itself at inopportune moments.

Rational judgment told him that he should be able to travel wherever he pleased, given the passage of time. Who could possibly recognize him now, all these years later? Nonetheless, he had stayed put, even if he still longed for those days of Italian villas and small towns in the hills, a sunny landscape where everyone sipped wine at midday with big bowls of pasta and platefuls of fish, then napped until three.

A knock on the door interrupted his reverie. It was his assistant, Edin Azudin.

"Yes, Azudin. Come in."

Azudin was pale and thin. Matek was always telling him to eat more, then laughing when the man would blush and squirm. Matek had decided long ago, simply by appearances, that Azudin must be homosexual. It was just as well. Fewer temptations, at least around this valley. You'd as soon be caught sleeping with a goat as another man, given the local attitudes, so Matek never worried about his quiet little assistant causing trouble. It was almost like having his own eunuch at court. Had Matek known the truth he would have laughed aloud; the meek, undersized Azudin kept two mistresses in Travnik, not so surprising when one considered the ready supply of hard currency he earned from Matek. But it was also his manner, a calm, mouselike obeisance, practiced daily, that placated the women in its quiet way, and he was discreet enough in his comings and goings to ensure that the affairs never got complicated. If you had secrets, they were safe with Azudin, which is why Matek valued his services.

"There is a caller for you," Azudin said. "He says it's about a new demining contract for the municipality. He believes you may be the right man for it."

Matek perked up. "Does he, now? Well, leave him on hold then. For"—he mulled the timing—"for exactly ninety seconds. Then get back on the line and tell him I won't be available for a while. But take his number. And an hour later you're to call and arrange a meeting for tomorrow. In the morning. Ten, if possible. If he can't do it then, you're to check with me. And the meeting is to be here. Understand?"

"Yes, sir, but . . ." Azudin halted, uncertain whether to exceed his usual responsibilities.

"Go on."

"He insisted that I make sure you knew who you were doing business with. Vlado Petric, the son of Enver Petric."

And for the first time in as long as Azudin could remember, Pero Matek was speechless. Matek knew he must look a sight, sitting there with his mouth agape and papers dropping from his hand. He vaguely sensed Azudin scurrying to pick them up, but he shooed the little man away with a distracted wave of a meaty hand, then stood, pacing, barely aware of his surroundings, wondering at this strange and sudden shout from so deep in his past, not knowing whether to feel nostalgic or disconcerted.

Matek had known about Vlado, of course. Had known that

Enver, whom he still thought of as Josip, had married, had a son, and died without ever having made much of himself—not surprising, considering their past. The man had always been too earnest for his taste. His talents were effective only if you knew how to channel them, but otherwise the man had been too inflexible to be of much use. Enver's son, Matek had heard, had become some sort of policeman, had even had to leave the country, something to do with smuggling and corruption. Had he been a dirty cop, or too idealistic? Probably an amateur, either way, like his father. But he, too, might be useful if channeled. Matek had heard rumors that a change was in the works in the management of the demining concessions, but the selection of a Bosnian seemed almost too good to be true. Suddenly he sensed new possibilities, even if the boy's name made him uneasy. What vexed him most of all was how the boy could have found out about him, or his past connection to Enver. Enver and he had agreed long ago to go their separate ways, vowing no further contact. Yet, here was Enver's son on the phone. It was puzzling, and more than a little worrisome. Had Enver blabbed something on his deathbed long ago, some father-son confession, complete with names and bodies? He doubted it. And at least the boy hadn't referred to his father as Josip.

"Shall I put him on hold, sir?" Azudin was still awaiting an answer, looking far too curious for Matek's taste.

"No. Put the call through. And why don't you go down to see Silovic and pick up this week's take. If he grumbles about doing it a day early, tell him this is a test. That I'm making sure he isn't raking the till and juggling the books at the last minute, or taking midweek loans at my expense. Tell him it's a pop quiz. Tell him whatever you like. And take your cell phone in case I need you."

There, Matek thought. Azudin hated chores like this. It would take his mind off this phone call. No sense piquing his interest in anyone named Petric. "Go now. And put the call through."

"Yes, sir," Azudin said, departing with the helpless expression of a driver of a tiny car about to be crushed between two careening trucks.

Matek returned to his desk, anticipation building to a boil and, he had to admit, his merchant's sense of an impending bargain prickling as well. If the son of an old colleague was in charge of a new demining contract, well, that was good news on a front he'd been trying to make gains on for months. But the very fact that Enver's name had been spoken over his telephone seemed alarming. Although, why worry? Azudin wasn't in the habit of reading anti-Ustasha tracts that named names and dug up old history. He was twenty-six, and about as interested in history as any young man on the make, meaning not at all. Even if he had been, the most detailed published accounts available never mentioned young officers who'd been so far down the pecking order. Matek had checked the books and pamphlets himself, looking always for the names Rudec and Iskric, just in case, scanning with a frantic thump in his heart that was always pacified in the end.

He could probably resume using his old name tomorrow without turning a single head, if he wanted. Well, maybe not. There were always the old heads to consider, the gray women in the streets or the men leaning on their canes. Funny how he thought of them as old when they were his contemporaries, and once or twice in his travels around the country he thought he'd noticed some of them eyeing him strangely—probably nothing but the idle curiosity of the rube, but you could never tell for sure. He remembered that American movie about the old Jews stumbling through the streets of New York, bony fingers outstretched, calling the name of some aging Nazi who tried to race away. A horror to have it end that way, which was one reason he seldom strayed beyond his region, and almost never journeyed to places where lots of Serbs lived. The war had made that easier, thank goodness, sending each side streaming for its own ghettos and enclaves, the crescents and the crosses once again penned in their own cantons. Now he could drive for miles without fear of meeting some unwelcome face from his past.

Azudin transferred the call. Matek lifted the receiver, wondering if he might begin to tremble, either with worry or anticipation. But his hand was steady, his voice calm. "Matek," he said.

His caller turned out to be the one who was tremulous—from anger, from nerves, from dismay. Vlado had dialed quickly, as soon as he and Pine had reviewed the approach he should take, but he realized as soon as he heard the man's voice that he should have waited, if only for an hour, giving his emotions time to subside.

Hearing the man speak his name, he wanted to shout, "Who are you?" if only to calm the flutter in his stomach, the pressure in his fingertips. Instead he stuck to the formalities, working to keep the quaver out of his voice. "Mr. Matek?"

"Yes. And you're Enver's boy?"

"Undeniably."

Curious choice of words, Matek thought.

"But I'm not calling to relive old times, because frankly my father never told me much about those. It's business that brings me to your doorstep."

"You're hooked up with the EU, I take it?"

"Yes. Demining contracts. You're in the market for one, and I'm the new regional administrator."

"I thought the EU was convinced I didn't measure up."

"That was under the previous management. Now I'm in charge."

"Glad to hear it. And with a name I can trust. You should visit."

"The sooner the better."

"Tomorrow, then. Early, if you can make it. Eight o'clock? We can have breakfast."

"I'll be driving up from Sarajevo."

"Make it ten, then. A more civilized hour. We'll have coffee, maybe a glass of wine."

Matek was momentarily at a loss for what to say next. He wouldn't be laying on the usual spread, not for a local, much less one who was practically family. No need for any grand poses with this one, yet he'd still need to do some acting, given the circumstances. "We'll have more to talk about than just business, of course. So plan on staying awhile."

"Sure. I'll count on it."

I'll have to play this one carefully, Matek thought. He'd be trying to gauge exactly what the boy knew before committing himself to one truth or another. He'd need to do some thinking between now and tomorrow morning.

He gave Vlado directions, then they said good-bye. Tomorrow would be interesting indeed.

CHAPTER TEN

Pine and Vlado drove north on the highway out of Sarajevo, up through Kiseljak, Busovaca, and Vitez. During the war the road had crisscrossed territory held by all three warring factions, with sandbagged checkpoints and scattered mines. Travnik was about sixty miles away, but they'd allowed an extra hour for bad roads and slow traffic, saying little to fill the awkward silence as the miles passed. The mountains shouldered the route as the pale winter sun climbed the sky to their right.

Vlado had a slight hangover, less from three shots of the hotel's plum brandy than from the evening's revelations, which had called to him throughout the restless night, a gruff whisper through the pillow.

"Guess we ought to review some of the details," Pine said, clearing his throat. Their hope was that Matek would want to sign the contract the following morning, a Friday, the day of the Andric raid, coordinating the timing to please all sides. The key would be luring him onto neutral ground at the Skorpio.

"It's a little rat hole near the Suleiman mosque," Pine said. "Cheap *rakija* that will melt the paint off a wall. Matek supposedly has a stash of Italian wines they keep in the back. They don't even need to lock it up. That's what a reputation will do for you. Nobody would dare touch it.

"There's a *cevapi* stand where he usually likes to stop, too, up an alley around the corner. Then he usually meets one of his mistresses at the Skorpio. Spends an hour filling her up with Chianti or something stronger before they go upstairs for an hour of fun."

At one level Vlado was listening. At another he was wondering what he might be able to learn from Matek about his father without revealing the true nature of his visit. Pine probably had more information worth knowing, too. But he was still talking, still reviewing every possible detail of the day ahead. Maybe it was his clumsy way of softening the blow. Or maybe he was just embarrassed about having strung Vlado along.

"Pull over," Vlado interrupted. "I need to check something."

"We'll be late," Pine said, plowing ahead.

"Which would make me like every other Bosnian," he said icily. "It's you and the Germans who are obsessed with punctuality. We're way ahead of schedule. Pull over."

Pine complied with a frown, yanking the wheel, the car shuddering to a stop on the graveled shoulder.

"I want to see anything else you might have with you about my father," Vlado said. "Even if I only have time for a glance."

"You've seen the file."

"But there's more, isn't there. Someone must have wondered what would happen if I needed more convincing. That was pretty thin stuff, really. Just a few dates and assignments. If I'd demanded more proof, what would you have shown me?"

Pine sighed but never took his eyes off Vlado. "It's in my bag," he said. "Just a few pages. There's more back at The Hague, but we figured this would do it. If you really want to see, that is. If I were you, I wouldn't."

"You're not me. Get it, please."

Pine nodded, reaching for his briefcase. He snapped it open, foraged a moment, then pulled out a thin, stapled report stamped EYES ONLY below the tribunal letterhead. It was an old report from a U.S. Army counterintelligence officer.

"It's a witness report," Pine said. "From Jasenovac. Taken at a DP camp in Italy in 1946."

Vlado had second thoughts as he scanned the cover page. How much did he really need this? He decided to plunge in before losing his nerve.

"I'll take a little walk," Pine said, opening the door. "If you don't mind."

"Watch for mines," Vlado said absently.

"I know."

The name of the witness was Dragan Bobinac. He was a musician, a cellist from the Serb village of Crveni Bok on the banks of the Sava River, not far from Jasenovac. His account began with the day he was rounded up near his home along with several hundred of his neighbors, and he had plenty to say about the man known as Josip Iskric, who later became Enver Petric:

The soldiers came into our village in early morning, about a hundred of them, led by two lieutenants. I later learned their names were Rudec and Iskric. Iskric was the one giving orders, shouting at his men to keep anyone from escaping into the river. Some of his men shot people as they ran from their homes. Anyone who resisted was clubbed or stabbed on the spot. Children who didn't come fast enough were shot or struck in the face with sticks or bayonets. Some were dumped immediately into the river, still bleeding and alive. As we were marching I saw the naked body of a woman on the riverbank. Her eyes had been gouged out and a metal rod was shoved in her genitals. Iskric ordered me and another man to throw her into the river. The other man's name was Cedomir, he was a baker in the village. When Cedomir saw the woman he fell to his knees and said she was his niece. Iskric took a sidearm from a holster and ordered Cedomir to get up or he would be killed, but he stayed on the ground, crying. Iskric walked in front of him and shot him in the face, then rolled the body over with his boot. He ordered me to push both bodies into the river. I got them into the water, but the woman snagged on a branch after floating a few feet downstream, and Iskric ordered me into the river to pull her free. All this time the entire column was halted, watching everything, while some of the children were crying. I waded into the river up to my knees and pulled away the branch, then I watched the woman float toward the main current, which carried her downstream.

Vlado couldn't bear the scene any longer. He skipped ahead to an account from inside Jasenovac itself.

I was one of 10 people employed in the carpentry shop in the main camp. We were marching to the shop from our barracks when we were ordered to halt to allow a large column to pass in the opposite direction. They were young women— 150, maybe 200—led by several guards and Lieutenant Iskric. Someone shouted an order for the women to stop as well, and we looked at each other. Tears were falling from their eyes, and Iskric made a speech, telling our column to look closely because in an hour all these women would be dead, and that the next morning perhaps we would be killed as well unless we worked hard enough that day. We were forced to watch while the women were marched to the river. They were loaded onto rafts that took them to the other side, where the current was stronger. As they stepped onto the bank they were pulled aside by guards, who stabbed them with bayonets, and cut their throats and stomachs with knives. We could hear their screams and groans very clearly when they were stabbed or clubbed. Their bodies were then thrown or pushed into the current, sometimes while they were still alive and screaming.

Bobinac's account ended a few pages later with his escape the following month. He, too, had finally been ferried across the river with a hundred others. He got away when one of the guards hastily shoved him into the current with only a superficial wound, from a bayonet to the stomach.

There was more, but Vlado had seen enough. He gingerly placed the pages back into Pine's briefcase. Then he rolled down the window, the air cool and damp on his face, which boiled with shame and revulsion. So how much more of this sort of material was on file at The Hague, he wondered? How many chapters of such unbearable tales? He would need to see each and every one, no matter how agonizing.

"All done," he shouted in a quavering voice. What he needed was a brisk walk to collect himself, but he figured he didn't deserve it. Better to take it like this, stewing and guilty in a seat next to someone whose hands were clean, while driving across this tired landscape where armies had marched for generations, from one war to the next.

Pine was about twenty feet in front of the car when Vlado called out. For a moment he paused, facing the other way like a forlorn hitchhiker. Then he turned and slowly strolled back, rubbing his hands together for warmth as he slid into the driver's seat. He started the engine without a word.

It was a mile or so before either of them spoke.

"You okay?" Pine said softly.

Vlado nodded. "No worse than yesterday." Then he shrugged, exasperated. "But I'm still not really sure how I felt then. So how can I say what's going through my head now? Don't expect me to be okay. Just expect me to do my job. Just get me to the meeting. At least now I know the sort of person I'm dealing with."

"Sure." Pine kept his eyes on the road.

Vlado waited a moment, then asked, "This witness, Bobinac. Is he still alive?"

"Living in Novi Sad, I think. He's prepared to testify at Matek's trial."

After a few minutes of silence, Pine tentatively resumed his impromptu briefing. "There's a wide street out front of the Skorpio," he said, "and no way to exit through the back without having to go through the kitchen. They keep the kitchen door in the rear padlocked. Firetrap, but perfect for us 'cause he has to come out the front even if he decides to bolt. Try to let the Skorpio be his idea. But if he starts making noise about another meeting at the house, insist that your boss never meets the locals on their own turf, that the meeting has to be in town. That should steer him where we want him."

"Plus, I'm his old friend's son, and his new partner in crime. So how can he possibly say no?"

"Yes. That, too."

Vlado wouldn't let it go. Not yet. "So tell me. What would you have done if you hadn't found me? Or if I didn't exist? Would this swap still have been arranged? And don't give me any of that 'Plan B' business."

Pine didn't look up. "Probably. Just would have been harder. We might have just waited until he went to the café on his own, then jumped. But SFOR doesn't like doing business that way. You have to get paid informants involved, and once you've done that the whole thing tends to leak like an old pirate ship. So we were looking for something to simplify this, and that's when we found you."

"How did my name turn up?"

"Harkness or LeBlanc, apparently."

The names chilled him, especially Harkness's, remembering the man's face in the dark as he'd muttered about Popovic. For all he knew, LeBlanc had been poking around in his affairs as well. Either of them might have been the man who'd shown up on Haris's doorstep in Berlin. LeBlanc was simply too clever to have asked him directly about Popovic, the way Harkness had. But now it seemed more unlikely than ever that any of that should matter to this operation.

"I heard they came across your name while researching Matek," Pine continued. "I guess through your father's file. We checked records for any living relatives of either. We couldn't believe our luck. They had me on a train to Berlin within a week. Contreras wanted it moving fast. The French did, too. Didn't know how long they could hold together the political momentum in the defense and foreign ministries. That was LeBlanc's doing. The French still aren't exactly keen on the idea of picking up Andric. It'll be the first arrest in their sector since the Dayton agreement. But at least they'll be starting with a bang. He'll be the biggest suspect yet to go to trial. But the main reason you made the pieces fit is because SFOR loved the idea. There's nothing they like better than ordering up a time, a date, and a secure location for bringing in a suspect. I'm not even sure we could have talked them into this one without the kind of assurance you'll provide. If you can provide it."

"And if I can't? What if Matek says we close the deal at his place or no place?"

"I can't imagine he would, given the stakes. He's wanted this contract a long time."

"But say that he does."

Pine turned toward him for the first time, the tires thrumming on the road. "I don't know. You tell me. We're flying by the seat of our pants as it is."

"Like you said. Half-assed."

"Sometimes that's as good as it gets down here."

Vlado wished Pine would quit saying "down here," as if it were some quaint corner of hell.

"How many SFOR people will be involved?"

"The soldiers? Hard to say. We're never privy to that. I'd guess at least twenty. Two APCs and maybe a Humvee with a big gun mounted on the back. It'll look like they're coming after Genghis Khan by the time they're in place."

"Won't that be kind of . . ."

"Stupid? Ridiculous? Noisy? Enough to panic everyone in the neighborhood and maybe him, too? Sure. You ever seen cops or soldiers do it any other way?"

Vlado smiled ruefully. "I guess not."

Vlado wondered how many other people back in The Hague must have known about his father when they'd met him. Harkness and LeBlanc had, of course. Contreras and Spratt had presumably known as well, smiling and chatting as if none the wiser. Perhaps Janet Ecker, too. All of them looking him in the eye and not wavering a bit. And these were the good guys. No wonder Pine had been so irritated when LeBlanc made the crack about "surprises" awaiting Vlado in Sarajevo. Maybe the Frenchman had been trying to warn him in some oblique way, although it struck him more as a clumsy joke, something to get under Pine's skin.

Everyone had fooled him, and now he was about to fool Matek, all in the name of family. He wondered how he'd feel when the moment of truth came, and the old man—his father's friend, for better or worse—looked into his eyes, realizing what was happening. Just what Vlado needed this morning. Another reason to feel rotten. At least after tomorrow he'd be able to call Jasmina. Who knew what she and Sonja were thinking by now? More than two days without a word, except from some tribunal secretary. And so much to tell her, so much that would be difficult and embarrassing. She'd never met his father, had only seen his picture.

"Here's the turnoff to Travnik," Pine said. "Nine-twenty. We're in good shape."

Travnik was long past its prime, worn down in past years by cataclysmic fires, and more recently by wearying tides of refugees. A century ago it had been a hub for the Ottoman viziers who ran

Bosnia for the sultan. European diplomats came and went, observed by the young Serbian novelist Ivo Andric, who skeptically recorded their doings in his *Chronicles of Travnik*. His home there, once a popular museum, was now largely ignored. Never mind his Nobel Prize. He was the Serb who'd portrayed the Turks and their local Islamic converts as bloodthirsty tyrants, deserving of vengeance.

About all that was left of those days now was a few old mosques, like the Suleiman, and the fifteenth-century castle overlooking the town from Mount Vlasic, the onetime stronghold of Bosnian kings.

They wove through the crowded narrow streets until they found the small hotel. Vlado dropped off his bag with Pine in the lobby, taking the car keys as Pine wished him luck. He was on his own now, could drive the Volvo off into the hills and never come back if he wanted. But Matek was waiting up on his mountain, the only one left who could escort Vlado into the past. As awkward and uncomfortable as the meeting promised to be, there was no way Vlado could refuse the invitation.

He easily found the turnoff to Mount Vlasic, climbing several miles before swerving onto a dirt road, the Volvo's underbelly bottoming out in the deeper ruts. At higher elevations the bare trees were coated with ice. On some curves he looked back down onto Travnik and remembered Pine's mentioning that Matek could see much of the road from his house and always knew when a visitor was approaching. Vlado thought he caught a glimpse of a red rooftop looming high up ahead, but the road was too twisting and narrow to allow the luxury of a longer look. Meanwhile, some rear chamber of his brain was still sorting through every retrievable memory of his father, looking for missed signs, gathering little threads from the past to see if they added up to anything meaningful. His father had passed himself off as a Muslim who never went to mosque, a Muslim who drank. Neither characteristic was unusual "down here," as Pine would have said, but Vlado remembered that his father had also been talked into attending Catholic mass on occasion with his wife and son, and those Sundays now seemed significant. In addition, he had given his son a good Christian name, Vladimir. He must have sneaked off at times to confession, Vlado supposed, if he was any sort of Catholic. The parish priest had probably been happy to conspire with him, hearing his petty sins but probably never the big ones.

And what about that trip long ago to his Uncle Tomislav's? That night out back with all the shouting and drinking. Now, what had that been about? Had his uncle fought in the war as well?

He remembered a wooden crucifix hanging in his aunt and uncle's bedroom, the bleeding Jesus with the agonized upturned face that had always seemed to be staring at a crack in the ceiling. Of course. His father's family had all been Catholics. The stupid son could have added it up as simply as the beads on a rosary if he'd ever bothered to think. But such details had run together when he was a boy. Tito had asked that crosses and crescents be considered little more than quaint symbols of their past, and Vlado had obediently obliged, never pausing to note their significance.

Vlado glimpsed the tile roof again, much closer now. Matek was probably watching his car, the engine rumbling like something tunneling toward him through the mountain. The Volvo's springs creaked through another set of curves, and there it was, a small guardhouse with a rusted iron pole barring the way. A man with a Kalashnikov slung on his back emerged from the guardhouse in a burst of gray smoke. No uniform, just blue jeans and a dark sweater, cigarette drooping from his lips. He sauntered to the car and checked Vlado's papers. Vlado had an EU identification card plus some other documents. If there was one thing the EU people had easily been able to spare for them, it was paper. The guard pulled a cell phone from his back pocket and punched in a number. Then he tugged at a rope to haul the pole into the air, clearing the way.

Waving Vlado through, he shouted, "The big house at the top. Go in through the front. Azudin will take you to Mr. Matek."

Mr. Matek. How long had it taken to train this one to say "Mister," Vlado wondered. If he wasn't working here, he'd probably be pulling up turnips and cabbages, or drinking in the loft of a barn, falling asleep and setting the hay on fire with his smokes. Instead he was waving an automatic weapon, empowered to kill by the man Vlado was about to visit.

It never hurt to remind yourself of exactly who you were dealing with.

CHAPTER ELEVEN

Matek watched Vlado approach from his window, unsure how to greet the boy. He'd been irritable all morning, shouting at Azudin when the coffee wasn't hot enough, griping about the bread, although it was the same bread as every morning.

When he saw the face emerge from the car, he knew there was no doubting the bloodlines. Sometimes, he knew, you saw the father in the son because you went looking for him. But in this one the resemblance was obvious, not so much in the features as in the way he carried himself, purposeful, head held high. This was not the sort of person who would ever apologize for what he believed in. Just like his father. But what did this one believe in? That was the morning's top question, and he intended to find the answer.

Then he chuckled in spite of himself at the idea that they might actually do business together, and he was still smiling when Azudin shepherded the boy—he had to stop thinking of him as a boy, the man was in his thirties—into the room. The smile broadened as he saw the uncomfortable look on Vlado's face. Good God, the boy was embarrassed. So he stepped quickly across the room and, without a word, grabbed him around both arms, bear-hugging like some Russian grandfather, feeling the young man's sinew and bone beneath the wool sleeves. And in spite of himself he felt tears spring to his eyes, so he pulled the man closer and spoke into his ear, silently reminding himself not to use any of the wrong words from the past.

"Ah, Vlado, your father and I. Your father and I. Such times we had together. But too long ago now."

Then the wave of nostalgia crested and broke, and Matek let go, stepping back to look into the boy's face, inspecting the cool reserve in the eyes that he knew so well.

Vlado had feebly attempted to return the man's warmth, although it was hard while the big arms gripped him so tightly. Now at least he could offer a smile, not a grand one but enough to do his familial duty. Then the big man withdrew and, in a rolling gait, eased behind the bulwark of his desk.

He had opened a bottle of red wine and set aside two glasses, polished to a sparkle. None of the usual smudges today. "I know it is early," he said, "but please." He poured Vlado a glass. "We must drink to your father."

A Chianti, Vlado noticed, figuring he'd be better off trying to act as an observant cop than as some sort of unofficial nephew. Look for details. Concentrate on the business at hand. But his father's presence was unavoidable, as if he were looming in a corner, nodding sternly, reminding Vlado to be respectful and polite.

The décor was not what he'd expected. It looked standard issue for some small-town mayor or party hack. Nor did it go with this wine. Matek noticed the glances of assessment and spoke.

"For the Europeans and Americans it is usually only *rakija*, because they expect it of me. For you, something I really like." Matek raised his glass. "To your father."

Vlado raised his own, then sipped.

"And also to his son," Matek said.

Vlado knew it was his turn, but it took an effort. "And to his friend," he finally said, which seemed to please Matek.

Neither spoke for a moment. Vlado decided to let Matek take the lead, knowing his own mind was still darting too many places at once.

"Yes, you are your father's son," Matek finally said. "He is the only other person I know who would sit there for so long without a word, determined to make me speak first, even with important business to be done."

Vlado blushed, wondering what else Matek must be thinking.

"I'm sorry," Matek said, "but there is one thing I must ask you straightaway. How did you know about me? From your father?"

Vlado had strict instructions on this point. He was to be as vague as possible, an approach that had troubled him all morning, because it seemed obvious that Matek would smell a rat. Why indeed would the son of Enver Petric not be able to provide a simple and concise explanation, especially when he'd been empowered to offer a contract to a man whom the EU had deemed unsuitable only a month ago?

He also preferred not to begin their conversation with a lie, feeling it might throw him off balance for the duration. And this first question, at least, he could answer honestly enough without revealing a thing. So he broke with the plan.

"My father never said a word," Vlado replied, looking Matek in the eye, feeling as if he'd been hooked up to a polygraph. "I didn't know you existed until years after he died."

"Then it must have been your Uncle Tomislav. He's the only other one who knew me from those days." Matek had a faraway look as he spoke, then seemed to snap back to attention, and Vlado sensed that the man had momentarily dropped his guard, letting the name slip.

"Yes," Vlado answered, going with his instincts. "It was Uncle Tomislav. He told me in a letter, not long before he died. He said I was not to trouble you. But he said that you would always be there if I needed help, after he was gone. Then when I took this job last month it wasn't long before I saw your name on a list. I couldn't be sure it was the same Pero Matek. But when I found out how old you were . . . well, it all seemed to fit."

"He must have told you many stories in that letter, your uncle."

It now seemed likely that Matek was acting. There was a change in his tone, all business now, and it put Vlado on his guard.

"No stories at all. He just said that you and my father were old friends, but that was all. So of course I wrote him back, asking for more, because my father had always been too shy to talk about the past, the years during the war. He wasn't one of those men who went around claiming to have parachuted into every valley and cave in Yugoslavia, fighting with the Partisans. But by the time my letter reached him, Tomislav had died. My aunt sent me a reply. And she didn't remember much."

"But Tomislav. If he was dying, surely he must have told you more than just my name?" Matek poured more wine, suddenly striking Vlado as an old lecher trying to get his young date drunk. They gripped the stems of their glasses tightly. Outside a tractor lumbered into motion, the diesel chug stroking like a jackhammer.

"No," Vlado said. "No stories."

Matek nodded, seemingly relieved. Vlado decided this was a good time to get down to business, but he couldn't resist the opening Matek had just offered.

"In fact, I was hoping you'd be able to tell me some stories. To fill in all those blanks my father left behind. To tell me what he was like when he was growing up. What he did later. You know how quiet he was. He hardly told me anything."

Vlado knew he'd just veered dangerously from the script. Pine had been explicit on the point. If Matek wanted to talk about the past, fine. Just don't bring it up yourself. But to hell with them. They'd opened this box, and he'd be damned if he'd shut it before pawing through the contents.

"Oh," Matek said, picking up the bottle to pour, then setting it down as he saw both glasses were still full. "Well, the usual things that you find in a small village. Playing sports together, going to school. Then there was the war, which changed everything. There was very little fighting for us, of course. I wouldn't even call it that. Just marching, mostly. Moving people or supplies from one place to another. And always in the rain, it seemed. Always in the rain and cold. Marching and waiting and digging. Very little action. Just grunt work. The sort of things that never make it into the history books. We left the country after the war, you know. For a few years. Surely your father told you that?"

"No. He never did."

"He never told you that we crossed the border?"

"My father never said anything about those years, no matter how much my mother and I asked. So we stopped asking."

Vlado felt free to finally take a good, long sip of his wine. This was going more smoothly than he'd expected. "Where did you go?"

"To Austria first. Marching with thousands."

Vlado remembered the tale about trucks. A convoy heading north from Zagreb with a few high officials aboard. But Matek was continuing, still embroidering the truth.

"The roads into Austria were jammed for miles, everyone trying to get out before the Russians arrived from the east. We hadn't been with Tito's men, you know. Just some local militia. And by the end everyone was fighting everyone else. Mass confusion, and you knew there would be retribution, no matter who you'd been fighting for. So the best thing to do was leave, and we finally made it across the border. We worked on a farm for a few months, in Austria. Finally some British soldiers came along and asked for our papers. They took us off to a DP camp in Italy. In Fermo. Awful place, but your father and I were still together. Thousands of people there. Food was terrible. Lice. Disease. Terrible. Then they finally sent us home. Through the Red Cross. It was not a good time to admit you'd been in the 'wrong' army, even if you'd only been privates digging ditches. So we returned the way we'd left, on foot. Crossing the border through the hills at night, and settling in places far from where we'd grown up."

Vlado was unable to resist a little test, having already heard a boatload of lies. "And this was when?"

"Nineteen forty-six."

A full fifteen years earlier than what Vlado knew to be the truth. Now what would be the point of that lie, other than to erase the years in Rome?

"I came here," Matek continued. "Your father went to a village near Sarajevo, each of us with nothing. We figured it was better not to stay with each other, or even to stay in touch, the political situation being what it was. So we drifted apart as the years passed. I think I only heard from him once, maybe twice, though I did hear he had a wife and son. And as you can see, I never had a family. Never had a son, though I wanted to. I envied him that, when I heard."

It was clear Matek was finished with the subject of the past. But Vlado was unable to resist a final question. "My father, what was he like then? As a young man."

"An idealist. Always too much of one, I thought. You might have even called him a zealot."

Vlado's heart sank. He'd seen enough handiwork of zealotry in the last war.

"He was always more of a patriot than me. I was only along for the adventure, and, later, for the opportunity. Because I learned something then about war. And I'm sure it's no secret to you, with the business you're in now. War is a terrible thing, but it comes with built-in opportunities, and you have to either seize them or be swept along with everyone else who has given up all control of their lives. Your father never liked that in me."

Soon afterward they began discussing business, the supposedly crucial part of their conversation. It turned out to be the easiest part. Matek confessed he'd been eager for a piece of the demining action for some time and had no trouble with agreeing to meet in town the next morning with Vlado's "boss," ostensibly the one who would have to approve Vlado's choice. Matek even suggested the Skorpio.

Vlado brought out a sheaf of papers, an agreement in principle, for Matek to peruse and then bring to their meeting to sign the next morning. It was boilerplate stuff from the EU office, the real thing. No sense risking the operation with fakes.

They said farewell at the door, their parting more subdued than their introduction, with Vlado vowing that tomorrow the food and drink would be his treat. Then he was on his way back to Travnik, grinding down the hill while Matek watched the white car descend the switchback curves, beetling through the dust.

Already Matek was working over their conversation like a piece of gristle, rolling it in his mouth, wondering what it was that just didn't taste quite right. There was no doubting the boy's provenance. He was Enver's son, all right. Maybe that was the problem. Earnest to a fault, just like his father. Wanting to do things for the right reasons, not because of how they'd serve his interests. But what would the right reasons be for a young man like Vlado?

Matek decided he needed a walk to think it over. He threw on a coat and shuffled wordlessly past the staring Azudin, out past the goats toward a high rocky knoll up in the trees, where the views of the valley were best. He listened to the few birds that had remained here for the winter, faint chirping noises in the icy gray brush. What was it that was sticking in his craw, refusing to be digested?

That bit about his Uncle Tomislav. Now, when the hell would the boy's father ever have told Tomislav Pero's new name, Matek? And why would he have taken the risk? It was possible, he supposed. But Enver was a careful man, who knew as well as anyone the consequences of leaking sensitive details. The boy had to have learned it from somebody, though, and if not Tomislav, then who? Growing chilly, Matek returned to his office and dialed the number of the Skorpio.

"Yes?"

"It's Matek. Is Osman around?"

"Isn't he always?"

"Is he still sober?"

"As much as he always is this time of day. He won't be completely worthless for a few more hours."

"Put him on."

There was a pause, then the sound of a chair scraping the floor, a clatter of glasses, followed by another voice. "Osman."

"This is Matek. Listen carefully because I have some work for you. There is a man staying at the Hotel Orijent who I'd like you to check for me. Discreetly, please. His name is Vlado Petric, and I'd like to know what he's up to. If he's traveling with anyone. If so, how they're registered, who's paying the bills. What their business is. Follow him awhile, and ask around. Learn what you can. But you're not to approach him, not to speak with him. Understand?"

"Sure."

"And no talking about this. Not with anyone. Not if you ever want another drink in this town."

"Understood." Osman was a drunk, but he wasn't a fool, and he'd always kept his mouth shut before.

"I want to hear back from you by day's end. Six o'clock at the latest, and before you've had anything else to drink."

"Yes, sir."

Matek didn't need to add that his instructions were an order. Orders were the only way Matek dealt with people, and it was well known that disobedience was often followed closely by terribly unfortunate accidents.

"If you're successful, your bar tab will be paid up for a week. Just have Selak add it to my tab. Azudin will deduct the amount next time he comes round to collect. Got it?"

"Sure."

"Good. Get to work."

Osman was better than his word. The staff of the Hotel Orijent was always an easy mark, and a few phone calls did the rest. By 5 p.m. he was thirsty and back on the phone, bursting with information.

Matek was outdoors when the call came, returning from another walk, having been too stirred up to get much work done. This time he'd walked a mile, straight up the goat path toward the summit, motivated by the day's events to check on a place he hadn't visited in years. But now he heard the phone ringing, and Azudin appeared at the front door, out of breath.

"The telephone, sir." It was still ringing.

"Well, then answer it, idiot!"

"I just thought that now that you had returned that . . . yes, sir."

He disappeared down the hall while Matek knocked mud from his boots, recalling his first walk up that hill so long ago, on a summer night of fireflies and the distant barking of farm dogs. It was 1961. The house had only been a single story then, and he'd made the journey at midnight, barefoot in the dew and a little drunk, serenaded by crickets as his trousers rasped in the high grass. It had been an easy walk then, even for someone foolish enough to be traversing a stony hillside without shoes. Too much drinking alone in those days, too much time going through his papers and his passports, wondering where to keep them all, knowing they were a sort of dynamite but also a sort of insurance, a retirement plan, even.

So he'd resolved the matter by climbing the hill with a shovel in one hand and a box in the other, and inside the box was an oiled leather pouch. By now, perhaps, the leather was mildewed and stiff, but perhaps he would know for sure soon enough, depending on what Osman had to say.

He reached his office, shouting down the hallway to Azudin. "I'll take the call in here. You go home early today. I'll take care of any loose ends."

Then he picked up the receiver, listening closely for a few moments, saying little. The news was unexpected, but he tried not to betray his shock to Osman. No sense letting the village drunk know he was disturbed, or soon everyone would know it. So he kept his voice even and thanked the man as always. But as he quietly replaced the receiver Matek realized that his hands were shaking. It was partly out of anger, perhaps, partly out of fear as well—fear of the unknown. Because for the first time in more years than Matek cared to remember, his future was in doubt, and this time none of the usual remedies would work. Extraordinary measures were called for. But which ones? And on this point he foundered, again uncertain, until it dawned on him that the answer might be as nearby as another walk up the hill, back to that place where he'd buried an unspoken shred of his life. If the road to your future was blocked, he mused, who was to say you couldn't flee instead into the past? After carefully disposing of a few impediments, of course. But that would be the easy part. That sort of business always was.

CHAPTER TWELVE

On another hillside some two hundred miles to the east, another soldier answered a ringing telephone. He was a general, a Serb in a bunker. He, too, had just been for a walk, and was about to go on another. He instantly recognized the caller, who spoke accented Bosnian with a habitual conspiratorial tone. This time, at least, the tone was warranted.

Andric answered in a low voice. He always kept a window open, and you never knew how close one of the sentries might be. A bored man can be a dangerous eavesdropper.

"It begins tomorrow," the caller said.

"So. They really mean to do it."

"Yes. And it will be early."

"How early?"

"Six. Maybe six-thirty. About an hour before sunrise. You still have your plans?"

"Of course. And you're certain of the route?"

"Yes. Just avoid the village. No good-bye fucks with the barmaid. Not even tonight. And don't move too soon. They have to practically be at your door. Risky, I know, but don't panic."

"I'm not the type."

"Yes." The caller chuckled lightly. "I'm quite sure of that."

"And you're sure of the time?"

"Positive. Any changes and you'll be notified. Just don't forget our terms. Or our schedule."

"As discussed. But there could be delays. This isn't the sort of work I'm used to."

"Understood. But I've allowed plenty of time. And you remember the name of the place, of course."

"Of course."

Both knew not to utter any names, not with the possibility that others might either intercept or overhear their conversation.

"Good. As long as I'll know where to find you, neither of us should have any problems. Good luck."

"Yes. For both of us."

They hung up without a further word. Andric checked out the window. The sentry was twenty feet away, seated on a barrel, blowing smoke rings and reading a porn magazine. The poor stupid bastard should have stayed in the army, but Andric paid on time, and with hard currency. Not that he got much for his money. What a waste of time and expense this had all been, three years of wages for these ignorant boys who talked of nothing but sports, women, and booze. Nothing else left to talk about in this ruined land that produced only cigarettes, bread, and whatever you could grow with your hands.

He checked his closet for what must have been the twentieth time that week. Everything was in place. The small backpack with a change of clothes. A compass. A filled canteen. Knife. Flashlight. Holstered pistol, loaded, plus a box of extra rounds. He didn't think he would need it tomorrow, but he would kill if he had to. Then, or any other time in the days to come. There were two maps, one of this country and one of another. Last, the most valuable item of all, the small pouch with passports and visas, plus the packet of the privileged information that had nearly cost him his job to obtain, and inside it, a tiny key, in the old style, such as you might have used to open a door long ago. Perhaps it would finally prove its worth.

There was still mud on the pouch, the slightest bit at the edges. He had dug it up late last week at the first word of possible trouble, trudging through the grove of plum trees and over the rail fence, down the path and past the stump, next to the field where, years ago, old Jelisic had grown his pumpkins. Two feet deep, but just as he'd left it. Now he'd see how far it could take him, how good the man's word had been, all those years ago.

There was a pile of old clothes on his closet floor. They were part of the plan, too, because if you rummaged beneath them you soon found a handle that pulled up a small door. The door opened onto an air shaft, with ladder rungs down the side; it dropped fifteen feet to a tunnel, an old route from Tito's darkest days of paranoia as he prepared to repel a Red Army invasion that never came.

Thank goodness for that paranoia, Andric thought, and he felt like celebrating with a drink, driving into the village for a final toast to his good fortune. But he was not the type for unnecessary risks. You never knew when some young French officer might decide to jump the gun.

He reviewed the route in his head. A hundred yards beneath the forest floor to the back of the hillside, then up out of the ground through another lost and forgotten door that opened into a tangle of weeds. Then down the hill through the trees to a farm, where a truck sat parked in the underbrush, looking abandoned and worthless, but he knew better. He'd rechecked the engine and the ignition three days ago. New battery and cables. Fresh gas in the tank and two full jerry cans in the back. A new set of plates in the glove compartment, plus a Croatian pair for farther down the road. Even at that he'd have to move fast, quietly, without fear. But he had no doubt he could pull it off. He hadn't been boasting to the caller when he'd said he wouldn't panic.

He simply wasn't the type.

CHAPTER THIRTEEN

The phone was ringing, muffled, seemingly a thousand miles away. But when Vlado opened his eyes he realized the sound was coming through the wall from Pine's room. It was seven o'clock, so he figured he might as well get moving. They'd be closing the deal with Matek today; just thinking about it made him nervous.

Pine knocked at the door before he was even dressed, and the news wasn't good. "Spratt just called." He looked flustered, hair in every direction and shirt unbuttoned. "The raid was a disaster. Andric got away."

"From a hundred soldiers? What happened?"

"Who knows. His sentries—the ones who survived, the damn French killed three of them—said he'd been asleep in his bunker. They were sure of it. But when they checked there wasn't a soul inside."

Vlado's heart sank. All the planning, deception, and revelations about his past had supposedly been part of the larger, higher motive of bringing Andric to justice. All that remained was the chore of arresting the old man, if that was even still part of the tribunal's plans.

"Where does that leave us?" he asked.

"Spratt said to go ahead. For the moment Matek is the only thing in the pipeline, and we could use a little face-saving. Our sponsors apparently want it, too."

"Sponsors?"

"Harkness and LeBlanc. It's probably all tied in with budget stuff. The tribunal needs a win, in other words, and we're it. So let's get it over with. Pick up the old bastard, let Harkness and LeBlanc have the debriefing we promised, then turn him over to the Croatians and get the hell out of here."

Vlado was too stunned to speak.

"Jesus!" Pine exclaimed angrily. "We finally get the French to make a move, and this happens. Now they'll never lift a finger again. Never. And the press will kill us. SFOR or no SFOR, the tribunal will get the blame."

Pine sat down on the bed. He seemed to realize for the first time that he was barefoot, and in need of a shave. "I better get dressed," he said, collecting himself. "And I could use some coffee. We need to go over everything again before we head out. Make sure we don't fuck it up."

They arrived at the Skorpio ten minutes ahead of schedule, just to be on the safe side, which meant they'd be sitting at their table for forty minutes before Matek was due. The place was virtually empty. Only the bartender and a single customer sipping coffee toward the back. A Humvee and an APC were parked about thirty yards around the corner, in the opposite direction from which Matek would presumably approach. The vehicles were a fairly common sight around the valley, and had been since the Dayton Accords, so no one was likely to be alarmed.

When Matek arrived, Pine was supposed to make sure he wasn't accompanied by bodyguards. Neither Pine nor Vlado was carrying weapons or a radio, in case Matek had a notion to search them, which Pine didn't expect. As soon as everything seemed in order, Pine would excuse himself to the men's room, where he would call the SFOR unit from a cell phone and retrieve a .45-caliber pistol from a towel box.

Vlado thought the entire setup was full of holes. What if bodyguards arrived first? What if Matek himself had a gun? Would anyone else in the bar be armed? They were counting on the shock value of a few M-16s to keep matters in hand.

The door to the bar swung open, and Vlado looked up. It was just some drunk, squinting into the dimness, getting his bearings. He glanced at their table and seemed to smile. He looked vaguely familiar from the day before in the hotel, but Vlado found it hard to imagine the man had been a guest. Probably an employee. Then the man strolled to the bar, where he rapped the counter once with his right hand. The bartender produced a bottle and a glass without a word, and the man began to drink.

"Local character," Pine muttered. "Shouldn't be a problem."

Vlado checked his watch. Matek was five minutes late. The delay stretched to ten minutes. Then fifteen.

"He's not coming," Pine said.

"He's probably just on Bosnian time," Vlado said, wanting to believe it. "Or he's just making us wait. Relax."

"No. He's not coming. This whole operation has been fucked from the start, and this is the perfect finish. He's a no-show."

Ten more minutes passed, and Vlado was convinced Pine was right. He saw Pine looking at him and didn't like the expression.

"What did you tell him?" Pine asked, not accusingly or sharply but not in a friendly way either.

"Nothing," Vlado said with some heat. "You think I warned him off? Told him this was all a big trap? As a favor to an old friend of the family?"

"Of course not. But what did you ask him about your father? What did you talk about? Something must have tipped him. Something you said or did. Your body language. Your embarrassment. Hell, what did you say to him?"

Vlado might have been angrier if he hadn't just been wondering the same thing. Matek had seemed eager to meet again, so what the hell had gone wrong?

"I don't know," Vlado said at last. "I really don't."

"We're screwed. And there are twenty soldiers outside to break the news to. Their CO will leak it across the chain of command, and within a couple of days we'll be right there in the headlines with Andric." He shook his head. "A flying start for Contreras and the 'new aggressiveness.' He'll end up as tame as any of them now, and God knows what will become of our budget."

They decided to wait until Matek was an hour late, but both knew it was an empty gesture. At noon Pine went the washroom to retrieve the .45. Then he dropped some bills on the table and turned to leave.

"C'mon," he said wearily. "Let's find the officer in charge. Who knows. Maybe they'll give us an armed escort up the mountain to Matek's compound. Stranger things have happened."

The soldiers were loitering around the Humvee, a few of them stamping their feet in the cold. Pine was directed to a tall American lieutenant with the name Hundley on his uniform.

"We've had a change in plans," Pine began optimistically, explaining the plan to head up the mountain. The officer saw right through it.

"What you're saying is that the operation's a bust. Which means we'll be pulling out. Our orders pertained to the town only. Nobody said anything about going up a mountain road that we haven't scouted or reconned. It could still be mined for all I know."

"This man was just up there yesterday," Pine said, nodding toward Vlado. "All by himself. So it's not mined. There's only one guard at the gate. Maybe two more inside, plus a suspect who's seventy-five. There's your recon."

"Sorry, sir," the lieutenant said, with no change in inflection. "No go. But you're welcome to speak to my colonel." He offered Pine a radio handset.

"He'd tell me more of the same, wouldn't he?"

"Can't speak for my colonel, sir. But that would be my guess. Unless he offers to let you speak to *his* CO."

"I could spend the whole day climbing the chain of command. Think I could reach the Oval Office by sundown?"

This finally got a smile out of Hundley, but nothing else.

"Yeah, I know," Pine said. "Just following orders. Have a nice day, Lieutenant."

"Will do, sir," the officer deadpanned. "Let's move out, men."

And with a rumble of engines and a wintry swirl of dust, the soldiers left, stranding Pine and Vlado at the curb like hosts of a failed dinner party.

After four cups of the Skorpio's coffee, Vlado was edgy and irritated. He had half a mind to drive the white Volvo up the hill to find out for himself. Maybe Matek was testing them, playing hard to get. But he doubted it.

"What we need is backup," Pine said, "at least enough to go take a look. Didn't Benny say he'd be in Vitez?"

"For the rest of the week."

"Worth a try, then. That's only twenty miles. And if anybody would enjoy mixing it up after an SFOR bail, it's Benny."

Pine punched in a number on his cell phone and waited, then spoke. "Benny? Calvin Pine. We've just had a major fuckup, and if you're anywhere near Travnik, we could sure use some help. Yeah? Perfect."

Pine filled him in on their morning, and Vlado could hear nearly every word of Benny's requisite tirade on the impotence of SFOR. He had an interview to finish, then he'd meet them at the hotel in an hour.

"He's the only one with the balls for something like this," Pine said.

Benny's other advantage was that he regularly carried a gun. It was against tribunal policy—Pine's borrowed .45 had been sanctioned only for the occasion of the arrest and he had already handed it back to the SFOR troops—but just about everyone below Spratt at The Hague knew that Benny's local interpreter kept a Beretta pistol for him, hidden in his cellar.

"You think one gun is enough?" Vlado asked. To him the operation was degenerating from half-assed to harebrained.

"It's not like we're going to storm the place. I just want a peek at the front gate."

"He'll see us approaching. From up in his house."

"Which is why I want Benny along. He's got that street-cop mentality from Brooklyn."

"The Bronx."

"Whatever. We can get the lay of the land, see if Matek's taking visitors. Maybe we'll even get lucky and bump into him on his way down the hill."

"If he's still around."

"Yeah." Pine frowned. "There's that possibility, too."

Benny arrived every bit as eager and gung-ho as he had been at his desk, which made Vlado wary. Still jittery from the caffeine, he envisioned barreling up the mountain into a phalanx of bodyguards with orders to fire on any EU car. A pistol wouldn't be much good against a few Kalashnikovs.

"Have you ever used it?" Vlado asked.

"Only once. Waved it at a nasty checkpoint a few years ago. Drunken Croats who wanted a 'toll' and maybe my car. Changed their tune in a hurry when they saw the barrel. Tried to act like it had all been a big joke. But that was years ago, right after Dayton. Now you never really need to be armed unless you're going after somebody like Andric. Who escaped this morning, by the way. It's all over the radio. But I guess you guys already knew that, huh?"

Pine nodded.

"So it really was a two-for-one, then?"

"Only now it's a none-for-two. Unless we get lucky."

"Fuckin' French." Benny shook his head. "Wonder who the loose lip was on this one. LeBlanc, maybe? I never thought this deal would go through from the moment I heard about it."

"You weren't supposed to hear about it at all."

"The names were making the rounds the day before Vlado showed up."

"Great."

"What do you expect when you let Harkness and LeBlanc call the shots? Lie down with dogs, get up with fleas."

Pine explained the likely setup awaiting them on the mountain. They agreed to err on the side of caution, vowing to reverse tracks at the first sign of a hostile reception.

The trip seemed longer to Vlado than it had the day before, but with Pine driving he was able to watch the view ahead. They got their first glimpse of the house about fifteen minutes after the turnoff. Benny pulled out a small pair of binoculars.

"Here. Somebody else take a look. Seems quiet to me, but I've never been there."

Vlado focused on the big upstairs window in the back, looking down the mountain from Matek's bedroom. Below was his office. The curtains were drawn on both.

"He's either not expecting us or doesn't care," Vlado said, not sure whether to feel relieved or disappointed. The place looked dead. Not even the goats were out.

Nosing around the final curve, they slowed to a crawl as they approached the guardhouse. A door was open on the side. The bar across the driveway was raised, and a dust-covered BMW was parked on the shoulder. Inside the guardhouse someone stood, as if he'd been hunched over looking for something. Benny pulled the Beretta from a shoulder holster.

"Know him?" he asked.

Vlado saw sunlight glinting off glasses. The man didn't seem to be armed. "Yes. It's Azudin. His assistant."

Azudin stepped outside, squinting into the pale sunlight. He looked helpless, out of place. He wasn't even wearing an overcoat.

"It's okay," Vlado said. "This one doesn't bite."

"They all bite," Benny said.

"And something's wrong if he's on guard duty. The others must have gone."

Azudin strolled uncertainly toward the car as Vlado rolled down a window.

"He's gone," Azudin said in the plaintive bleat of a lost lamb.

Vlado translated for Pine, who shut off the engine. The three of them climbed from the car while Azudin stood at the edge of the lane barely paying attention, as if pondering what to do next.

"Where's everyone else?" Vlado asked.

"I paid them for the month and sent them home."

"What about Matek?"

"He left last night. He sent me home around five, so it could have been anytime after that. When I got here this morning he'd cleared out. The overnight sentry must have been asleep, because he didn't see a thing."

"Is that his car?" Vlado pointed to the BMW.

Azudin shook his head. "Mine. His is gone. So are his guns, and most of his money. He left this."

Azudin held out a scrap of paper. Stepping closer, Vlado saw that Azudin was pale and drawn, clearly shaken. Vlado gently took the note from his hand.

"What's he saying?" Pine asked.

"Matek took off last night. I'm translating the note he left." Vlado squinted at the cramped handwriting of a man used to bashing a keyboard. Once he had the gist, he read aloud the English version to Pine and Benny. "'Edin, there was always a possibility this day would come, and now I must go. All of the keys are in my upper desk drawer. The combination to the safe follows. I have signed the necessary documents, which you will also find on the desk. Sendic will notarize them in town. My businesses now belong to you. My bank accounts do not. There is enough cash in this envelope to pay the staff for a month. The rest is up to you. You will not be able to reach me, so do not try. When the son of Enver Petric comes calling, give him and his American friend from The Hague my best. They should be able to answer the rest of your questions. Good luck. Pero.'"

"Sounds like he knew all about you guys," Benny said quietly, rubbing his hands to stay warm. He'd holstered the Beretta.

Vlado and Pine were silent. The mountain suddenly seemed a vast and empty place.

"This safe," Pine asked. "Has he opened it yet?"

Vlado translated. "He says no," he reported to Pine. "He's hardly touched a thing."

"Tell him we'd like a look around, if he doesn't mind. And we'd like to use his phone."

Surprisingly, all that seemed okay with the stunned Azudin, but as he turned to lead them up the lane it finally seemed to dawn on him to ask for an explanation. He stopped, turning robotically. "Why are you after him?"

"Matek is a suspected war criminal."

Azudin frowned, more confused than ever. "But he was here throughout the war. He did nothing, except make a little money. I know, I was with him."

"Not this war. The last one. Your boss was an Ustasha officer. At Jasenovac."

Azudin was unimpressed. "And because of this he is running? Because of something fifty years ago?" He shook his head, more baffled than angry. "I thought the world wanted us to forget all that. Come this way." He continued their tour with the air of a funeral director.

"Christ," Benny muttered. "You'd think he'd lost his father."

A black look from Pine and Vlado made him realize it was a poor choice of words, but he was the only one who didn't understand why.

"Relax, guys," Benny said. "The hard part's over. Just your Ichabod Crane here and a bunch of file drawers. Tell him we'll be out of his hair in a few hours."

Vlado wondered vaguely who Ichabod Crane was. It did seem that the worst of the danger had vanished along with Matek and his thugs, but he couldn't escape the sense that they were overlooking something in their blithe stroll toward the house. Jasmina's words of warning flitted through his head, and he tensed as they entered the front door, half expecting Matek to lunge at them from the darkened hallway, Kalashnikov in hand. But all was quiet save the humming of a computer from a room down the hall.

When they reached the office, Pine picked up the phone.

"Might as well get the dirty work over with."

"Hope you don't mind if I listen in," Vlado said, heading to Azudin's phone in the adjoining room before Pine could say no. There was no way they were keeping him in the dark on any further operational details.

Spratt deflated like a punctured tire when he heard the news, emitting a long, despairing sigh that even the static couldn't disguise. It was clear he was still in anguish over the Andric fiasco. "What the hell's going on?" he said tiredly. "First two moves we make in months and it all goes to shit."

"We're searching his place," Pine said. "I guess we should notify the borders, the airports, and the rail stations. As if that will do any good."

"Leave that to the field offices. I'll make some calls. You see what you can come up with. Then we'll plan our next move, if we've even got one."

"Still no sign of Andric?"

"It's like he never existed. The idiots searching his bunker didn't find the trapdoor for four hours. Four bloody hours! Can you believe that?"

"Trapdoor?"

"Under a pile of clothes in a closet. Down an air shaft to some old tunnel that led through the hillside to some woods."

"Tito," Vlado said without thinking, startling Spratt, who hadn't even known he was on the line.

"What do you mean, 'Tito'?"

"One of his old escape bunkers. So he and his officers could get away when the Russians came. All of them had tunnels."

"Well, hell, that's what we get for not consulting locals enough. We finally got some dogs in to trace a scent. They spent an hour leading us to an abandoned farm. Fresh tire tracks, probably a truck. It's beginning to look like he'd planned it pretty well. Now the question is whether he knew we were coming or if he was always this prepared and just got lucky."

"What do we do next?" Pine asked.

"I'll have to phone LeBlanc and Harkness," Spratt said. "They're both waiting in Sarajevo for you and the suspect. We'd promised them a private debriefing with Matek. Now they may want to debrief you."

"And we'd allow that?" Pine said.

"You'll also need to speak to Janet," Spratt said, ignoring the question.

"Why?"

"She'll tell you. Sit tight until you've heard from her. Where are you, anyway?"

"Matek's office. Up in the hills."

"Give me the number. I've just been summoned upstairs. Third time today, and this time I've got more bad news to deliver. Stay there until you've heard from Janet."

"No problem. We'll be searching the place. His little assistant's been pretty cooperative."

Pine turned to Benny after hanging up. "Sorry, but it looks like we might be stuck here awhile. You game for helping us look around?"

"Got nothing else to do. Where you want me to start?"

"Well, you're guest of honor. Why don't you take the safe. Matek wrote the combination on the note, as long as our host doesn't mind." Vlado looked around for Azudin, but the man had apparently wandered off in a daze, so he handed the note to Benny. "I'll take the file drawers in the back room. Vlado, why don't you check the rooms upstairs."

They nodded, glum but resigned to the slow hours ahead. So much for their three-man commando action, or any hope of catching Matek on his way out the back door. The old man had been cagier than they'd thought.

Vlado was curious to see what Matek's living quarters would look like, especially in comparison with the set-piece décor of the downstairs. But as he reached the top of the stairs, a movement out the window caught his eye.

It was Azudin, walking briskly across the barren grounds, no longer looking either lost or confused. A small bag was in his right hand, and he glanced furtively over his shoulder toward the house, quickening his pace toward the front gate. In stride and demeanor he was nothing at all like the meek man who had seemed on the verge of tears just a moment ago, and Vlado's nagging worries converged into full-blown fear. A rambling and incautious search suddenly struck him as a very bad idea, and he spun to head back downstairs, taking the steps two at a time and lifting his voice to shout a warning.

His first words were swallowed by a heaving blast that lifted him in the air, as if a gust of pressure had bolted up the stairs. The next thing he knew he was sitting at the bottom landing, head hurting and ears ringing, his left knee feeling wrenched half from its socket. A fine white dust drifted from the ceiling like mist, already coating the hairs on his arms. The house was dreadfully still.

"You all right?" It was Pine, in a croaking call from the back room. "Benny? Vlado?"

"I'm at the steps," Vlado shouted, finding his voice, feeling as if the wind had been knocked out of him. He stood, quivering like a fawn. "I think I'm okay."

"Benny?" Pine said, again without reply. Then, louder, more frantic. *"Benny?"*

Vlado limped into the ruin of Matek's office. Benny's legs protruded from beneath splintered varnished wood and a jumble of paper and plaster. They weren't moving. The ceiling above him was cratered. The door of the small safe in the wall above was open, but the gray metal was scored and blackened, radiating arms of blackness as if a small meteorite had struck. The computer screen was shattered, and the big desk was splintered, the top heaved up like the deck of an icebound frigate. But the worst sight was the red spatter across every wall, some of the heavier markings just beginning to drip and ooze across pockmarked fields of white plaster.

"Jesus!" It was Pine, who'd just staggered to the rear door, covered head to toe in white dust that made him look like the walking dead. From the way he flinched, Vlado must have looked the same. But it was the silent Benny who drew their attention now, and they converged on the still-motionless legs, no longer calling his name. They crouched and began pulling away pieces of the desk and chunks of the ceiling, working gingerly, worried they'd do him further damage.

But it was soon clear that matters could get no worse for Benny. They pulled back a chunk of the desk to see that from the waist up he was a shredded welter of cloth, pulp, and flesh. Ragged shards of bone poked through in one or two places. He was facedown, his black hair matted and splayed. It was all Vlado could do to keep from gagging, and neither of them had the nerve to turn him over.

"My God," Pine gasped. "Oh my God."

He stood, stumbling backward and nearly falling on a bloodied pile of debris. Vlado had seen bodies in this sort of shape during the war, and the culprit had always been the same: an antipersonnel mine that sent hundreds of pieces of metal flying into the victim. This was no homemade explosive of nails and fuel oil. This was military-grade hardware, the same sort Matek had been hoping to acquire more of with a demining contract.

Vlado remembered the odd fleeting expression of wariness that had crossed Azudin's face as Vlado left the office to listen in on Pine's call. Azudin, having carried out his last set of instructions for his boss, had obviously wanted all three of them to be nearby when the safe was opened. That thought made Vlado want to hurry toward the door in pursuit, but Pine shouted, "Don't move!"

When Vlado took another step Pine shouted again. "Don't move, damn it! For all we know there are more, and we don't even know what that one looked like, or what triggered it. Look for any wires. Any kind of metal box. Hell, it could be anything."

Pine looked around, glaring like a cornered street fighter, a sight made surreal by the coating of dust. Vlado wanted to sit but didn't dare, not with all the rubble around him that might conceal something.

"Where's Azudin?" Pine asked, the volume down a notch.

"I saw him out the window, leaving in a hurry. I started to shout something, but that's when the mine went off."

"Weaselly bastard. Probably halfway down the mountain in his BMW, counting his inheritance. For all we know he wired the front door behind him. We may have to crawl out a window."

"Or maybe he's sending the bodyguards back up the mountain to finish us off."

"Yeah, there's that, too."

They paused, as if listening for intruders or the approach of a truck. But the only sound was a car engine cranking to life, then a purr as the gears engaged, followed by the crunch of gravel. Azudin was leaving now, and from the sound of it he was in no hurry, having heard the blast. The quiet little man had fooled them all, and so had Matek.

Pine gingerly reached down beside Benny, poking around in the bloody rubble. "I'd look for the gun, but—"

"Don't bother. I've seen what these things do. It'll be destroyed. Besides . . ."

"I know." Pine was now transfixed by Benny. "My God. Of all the people. We go the whole goddamn war without a scratch. Then some old man, not even from the right war. Some fucking profiteer." Pine then glared toward Vlado, as if he, too, were somehow implicit. Vlado thought he knew why, because even he felt a bit of the same emotion. His father's old pal had done this, the bloodlines running straight to him. His country and his people, in a cycle that never stopped. But what was there to say or do, other than nod slightly, as if he understood completely?

Then Vlado shook his head in the manner of a wet dog, trying to clear his mind. Tears were snaking through the dust on his cheeks. He sagged into a crouch, still not daring to test his weight on any of this mess but feeling as weary as he had in years. He glanced back at Benny's legs. The great and glib blusterer, a generous man, so zealous about his work. Vlado had barely met him but had liked him right away, and now he was gone. Just like that. Jasmina had been right to worry. So much for their "foolproof operation," as Spratt had so cavalierly described it while rattling the ice in his cocktail. The evening of suits and chandeliers at The Hague now seemed a year in the past, and it was certainly a world removed from here.

"Okay," Pine said, calming. "Let's think this through. Let's start moving, just be careful where you step. Don't open any drawers, cabinets, doors, or anything. Maybe one of the phones still works in another room. We need to get a UN demining team up here before we even try leaving the building. Otherwise it's Russian roulette." He paused. "Then I'll have to call Spratt. This will change everything. Jesus, Benny. Jesus." He shook his head. "I guess we better get an ambulance up here, too. To take the body away."

The phone rang in Azudin's office. For a moment Vlado and Pine just stared in that direction, as if Matek himself were calling to taunt them into another fatal blunder. On the fourth ring Pine collected himself and began hopping carefully through the mess like a man negotiating an ice floe, looking for safe places to step.

"Maybe it's Janet," he muttered hoarsely. Even then he hesitated before lifting the receiver. Now every object seemed poisoned, a potential booby trap. "Hello?"

Vlado made his way to the phone, and without any prompting Pine angled the earpiece outward so he could listen in. The awkwardness and secrecy that had held them at arm's length was gone. For better or worse, they'd become a team, united for the moment by their grief and their edgy suspicion of everyone and everything.

"Well," Janet Ecker said breezily. "All hell has broken loose here."

"Benny's dead," Pine answered bluntly, putting a stop to everything. "He was with us, and he's been killed by a mine explosion. It was a booby trap. Matek had mined his office."

For a moment Janet said nothing. You could hear the creak of her chair, office sounds in the background. The connection was startlingly clear. Vlado looked through the doorway and could see Benny's black shoes, covered in dust.

Pine filled her in on the morning's details and their plans on what to do next. "We were searching the place," he said. "But I think it's best now if we don't touch a thing."

"Is Vlado all right?" Janet asked.

"I'm fine," he answered.

"Your wife called this morning. She was worried. I told her you were alive and well. Glad I don't have to call her back for a correction. My Lord. I can't believe it's Benny. What the hell were you doing calling him in, anyway?"

"Let's sort out the blame and the screwups later, okay? Right now we've got a body and no mission. We're a little out of it, as you might guess. Some sense of direction from whoever's in charge these days might be welcome."

"I'll call back. Stay put."

"Believe me, we're not moving."

Pine then phoned the UN's local demining office, an irony lost on neither of them. The blast had served several purposes for Matek. His Rolodex, if he'd had one, was gone. The file drawers in the back—Pine had only had time to open one—now seemed likely to be wired for destruction. Vlado headed back upstairs, watching carefully for trip wires, if only to take a quick look and to give himself something to do. His suspicions about the décor proved to be correct. Upstairs was all chrome and leather. Cool marble floors with bright throw rugs in modern geometric designs. Just as tasteless as the downstairs in its way, but with a more Mediterranean flavor. Matek had deemed his own culture beneath him and gone in for a garish imitation of Italian. And why not? If Vlado had spent an entire war trying to wipe out a major part of that culture, then he, too, might have sought some way to figuratively shed his skin. But if that was so, then what had his father been up to for all those years, returning home simply to resume the life of a Balkan peasant, acting as if he were still a naïve and innocent toolmaker hovering reluctantly at the fringes of the twentieth century?

Downstairs the phone rang again. Pine waited for Vlado to return before answering, and they again shared the earpiece. It was Spratt, and both of them braced for a chewing-out. But Spratt swallowed his bureaucratic instincts. "The first thing you need to do is get the hell out of there," he said. "Let a demining unit do the rest."

"I've already called one," Pine said.

"You also don't know what other sort of greeting Matek might have planned for you. His goons could be waiting on the road to finish you off for all you know. Go back to Sarajevo and await further instructions. From here it's going to depend on how Contreras reacts. My call would be to drop the thing entirely. Let international law enforcement pick up the chase, and get the hell out of the way. But from what I've seen of him so far, he's liable to take this personally."

"I sure as hell do," Pine said.

"I'm not saying you shouldn't. So do I. But operationally you know our limits. The other bit of news, unfortunately, is that our sponsors still want a debriefing, and they're waiting at the Holiday Inn."

It took Vlado a moment to realize that Spratt was talking about Harkness and LeBlanc, the last people he wanted to see right now. He just wanted to board a plane and go home.

"Why?" Pine asked.

"They're trying to pick up the pieces, too." Vlado winced at the wording. "This was their baby, so they'll want to know every detail about how it went wrong."

"Just what we need. When do we meet?"

"I put them off until this evening. Seven. That should give you time to collect yourselves."

"What about arrangements for Benny? Getting his body home?"

"Let me worry about that. You just get back to Sarajevo. I'm sending reinforcements for the meeting."

"Reinforcements?"

"Janet Ecker. She's catching a two p.m. flight. She's the only one who's seen the whole file. Depending on what's decided in the meantime, you may need to know more. Either way she can help fend off Harkness and LeBlanc."

"What makes you think we'll have to fend them off?"

"Previous experience. Plus the entire way this operation has gone. Why should things get any easier?"

"Fair enough."

"For now, get yourselves down the mountain safely. One casualty is more than enough, God knows."

After hanging up, they decided to wait outside for the demining unit to arrive, but found themselves momentarily unable to leave the house. Neither said a word, both unwilling to simply walk out while Benny's body still lay in the next room.

"Doesn't seem right, does it?" Pine said.

Vlado shook his head. "None of this has seemed right from the beginning," he replied. For him that included the past four weeks, all the way back to when Haris and Huso had arrived on his doorstep, bloody and grimy in the darkness. Now all the events seemed part of the same awful package, and he questioned his own role at every turn. The trail of bodies seemed uncanny, it was so diverse and multinational—you could even begin with a small boy from Sarajevo, dying of whooping cough; then a young thug in Berlin, and now a loud, likable cop from New York. Yet he remained standing, like a man walking unscathed from a plane crash, a freak of fate. A sudden wave of nostalgia for his old life—the one before the war, before everyone had become either a casualty or a refugee—rolled over him heavily, and he averted his face from Pine.

But Pine's attention was elsewhere. He walked slowly into Matek's ruined office and knelt by the legs. The smell of blood was stronger now. Vlado watched as Pine placed his right hand gently on the back of Benny's leg, then bowed his head with his eyes shut tightly. He mouthed a few words, too quietly for Vlado to hear, then paused, still in a crouch. Finally he exhaled deeply and rose slowly. The UN vehicles were just pulling up outside.

"Okay," Pine said calmly. "Nothing more we can do here."

They left without another word between them.

CHAPTER FOURTEEN

They were jittery for the entire ride to Sarajevo, flinching whenever another vehicle approached from behind or slowed down in front of them. Even a creaking farm wagon blocking the road seemed suspicious, part of a possible ambush, given Matek's reach and connections along the valley road from Travnik.

As a result, they said little along the way, giving Vlado plenty of time to think. He decided on a plan for the afternoon, announcing his intentions as they finally reached the outskirts of the city. "I was thinking I might go by my old apartment," he said softly, breaking a long, dazed silence. "To look for some old photos and family papers. Things my mother left me when she died. Not much. I just sort of glanced through it after the funeral and put it away in a closet."

"Names and addresses?"

"That's what I was wondering. If any of my father's relatives are mentioned. Maybe some of them knew Matek."

"Like the uncle you mentioned?"

"Uncle Tomislav. His wife was my father's sister. Maybe Aunt Melania is still alive. But for all I know our old apartment is either gone or cleaned out."

"Would somebody have moved in?"

"I can't imagine it would have stayed empty. With all the refugees coming in, the government took back a lot of housing. Or else people just took things for themselves. Whoever took our place probably assumed we were dead. Maybe they sold everything. It's worth checking, though."

Pine shrugged. "Better than doing nothing, I guess."

Vlado wondered how long it would take them to recover from the shock of the morning's events. They hadn't even had time to wash out the plaster dust from their hair. Pine's right sleeve was still stained with Benny's blood. An hour earlier Vlado had been ready to give up and go home. But now he was itching to do something, anything that might help track down Matek. He was still curious about the link to his own past, and now there was Benny, making Matek's crimes more fresh and personal than ever, whether the tribunal was ready to drop the case or not. Pine had been silent on the subject so far, but Vlado was certain he'd feel the same. Both felt foolish, even guilty, for having underestimated Matek, a miscalculation that had cost a friend his life. Checking Vlado's old apartment might not uncover a thing. But, like Pine said, it was better than doing nothing.

They checked back in to the Holiday Inn, which gave them a chance to shower and change clothes. With a few hours remaining before they were supposed to meet Ecker's flight, Vlado set out on foot, retracing one of his familiar routes through the city, the old apartment key in his pocket. Jasmina had insisted that he bring it, hoping he'd have time for a look. He wondered what she and Sonja must be up to, back in Berlin. A fleeting thought of Haris crossed his mind like a small cloud, but the name troubled him more for its association with Popovic than with Jasmina.

Their apartment squatted in a block of fairly new buildings on a slight rise, overlooking the fields that led to the Olympic Stadium. The fields had once been playgrounds, but during the war they were pressed into duty as a cemetery, offering Vlado a daily census of the body count from the front window. The area had been vulnerable to shell fire from three sides, and Vlado had lived mostly in the living room, next to the kitchen, sleeping on a couch. With neither running water nor electricity during much of the siege, he'd tapped into a natural-gas line, bootlegging a supply into his house through a garden hose that he'd tacked to the wall. There had been a nozzle on the stove and another spouting from the wall, for light.

He supposed all that was gone now, but he had no trouble recalling the mood of the lonely nights, when there had been little to do but paint a set of tiny lead soldiers arrayed before him on a bench, tedious work that made the hours pass until he was weary enough to retreat into sleep. He didn't wish to relive those times by any means, although they now seemed almost tranquil by comparison, the occasional shell bursts and sniper fire reduced in his memory to annoying background noise, like the dripping of a leaky faucet.

Rounding the last corner, he was pleasantly surprised to see the building still standing. The windows to their apartment had been repaired. So had a small hole in the roof. New tiles marked the spot with a brighter shade of red.

He knocked, still not sure what to say, then was surprised to recognize the face of the man who answered. The last time he had seen it, the man's beard was powdered with plaster, his eyes dazed. That was five years ago, a snowy morning when a shell had fallen on an apartment block next-door, scattering a refugee family that had moved in only a week earlier. Vlado had been jolted awake by the explosion. Then he had invited all six of them inside to recover from the shock.

Shortly after that Vlado had smuggled himself out of the city in the cargo plane. Now here they were again, this time on the other side of the door, if he could only recall their names.

"Konjic," the man said, smiling as he refreshed Vlado's memory. "Alijah Konjic. And you are Vlado Petric."

"Yes," Vlado said, hoping his sudden arrival wouldn't be seen as a threat. Through the doorway he could already see the old couch, the one that had been his bed for two years. The Konjics had arrived in Sarajevo without furniture, so his abandoned home must have seemed like a godsend.

"Please come in," Konjic said with genuine warmth. He made a sweeping gesture with his arm to usher Vlado across the threshold. "My wife, Nela. My children. Everyone is here, and we owe you so much."

"Hello," a woman's voice piped from the kitchen, and Vlado turned to see Nela in an apron, a wooden spoon in hand. Two children sat on the couch, riveted to a small black-and-white television propped on an end table. A third, older child sat on the floor doing his lessons. Konjic had said everyone was here, but Vlado remembered six of them. The fourth and smallest child was missing, and he readied himself for another dose of what now seemed an endless supply of bad news.

Then a small voice spoke up from around the corner, and to

Vlado's immense relief he recognized the face as the boy trooped into the room, a good foot taller by now, yet still carrying one of the tiny soldiers Vlado had left behind. Vlado smiled, and Konjic seemed to realize why.

"Ah, your soldiers. Yes! He was playing with one of them the first time we met. After the shell landed. It was the first thing he went looking for when we came back."

And here Konjic's enthusiasm turned sheepish, as if he suddenly realized the implications of Vlado's return. Pretty much everything in the room, except the small TV, had belonged to Jasmina and him before the war. By all rights everything still did, even if they now seemed like items from a museum—the couch, the chairs, the small oval rug that had been a wedding gift from Jasmina's mother, the old photo on the wall of the Mostar bridge. It was like entering a time capsule, and Vlado moved quickly to put Konjic's fears to rest.

"I am only here for a few days," he said, seeing Nela relax. "We live in Germany now. My wife was able to take the most valuable items when she and my daughter left, two years before I did. I'm not here to claim anything. But I did want to look for something. An old box with photos and papers. Old family records. Some personal things that may have been left behind."

"Yes," Konjic said, effusive in his relief. "Yes. I know that box. We've kept it. We've kept everything, you know. Some things because we've used them, of course, but all of your clothes and everything else, it's all still here."

"Please," Vlado said, "just the one box. Keep the other things. Sell them if you want. The rest of the personal items I may come for later, if I bring my family back. But today there isn't time."

"Yes. Yes, of course. Come. It's back here."

They walked to the rear bedroom, Vlado spooked by the familiar hallway, the smells, the rugs on the floor. Konjic ducked into a closet and raised himself on his tiptoes, tugging at a cardboard box. Yes, that was the one Vlado remembered.

"We thought that you had been killed," Konjic said. "Someone told us you were a policeman, and we heard a policeman had been shot down by the river on the night after we met you. Later we heard that it wasn't you, that maybe you had gotten away. There was nothing in the newspaper, and no one seemed to know much. So we decided to keep everything. In case you ever came back." Konjic shrugged.

He seemed like a good man, Vlado thought. He was glad they'd ended up with the apartment, but he did wonder what his old neighbors—if any were left—must think of this tribe of peasants from a faraway village, bringing their country ways to the middle of the city.

"Some people did try to kill me," he told Konjic. "Smugglers. They took a few shots, but they missed. It's a very long story." And one that keeps repeating, he thought. "But we're in Berlin now. Maybe we'll come back, maybe not. But not here. The place is yours."

As if to seal the deal, he reached into his pocket for the key. He solemnly handed it over, the closest thing to a deed available. With that, Konjic's relief was complete, and Vlado wondered how often the family must have dreaded this very sort of visit. If the trip accomplished nothing else, at least it would leave these people at peace.

Konjic set the box on the bed. "Take as long as you want," he said. "I'll be with the children."

He shut the bedroom door behind him, giving Vlado his privacy. Only the muffled noise of the television leaked beneath the door, a faint sound of gunshots and squealing tires.

On top were old bills and receipts, instruction manuals for radios, a television, a small hand drill. There were photos, a few infant shots of Sonja. He set those aside, knowing he shouldn't slow down until he found what he was looking for but unable to resist the occasional detour of memories. Their marriage license. Some photos of friends at a party, from '89. A stack of handwritten compositions from his childhood that his mother had saved, then given to Jasmina just before they were married. He remembered sitting up in bed late one night—this bed—reading them while she laughed, a strand of her hair fallen across her face. Old magazines that he'd saved for one obscure reason or another. And then, about halfway down, there it was, a large brown envelope with his mother's handwriting on top: "For Vlado."

He remembered the short woman who'd been a friend of hers bringing it to him the day after his mother's funeral, after he'd helped move the furniture out of his mother's apartment. It had been a big Catholic service, the priest swinging a censer as he marched slowly down the aisle. He wondered what his mother had known about his father's past. Had she, too, kept his secrets, or had she been fooled along with Vlado, believing in the man's essential goodness and honesty—the quiet virtuous worker who made a living with his strong but gentle hands?

His mother hadn't come from the same village or even the same part of the country. They'd married only a year after his father returned from Italy. She'd been a devout Catholic. He wondered now if she had known all along that his father was secretly a Catholic as well. Perhaps she, too, had been a sort of ethnic nationalist in her own quiet way, which would explain why she had later become so frustrated with her son, the nonbeliever who worshipped only soccer stars and his own future.

There wasn't much inside the envelope, maybe twenty or thirty pages in all, which was pretty much the way Vlado remembered it. Part of it was a technical manual, old instructions for the equipment in the machine shop where his father had worked. There was a diagram of a metalworking lathe, with all the moving parts numbered, and Vlado could easily picture his father behind the machine, hard at work, the bright curly shavings collecting in the hair of his forearms.

There was an old soccer program, perhaps from the game in his dream, for all he knew. He scanned the photos of the players, most of whose names he'd forgotten, although they'd once meant so much to him. At the bottom of the pile were a few more photographs.

One in particular drew his attention. It was of four men in uniform. On the far right, propped against a giant oak, was his father. Who were the other three, and where were they when this was taken? The fellow on the left looked familiar, and Vlado realized it must be Uncle Tomislav. Yes, that long face with the jug ears. Definitely. He closely scanned the other two faces, looking for any sign of the man he'd met yesterday. But neither of the other men was Matek. He turned the photo over, looking for an inscription, but there was only the stamp of the studio that must have made the print, with an address from Mostar, down in the southwest, the city closest to his father's home village of Podborje.

The topography made it clear the photo hadn't been taken anywhere near Jasenovac, where the landscape was flat and green. In the background were hills and more hills, and the men looked relaxed, at peace with themselves. There was no date, but he surmised it must have been taken early in the war, perhaps before anyone had even fired a shot.

But if this was indeed Uncle Tomislav, then maybe Aunt Melania in Podborje would know a little more about his father's movements during the war. Vlado placed the other papers back into the box, then slipped the photo inside the envelope before gently placing it in the inside pocket of his jacket. He heard the door opening behind him, the noise from the television rising in volume.

"Find anything good?"

It was Konjic, looming over his shoulder, curiosity having gotten the better of him. Vlado looked up from the old, familiar bed, clearing his throat.

"Not much. But enough, I guess. A few memories of my parents."

Konjic beamed, as if personally gratified Vlado's mission had been a success. "Please, when you are finished, I came to tell you that my wife has made coffee. My sons have gone out for cake. In honor of your return."

Vlado could have sworn that Konjic then made a slight bow, an oddly touching gesture by this man he barely knew. In the larger scheme of things these people owed him nothing. They'd have just as easily found a vacant apartment elsewhere. But if they wished to show their gratitude, he would accept it. So even though he had little time to spare, he said yes to their invitation. Or maybe he simply felt like being among a family right now, with sons and daughters and their parents, crowded together around a table to eat and drink.

"Thank you. I'd like that."

They gathered in the kitchen, the children elbowing one another for position as everyone made way for their guest. The table was new, rough-hewn but sturdy, with clean lines and well-fitted joints. The one Vlado and Jasmina had owned wouldn't have been large enough. Vlado rubbed his hands along the sanded, polished top.

"I made it," Konjic said proudly. "All with hand tools. Wooden dowels and my own joining. You can't get things like screws and power tools anymore. Not without a lot of hard currency."

"It's very nice work."

Konjic then got a look on his face as if a lightbulb had gone off in his head, and he leaped to his feet. "I almost forgot!" he said.

He disappeared down the hallway. Following a brief metallic clatter he returned holding a battered toolbox that Vlado recognized as his father's—his lone inheritance. It made him quail slightly to see it now, and he couldn't help contemplating the destructive power of the hammers, the screwdrivers, the wrenches, even though he doubted the toolbox had even belonged to his father until well after the war.

"It was my father's," he said faintly as Konjic set the box heavily on the end of the table.

"Then you must have it," Konjic said, beaming yet again, although the toolbox was undoubtedly one of his most prized and valuable possessions. Whatever those tools symbolized of his father's past, they had at least built this sturdy and beautiful table.

"No," Vlado said, mustering a smile and shaking his head. "It's yours now. I have no use for it. Please. You keep it."

Konjic nodded, not saying a word, as if sensing that there might be more attached to these objects than function and utility. He didn't open it, nor did Vlado want to look inside. Instead he looked around the table and noticed the smallest boy watching him from the end, the one who'd played with his soldiers. Vlado smiled back.

"I hope you're enjoying those soldiers," he said, wanting to change the subject. "I painted them all. But it was only a hobby for passing time. I don't want them back. Too many memories of the war. So I am glad you can make some use of them."

"Tell him the story, Daddy," the boy said. "Tell him about the soldier."

The father's eyes were sparkling. Vlado wondered what this could be about.

"Do you remember that morning, when you invited us in?" Konjic began.

"Yes. The explosion woke me up. I wasn't sure you were all okay, and I was worried there might be more shells."

"We went from here to the hospital. Just to check things out, like you told us. Everything was fine. Then we decided to get our food for the day. Bread, water, and rice. You know, the usual. So we divided up the chores. Nela and Mirela would stand in line for the rice, the two older boys would wait on bread. Me and this one here"—he mussed the small boy's hair—"me and little Hisham would get in line for water.

"That was when I looked down and saw Hisham playing with one of your soldiers. He had picked it up off the table when I wasn't looking. I'd asked him to put it back, and I thought that he had."

Vlado remembered that he had thought so, too, even recalling that he'd been disappointed that the boy hadn't kept it.

"I almost said something about letting him keep one," Vlado said, "but you seemed pretty stern about it, and I know how it is when you're trying to discipline your children. You don't want somebody else contradicting you. So I held my tongue."

"Which was the right thing for you to do. But little Hisham here, when no one was looking he took one anyway. And as soon as I saw it I said, 'No. You must return it now.' So Hisham and I walked back to your apartment. You were gone, but the door was unlocked, so he put the soldier back on the table with the others. I saw to it myself. By then of course we were a good ten minutes late for getting in line for water. And then what do you suppose happened?"

Vlado shook his head.

"We arrived at the water line to find that a shell had landed, only five minutes earlier. Four people were killed, including two boys. So, you see, if it had not been for your soldier, well, that might have been us standing there. Your little man in blue, Mr. Petric, he saved our lives. So whenever Hisham plays with them, they remind us of the war, but they remind us of you, too, and all of the memories are good ones."

Konjic nodded curtly, as if that was his final word on the matter, and even though Vlado knew that a dozen other events had played equally important roles in that single moment of fate, he felt that the scales had finally begun to rebalance in his favor. In the wake of his departure one child had died. Earlier today a colleague had died as well. But now, at least, there was this child who had lived, sitting at the end of a table built with his father's tools, grinning, icing on his cheeks.

"Thank you for telling me that," Vlado said quietly, placing his empty cup on the saucer. "And thank you for all of this, too."

They didn't talk much after that. Mostly a lot of smiling and laughter over silly things the children did. A half hour later Vlado rose from the table.

"I'd better be going. There's a lot of work to do."

The family escorted him to the door, waving good-bye as if he were an old friend who'd come bearing wondrous gifts. It was a better homecoming than he ever would have expected, and not until he was halfway down the hill to the Holiday Inn did he remember the photo stuffed in his pocket. He quickened his pace, rubbing the edge of the envelope with his fingertips, wondering what might be waiting for him, if anything, at Uncle Tomislav's house in Podborje. Perhaps the tribunal was finished looking for Pero Matek—he'd know for sure this evening—but he wasn't finished, and Podborje now seemed worth a visit.

CHAPTER FIFTEEN

Janet Ecker's flight was nearly an hour late, leaving them barely enough time to make the scheduled meeting with Harkness and LeBlanc at the Holiday Inn. Janet had to brief Vlado and Pine on the ride from the airport.

"First things first," she said to Pine. "Contreras wants you to stay on the case."

It was a surprise, but a good one.

"Officially, of course, we're not calling it a manhunt. For the record, you're pursuing leads on the whereabouts of a material witness. One who just happens to have murdered a colleague. But with that in mind . . ." She pulled an envelope from her briefcase. "You're ticketed on a noon flight tomorrow."

"To where?" Pine asked, sounding on edge.

"Rome. Both of you." She looked at Vlado. "As long as you're still along for the ride."

Vlado nodded. Anything to keep him in pursuit of Matek.

"Why Rome?" Pine asked, a stirring of interest in his voice.

"Someone there you need to see. Robert Fordham. Army counterintelligence. Or used to be. He was Matek's handler in postwar Rome. Vlado will need a visa, of course. The Italians promise to have one ready by tomorrow morning."

"What about Andric?" Pine asked.

"We've got a dozen people on it. Chances are he's in Serbia by now, anyway. As for the rest, Spratt's got somebody flying down to handle arrangements for Benny. He's got family back in New York. They're going to fly the body home. There will be a memorial service next Friday in The Hague."

That silenced them for a moment before Pine spoke up. "I still don't get our priorities, though. Personally, I'm all for it. After what happened to Benny, there's no one I'd rather pursue more than Matek. But if I'm some tribunal bean counter, I'd be saying, wait a minute, we're throwing an awful lot of limited resources after some old guy who's not even ours to try. Even for murder."

"Somebody may yet say that. But for the moment the only one who wants us off the case is Harkness. That's the word, anyway. So be prepared for a lecture."

"I thought this was all his idea? His and LeBlanc's. And now we lose a good man and he expects us to just drop it? What the hell's up with that?"

"Maybe you should ask him. But something about this seems to have him spooked."

"What do we say when he asks what we're doing next?"

"We mention Rome, and that's it. And we don't back down on anything."

They arrived at the Holiday Inn with only minutes to spare, hustling upstairs to a small conference room where the two envoys were waiting. LeBlanc sat calmly to one side, with a prim smile that was almost a smirk. Harkness wore tweeds. He really did bring to mind a British country gentleman, Vlado thought, hoping there would be no further asides about Popovic. They seated themselves around an oval table, Harkness striding to one end as if he were the master of ceremonies.

"Something to drink, gentlemen?" he asked. "And lady, of course."

Vlado half expected gin and tonic to be in the offing, given the man's bearing, but a bottle of mineral water was the only drink in sight.

"I'd like to begin by expressing my sympathy," Harkness continued. "I suppose we've all learned a sad and costly lesson this morning, and on two fronts no less."

"And what lesson would that be?" Pine asked sharply.

"That this is still a very dangerous place, for one thing. But also that the tribunal, for all the growing up it's done, really isn't equipped for the manhunt business. We never should have pushed you into that role. Our apologies. And our deepest condolences on Benny. He was a splendid fellow."

Presumably he was also speaking for LeBlanc, although it wasn't clear from the Frenchman's expression whether he shared Harkness's willingness to accept blame. Janet and Pine were tight-lipped, and Vlado couldn't help but contrast the chilly atmosphere with the warmth of the home he'd visited—his own home, he had to remind himself—only a few hours ago. He also wondered at the way Harkness had taken charge, as if the operation were his to run.

"Obviously," he continued, "our main priority now is Andric, despite the personal stakes involved. I plan on having a word with Contreras first thing to make sure he's on the same page. State has been informed, of course, and that's their position as well. If we're going to have police searching half the rail stations and airports of Europe, we might as well focus on the bigger prize, notwithstanding this morning's events in Travnik. And not to mention the obvious problems of jurisdiction and authorization."

"Actually," Pine said, color rising, "this meeting is only a courtesy, and our marching orders from the tribunal make it clear that Vlado and I are to keep pursuing leads on Matek. Janet will back me up on that."

"'Jurisdiction be damned,'" she said. "Contreras's own words, as of this afternoon."

"He'll come to his senses soon enough," Harkness said, polishing his glasses with a handkerchief, "either once the sting has worn off or when he's got another dead operative to answer for. Let's just hope it's the former, not the latter."

"We're not operatives," Pine said, redder still. "That's your world. We're just investigators and prosecutors. And if I didn't know better, I'd say you'd just threatened us."

Now it was Harkness's turn to get angry. He slapped his glasses on the table almost hard enough to break them, then leveled a pink finger at Pine.

"Not a threat. Not in the least. Benny Hampton was a good man. No one here disputes that. But lurching into matters that are none of the tribunal's damn business is hardly a fitting memorial and can only create more problems. Pursue this if you want. Just don't expect the same enthusiasm from the State Department when it's time to pony up for another tribunal budget. And that *is* a threat. At this point anything that drains resources from apprehending Andric is a waste and a hindrance."

"As if none of us knows where Andric has gone," Janet said.

"To Serbia, you mean," said LeBlanc, who up until now had been content to watch the Americans rip into each other. "It would only make sense. Milosevic is taking everyone he can and sending them toward Kosovo. A cable this morning—and I'm sure that Monsieur Harkness has received the same information—says they've just moved another twenty thousand."

"Why, Guy, I thought the Serbs were your friends," Harkness said, affecting a bluff manner. "And while we're on the subject, you're not going to tell us someone on your side didn't tip off General Andric, are you? I wasn't going to bring that up out of politeness, but with you so certain about his current destination it seemed appropriate."

An awkward silence followed. From the beginning of this operation Vlado had wondered about the exact nature of the work done by Harkness and LeBlanc. When he was a teenager it had been popular to label all visiting Americans as CIA agents. Every Brit was MI-5, and all stray Russians were of course KGB. It had been more of a game than a belief, to the point of becoming a silly cliché. When the Olympics had come to Sarajevo in '84 his friends had made a game out of "tailing" certain athletes and tourists through the evening bar scene, pretending they'd actually identified an operative. But with LeBlanc and Harkness, Vlado sensed, the parlor trick was far more sophisticated. On the one hand, they seemed to do everything but nudge and wink to convince him that their connections ran deeper than the mere diplomatic world. Yet, they prattled on with straight faces about their bosses at "the State Department" or "the Foreign Ministry." It was unnerving, mostly because he wasn't sure whom he was dealing with—the representative of a nation or of some agency with a more secretive agenda. Or perhaps with these two, he thought, the stakes were personal.

"Maybe you guys could argue later," Janet said. "But until we hear otherwise—from The Hague, not from Washington or Paris— we're still on the Matek case. This is a briefing for your benefit, not a planning session for you to direct."

"All right," Harkness said. "I'll play along. And what might your next move be in this vital pursuit of Matek? As a courtesy only, of course."

"We're thinking Rome as a possible destination."

Harkness chuckled mildly, then sipped his water with a satisfied slurp. "You're not really going to waste your time talking to that old windbag Bob Fordham, I hope?"

Janet flinched but said nothing.

"I know he's on all those old cables. But the man has proven notoriously unreliable. It's why he washed out, you know. No one could believe a word he said. The priority for all of us should still be Andric. And if I may add my two cents—merely in an advisory role, of course—then I'd say the key to finding Andric is finding Branko Popovic."

Vlado looked away from Harkness while trying not to show his surprise. He flashed on an image of Popovic's body in the trunk, face-down like Benny's, flesh pale and lifeless like Benny's, the dark blood-stain across his back.

"Now there's a man with some real army connections who, if we find him, can help us," Harkness said. "Not just with Andric but with Matek, too. Same shady friends. Just a rival ethnicity. And from what I've heard, certain parties have already been working on cutting an immunity deal in exchange for Popovic's testimony. I don't want to say it's us and I don't want to say it's your people, Guy. It might even be all of us, under the auspices of the tribunal. Or so I've heard."

This was news to Pine, apparently. "A deal?" he said. "He's been under indictment for more than a year, if that's what you mean. A sealed indictment, granted. But there's nothing beyond that."

Janet, looking pained, spoke up. "Actually, Calvin, there have been talks going on at levels well above us for quite some time. I can't speak with authority, but Spratt and Contreras have wanted to reel him in for reasons other than prosecution. Popovic apparently knows things about a lot of higher-ups, and not just Andric."

"I won't disagree," said the Frenchman, still looking down at the table.

"Excuse me," Harkness said. "But might this be a good time to ask our Balkan friend Mr. Petric to leave the room?"

Vlado didn't like the sound of that, considering the subject. He wondered what more Harkness had learned during the past few days about Popovic, and what that might mean for him. There was no way he was leaving the room voluntarily, but he needed someone to speak up for him. When help arrived, it came from an unlikely corner.

"Personally," LeBlanc said, "I don't see why anyone should have to leave."

"*Personally*, I'd agree," Harkness answered testily. "Professionally, the smaller the loop the better."

"But Paul," LeBlanc continued, with a look that said the conversation had gone right where he'd wanted, "as far as Vlado is concerned, all of this *is* personal. Or have you forgotten the connections that brought him to our attention? Don't you think he's earned inclusion?"

Vlado hoped the only connection they meant was his father. Judging from Harkness's sudden embarrassment, that seemed to be the case.

"Yes, of course," Harkness said, reddening. "I guess I'm just not used to including locals on matters like these. No disrespect intended, Vlado."

"None taken, Paul," Vlado said, lingering on the name. "After all, it's only our country."

LeBlanc bowed his head, suppressing a laugh.

"Now that we've settled that," Pine said, "what does any of this have to do with Popovic, other than his status as a material witness against Andric?"

Harkness looked across the table to LeBlanc. "Guy, you want to take a shot at that? While being careful, of course."

LeBlanc shrugged. "He's done work for both of us. Apart from whatever he's offering the tribunal."

"He's given us some pretty good stuff," Harkness said. "Help with military targeting. The latest word on the thinking of Yugoslav leadership. He's become quite the turncoat. For a price, of course." He stared at Vlado. "And it could certainly cost him his life if word ever got out. Assuming it hasn't already."

"You think he might be dead?" Pine said. Vlado pressed his hands together beneath the table.

"It's a possibility," Harkness said.

"Unless he's dropped out of sight in order to help Andric,"

LeBlanc added. "Another possibility. Maybe Andric outbid the tribunal for the man's services."

"Wouldn't make sense," Pine said. "Not if turning evidence against Andric was really his ticket to freedom."

Harkness and LeBlanc exchanged glances, Harkness with what appeared to be a look of warning.

"There are other factors," LeBlanc said. "But I'm afraid I can't share them just now."

Pine turned to Janet. "Do you know what the hell they're talking about?"

She lowered her head. "No."

"Sure about that?" he said testily. "Given your connections with 'the community'?"

When she looked up, she was clearly angry. "Positive. And don't question my word again, especially with regard to my so-called connections."

Vlado was still trying to put the pieces together when he looked up to see Harkness chuckling at him.

"You're looking a bit flabbergasted, old boy," Harkness said. "Welcome to the wilderness of mirrors."

"Wilderness of mirrors," Vlado repeated. It was an interesting phrase.

"A paranoid old spy said that once about the intelligence community," Janet explained. "Mostly because he never learned to tell the difference between the real images and the reflections. Pretty much sums up this situation, I'd say."

"As long as we're on the subject of bewilderment," LeBlanc said, "in my opinion, all three of these disappearances may be connected. Matek's included."

Harkness shot him a dark look. "I believe we're talking out of school now, Guy."

"We do all want the same thing, don't we, Paul?"

"You tell me. But as long as that cat's out of the bag, may I offer some more advice?"

"Why not," Pine said, "since you're going to tell us anyway."

"Wherever you go, watch your step. You're fooling yourself if you think Matek doesn't have any international reach. You've already whistled past the graveyard once, gentlemen, and look where that got you. Blunder into Italy, and it might be worse. So why not leave it to the professionals?"

"I thought we were professionals," Pine said.

"You know what I mean. Besides, it might be more productive looking for Popovic first. And from what I know of the man, there are already plenty of good leads in Vienna. In Zurich. But especially in Berlin. You're a Berliner, Vlado. You must have some contacts in the Yugo community there. Surely someone would have spotted Popovic by now, no matter what name he's traveling under."

Vlado wondered if he was the only one in the room who thought Harkness's smile suddenly seemed predatory. Who should he fear more, he wondered—Matek or Harkness? Yet he was about to further entangle himself with both, drawn deeper into their interests by the tether to his father's past. The challenge was to keep the tether from becoming a noose.

"I have a better idea, Paul," Janet said. "How about if you show us how the pieces fit, then we'll be able to help you even more. Seeing as how you think that's our job."

"We've already offered more information than I'd wanted," he said, glancing pointedly at LeBlanc. "But if you can be specific about what you want to know, maybe I can help."

It was the old bureaucrat's trick. I'll tell you what I've got as long as you already know. But Janet called his bluff. "I'll be very specific. There is a piece of Matek's security file I can't get my hands on. His repatriation documentation from '61. Apparently you've seen it, but every request I make comes back empty."

"That's not ours to deliver, I'm afraid. You'll have to ask the Yugoslavs."

"Well, maybe you should make a little better effort to free it up, especially if Belgrade still wants old Ustasha criminals like Matek taken care of."

"I didn't say they hadn't delivered it. I said it wasn't ours to deliver to you. Some things are given to us conditionally. With certain restrictions."

Her face was rigid. "That's nonsense."

"No. It's called diplomatic protocol. Happens all the time."

"You know damn well there are ways around that kind of protocol. Especially from where you sit. And I'm not talking about your desk at the Department of State."

Well, at least someone had finally stopped dancing around the subject, Vlado thought. Harkness was clearly displeased, although LeBlanc wore a prim smirk.

"No need to make this personal," Harkness replied coolly. Then, leering at Pine, "You, of all people, Janet, should know not to make things personal. Clouds your judgment."

Janet went scarlet, Pine as well. LeBlanc shuffled through some papers, his expression as bland as if he'd just sat through the world's most uneventful meeting.

"Well, then, ladies and gentlemen," Harkness said with a note of triumph, rising suddenly from his seat. "We seem to have covered the necessary ground. Best of luck in your misguided pursuit, however far afield you might stray. And cheers."

He raised his water glass as if toasting the end of a cricket match with champagne.

No one joined him in the gesture.

"Well, that was an experience I could have lived without," Pine said a few moments later, still steaming. He, Janet, and Vlado were in the hotel coffee shop. "Do either of you have any idea what they meant about connections between the suspects?"

Janet shook her head. "But it's bound to be in the files somewhere. Or maybe Fordham knows. Why else would Harkness want to steer us away from Rome? I'm betting Popovic is nothing but a dead end."

He was certainly that, Vlado thought darkly, wanting only to change the subject. "Tell me," he said. "Harkness and LeBlanc aren't just diplomats, are they?"

Pine smiled. "They're spooks, you mean."

"Spooks?"

"Spies. Intelligence. Or in the case of Harkness, CIA, with diplomatic cover."

"Yes. Spooks, then."

"Maybe. It's always been the assumption, even if nobody talks about it."

"Why doesn't anyone just come out and say it?"

Janet laughed. "You mean, 'Hello, I'm Paul Harkness, CIA'?"

"No. But one of you might have told me."

"I guess you get used to dealing with people like them when you work in places like this," Pine said. "Besides, you never know for sure."

"So you just deal with them the same way you would with any outsider," Janet added. "Even if they're straight-up diplos, they're going to have their own agenda, and believe me, some of them are every bit as devious as any spook. So we cooperate when we have to but otherwise keep to ourselves."

"But you're both Americans. So you must be on Harkness's side. At least a little."

"Sometimes I wonder," Pine said.

"Just think of it as us, the tribunal, versus everybody else," Janet said.

Vlado shook his head. Everyone on the same side, yet all of them working for someone else. Perhaps this was Bosnia's future, a conflict that would mature from a bludgeoning match to a sneaky and surgical meddling. "You were right, Calvin. Our politics are nothing compared with all of this."

"So, tell me more about Robert Fordham," Pine said. "Is he really a lying windbag?"

"If so, then he's the most reluctant windbag I've ever come across. It took me a good half hour to convince him I was legit. He even called to verify I was on the level. I guess his reliability depends on how good his memory is. But he's about the only person left from Matek's Roman days. Strange bird. Bit of a hermit. Was a foreign-service brat growing up—that's where he learned his Italian—but didn't move to Rome full-time until six years ago, after his wife died. In '44 he made it to Rome the hard way. Landed at Anzio with the U.S. Fifth Army, then slogged his way north. When the war ended, his State Department daddy wangled him a posting to an army counterintelligence outfit. The 428th. The rest is in here." She handed them a cream-colored folder stuffed with papers.

"What did Harkness mean when he said Fordham had washed out?" Vlado asked.

"In '46 he seems to have run afoul of his superiors. The details are hazy. He also didn't get along too well with Angleton and some of the early CIA people."

"Who's Angleton?" Vlado asked.

"Funny you should ask," Janet said. "He's the guy who came up with 'wilderness of mirrors,' mostly because he ended up lost in it. He was fighting the cold war before most people knew it existed. By the end of his career he was seeing double agents under every bush. Anyhow, I guess in Angleton's view Fordham didn't exactly graduate with honors. Went back home and became a banker. Wanted to join the foreign service but flunked his security clearance. Probably due to Angleton."

"So he has an axe to grind," Pine said.

"Possibly. But it's him or nobody."

"There is one other thing," Vlado said. "Maybe it's a lead, maybe it's not."

He pulled the old photo from his coat pocket and told them about his Aunt Melania.

"If she's still around, she might be worth talking to. Her house is in Podborje."

"Interesting," Janet said, studying the photograph. "Where's Podborje?"

"Two-hour drive at the most, even on bad roads."

"You think she's still alive?"

"These farm women are pretty tough," Vlado said. "There's an old joke about Herzegovinian women. 'Why do the husbands always die before their wives? Because they want to.'"

Pine laughed loudly, Janet less so. But they agreed that the trip was worth a try. Vlado and Pine would make the drive in the morning.

"Okay, then," Janet said, bringing the meeting to a close. "Then you'll be heading south before I'm up. Just make it back in time for your flight to Rome. Then we'll see how far you can burrow into Matek's past."

Vlado smiled grimly. He'd never been to Rome, but the past was becoming familiar territory.

"Time travel," he said. "I seem to be doing a lot of that lately."

CHAPTER SIXTEEN

They left before the sun was up, driving through the darkness into high mountain passes where dirty piles of snow lined the roadside. But by the time they reached the turnoff south of Jablanica, steam was rising from the pavement into the early light of what would be an unseasonably warm day.

"From what I remember, it's a stretch to even call it a village," Vlado said. "A few farms and houses, pretty scattered. But I do remember you can see my uncle's place from the top of a hill, just before the road goes into the valley."

After they turned off the main highway, the roads were more like glorified goat paths, all dirt and gravel, even more rutted than the one to Matek's compound.

"Jesus," Pine shouted as the Volvo scraped its undercarriage on yet another hump of stone. "Hope the EU doesn't mind investing in another exhaust system."

A few turns later, Vlado shouted, "Stop!" and Pine brought the car sliding to a halt at the edge of a hairpin turn. Vlado climbed quickly from his seat, stepping onto the grass verge of an overlook above a deep, narrow valley. Pine joined him, taking in the view. The morning breeze was soft in the rising heat.

"There. The second rooftop. See?" Vlado sounded as enthusiastic as a small boy. The morning had the feel of a fresh start, the beginning of an adventure, especially with Rome awaiting them at day's end. "I can't believe it," he said. "I remember this exact view. My father made us all get out of the car. I think he even took a picture."

"Let's just hope your aunt's still down there."

"Oh, she's there," Vlado said, smiling broadly. "Look at the chimney."

Wisps of white smoke swirled from one end of the red rooftop.

"Maybe it's somebody else," Pine said.

Vlado shook his head. "Not in Podborje. When people die, there's nobody else to move in. No one moves to places like this anymore. Let's go."

The descent took fifteen minutes. They hadn't passed another car for at least an hour. They pulled up in front of a plastered brick house with a red-tile roof. Just to the right was a weathered wooden barn. Beyond were brown fields, stubbled with weeds and the remnants of last summer's corn. The valley was quiet, no sound but the wind across the fields, and the air smelled of smoke.

Snow still covered some of the small lawn, melting fast. From the barn came the slapping sound of a wooden door, and they turned to see a short, stooped woman in a long skirt emerge with two steaming pails of milk, one in each hand. She eyed them skeptically, these visitors with their white European car, but she never stopped walking toward the house.

It was her, Vlado realized, although he'd remembered her face as smooth and brown. Now it was creased and collapsed, yellowed and spotted, like one of those handicraft dolls made of dried apples. But there was still strength in her movements.

"Aunt Melania?" Vlado ventured tentatively.

She stopped, carefully setting the pails in the mud, squinting into the morning light.

"Vlado?" she croaked, in a high but strong voice. "Is that you, boy?"

Vlado nodded, and she dropped to her knees as if shot, rapidly crossing herself and muttering words they couldn't hear. They rushed to her side, but she was smiling.

"Please!" she gasped. "Careful of the milk." Then she stood, wrapping Vlado in a wiry embrace before stepping back to look him in the eye as if he were the eighth wonder of the world. Pine watched dumbstruck while a rooster strutted forward, clucking nervously as it inspected the intruders.

"I never thought I would see you again," she said. "Especially when I heard your father was dead. He must have told you how much he never wanted to see us again."

"No," Vlado said. "He never did. But I do remember coming here."

She continued peering at him, as if searching for signs of falseness. Appearing satisfied at last, she said, "Come inside. I have something for you, but first I'll make coffee. And I am baking bread. You will eat."

Once inside, Vlado introduced Pine as his "friend from America. He won't know anything you're saying, though, so don't worry."

She laughed. "It will be just like your father, then. He never understood what I was saying, either, or pretended he didn't. Your mother, though, she always knew I was talking sense."

The house smelled of warm bread. She seated them by a rough table, built much like the one Konjic had made, and pulled a brown steaming loaf from the mouth of a huge oven. Then she put a pot of coffee on to boil, making it the Turkish way, from a grind finer than dust that left a muddy sediment in every cup.

"Me and the woman at the next farm, we bake for each other," she said. "She's a widow, too. We live a mile apart, so we take turns making the walk. She won't be here for another hour, so we have plenty of time to talk. But first, some eggs. Come."

They followed her back outdoors, trooping past the barn with its smell of manure and damp coldness to a weathered henhouse, where she stooped among the birds, their wings flapping as she pulled an egg from each of six nests. Returning to the kitchen, she took a blackened iron skillet from a hook on the wall and began scrambling the entire batch. She lay plates and forks before them, seating herself at the end.

"I guess I shouldn't be so surprised to see you, coming across the mountains with the sun barely up. And with an American, no less." She smiled, eyes gleaming with mischief. "You were always going to be an explorer, you know. A traveler on the seas. Or that's what all your books were about when you were a boy. Is that what you've become?"

"I'd forgotten all that," Vlado said, laughing. "Wasn't Magellan my favorite? Because he was the first to go around the world?"

"Yes. You wanted to be the Yugoslav Magellan. You said you wanted to sail for Tito. You should have seen your father's face when you said that. It was all he could do not to shout at you, but he held it inside. Your mother and I had a good laugh and just egged you on. We were terrible."

"And Uncle Tomislav?"

"Oh, he didn't worry about those things anymore."

Vlado paused long enough to interpret for Pine, who had been silent up until then. That prompted a question from Aunt Melania. "I saw the EU symbol on your car. Is that who you're working for?"

When Vlado told her they were working for the war crimes tribunal, her eyes widened. She reappraised Pine with greater scrutiny, then asked, "Is that the reason you're here? War crimes?"

"Yes, but it's very complicated."

"Those things usually are."

She was looking down now, cradling a coffee cup in her lap. "How much did your father ever tell you about the war?" she asked.

"Nothing, really. But I've learned a few things in the past week. About what he did. Where he was. That he went to Italy afterward, things like that."

"Then maybe you can understand why he and your Uncle Tomislav never really got along later."

"Because of the war?"

"Mostly because of what happened afterward. Your father had been traveling with another boy from here. Pero Rudec." ·

Pine heard the name, and Vlado flinched as he noticed the American straining to figure out what was being said. It wasn't a good time to interrupt for interpretation. He hoped Pine would have the good sense to be patient.

"Yes. I've heard of him, this Rudec."

She shook her head, sipping her coffee, then spoke very slowly, gravely. "Then maybe you also know about a man named Josip Iskric?"

"Yes. He's my father."

She nodded, saying nothing for a few moments. "Iskric was my name, too, of course. Until I married your Uncle Tomislav. Our family was all through this valley. Only a few of us now. A lot of them were killed in the war."

"Tell me about the war. And what happened around here."

"Afterward was the worst. That's when your father and Pero left the country. But your uncle stayed, and the new authorities, Tito's people, put him in jail for a while. Him and some others from the local militia. He had never gone in for the politics. He'd just fought in the Home Defense Army because all his friends were doing it. But he had never sewed a big *U* on his shoulders like some of them. Like your father, for one, at least for a while. And like that Rudec for another, as if he ever cared about any cause but his own.

"But your uncle wasn't interested in causes, and I think that is what saved him. Some of our friends in the village, the Seratlic family, they were Serbs. They had survived. Someone must have hidden them during the war, because by the end of the fighting the other Serbs in the valley were all either dead or gone. Taken north. But Seratlic vouched for Tomislav. Why, I don't know, because Tomislav wouldn't have spoken up for them, and he certainly wouldn't have hidden them. He always did as he was told. But we'd once sold them milk at fair prices, when their father had a dairy. So your uncle got out. Some of the others stayed in jail. A few were shot. Quick trials that no one ever saw. You'd read a paragraph in the newspaper, and that was it. It was a bad time.

"We thought your father was dead. Rudec, too. And when we didn't hear from them for a few years, we were sure of it. My only brother, gone. Then in 1961 we got a letter from him. He told us to burn it after we'd read it. It didn't even come by the regular mail. Some old man on a mule who'd gotten it from someone else on a train. It didn't have his name in it, but we knew who it was from what he said."

"Do you still have it?" Vlado asked, more as a son than an investigator.

"We burned it, as he'd asked. He told us that someday he would visit, but that for the moment it was too dangerous. He said he was near Sarajevo, that he'd learned a trade and met a woman. But he didn't tell us his new name, or his village. When you were a boy, I knew you only as Vlado. Maybe now you can tell me your last name. I have always wondered. Can you tell me?"

"Petric," said Vlado, feeling fraudulent as he stated it, a creation of forgery and deception. "Vlado Petric. It has always been my name."

She nodded curtly, accepting it.

"Excuse me again," he said. "I have to tell my friend a little of what we've been saying." He brought Pine up to speed, leaving out the part about his name.

"Ask her if your father's letter mentioned Rudec," Pine said.

It hadn't.

"But Rudec is alive, isn't he?" she asked. "This visit is about him."

"Yes. Only now he goes by the name Matek. We're looking for him. Partly because of the past. Partly because he killed one of our colleagues."

She shook her head slowly, regretfully. "Then I will help if I can. But I'm afraid I don't know much. He never returned. Never wrote or sent word to anyone. Only your father came back, and even he had to sneak into the valley. He said that if anyone ever found out his real name, they would put him in prison, or shoot him. But of course Tomislav, being a man, had to talk about the war. So after dinner, and after the third glass of brandy, Tomislav began asking questions. About the war, and the year your father went north."

Vlado knew where north led—straight to the Sava River, and Jasenovac.

"He wanted to know what had become of Rudec, and where they'd gone, what they'd done all those years. Maybe your father had been led astray by all of the bad politics, Tomislav said. By all those men who went goose-stepping with the Germans, wearing their big U's. Bowing down to priests and politicians, like it was some kind of crusade. Because by then, of course, your uncle was only listening to what Tito had to say. So he and your father argued, then they fought. Fortunately by then they were so drunk they couldn't do much harm. They broke a few glasses, knocked over some chairs."

"I saw them out the window. Like two bulls in a ring. Snorting and pawing."

"Two *drunken* bulls."

She smiled, showing her missing teeth. "But your mother and I got them to bed. You only had to lay them down and they passed out."

She paused, as if that was all she had to say on the matter. Vlado sipped at the strong, bitter coffee, feeling the pleasing familiar grittiness on his tongue. Somehow it tasted better here, in this quiet valley hidden in the hills.

"Tell me more about Pero Rudec," he said. "You knew him?"

"Oh, yes. A handsome boy, especially when he wore his uniform from the officers' academy. But he was always a little unsettling, too."

"How so?"

"Oh, you know. Always the first to do everything, especially when it came to girls. Always looking for the easiest way to do something. The shortcuts. But he also knew how to make the parents like him. Being sweet to your mother while trying everything under the sun with her daughter. Some of the fathers saw through it and chased him off, but he was pretty sly."

"You went out with him?"

"Oh no. He was forbidden fruit. And I was already promised to Tomislav. A good thing, too. Soon everyone knew that a girl down the valley, Mirta, was pregnant. But it was just after the war had started, and that gave Pero a chance to get away. Tomislav and your father signed up for the local militia. But Pero volunteered for a special unit heading north. Sort of an Ustasha SS, only they didn't call it that, but I think he liked the idea because it took him away from Mirta and her father. Of course he had to put a different face on it, talking about his valor and his duty. But no one believed him. I think he also liked the idea that he might collect some booty. Like a pirate."

"People knew there would be booty?"

"People had already heard what these units were doing. Burning villages and taking everything. Trying to wipe out the Chetniks. Some volunteers had already come back because they couldn't stand it." She shook her head. "I don't think Pero felt one way or the other about the Chetniks, but he never came back."

"What was it like here?"

"There were raids by all sides, back and forth across the hills. In the last year of the war a group of Partisans or Chetniks, no one was sure which, attacked and burned a village near here. Tomislav and your father were with the first men to get there afterward. Every family had been murdered in their beds. Everyone wanted revenge. And that was when your father went north."

"In the last year of the war?"

"Yes."

Vlado was puzzled. The file had clearly said his father went north two years earlier, at the same time as Matek. He attributed the discrepancy to the haze of his old aunt's memory, knowing how these things could get jumbled over time.

"But Tomislav stayed?"

"His father wouldn't let him go. Our father felt the same way. But Josip went anyway. He was determined."

Thus was a war criminal born, Vlado thought. Seeking vengeance and finding it, but a vengeance of the most terrible sort.

"And he ended up at Jasenovac."

"Is that what you've heard?"

"Yes. Right there along with Rudec."

She was silent a moment, playing with her napkin. "I'd always heard that about Rudec," she said. "But I was never sure about your father."

"Is that what he and Uncle Tomislav were arguing about that night?"

"Who can say? Your mother and I couldn't stand the noise, so we left them alone out there in the back. Then we heard things getting worse, but by the time I got downstairs they were on top of each other."

"So you never really found out what set them off?"

She paused, as if reluctant to continue. "Something about Rudec, if you really want to know." She stared at the floor. Pine must have sensed the change in her tone, because he was suddenly more attentive, leaning forward in his chair.

"What was it?"

"Oh, Vlado, you really don't want to know all this. The past is the past. Let it stay in the ground."

"Someone else has already dug it up, I'm afraid."

She sighed, then placed her coffee cup on the table and straightened in her chair. "Tomislav told me about it the next day, after you had all gone. Even then he couldn't quite remember why things had gotten so out of hand, once he started explaining it. But Rudec's name had come up. Tomislav had heard some things after the war. About that place you mentioned."

"Jasenovac."

"Yes. Rudec and a few others had apparently been some of the worst. All the wild stories about the killings, the torture. I'd always wondered if maybe it was just Tito's people making it up. But the Seratlic family, the ones who'd helped Tomislav, they'd heard it from cousins who'd survived the place. They said all of it was true.

"But your father told Tomislav to stop repeating those things, especially the ones about Rudec. He said it was too dangerous. And Tomislav thought your father was being a coward. But your father insisted, and said Tomislav should never repeat those names to anyone. Not his, and not Rudec's. So Tomislav lost his patience. And, well, you saw the rest out your window." She paused again. "But the oddest part was what your father did the next morning."

"Leaving early the way we did?"

"Before that. Before you were even up. Tomislav was still asleep, snoring. Your mother was packing. I was already in the kitchen, still restless from seeing them the night before, my husband and my brother rolling on the ground like a couple of animals. So I was making bread when your father came down. He told me he was sorry things had gone so badly. But that he really was worried about what would happen if we talked about Rudec, or whatever he was called now, because he had some sort of new name, too. Your father said it would hurt him more than Rudec, because of things that had happened after the war."

"*After* the war?"

"Yes. In Italy."

"But not during the war."

"No. Your father wouldn't talk about those years. Not a word. Especially about the time after he went north."

"To that place."

"Yes. To that place." She lowered her head.

"They were in Rome fifteen years," Vlado said. "I guess a lot could have happened. He could have been talking about anything. Work that they did against Tito, maybe."

She shook her head. "Not in Rome. Later. When they were on the coast. In some other town. It's where he and Rudec were for years, your father said."

There had been nothing in either file about that.

"I didn't know they lived anywhere but Rome," Vlado said.

"They only stayed in the city a year or two, he said. Then they went south. Looking for work, I guess, or maybe because it was cheaper. He didn't say much beyond that. But he did say he hadn't wanted to leave. He said he was happy with his new life, with you and your mother. But—and I'm trying to remember exactly how he said it, because it was so strange . . . it was something like 'I love my new life, but I never really finished my old one.' Then he gave me something, and I understood at least part of what he meant. But not for sure, because he never said anything more. He just gave it to me and told me to never throw it away, but to never let you or your mother see it. I think he couldn't bear to destroy it but was afraid to keep it anywhere that one of you might find it."

"What is it? Do you still have it?"

"Yes. And maybe I should have kept his wish and not told you about it. But if it will help you find Rudec . . ." She shrugged. "Because he is part of it, too."

"Show me, then. Please."

She nodded, placing her palms on the table and slowly pushing herself to her feet. In passing she laid a hand lightly on Vlado's head, in the manner of a priest offering a blessing. "It's in my dresser drawer, where it has been since that night. I never even showed it to Tomislav." Then she hobbled off, stiff after their hour at the table, seeming years older than when they'd arrived.

"What's happening?" Pine whispered. "Where's she going?"

"She's getting something my father left here, years ago. When I was a boy."

Pine said nothing. There was only the sound of chickens outside the window, clucking and scratching, heads bobbing in the sunlight. Aunt Melania returned with a small square of paper. When she turned it over, Vlado saw it was an old photograph. She handed it to him. The tones had browned but the focus was sharp.

It was his father, smiling broadly, a young healthy man standing with his arm around the shoulder of a smiling woman whom Vlado had never seen. They stood by a ladder, which was propped against a lemon tree. Gauzy netting was stretched across the tree-tops, filtering the sunlight. Next to them was another couple, and it took only a few seconds for Vlado to recognize the features of Pero Rudec, or Matek, as they knew him now. His aunt was right. Matek had been handsome, with just enough of the rogue in his expression to seem mysterious. The foursome was in a small grassy clearing, surrounded by citrus trees. On one side of the grass was a ring of white stones, darkened in the middle, as if someone had made a campfire.

The woman with his father was thin and dark-haired. They

seemed quite comfortable with each other, whereas Rudec's companion seemed stiff, ill at ease, or perhaps that was Vlado's imagination.

"Do you know her name?" Vlado asked.

"No. He never said a word of explanation. He only asked me to keep it."

"May I have it?"

"Please," she said. "And take this one, too. He sent it later."

It was a picture of his father and him standing by a wooded mountain overlook. Vlado recognized the view, a few miles outside Sarajevo with Mount Jahorina in the background. Vlado looked about six, in shorts with knobby knees and blocky shoes. His father stood behind him. Both were smiling broadly, the same look of ease that his father wore in the picture from Italy, only in this one you couldn't help but notice the man's large, strong hands placed protectively on the boy's shoulders. Were they the hands of a killer? Vlado felt his eyes brimming, so he took a deep breath and looked again at the other photo, turning it over to search for an inscription. There was only a stamp from a studio where it must have been printed: FOTOGRAFIA MARTELLI. CASTELLAMMARE DI STABIA. 1958. He'd never heard of the place. Perhaps it was the town on the coast his aunt had mentioned.

"Just pictures?" Pine asked from behind. He sounded disappointed.

"Maybe we'll learn more in Rome," Vlado said. "And this other place." He turned the photo over again, saying the name slowly. "Castellammare di Stabia. Maybe we should go there, too."

"Maybe," Pine said, sounding skeptical.

Aunt Melania, who hadn't understood a word of their English, then spoke up. "Would you like a piece of advice from an old woman, Vlado? Something that will last longer than just a cup of coffee and a warm slice of bread?"

"Sure," he said, smiling back. But he saw she was serious.

"Don't go there." She pointed to the photo. "Leave those things where they belong."

"I'm afraid it's too late for that now."

She nodded, as if resigned to his answer. "If you have to, then. Maybe it will even be for the best."

The look on her face said she didn't believe a word of it.

CHAPTER SEVENTEEN

Robert Fordham gazed down at the streets of Rome from his balcony on the fourth floor, wondering what he'd gotten himself into. On a warm November Saturday like this it was easy to forget the weary dishevelment that had reigned a half century earlier. Today the view was of nothing but prosperity—stylish hordes out for fresh air in sleeveless majesty. Older women squeezed vegetables in the market; the younger ones window-shopped. Close your eyes and the exotic orchestra of the streets kicked in—buzzing Vespas and honking cabs, a tinny choir of cell phones.

Yet, within the hour, and by his own free will, he would be conjuring up the grim postwar mood of 1946. For a pair of strangers, no less—an American and a Bosnian, the same sort of tandem that had once done him so much harm.

He sighed at his foolishness. Ever since he'd given his consent the previous morning his cautious nature had been on overdrive. Already wary of phones, of repairmen, of any visitor other than his housekeeper, Maria, he was now seeing threats in every strange face. Before taking his regular walk that morning he'd found himself reverting to the small tricks of a very old trade, leaving behind markers and telltales to determine if anyone had entered his apartment—or tried to—while he was out. He'd stopped at every corner to look over his shoulder, guarding his flanks. He'd scanned every parked or passing car, looking for an excessive number of antennae, and he'd been more relieved than he cared to admit to find his front door undisturbed on returning.

Stir up enough memories from a brief and intense time in your past, he supposed, and the old habits and fears returned with them.

But part of him believed that it was only prudent to feel this way. There were still too many unforgiving people out there, with memories as long and clear as his, and Rome was his last refuge. He had long since given up the stern clapboard villages of New England for the eternal mess and glory of this ancient sprawl along the Tiber, having made it his solemn duty to live and eat well, while worrying as little as possible about the past.

Why, then, had Fordham agreed to venture back to that era when the city had been exhausted, creaking along on pushcarts and horse-drawn cabs in a medieval gloom of hunger and want? The lure certainly hadn't been the woman who had telephoned to make the request. Janet something or other, supposedly with the war crimes tribunal. She'd been friendly enough, and her bona fides checked out. But something in her manner had carried the unmistakable whiff of the Agency, or some similar organization.

The tribunal was only the latest outfit seeking to tap his memory. Earlier supplicants had been nameless men in suits, still trying to tidy up after so much sloppiness. They'd knocked at his door, said little, then left with curt nods when he politely declined. A later one had posed as a journalist—a clever effort, but no, thank you. Another had approached him at a café, unannounced, with the bluster and bonhomie of a long-forgotten acquaintance. "Just happened to be on vacation, old boy, so imagine bumping into you here. Let's talk about old times, shall we?" No sale for that one, either. Fordham had learned the value and safety of silence as well as anyone. After all these years, why give them reason to move against you?

He would have said no this time, too, until he'd heard the name that finally flushed him: Petric.

Could there possibly be a connection? And in such an unlikely quarter as the war crimes tribunal? He hadn't spoken their language in years, and for all he knew there were thousands of Bosnians named Petric. But he doubted it, and for the briefest of moments as he scanned the sidewalks below he saw not the shoppers with their strollers and motorbikes but wispy visions of that other time: thin, grimy boys in dark shorts siphoning gasoline from his motor-pool jeep, hunched old men peddling rerolled cigarettes at the curb, and, yes, the raven-haired prostitutes in all their rumpled glory, offering a half hour of tenderness for a pittance of lire or U.S. Army scrip. For a little extra they would even accompany you afterward on a stroll, arm in arm through the Borghese, where giggling boys by the duck pond climbed trees to toss pebbles at the GIs and their dates.

The shadow that inevitably fell on such memories was a hunched Balkan figure disappearing around a corner, a sharpened, underfed face with dark eyes, a face that could read your deepest ambitions and play them to the greatest possible advantage.

"Signor," a woman's voice said, returning Fordham to the here and now. It was his housekeeper, Maria. "Your guests have arrived."

He turned from the sunlight and stepped indoors, where the plaster walls always seemed to retain their midwinter chill. "Yes," he said with resignation. "Buzz them up."

A maid met Vlado and Pine at the door when they reached the fourth floor. Signor Fordham had only recently completed his nap, she informed them gravely, although the man who emerged around the corner looked far from groggy or ill prepared. He regarded them warily, his gaze lingering a shade too long on Vlado. Then he advanced in a courtly stroll, hand outstretched but quavering slightly, as if shaken by what he'd just seen. China blue eyes shimmered. A full head of white hair swept back neatly from a high forehead. He was tall, about Pine's height, and in spite of a slight stoop there was something military in his bearing. Considering the occasion, he was dressed almost formally, in wool slacks and blue blazer with a starched white shirt.

"Welcome to Rome, gentlemen. I'd hoped the subject of Pero Matek would never come up again in my presence, but I'm hardly surprised it has. Too nice a day to stay indoors, so I thought we'd go out on the terrace. Coffee?"

"Please," both men answered, and he nodded to Maria.

"One little matter first, if you don't mind. If you brought any identification from the tribunal, I'd like to see it."

Vlado glanced at Pine as they pulled out their wallets, fishing ID cards from the small stacks of lire they'd picked up at the airport. Fordham gave the cards a long look, comparing their faces to the photos before handing everything back, offering no apology for his apparent mistrust.

They took seats on the balcony, a trifle uneasy after that display.

From Vlado's quick inspection the apartment seemed a spartan place, with few signs of the chockablock décor that usually fills the homes of the old, especially the prosperous ones who've traveled widely. No collections of photos or relics or memorabilia. Only one or two paintings. The furniture might have been from an upscale hotel, it was so generic. The terrace offered the lushest display—a floor of painted tiles with an ironwork table and chairs, enclosed by tall, hovering plants in giant terra-cotta pots. It was like some nook in a forest. Vlado briefly sampled the view before sitting, glancing at a torrent of pedestrians and mopeds streaming downhill from the nearby Colosseum, which glowed in the amber of late afternoon.

"One more bit of housekeeping before we start," Fordham said. "Were you followed on your way here?"

Pine seemed taken aback, glancing at Vlado for guidance. "We, uh, pretty much came straight from the hotel," he finally said. "And we'd pretty much gone straight from the airport to the hotel. I guess I wasn't really looking out for it. It's not exactly part of our training."

"I suppose not," Fordham said, sounding disappointed. Pushing himself to his feet, he stepped gingerly toward the edge of the terrace, leaning outward to allow a view without revealing himself to anyone below. "There's a man down there," he said, returning to his seat. "Doorway across the street, reading a newspaper. Blue jacket, green tie. Showed up just before you arrived. He with you?" He looked first at Pine, then at Vlado.

Neither had any idea who he meant. Pine got up for a glance, but Fordham hastily motioned him back to his seat.

"No sense attracting further attention. Probably nothing. Just a feeling."

"You know, it's *us* looking for *him*," Pine said, trying to strike a note of levity. "Not the other way around."

"It's not Pero Matek I'm worried about. It's the other ones."

"The other ones?" Vlado said.

"The problem is that neither of you has any idea what you're dealing with. Just like I didn't."

"That's why we're here," Pine coaxed. "To find out."

"But I may be doing us all a disservice by telling you. These things happened a long time ago, but in some quarters they haven't lost their currency, or their potency. Long half-life, this kind of information. Some of it should have been buried in lead and locked away." Then he turned toward Vlado. "You should know that as well as anyone, I'd expect. Are you his son, or is the connection more distant? I'm referring to Enver Petric, of course. Né Josip Iskric."

"My father," Vlado said, feeling as if his one advantage in the interview had been stripped away. How had the man figured it out so easily? Surely not from the tribunal, he hoped. Maybe it was the sort of deductive leap possible only for the overly suspicious, even paranoid. Yet, for an irrational moment, Fordham seemed like some sort of spirit guide, an eccentric old mystic who could gaze through the foliage of his balcony into the mist of the past. The man's blue eyes shimmered. Powerful emotions were at play, but Vlado couldn't read them.

"I suspected you might be his son the moment I heard your name. When you walked in the door I was certain. Those eyes. The way you listen. That earnest quality." That word again. Vlado winced. "It's the only reason I agreed to see you at all. Even then, that woman who called nearly put me off enough to refuse."

"Janet Ecker?" Pine said. "What'd she say?"

"It's not what she said. It's the way she was. Like the man I just saw across the street. Again, nothing definite. Just a feeling. Schmoozed me just like they would. People from the Agency. The ones who've been coming round here for years, trying to get a rise out of me. I guess I was worried she might be from their world instead of yours."

Vlado and Pine exchanged glances. The old man's precautions suddenly didn't seem so fussy, and certainly not laughable.

"It's not easy," Fordham said. "Breaking cover like this. Maybe I'm still seeking expiation. Forgiveness of sins. Though God knows I'm not Catholic."

"Expiation?" Vlado asked.

"That part comes later," he said, still unreadable. "Patience."

He stood, creeping again to the edge of the terrace, leaning the way he had before. Apparently satisfied but revealing nothing, he returned to his seat.

"What do you know about those days, anyway?" he asked Vlado. "Your father ever tell you much?"

"Nothing. I didn't even know he'd lived here until a few days ago."

Fordham nodded, seemingly not surprised. "Then I suppose the only way to tell you this story correctly is to take you to the scene of the crime," he said, Vlado wondering what the crime might be. "Besides, it's a fine Roman afternoon, and this weather won't last. Come on. I'll call us a cab."

When they emerged onto the sidewalk there was no sign of the man with the newspaper and the green tie. The ride was a strange one. They changed cabs twice, with Fordham speaking only to the driver for the first two trips, waving off their questions as they rode north through the city at dusk—up past the ruins of the Forum, then along crowded streets past the shoppers and off-season tourists, squeezing past the top of the Spanish Steps before veering west toward the river. Not until they caught the third taxi, by the Tiber, did Fordham stop turning incessantly to look out the back. Settling at last into his seat, he spoke again.

"What do you know about the way things worked here in 1946?"

"Just what we've seen in the cables," Pine said. "And those weren't rich in context."

Fordham nodded. "The city itself wasn't so different," he explained. "It was the people who were an unholy mess. Refugees from half of Europe, and nobody had a dime. But if you were on the run or had something to hide, it was a great place to be. The Italians were too busy purging one another to worry much about other nationalities. The politics would go left one week, right the next. Just like today, only now it's every month. So, the carabinieri pretty much left it up to us and the British to sort out the foreigners. Croatians and leftover Ustashi were my department. I was one of eight officer-investigators with the 428th CIC detachment, Army counterintelligence. We had a little office at 69 Via Sicilia. British Intelligence was just upstairs, thinking they still ruled the waves. Then there were the leftovers from OSS, James Angleton and his people, technically still working for the army even if officially without portfolio. The CIA wasn't born yet. He was a strange one. Tall and skinny. Wore a big coat, big hat. One of our people went to see him once and found him crawling on the floor, checking for microphones. Which of course made us wonder if he'd bugged *us*. He was already more worried about Moscow than any leftover Nazis. Hated Tito. Saw any Ustasha types as potential allies."

"There were a lot of Croatians here?" Vlado asked. "And Bosnians?"

"Thousands. Coming out of the DP camps or up through Austria. A lot of them wanted to get down to Argentina or over to America. Ante Pavelic himself ended up as Juan Perón's security adviser, you know. There should have been a song about him in *Evita*. We were supposed to be rounding them up, but somehow they kept slipping through the cracks, mostly with the help of an evacuation network run by some Croatian priests, over at the Confraternita di San Girolamo. That's where we're headed. San Girolamo. Father Krunoslav Draganovic ran the show there. He also happened to be head of the pope's Pontifical Relief Commission for Refugees, which tied him into all the DP camps. Sometimes they sent people back across the border—with our help—to plant bombs or generally raise hell. But mostly they shipped all their bad eggs to safety overseas. Gave them new names and put them on freighters to Argentina, America, Canada, you name it. Everybody called Draganovic's network the ratline. It's how Klaus Barbie got away."

"The Butcher of Lyon?"

"Yes. And it was more than a little embarrassing when it came out later that we'd helped him get away, with Draganovic pulling the strings. The cover-up said Barbie was the exception, not the rule."

"You don't agree?" Pine asked.

"Nobody would who was here then. But the proof's gone by now, of course. Which is why I keep my mouth shut."

He paused to give further instructions to the driver. They were still headed up the Tiber, in traffic growing heavier by the minute. The dome of Saint Peter's loomed in the distance to their left.

"The day I met Matek I was looking for a Nazi. An old SS man we kept rounding up and the British kept letting go. Fiorello, our CO, was determined we were going to keep picking him up until the Brits kept him locked up. That's the way it was then. You were never sure who was on your side one day to the next. We had a list of his mistresses, and we'd visit them one by one until he turned up. I drew Inge, whom I always thought of as Marlene Dietrich, mostly because of the way she talked. She lived in a run-down old pension on Via Abruzzi, place full of exiles. Always smelled like boiled cabbage.

"Well, Inge was in, but our SS man wasn't. He'd dumped her for some new gal across town, so I phoned in the name from downstairs and decided to check the books. That's how we made the rounds then, checking registration records, then visiting the newcomers, making sure their papers were in order. Just about everybody had some kind of information, and usually all it took to get it was a few cigarettes. And that day, Matek's name was the latest entry. So I paid him a call."

"You spoke the language?" Vlado asked.

"Serbo-Croatian? Some. But Matek had learned some Italian at Fermo. He'd just arrived and was pretty skinny after all that time in the camp. It was pretty clear his papers were a rush job, but he had that look in his eye that dared you to do something about it. He said Father Draganovic himself had gotten him out of Fermo, so right away he had my interest. The father had driven down to the camp in a U.S. Army staff car, which somehow didn't surprise me. He'd held a mass for a few hundred Croatians, then prayed the rosary and asked anybody with special requests to see him afterward. Matek had gotten a job at San Girolamo working as a typist and driver, which piqued my interest further. I'd been trying to get a hold of some information there for months."

"What kind of information?" Vlado asked.

"They kept a master list of all the émigrés—names, aliases, military rank, you name it—everybody they'd ever housed or fed or were trying to ship out, including all the big Ustasha types in hiding. We'd turned another worker who was supposed to slip us a copy, but a week later they fished him out of the Tiber. So you had to be careful."

"Did Matek tell you his military background?" Vlado asked.

"A few lies. But we didn't concern ourselves too much with that, because within a few days an order came down from Washington to go after Pavelic, the dictator himself, and suddenly Matek was our best bet for an insider."

"This was when?" Pine asked.

"June of '46. Tito's people had been screaming for months that we were hiding Pavelic in Italy. I think somebody in Washington finally got tired of hearing it."

"Were we?" Pine asked. "Hiding him?"

"We certainly hadn't been looking for him. Especially people like Angleton. But our guys were game for the chase, and the word around town was that Pavelic was holed up at Castel Gandolfo, the pope's summer residence, out with the peacocks and chicken coops. Supposedly some of his old security chiefs and cabinet members were there, too. The only way to know for sure was to get that list out of San Girolamo. And damned if we didn't, with Matek's help."

The taxi reached its destination, stopping by a bridge, Ponte Cavour, beneath the leafless sycamores lining the Tiber.

"Best to keep moving as we talk," Fordham said, looking around quickly as they crossed a busy boulevard. "Makes it harder to eavesdrop." Pine rolled his eyes.

They strolled into a modest but spacious piazza with one side facing onto the boulevard by the river. A high grassy mound at the center of the square seemed to glow beneath the fading orange sky. Bordering the other three sides were long five-story buildings of fairly recent vintage, by Roman standards, boxy and severe, with rows of narrow rectangular windows. The ones on the north and east sides were made of scrubbed white marble, but the one at the south end was ugly brown brick. It was joined to a faded dark chapel that looked centuries old.

"The mound is the mausoleum of Caesar Augustus," Fordham said. "Everything else in the square is a Mussolini creation, and that damned ugly hunk of bricks at the south end is San Girolamo. The Croatians couldn't afford the marble, I guess. But it worked well enough for Draganovic and his ratline." He pointed to the marble walls of the nearest building, just behind them. Beneath the windows there were carvings of ancient Roman armies but also of the Fascist armies of World War II. Latin inscriptions ran overhead, with Mussolini's name prominent, along with a reference to his distant predecessor, Augustus.

"Hard to believe it's still here," Vlado said, having grown used to Berlin, where every remnant of the Nazis had been either bombed, buried, or annotated to museum status.

San Girolamo also displayed art of the era, in three huge, colorful mosaics looming above the fifth-floor windows. Jesus was in the centerpiece, a fawning crowd at his feet. The two flanking pieces featured priests ministering to crowds, presumably in Croatia. The inscriptions on this building were also in Latin, although the checker-board symbol of Croatia was featured prominently. Vlado saw spray-painted graffiti on the bricks as they approached—a skull and crossbones topped by the words GIOVENTÙ NAZISTA.

"What's *Gioventù* mean?" Vlado asked.

"Youth," Fordham said. "'Nazi Youth.' Guess they still feel com-fortable here."

The place made Vlado edgy, and for the first time in all his trav-els he could sense his father's lingering presence, a wan ghost in worn clothing drifting beneath these words and images, saluting an armed guard on his way through the door. Such petty players, his countrymen, in these great struggles of the continent—instigators and assassins who lit the bonfire of Europe, then went off to fight among themselves. Even the great Pavelic, killer of millions, had been a sort of nothing here, hiding in cassocks and convents, then sailing in the belly of a freighter under a forged name.

"Looks like the Croatians felt right at home here," Pine said.

"Oh, they were great allies. Another Catholic nation making nice with Germany, and right across the Adriatic. It was a friendship for the ages, which is why the Vatican took it so hard when Tito took over."

"But if they couldn't afford the marble," Vlado asked, "how'd they afford the ratline?"

"Draganovic," Fordham said. "Supposedly had a few crates of gold right there in his office. Looted from the State Bank of Croatia as the war was ending." Vlado remembered the references to Matek and the strange convoys out of Zagreb. No wonder the good father had helped him get out of the DP camp. "Probably had two hundred pounds of it. The British had helped him bring it up from a mon-astery in Austria."

They paused, facing the brown walls of San Girolamo. The mosaics were barely visible in the fading light.

"Can we go inside?" Vlado asked.

"You might be able to talk your way in. But everything would be locked up. Just like on that weekend in '46."

"Matek had a key?"

"Several. To file drawers and offices. He'd stolen them, of course. Just for a day or two. Had us copy them, and kept a few of the copies for himself. That was part of his bargain."

"What else did he ask for?"

"Oh, he wanted the moon. But no cash, we insisted. So he came up with a wish list. Quite eclectic. A few tools. Some cigarettes. But mostly a lot of passes and travel documents, for freedom of movement. We weren't giving him those until he'd gotten us the goods, of course. He also wanted documents for a friend. A confederate. He'd concluded he couldn't pull it off without an extra set of hands."

Vlado let that sink in a moment. "My father," he said.

"Yes."

"So that's when you met him."

"Just before the break-in. I had to make sure we approved. And I did, with reservations."

"Having to do with his war record?"

Fordham nodded grimly. "But probably not in the way you think." He looked around, as if worried again about eavesdroppers. No one was in sight, but darkness was falling. The air was chilly. "Gentlemen, if we're to continue, and if I'm to give you what you really came for, there are better places to talk about things like this. That blue van over there's been giving me the creeps since we got here." Neither Vlado nor Pine had noticed one. "And some of it, I'm still not sure I should be telling you. For your own good, as well as mine."

"Meaning what?" asked Pine, who was still looking around for the blue van.

Fordham pursed his lips, suddenly looking older than he had all afternoon. "Meaning that just because it's fifty years old doesn't mean it's lost its ability to do harm. Even to kill. And meaning that after fifty years, I suppose it's finally time for me to come clean." He turned toward Vlado. "With you, in particular."

CHAPTER EIGHTEEN

Another three-taxi relay took them to a restaurant called Rimini's. It was one of Fordham's favorites, and he apologized personally to the proprietor for arriving so early. It was barely 6 p.m.

"No better than tourists. But we'll pretty much have the place to ourselves."

Even so, Fordham was edgy whenever a waiter approached, eyeing the kitchen door at the sound of every coming or going. Rimini himself seated them, putting them near the back, then pacing awhile nearby, as if unsure of what to make of these sullen early arrivals. As if correcting for their mistake, he waited a good ten minutes before delivering menus.

Vlado was hungrier for information than for food, but not until Rimini took their orders did Fordham return to the subject. "Meeting your father was Matek's idea," he began. "He'd told your father I might be able to help him return home. Of course, Matek didn't tell me any of this until five minutes before the meeting. Said it would be up to me to bring up our plans for San Girolamo. So I handled it very clumsily."

"Was Matek there?"

"In the hallway. It was at your father's pension, which was worse than Matek's."

Fordham flinched as a waiter materialized with the first course, a bounty of antipasti in bright reds and greens. Vlado tried to imagine Fordham as a young man, with a face smooth and well fed and the swagger of a soldier whose war was won.

"So you told him about the plan," Vlado prompted.

"Not completely. Didn't want him running back to Draganovic with the details."

"Did you think he might?"

"Not really. As a driver he'd ferried around enough of the father's guests to realize the sort of business they were in, the power they could wield. And everyone had heard about the poor fellow fished out of the Tiber. So the minute I raised the possibility of procuring a little information, he shut down. Asked me to leave."

"Did you?"

"I was too defeated and embarrassed not to. But I came back."

"He changed his mind?"

"No. Turns out Matek had been counting on your father to refuse, but he'd wanted me to see what we were up against. Matek believed your father's reluctance only made him more desirable. He didn't want to work with anyone who didn't have a healthy fear of Draganovic. He said the key was making your father fear us more."

"How?"

"With his security file. By putting him in a position where he'd either have to help us or be revealed to the authorities. Your father had spent some time as a guard at Jasenovac." Fordham hesitated, lowering his fork. "You knew that, I hope?"

Vlado nodded. His stomach clenched, and he gently put down his fork.

"But of course that wasn't enough for Matek," Fordham continued. "He wanted to rig up the worst possible dossier—massacres, atrocities, eyewitness accounts—then show it to him and say, play ball or else."

Vlado flushed, glancing at Pine, who had also put down his fork and was staring intently at Fordham. They caught each other's eye, Pine with an expression that seemed both embarrassed and angry. Remembering the vivid account he'd read two days earlier, Vlado wondered now how much had been fiction. He felt a jealous anger brewing, this time on his father's behalf.

"So his father's file is all a lie?" Pine said, barely in a whisper.

"Pretty much. As far as anything detailed goes, anyway."

"And you agreed to this plan?" Vlado said, leaning forward, his voice rising.

"Please." Fordham looked around nervously. "I didn't, in fact. I checked with Fiorello, just in case, and he felt the same. Matek would have to find somebody else. Someone we could lure with a carrot, not a stick."

"But that's not how it worked out, was it?" Vlado said.

Fordham shook his head, looking doleful. He dabbed his mouth with a napkin. "We were pressured from upstairs. Someone at the embassy. Young hotshot from Washington on special assignment from State. He'd been making the rounds in Europe and had taken a personal interest in the hunt for Pavelic, so he calls me over to his suite at the Grand Hotel. Big corner room with the windows open and the shutters thrown back. 'You have a job to do, Robert,' he says. 'And I'd hate to see a fine career ruined because of some philosophical objection.' It was get in line or get out of the way. So we got in line. And it turned out that Matek and your father weren't the only players in the deal."

"Who else?" Vlado was terse now, an interrogator in pose and demeanor. All that was missing was the bright lamp. If he could have, he would have tied Fordham to the chair, making him stew until it hurt.

"There was an agent Angleton wanted to run. Some low-level Ustasha hiding out at a convent. He was going to take a radio, explosives, cross the border and raise hell. After a year of good deeds, they'd give him safe passage to the United States. But he had a dirty file. Dirty as they come."

"So you switched his file with my father's."

"Not switched. We wouldn't have wanted any Jasenovac reference in his dossier. But his records made a convenient case history for your father. Real witnesses talking about real events."

"I know," Vlado said. "I've read them."

Fordham swallowed heavily, then nodded. "It let us kill two birds with one stone, as it were. Gave our operative a new identity and put your father in chains, figuratively speaking. Not that the operative ever amounted to much. Tito's people caught him inside a week. Shot him."

Fordham turned his eyes to his plate, sopping up a puddle of oil with a crust of bread. Vlado reached across the table and grabbed the offending hand, squeezing the wrist, then leaned into Fordham's face while speaking in a rasping whisper. "Stop it. Stop it! You're not eating anything until you're finished talking!"

Pine watched openmouthed but did nothing to stop Vlado. Fordham glanced nervously at a couple who had just entered the restaurant, but this only drew further ire.

"Don't look at them!" Vlado hissed. "Don't look anywhere but at me until you're done. I want to know exactly what happened next. Every detail. When did you tell my father?"

"The following week." Fordham's voice was shaky, barely audible. He looked at the hand gripping his wrist with an expression of alarm. Vlado eased his grip but not his gaze. "I took the file over to his pension."

"What did he say?"

"Told me it wasn't him. Said he'd heard stories, of course. Seen some things he hadn't liked. But nothing like this."

"Did he say what he *had* done?"

Fordham shook his head. "And I didn't ask. That would have been admitting we'd doctored his file. But at some level he must have known what had happened, because he said, 'This is Pero's doing, isn't it?' I said I didn't know what he was talking about. That we'd pushed Matek the same way we'd pushed him. I knew he didn't believe me. He was angry. He . . . grabbed me for a minute. By the wrists." Fordham looked away, and Vlado flushed in spite of himself, gently and slowly letting go. "Then he let go and sat down on the bed."

"And he agreed."

"Not at first. Said he could embarrass us as much as we could embarrass him. I told him to go ahead and try. I told him we'd throw him back across the border with a big *U* sewn to his britches and a rap sheet a mile long. They'd shoot him at sunrise. And with that he gave up. Besides, we were still offering what he wanted most. The opportunity to go home. Work for us, I told him, and we'd make the file go away. Give him a new identity, clean as a whistle: Enver Petric, the village farm boy who'd sat out the war, and an ethnic Muslim into the bargain."

So this was where Vlado's name had come from: a lying spy and a murderous scoundrel. Vlado then asked the question that had been lurking behind his anger all along, although he wasn't yet sure he was ready for the answer. "What was my father's actual record, then?" His stomach fluttered as if he'd just leapt from a diving board.

"I never allowed myself to read it," Fordham said.

"Never *allowed* yourself?" Vlado's fist struck the table. Pine placed a hand lightly on his arm. The couple at the front table looked up with startled expressions, and a waiter approaching briskly with a tray full of steaming platters paused in midstep. They waited in silence while he distributed the food, but Vlado didn't take his eyes off Fordham.

"I was afraid of how clean it might be," Fordham said quietly, after the waiter departed. "Although he *had* been at Jasenovac. That I knew for sure."

"But only for a few months," Vlado countered, some of the steam gone from his voice. "And it was right at the end of the war."

Fordham flushed, and for once he didn't seem to care if he was overheard. "Look," he said, leaning forward. "I don't defend what I did. But do you have any idea how many people they could kill at Jasenovac in just a month? Let alone two. Or by what means? Are you at all familiar with how they concluded their business at the time your father would have been present?"

Vlado said nothing, dazed by the blow.

"Well, I'll tell you, since you're so eager for *every* detail."

Now it was Vlado who was looking around the room.

"Look," Pine interrupted, "I really don't see any need to—"

"I do," Vlado said. "Let him finish."

"As well you should," Fordham said, nodding soberly. "I've been feeling guilty about this for more than fifty years. I should have owned up to it long ago. Should have never been a party to it. But even if your father did nothing but dig latrines, he knew what he knew and held his tongue. He kept it all to himself while murderers like Matek walked free. Okay, so we found a way to shut him up. But why hadn't he spoken up earlier? As an investigator, you know as well as anyone what it means to conceal the guilt of others."

"Believe me," Vlado said, feeling a queasy kinship. "I know."

"So did they even carry out the burglary?" Pine asked.

"Oh, with flying colors. First Saturday night in July. While I waited across the square in a jeep. After an hour they came lumbering out with a couple of boxes like they owned the place. None of the guards even raised an eyebrow. Amazing. Matek had a big bulge in one of his coat pockets, a fat envelope he'd stuffed in there for himself. We spent the rest of the night photographing everything so we could put it all back Sunday. It was a windfall—every name of every émigré, including their aliases. Enough to keep us busy for weeks. But of course there were gaps, too. Correspondence with the Vatican that we'd expected to see. Correspondence with Angleton, too, which, personally, I wanted as much as anything. I wanted to put him out of business."

"You think that was the sort of thing Matek kept for himself? The envelope in his pocket?"

"That's my bet. At first I thought he'd turned it over to Angleton, that Matek had been working for him as well. Later I wasn't so sure. But it would have been some of the biggest sticks of dynamite in the whole barrel."

"Then why didn't you withhold his passes?"

"I tried. I was overruled. The man upstairs again."

"Who was he?" Pine asked.

Fordham smiled ruefully. "It's the one question I haven't yet decided whether to answer. It's the one name they'd still want me to keep to myself. But I suppose if I wanted to play it safe, I shouldn't have met with you at all. They'll assume the worst anyway."

He paused for a moment, as if collecting himself. He dabbed his face with a napkin, then gestured toward the newly arrived food.

"Do try some of this before it gets cold, won't you. It's quite the best there is in Rome. There's fish coming, too, along with a little veal."

Then he took a bite, Vlado willing to indulge him for the moment. Raising a glass of wine, hand quavering slightly, Fordham seemed about to propose a toast. But all he spoke was a name.

"Samuel Colleton."

"He was the man upstairs?"

"Well, well," Pine said.

"Who is Samuel Colleton?" Vlado asked.

"Number-two man at the State Department," Fordham said. "But the job he really wants—has always wanted—is to be head man at the Agency. And that job comes open when the current director retires in May. Colleton's not the only contender, of course, and he's the oldest, a disadvantage. But apparently a certain momentum has been building, a feeling that maybe the old man deserves one last moment of glory—a sort of lifetime-achievement award. Which is why any hint of scandal from his past would sink him. Reputations are at stake, gentlemen. And perhaps more."

"Harkness," Pine said.

"Pardon?" Fordham said.

"Paul Harkness. A State Department operative out of Sarajevo. He helped put together our botched operation. Technically, Harkness works for Colleton, and might still be working for him if Colleton gets the promotion."

"Ah," Fordham said. "*That* kind of diplomat." He chuckled mirthlessly, relaxing for the first time in a while, shaking his head as he scooped another bundle of noodles onto his plate. "These kinds of things always end the same, don't they? Just as you're ready to make your move, your operation goes to hell in a handbasket, and nobody on the ground ever knows why. Exactly what happened to us with Pavelic."

"Someone botched it?" Vlado said.

"New orders from Washington, right after the break-in. Our hunt was postponed until further notice, leaving us dead in the water. Then Matek sank us."

"Matek?"

"He skedaddled. And I got the sack. All after a big mess over at Draganovic's personal quarters, at 21 Borgo Santo Spirito, right next to Saint Peter's. Official Vatican property, so you couldn't touch him there. But the sidewalk out front was fair game, and Matek phoned me from over there a week after the break-in. Said if we came right away, we'd find the ones we'd been looking for, arriving in a car with diplomatic tags.

"We presumed he meant Pavelic, riding around in Draganovic's car. But it meant we'd have to grab him between the car and the front gate. Violating Vatican extraterritoriality was the great taboo. So, a couple of us rushed over there knowing it would be a close shave."

"I thought you'd been ordered off the case?"

"But no one had said what to do if he fell into our lap. So we drove over. Parked around the corner and waited on the sidewalk. Ten minutes later a black car with diplomatic tags comes cruising in. We grabbed the first two guys out. Didn't recognize either one, but we had to do something, so we said we were taking them in for questioning. But by then there was a huge commotion. A bunch of nuns had come down the steps to see what all the fuss was about. They're shouting and gossiping, lecturing us in Italian, Croatian, English. You'd have thought it was Christmas Eve in Saint Peter's, we had such a mob.

"Somewhere in the middle of all this I notice a truck pulling out from an alley just down the street. I got a glance at the driver, and I could have sworn it was Matek. Grinning. And all I could think was that we'd been had. But we took the two fellows back to Via Sicilia anyway. Checked their names against our list of suspects, and of course they weren't on it. So we apologized. And I think it might have blown over if not for the official complaint. The worst kind. An eyewitness claimed we'd violated extraterritoriality. Said we'd grabbed them inside the gates. And the complaint was filed directly to Angleton, who was going to make sure it stuck."

"One of the nuns?"

"No. A clerk named Pero Matek. With a corroborating account from Josip Iskric."

"But you were his meal ticket," Pine said.

"His *expired* meal ticket. From then on I could only have been a hindrance. The next morning we were hauled in to see the ambassador. I was packing my bags by the end of the week. Transferred to Vienna, where I spent a year carrying messages between the British and the Americans, in an office where everybody knew about my great fuckup. The following year, of course, Ante Pavelic caught a freighter to Argentina."

"Great."

"Yes. Perfect. So at the end of my hitch I went back to Harvard. Got my degree and put in for the foreign service. Passed the exam but never got a posting. Failed the security clearance. Thanks to my good friends back in Rome."

He paused, looking off into space, then resumed in a quieter tone. "Years later I ran into Fiorello in Boston. Ancient by then. Cataracts and hypertension. Died the following spring, so I guess he was wanting to square accounts. He told me a story that made the rounds after I'd shipped out. Around the time of the break-in, Draganovic had apparently gotten skittish about his crates of gold, the stuff they'd looted from Zagreb. Decided that the office wasn't safe enough, so he'd moved them to his place at Borgo Santo Spirito, where we'd made our famous 'arrest.' But both crates were stolen. Two nameless conspirators who vanished into the mist, destination unknown."

"Matek and Iskric."

"That was my guess. Since then I've always wondered if all we were doing that day outside the gates was providing a noisy diversion for a heist. Fiorello said no one came out of the affair very happy, including Angleton's people. They were kind of uneasy for a while, as if more than just gold had been lost."

"Stolen information?" Vlado said.

"Maybe. The best way to hurt an Angleton is to steal his secrets. And talk about a long half-life. That stuff would still be radioactive."

"So no one ever saw them again?" Vlado asked. "Matek or my father?"

"Not a trace. But I did hear something right before I left for Vienna. The Croatians had reported a stolen truck, and the morning before I caught my train they found it. Empty, of course, and out of gas. On the side of the road, just outside Naples."

Vlado thought of the photo of his father and the unknown woman, standing in the citrus grove along with Matek, near the town he'd never heard of.

"Calvin, where's your map of Italy?" he said. He pulled the photo from his satchel as Pine shuffled through a briefcase. They awkwardly unfolded the map, shoving plates aside with a clanking of china and silver. Vlado checked the name of the town stamped on the back of the photo. "Near Naples, you said?"

Fordham nodded, smiling now, as if suddenly caught up in the spirit of their chase.

"Yes. Practically at the foot of Mount Vesuvius."

"Castellammare di Stabia," Vlado said, thumping a finger in triumph against a spot on the map. "Right across the bay from Naples. Just around the bend from Vesuvius."

Pine broke into a smile, then looked across the table at Vlado. "I'd guess," he said, "that we'll be staying at least another day in Italy."

CHAPTER NINETEEN

Vlado was awakened the next morning by the sound of voices, a conversation drifting just beyond reach. The sensation was so vivid that he groggily got out of bed to open the door, half expecting to find a pair of young men dressed in 1940s garb, paused in the middle of a discussion. But the hotel hallway was empty, every doorway silent.

It was barely light, not even seven on his last morning in Rome—his first and only one, as well, he reminded himself. Time to get moving, if he was ever to catch up to the wandering spirit of his father. Lead me to Matek, he thought. Show me the way to your old enemy.

Coming more fully awake, he splashed his face at the bathroom sink, realizing that the voices he'd heard were the last snatches of conversation from a waking dream—the young Fordham and the young Enver Petric, squared off in his father's shabby room somewhere across the city. For a fleeting moment, as he inspected his dripping face in the mirror, he was oddly certain that if he were to climb to the hotel rooftop, he'd be able to pinpoint exactly where the conversation had taken place. It would stand out like a tiny beacon on the horizon, shining among the TV antennae in the blushing haze.

But Vlado had another destination in mind, a final stop before he and Pine journeyed south. He threw on his clothes, went downstairs, and headed into the street. He craved coffee but didn't want to waste time in the hotel. The strange weather was holding, so the morning chill was bearable, and within a few blocks his stride loosened. He unbuttoned his overcoat, taking in the smells of baking bread and brewing coffee. The Romans were throwing open their shutters to the morning, heeding the Sunday call of ringing church bells.

A few blocks later he crossed the Tiber, gazing down at the greenish-brown water flecked with trash. The same current had scoured centuries of empire and conquest, outlasting all the barbarians and fascists and occupying armies. His father had taken just such a walk, perhaps, on just such a morning, a devout young Catholic on his way to mass. Yet he'd been willing to forsake name and religion to return home. Why, then, had he remained in Italy for fifteen years? And what had finally driven him back across the border?

It took ten minutes to reach the periphery of Saint Peter's Square, where the cathedral's huge dome filled the sky. Cutting left up an alley, he reached a narrow cobbled lane, which he knew from his map would be Borgo Santo Spirito. Checking the house numbers, he made his way to number 21, at the end of the block, only a stone's throw from the colonnade around the massive empty square. The building was still a convent, five stories of beige stucco and arched windows, just as Fordham had described it. This was where Draganovic had lived, but more important, where Matek and his father had last been seen, presumably while making their boldest move, escaping Rome with a truckload of someone else's war booty.

Out front someone had just hosed down the brick sidewalk. An iron gate beneath a stone archway led up a long flight of marble steps to the entrance. There was a small plaque on the front wall: ZONA EXTRATERRITORIALE VATICANO. Even now, you couldn't make an arrest here, and Vlado smiled at the thought of the young Fordham standing at this very spot, cursing his luck. But the building itself was a disappointment. Somehow he'd hoped—irrationally, he knew—that it might offer some sign, or message. But the plaster walls were mute, the windows staring blankly. The same was true for the alley just down the lane, where Fordham must have spotted Matek's grinning face in the window of the departing truck. There were no portals into the past here. Nothing but the rainwater smell of the rinsed cobbles, the lonely whine of a Vespa from the next street over. His excitement from earlier that morning drained away. What could he have been thinking? The key to everything was not so much in the past, he realized, as in those who had survived it, then twisted history to their devices. Look forward, not backward, he told himself, unless you wish to be blindsided.

Vlado solemnly began walking back toward the hotel. By now,

a dull ache in his forehead was fairly screaming for caffeine, so he stopped at a bakery that was just opening for the day. He ordered a roll and an espresso, waiting at a small table out front. Stirring in a lump of sugar, he sipped from the tiny cup, strangely deflated, watching an aging priest in a black frock beetle his way toward Saint Peter's. Then a voice came at him from behind, strong and clear and very American.

"It's really a mistake, you know, going to all these old places. Your father's world is gone, and so is he. Let it rest."

It was Harkness.

He'd pulled up a chair and was leaning forward, the big pink face only a foot from Vlado's. Still looking every bit the country gentleman, he was decked out neatly in a sport coat and pressed slacks, looking as if he'd already shaved, showered, and read the Sunday papers. Harkness was still two steps ahead of them, Vlado realized, right where he must have been all along.

"I only say this for your own good, of course." The man was smiling now.

"Of course," Vlado said, too shocked to say much else. "So why are you following me?"

Harkness ignored the question. "A word of advice, if you care to listen. Not that anyone has so far. None of this will help you find Matek. It might lead you in the right direction awhile. But in the end he'll outsmart you or kill you. Or just when you're ready to make your move, the tribunal will yank back on your leash. Pine's bosses don't operate in a vacuum, you know, and soon enough they'll realize the two of you, as well as your little friend Janet Ecker, have wandered into places that have nothing to do with tribunal business and everything to do with mine."

The name Colleton formed on Vlado's lips, but he resisted the temptation to speak it. "So you don't want Matek caught?" he asked instead.

Harkness shook his head. "To the contrary. There's nothing I'd like better. You seem to forget that it was my idea to arrest him."

"Then what does it matter if we pursue him?"

"Let's just say that things got complicated once he headed for the hills. And it hardly helped when Branko Popovic dropped out of the picture. For good, I'm now told. Meaning that you, in particular, owe me one. Meaning that it would be a very bad idea mentioning any of this conversation to Calvin Pine." He leaned closer, lowering his voice. "Besides, you should be home with that family of yours, making sure the police don't get too nosy. LeBlanc's there already, you know. Poking around in Berlin."

Vlado had heard enough. He reached for the bill, but Harkness was quicker.

"Allow me," he said, laughing when Vlado tried to snatch it back. "I don't think Jasmina wants you blowing your paycheck in over-priced tourist cafés." Vlado flinched at the mention of his wife's name. "Which reminds me. He's been calling her again, you know. Our friend Haris? Berlin can be so lonely this time of year. Who knows, maybe he'll make it back there before you do. Unless someone else beats you both to the punch—Branko Popovic didn't operate in a vacuum, either, Vlado. Had plenty of friends. You really ought to call home more often, you know. And, please, let's not bump into each other again. The next time it won't be so pleasant. *Ciao.*"

Harkness turned sharply on his heels toward Saint Peter's, disappearing beneath the shadows of the colonnade without once looking back. Vlado was left standing by his table, where his roll lay uneaten on the plate. Stomach knotted, he walked slowly at first, then quickened his pace, and before he knew it he was running full tilt for the hotel, sweat beading on his forehead.

After a few blocks he stopped in confusion. What good would it do, hurrying back, when his phone line would be blocked, as it had been everywhere else? He pulled out his wallet, shuffling through the small stack of lire. There was just enough, only because Harkness had picked up the tab. He stopped in a small *tabacchi* shop where the proprietor was just rolling open the metal grille and bought a ten-thousand-lira phone card, hoping it would give him enough minutes to Berlin.

Jasmina picked up on the first ring, sounding sleepy and warm, speaking from their bed.

"Hello. Sorry to wake you, but I've got to hurry. There are only a few minutes on the card."

"Vlado? Finally." She sounded relieved. "It's so good to hear from you."

"I'm sorry I haven't been able to call."

"A secretary told me you weren't allowed. She said it might be a week or more, so this is a nice surprise. You're in Sarajevo?" She didn't sound alarmed, which was something, he supposed. Perhaps Harkness had been bluffing. If so, it had worked.

"I'm in Rome. Since yesterday."

"And you went without me? I'm insanely jealous." She laughed, but he thought he detected a nervous edge. Was she alone? Of course she was. Don't be a fool for the man's bluster. "Sonja will be jealous, too. I'd put her on if she was up."

Vlado checked the digital display on the phone. The card was draining alarmingly fast. He was already down to six thousand lire.

"No. Let her sleep." Vlado already felt guilty for doubting Jasmina. It was Harkness who'd been lying. "We're driving south today, leaving in an hour. I just wanted to make sure everything there was okay."

She must have detected the tension in his voice because her tone changed as well. "She really misses you, Vlado. And so do I. It's too much like during the war."

"I'm sorry. And I'm glad. It's good to be missed."

The meter had dropped to four thousand. He had to find some way of warning her, quickly, without either alarming her or having to explain too much. But she preempted him. "Vlado, a strange thing happened yesterday. It upset me."

"Yes?"

"You remember . . . Haris?"

"Yes. Go on."

"He telephoned. From Sarajevo. When I first heard the static I thought it was you. He had a message for you. It was you he wanted to speak with, in fact. But he seemed to know you were out of the country."

The coffee was burning a hole in Vlado's empty stomach. The meter was down to three thousand. He thought of Harkness, smiling, somewhere out on the streets of Rome, leisurely awaiting his next move.

"What was the message?"

"He said they'd come looking for him, and he wanted to know if you were the reason. I asked what he meant, but he said you'd know, and that he had to go. He sounded scared. Maybe for both of you. But it all happened so fast, then he hung up."

So. It hadn't all been a bluff. Maybe none of it.

"What did he mean, 'they'? Who's looking for him?"

"He didn't say. I thought you'd know. I couldn't sleep after he called. What haven't you told me, Vlado? What should Sonja and I do?"

Two thousand lire.

"Stay at home from work a few days. Keep Sonja with you. There's more we need to talk about, but there isn't time now. I've kept too many secrets from you. I'm too much my father's son. I'm sorry, I know I'm not making sense. Go to the Vrancics' down the hall if you think you need help. Go to the police if you have to. But try not to worry. Everything should be okay."

"Vlado, are you in trouble?"

One thousand lire.

"I might be. I don't know. But I should be finished here in a few days. I'll be home as quick as I can. I have to go, the phone card's running out."

"I love you. Good-bye."

The connection went dead before he could answer.

"Goddamn it!"

His shout drew the disapproving stare of a passing nun as he slammed down the receiver. Here he was, in a city where cell phones bleated from every pocket, and he couldn't even arrange a decent call home. He cursed Pine, the tribunal, the city of Rome. Then he cursed Harkness, but the thought of the man's face dimmed his anger with apprehension. His first impulse was to try to catch the next plane to Berlin. The hell with everyone else.

But that was exactly what Harkness wanted. And no matter how ruthless the man might be, Vlado doubted he was the sloppy type. His threats had hit home, but Vlado's gut feeling was that he'd exaggerated to make a point. Perhaps he'd even found Haris, and had put him up to making the call. How else would he have discovered by now that Popovic was dead? Did Popovic still have goons out there? Probably. But they'd be fighting over the leftovers, more dangerous to one another than to him or his family. Or so he hoped. What had Harkness called it, during the meeting in Sarajevo? "Whistling past the graveyard." Another American idiom that seemed all too apt.

He felt a keen sense of urgency, as if the meter on the phone was still clicking downward. He'd have to be more careful than ever, and faster, more efficient. If they didn't find Matek within the next day or so, they might never, and all remaining secrets would stay buried.

Reaching the hotel room, he found that Pine had slid a note under the door.

"Vlado," it read. "I'm picking up the rental car. Back by 9. Calvin."

Just as well. On the walk back he'd come up with an idea, and this might give him time to carry it out. If his father and Matek had indeed robbed Draganovic, he'd realized, they wouldn't have relied on fake identities from San Girolamo to help them make their way south. And if their booty included some of Angleton's most embarrassing secrets, then they wouldn't have wanted to use the identities furnished by the Americans, either. The case file had told him of only one other reliable source for bogus identity in those days, and that was the Red Cross. For once, he had an inside source. He pulled Amira's calling card from his satchel. Now if he only had a phone.

He checked the line, just in case, but it was blocked. Ducking into the hall, he saw a maid emerging from a room along the corridor. The door was open. Gently shutting his own door, he stepped toward the linen cart, where the maid was collecting a stack of fresh towels.

"Scusi," he said, brushing past her as if he owned the place. You did these things with confidence, or you didn't try them at all.

"Sir?" she said.

"I'll be right out," he said briskly. "Then you can finish."

Shutting the door behind him and setting the security chain, he saw a man's clothes and a newspaper spread across an unmade bed. He picked up the receiver, punching an eight for an international line. The dial tone sprang to life.

He punched in Amira's home number, grateful that she'd written it on her card, and as the phone rang, it really did feel like he'd gone back to his life during the siege—his wife had become a seldom-heard, distant voice in Germany, and he was again alone and in need of a favor from this woman in Sarajevo, only now he knew how dearly she had paid for helping him the first time.

He awakened her, just as he'd awakened Jasmina; her voice was drowsy and languorous.

"Yes?"

"It's Vlado. Vlado Petric."

"Of course." As if she wasn't the least surprised. She must have then cupped a hand over the receiver, because he heard her speaking to someone else, the words indistinguishable. Probably her foreign boyfriend. And Vlado again felt the irrational stab of jealousy, followed by a flush of guilt.

"Go ahead," she said, all business now.

"I'm in Rome. But I need some information the Red Cross may have. Old stuff, from fifty years ago."

"And you thought maybe I could look it up for you." She was not happy about it but she wasn't angry, either.

"It's just that, well, I'm not sure that going through official channels would do much good. It's not something they'd be proud of."

She laughed. Whatever reserve she'd maintained had dissolved. "And what will it be next time, Vlado? Will you need me to break into a building for you? Go ahead. Tell me what you need. Then I'll decide if you deserve it. Is it for the tribunal?"

"Yes. But it's personal, too, I guess."

"These kinds of things usually are in our country."

He told her he was looking for records of two Red Cross passports issued in Rome during the last week of June or the first week of July 1946—around the time of the break-in at San Girolamo. Most likely they would have been issued the same day, to males ages twenty-three and twenty-five, or thereabouts, in case they'd fudged their dates of birth.

"Under what names?"

"That's what I'm trying to find out. They would have wanted new identities. Evidently it was fairly common then."

"Common now, too. At least in some quarters of the IRC. But I never said that, of course. Let's just say that some employees don't always maintain their spirit of altruism when faced with the prospect of a windfall profit for a few mere documents. Especially during wartime. Especially in shitholes like this."

"Whatever you say."

"Do you have a nationality?"

"It was a pair of Yugoslavs, ethnic Croats. But if I had to guess, I'd say they'd want to be listed as Italian, so they could stay awhile.

Maybe with an address near Trieste, somewhere near the Slovenian border, so it wouldn't be implausible for them to have Slavic accents, or to know Serbo-Croatian."

"A lot of the older stuff has been computerized. Leave it to the Swiss to digitize every possible record. In which case it's lucky you reached me on a Sunday. I can surf around on the office computer with none of the administrators around to ask what I'm up to. Which is no guarantee I'll find it. If it's still only in paper form, I might not be able to track it down until Monday, if then. But you're right about going through official channels. Total waste of time. How'd you end up in Rome?"

"Long story. And we're heading south in half an hour."

"Still with the American?"

"Yes. Still with the German?"

She laughed. "I'll do what I can, Vlado. Try me back tomorrow at the end of the workday. Here, not at the office."

"Understood. And thanks."

"No need. The more of the bastards you can put away, the better. Talk to you tomorrow."

Vlado stepped into the hallway. The maid had disappeared into some other room. He shut the door behind him, wanting to pack up and leave before she saw him again.

He met Pine in the lobby a few minutes later. It was just before nine, and the rental car was parked out front. Vlado wondered what he should say, if anything, about the morning's events. Nothing, he supposed, given all the warnings. Somehow it seemed safer keeping it all to himself, although it made him feel guilty.

"I called and got us a hotel in Castellammare di Stabia," Pine said. "But damned if I've decided what we'll do when we get there, other than spend some more of the tribunal's money." Then he smiled, picking up his bags. "But I guess we've got three hours to come up with an answer. C'mon. Let's hit the road."

CHAPTER TWENTY

As Vlado and Pine were climbing into a rental car in Rome, Pero Matek was gazing out the window of a train.

It had been a long two days, he reflected, although much easier than the last time, when it had taken months, even years, and every turn had been fraught with either ambush or deception. One enemy after another, from armies to gumshoes to priests. But he'd had the energy to deal with it then, outwitting all comers even when operating without food or sleep. Now a mere day in a car and a second aboard trains had exhausted him.

He hadn't helped himself by making the journey longer than necessary. The most direct route would have taken him west by northwest to the Croatian coastline, then up along the shore, cutting the corner at Slovenia toward Trieste—a circuit of the upper Adriatic, like some tourist with his Baedeker. But he'd headed for Austria instead, spending the first night just across the border, awakening in Villach to a warm morning with steam rising from the streets. He'd dumped the car, which had been stolen anyway, and since then it had been trains all the way, zigzagging down the boot of Italy until he found himself in a second-class compartment crawling around the Bay of Naples. The view toward the water was blocked by industry and crumbling apartments, so he turned in his seat to look inland, up toward the imposing brown cone of Vesuvius.

The top was bare, leveled by its last great blast in '44, only two years before his own arrival. He remembered the way the mountain had been smoking then, a sulfurous steam that had made him uneasy, bringing to mind all those ancients fleeing for their lives at Pompeii and Herculaneum. Panic was the same no matter what its era, and the fear that drove mobs disgusted him.

He thought of the crowds along the northbound road out of Zagreb in the last month of the war, refugees clogging the highway with their carts and bundles, slowed by their belongings when they should have just cut and run.

Or worse, there were the crowds during the fighting in the Kosarev Mountains—a church full of people, all of them screaming while his men formed a line around the building. The mobs had started breaking their own damned stained glass just to try to save themselves, until a few machine-gun bursts persuaded them to remain inside. Then the fires had begun, his men pouring gasoline by the gallon, wasting it, an inefficient way to do business when you could sell your surplus at a premium. The noise made by the trapped crowd had reminded him of cavitation in the bottom of a kettle as water comes to a boil, the molecules excited with a clattering noise like fingernails tapping on the bottom. The angry buzz of hornets in a shaken nest. And you killed them the same way, with smoke and flame, to make sure none would ever sting you. Roasted alive, the propagandists had said later. Well, burned for sure. But by the time the roasting began they'd been dead enough.

He turned from the window. The man next to him was getting up, a bag of apples in his hand. Matek checked the stop. Still five more to go on this rattling local that seemed to stop every mile, dotting the arching coastline all the way to Sorrento, which even this time of year attracted vacationers. He spotted a pair of young Germans with backpacks, a few middle-class Brits and their pale brood. No Americans, though, thank God, so the only noise on the car came from the Italians, especially the two near the front, arguing loudly above the rattling of the car, their arms moving as if they were conducting an opera, some energetic scene from Puccini. It had turned into an unseasonably warm weekend, so he supposed he had to expect some holiday crowds. The views from the bluffs of Sorrento and Positano would be no less spectacular merely because it was winter. The swimming pools would still be heated, the restaurants still overpriced, the shops still full of everything that was coveted and useless. But for him, only a few calls at a few old stops, a brief interlude for collecting on an insurance policy of sorts, a retirement fund, something he'd set aside long ago for some vast unforeseeable emergency, for which his current predicament surely must qualify.

At last the train screeched and shuddered into his stop, a grimy and crowded port city that he had once called home. Hardly anyone else was getting off here, he noted with pleasure, and he stood with his small canvas bag, still a man who could travel light. But the journey had drained him. As he made his way down the aisle he felt the fatigue in his calves and at the backs of his eyes. He could never have made the pilgrimage of '45 now. He'd have become one of the thousands left for dead, strafed by the Russian planes and rounded up by the Partisans. Herded into long lines and shot. Then, the mass graves. Had there ever been an era when his countrymen hadn't been digging them?

He walked slowly into the town on narrow streets, and within a few blocks he found a small pension that seemed suitable. It was a bit down at the heels on the outside, but the room was clean and the rate cheap. The proprietor was kind enough. She was roughly his own age, probably a widow from the way she hovered over him, seemingly with little to do but talk and ask questions. Not that he was answering. His Italian continued to bloom, his fluency returning faster than he would have guessed. Yes, he would do just fine here.

After the woman finally left—a trifle too nosy for his taste, he decided—he threw open the shutters to let in the air. Looking past a church steeple he could just see a sliver of the Bay of Naples, glittering in the morning sunlight. And if he leaned just a bit to the left, there it was, the great cone of Vesuvius. He had forgotten the way the volcano dominated the entire basin, making every village seem vulnerable to her brewing and steaming. But she was quiet today, as she had been for years. Like his own life, he reflected. And surely one measure of greatness, whether you were a man or a mountain, was how well could you emerge from dormancy, how deftly, and with how much residual power and skill.

He had some time to rest now. No sense in acting hastily, especially when there soon might be others to contend with. Perhaps by now the investigators had discovered his old identity, and if so, they might have discovered other things as well. From the moment he'd heard from his informant Osman in Travnik he'd known he'd have to keep moving for a while. The boy, the son of Enver Petric, had been unnerving enough, turning up out of the blue like that. But then Matek had learned he was traveling with an American, and the name Calvin Pine had sounded familiar. A short search on the Internet had easily turned up the man's background: the war crimes tribunal in The Hague. Meaning that he'd have been a fool to wait for their next visit. Handcuffs and a show trial, the end of everything.

Thinking of them now only made him irritable. His plan to booby-trap his office with mines had seemed elegant at the time, but he realized now it had been too clever by half. Too imprecise. He'd been worried about sloppiness, about attracting too much attention with blunt force, when he should have realized that, for all intents and purposes, he was going back to war. Better to have simply sent a few thugs down the mountain to murder them in their beds, especially the son of Petric, with his father's eager eyes and earnest determination. The sort who wouldn't give up until you put a bullet through his brain. Instead he had killed neither of them. Just some third wheel. The other three mines hadn't even gone off. Or else Azudin had found some way to fuck it up. He'd cursed when he heard the victim's name on the radio. A fellow he'd never heard of, yet a killing that was just as likely to make them hunt for him. So much for elegance.

And what if they turned up here? Local talent could handle it, of course. It was as easy to find in Italy as it was at home. Perhaps easier even, once he'd had a day or so to get the lay of the land. Or he could take care of things himself. The gun was in his bag, and now that he was back on a war footing, it would only seem natural.

But he'd found other news even more disturbing. The radio bulletin yesterday from eastern Bosnia. A botched raid by the French. The escaped general still at large. It was too much of a coincidence that they'd both be on the run at the same time, and Matek was convinced there would soon be at least one other visitor to keep him company.

He unpacked his bag and sprawled on the bed. Later he would have a nice dinner, some wine. A decent vintage and a bowl of pasta, nothing too heavy. Then, early tomorrow, he would find the right place to begin doing business, a vantage point that would let him take stock before making his move. But for now, rest. He lay his head on the overstuffed pillow, feeling the surprising warmth of the coastal breeze in November, the shutters drifting and slapping lightly against the wall. By late tomorrow, a bustling Monday, there might well be quite a show to watch, and he wanted to be rested for his part in it. Closing his eyes, he tumbled toward sleep, still dormant for the moment, feeling like a man with all the time in the world.

CHAPTER TWENTY-ONE

Not long after Pine pulled onto the Autostrada heading south, Vlado, exhausted, fell asleep, with the windows down and the breeze in his face. He awoke later with a start, having no idea where they were or how much time had passed. It was warmer, the traffic heavier. To the right, the ocean glittered in the distance. Glancing left he was startled to see a huge brown mountain, lopped flat at the top. Vesuvius, no doubt. He wished Sonja were here to see it. They'd hike the trail to the top. Peer down into the crater.

Pine hadn't yet noticed that Vlado was awake, and Vlado watched him. He looked relaxed, steering with one hand, sunglasses shining, an elbow propped on the open window—the very picture of an easy-going American traveling without a care in the world, spiky blond hair tossing in the breeze. He was easy to work with, a pleasant fellow. But more important, Vlado trusted him, and he had a feeling that was going to be more important than ever in the next few days.

Pine glanced over, saw that Vlado's eyes were open.

"Quite a sight, huh? Wouldn't want to be around when she blows."

"How much farther?"

"Twenty minutes. Maybe thirty with the traffic. You had a pretty good nap. I think you needed it."

Vlado nodded, still groggy.

"I've been thinking," Pine said.

"About what?"

"Matek. Him and your father driving down here in that truck. Assuming that was who Fordham saw, of course. I guess we have to assume that, or we might as well not be here. Let's say they ran out of gas somewhere around here. Then they've got to find some way to keep moving with two crates of gold. Another assumption, of course, that they took the crates to begin with."

"Sounds right for Matek."

"If you had a bunch of gold bars at your disposal, you'd be able to afford any kind of help to keep you moving. Except you wouldn't exactly be able to melt into the landscape once you started spreading gold around. Matek strikes me as too careful to have done that. He'd have kept it hidden, at least for a while. I also doubt they'd have been able to take much of it with them when they slipped back into Yugoslavia. For that matter, why go back at all once you've taken fifteen years to build a life here, and have a nice nest egg salted away? Unless you had to leave, and leave in a hurry. Which is all my way of saying I think it might still be here. The gold. The envelope. All of it. Or whatever they didn't spend in fifteen years. Sound plausible?"

"Sounds like you want it to be plausible."

"Not much point in us coming here otherwise. Because Matek would certainly have no reason to come back."

"Except for the woman, maybe. The one in the picture."

Pine cocked his head. "You really think that's his style? To be pining away all these years for a woman?"

"No. Just trying to convince myself, too, I guess. I'd hate for this to be a dead end."

"Maybe it isn't, even if he's not here. Spend fifteen years anywhere and there's a good chance that somebody left behind will have an idea of how to find you later."

"Possibly."

"Or possibly not. I don't know. The more I think about it, the more I wonder about all our assumptions. They're mostly based on the recollections and conjectures of a paranoid old man. And if all his secrets are so damned dangerous, how's he lived to the ripe old age of, what, seventy-eight?"

That thought silenced them both, and Vlado couldn't help but remember what Harkness had said about their short tether. If he was right, this would be their last stop, whatever happened.

"At least the weather's nice," Pine said, speaking over the breeze. "At the worst we'll have a couple days' vacation."

"With a few more nice meals."

They drove on a few miles, watching the signs for Castellam-mare.

"So, what do you think you'll do when this is all over," Pine asked, "now that we've turned your life upside down? Think you'll move back to Bosnia?"

"Hard to say." He tried not to think of Popovic, or of all the people who might have worked for him, still in the country. Or of Haris, who'd gone back and may have gotten into a jam. He wasn't sure Jasmina wanted to go back anyway.

"Jasmina doesn't like Germany, but she likes what's happened to her there. You'd think it would be the ones who lasted out the whole war who'd be tougher now, but they're just worn out. She's stronger. More forceful. You ought to see her with a German butcher. Fights him by the gram, and comes away gloating about it. She was happy to have me back, but she's a different person. Sometimes I like it and sometimes I don't."

"Sounds like what she said about you."

"What do you mean?"

"We had a chance to talk in Berlin. While we were waiting for you to get home. She said the war had hardened you. And part of it was good. She said there would never be anything that could beat you or break you after you'd survived the siege. But she worried about you, too. All those emotions you'd stored up. She said you'd learned a little too well how to keep things from bubbling to the surface. It's what you'd expect a woman to say about a man, I guess. None of them think we can communicate. But still."

Vlado nodded, feeling his heartbeat quicken. He desperately wished he were home. If he were there just now, he'd finally be able to talk about everything, not just from the past few days but from all seven years. It would come out of him like an illness, a dark liquid purged from his system. Yet there would be sweetness as well. And then he would share a drink or two with Jasmina, and as the night grew still they would slink off to bed, and enjoy a welcome bliss where there was no past but their own.

"How'd you two meet?" Pine asked.

Vlado smiled. "Like peasants. I was the city boy visiting her village, staying with some old friends of my mother's. There was a big celebration for the Feast of Saint Damien, the village patron saint."

"I thought Jasmina was a Muslim name?"

"It is. But no one missed a feast like this. Lambs on a spit. A big dance. And it's where all the courtship took place. Especially if your parents were part of the old ways, and hers were. So there I was, the city boy in his blue jeans. I held myself above all that courtly business and the stupid traditional costumes. But they made a big circle and went round and round, dancing the *kolo*. Once that starts, you can't help but join in. And I saw this girl on the other side of the circle looking at me, so I smiled back. I think she liked that, liked it that a city boy so disdainful of it all still found time to do some shopping. She was fed up with all the farm boys with thick necks, especially the ones her parents kept picking out. So we spent the evening talking, way too much for her uncles and her aunts, but her mother was okay about it. The hell with tradition for a change.

"After that I started driving out from Sarajevo on weekends, borrowing my father's car. All very formal for a while, and always with a chaperone, but she minded it more than I did. I thought it was kind of charming. Romantic. And it was always such a victory when we managed to sneak away."

Vlado remembered one such time in particular, slipping off to a farm pond during another feast day, darting barefoot through the pines. Vlado tiptoeing on his city-boy feet in a way that had made her laugh. Then reaching the water's edge, shedding their clothes without out a word or a prompt, the entire village off somewhere else. They'd plunged into the cool water, laughing, playing like otters, lithe with their touches and feints. Then, drying off, they'd looked each other in the eye and understood what their future would be without even speaking, and they'd tumbled together onto the grassy bank, wet bodies molding to each other, sliding and warm. He'd pressed his face to her hair, smelling the pond, and afterward, as they held each other, they'd spoken of what their lives would become, adorning their futures with the sorts of dreams they had never before admitted to anyone. Four months later they'd married—more dancing of the *kolo*, then a golden age with a child and success, and no hint of war or upheaval or separation.

If Jasmina had known all the trials ahead, Vlado wondered, would she have come along with him anyway, especially if she could

have foreseen his latest and darkest secret? It was this painful question that at last burst the dam of his thoughts and made him realize he had to tell Pine everything, now, no matter what—that if he
didn't do it this instant, he might never, and somehow it would poi-
son them all.

"Calvin, there's something I need to tell you. Something that
may be related to the case. Or maybe not. Only Harkness and
LeBlanc probably know for sure. But you need to be told."

Pine furrowed his brow, obviously caught by surprise. "Okay," he
said. "I'm listening."

So Vlado told him all about Haris, Huso, and Popovic, and the
body in the trunk. He held back only when it came to Harkness—the
man's threats, and Vlado's worst suspicions. Those, at least, would
have to wait until he knew his family was on safer ground.

When he was finished, Pine shook his head slowly in apparent
sympathy. "Jesus, what a spot to be in. No wonder you looked so
wary when I showed up in Berlin. But don't worry. Nobody will hear
it from me. The tribunal needs to know Popovic is dead, but nobody
needs to know my source. They probably suspect as much by now,
anyway, given how long he's been missing."

"Thanks. But I can't ask you to protect me. Not once our work is
finished. You'll have to tell them what you know. Or maybe I'll tell
them first."

Pine scowled. "You think you're the only cop I've ever had to
cover for? In Baltimore it must have happened once a month. Planted
evidence? Look the other way, buddy. Botched warrant? Here, sign
this one instead, postdated. A little trigger-happy in that shoot-out?
Hey, that's the streets, the guy was dirty anyway. At least with you
the victim was truly deserving, not some fifteen-year-old from a
housing project with his mom strung out on heroin. It's why I left.
Why I volunteered for the tribunal. What could be a clearer and
cleaner mission than hunting genocidal maniacs? Even an old one
like Matek." He paused, shaking his head again. "But look at us now.
Wondering who's calling the shots, or how long we'll be able to stay
on it. Confess later if you want, but you might think first about your
wife and daughter."

It was exactly who he'd been thinking about, wondering with
each passing mile if they were still okay. Vlado nodded, relieved that

he'd spoken but still unsure of his next move, half wishing Pine hadn't let him off the hook so easily.

Pine, in fact, was soon moving on to other matters, such as how Vlado's revelations might figure into their pursuit.

"So, how was Popovic supposed to have fit into all this?" he asked. "It still doesn't make sense. From what I gather, Popovic has been a sort of glorified errand boy for Harkness since the war ended. When he wasn't out killing Kosovars, anyway. And he almost definitely had ties to Andric. The whole sick crowd of Serb generals and paramilitaries. It's why he was so valuable to the tribunal as a possible witness. But damned if I know how Matek fits that picture."

They drove a while longer in silence, turning over in their heads what they knew, or thought they knew.

"Then there's LeBlanc," Pine finally said. "I wouldn't underestimate his ability for mischief any more than I would Harkness's. For all we know Castellammare could already be pretty crowded. And if they know more than we do . . ." He shrugged. "Then everything might be over before we even get started."

"Like what happened to Fordham."

Pine nodded grimly. "Where would you go first then, if you're Harkness or LeBlanc?"

Vlado shrugged. "I don't travel in their world. I can only tell you what a policeman would do."

"Good enough for me. I'm just a prosecutor. What does the out-of-town cop do first?"

"Visits the local cops. Partly as a courtesy, partly to get a few more eyes and ears working for you. You don't mention any crates of gold, of course, unless you want the whole town in an uproar."

Pine frowned. "I don't exactly want the local yokels to know what we're up to. Not yet. I've had enough dealings with the carabinieri before. Too military. They're breathing down your neck until you're boarding the flight home."

"Then go to the *polizia di stato*. It's who I dealt with whenever we had to contact the Italians over smugglers or fugitives. You're more likely to get somebody in a suit. And they hate the carabinieri more than you do."

"You're kidding."

"Big rivalry. They monitor each other's scanners. Steal each other's sources. It's all very Italian."

"I should travel with Europeans more often. Broaden my world-view."

The Autostrada ended just as it reached Castellammare di Stabia, giving way to a winding two-lane road that crept up and over hills, hugging the rocky slopes that fell away to the Amalfi. The town—more like a city—was the gateway to a string of resorts, with the gray hump of Capri visible offshore in the distance. Castellammare had once been a resort itself, going back to ancient times when its mineral springs fed Roman baths. Then came the green parks and princely villas. Local boosters still liked to think of their town in those terms, but the dominant sights today were gantry cranes and bustling wharves. It was the last oily smudge of industry before the shoreline gave way exclusively to leisure.

It was also the home to citrus groves, terraced forests, mostly lemons, harvested for every sort of product, including a strong local liqueur.

"Look," Pine said, as they passed the first of the orchards. "Like the one in your photograph."

Vlado had been thinking the same thing, although at this time of year the trees held no fruit, so there were no workers up on ladders. Nonetheless, he felt strange seeing the orchard, as if he were moving ever closer to the heart of something he wasn't yet sure he wanted to reach.

CHAPTER TWENTY-TWO

They checked in to a small hotel with decent views and an atten-tive staff, which seemed to have little to do in the off-season. The bellman threw open a window to freshen the room, and Vlado took deep breaths of the briny air off the sea. His room faced the mountains, not the ocean. The manager had apologized—sea views were more popular, not to mention more expensive—but Vlado pre-ferred it this way. Who wanted to be enticed by sparkling green water when it was still too cold for swimming? Give him the hills and the terraces, with the narrow roads disappearing into rocky folds.

He rummaged in his satchel and pulled out the old photograph, studying it again while the piping chatter of children drifted in from the streets. For what must have been the twentieth time he gazed closely at the face of his father, then at the woman's. It was clear that their relationship had been no mere fling, even if it endured for only a summer. They seemed at peace with each other in a way that Matek and his companion clearly weren't. Or perhaps Vlado was reading too much into it, a troubled son trying to make the best of things. Maybe their contentment was just weariness, resignation, a moment of repose at the end of a long and tiring day, climbing those ladders and shaking lemons from the trees.

There was a knock at his door, followed by Pine's voice. "Ready to roll?"

"Be right there."

The regional headquarters for the *polizia di stato* was only a kilo-meter away, so they walked, stretching their legs after the long drive. The building was an eyesore of sharp corners and dark glass, tucked at the edges of the port. A din of clanging metal and whining fork-lifts drowned out the street noises as they approached. They entered to face a reception counter. Behind it, rows of desks were piled with papers. The few officers on weekend duty strolled about in two-tone blue uniforms, coffee in hand, cigarettes burning in their lips. Pine sized it up right away.

"Typical cop shop," he said. "You sure about this?"

"Maybe we'll get an atypical cop."

A woman up front asked them a question in Italian, but when Pine responded slowly in English she replied crisply in kind. "What is your business, gentlemen?"

"We're from the war crimes tribunal in The Hague," Vlado said, taking the lead if only because he'd dealt with the Italian police before. "We're here as a courtesy, and to alert you to the possible presence of two suspects."

"I have just the man for you," she said, picking up a phone.

"Two?" Pine said under his breath.

"Think big. They'll be more impressed. And Harkness did say the cases were connected."

"Just like he said Fordham was a lying windbag."

"Detective Inspector Torello will see you," she said. "Follow me."

She led them to a nearby door, then through a maze of desks to a glassed-in office in the back, where Torello was waiting in the doorway.

He was tall and slender and wore a suit—just what they'd wanted, unless he turned out to be some sort of glorified public rela-tions functionary—and seemed attentive and alert. The office eager beaver, Vlado thought, agreeable to overtime and weekends if that's what it took to get him out of this backwater.

"Please," he said, handing each of them a business card. "I'm assuming you'd rather speak English, and mine is quite good, if I say so myself. Welcome to Castellammare, gentlemen. When did you arrive?"

It was a social question with a point. He wanted to know how long they'd already been prowling around on his turf.

"Just got here," Pine said. "Drove down this morning from Rome."

"Well, I am of course at your service, although our usual run of international cases is smugglers and refugees."

"You could say these fellows are refugees," Pine said. "Suspects who've recently eluded us in Bosnia, and we have reason to believe one or both might be in your neighborhood."

Torello raised his eyebrows, then offered cigarettes from a desk drawer. Vlado took one while Pine shook his head, bracing for the inevitable onslaught of smoke. The man was handsome and wore no wedding ring. Yes, he was ambitious all right, or he'd be out on some beach with a young woman on a warm Sunday like this. Vlado looked for family pictures and found none but did notice a pressed dinner jacket, fresh from the cleaners, hanging from a hook in the corner.

Torello studied Pine's business card a moment. "So, tell me who it is you're looking for, and why you think they may have come here."

"We can give you two possible names for one of them," Pine said. Vlado knew he had no intention of answering Torello's latter question. "Pero Matek, aka Pero Rudec. The other fellow you may have heard of. Marko Andric, Serbian general. One of our ranking suspects. I've got particulars and a photo on each, if you've got a copy machine handy."

"Of course. And I'll check with some of the hotels and pensions this afternoon to see if any holders of Yugoslav passports have registered recently. I'll also provide you with official letters of introduction, if you'd like. They'd be helpful if you'll be making any inquiries locally. Will you be?"

The man was good. Offering a service while poking his nose a little deeper into their business. Pine hesitated, so Vlado answered.

"We might be. What can you tell us about the local citrus growers? Their hiring practices, and any employment records they might keep?"

"Right now they're not very busy. They won't be hiring seasonal help for a few months. As for records"—he shrugged—"same as everyone else, at least in name. But with the seasonal hires you can never be sure. We find some illegals now and then. Albanians. A few Bosnians, too. You think your men might be looking for work?"

Vlado looked at Pine, unsure whether to take it further. Pine nodded. "One of them might have worked in the orchard a while back."

"How long ago?"

"Fifty years. Maybe 1952. Or as recent as '61."

Torello raised his eyebrows. "Right after the war, then. Well. Those were interesting times here."

"How so?"

"In the usual way of wars, I guess. There were no jobs, really, so anyone making money was probably doing something illegal. Lots of people on the move. And the soldiers, of course. Occupation forces. Mostly Americans, who seemed to like hanging around on the beach. All this is secondhand, of course. From some of the older guys."

"You're not from here?" Vlado asked.

"Florence. Like night and day." That would explain why he'd want to get out of this place. "I can give you names of some of the larger growers," he continued. "Their offices will be open tomorrow. I doubt their records will be much help, if they even have any from that far back. But it's a start." He paused, knocking the ashes off his cigarette. "In the meantime, answer me this, please. Why would not just one but two Balkan war criminals on the run, with all of Europe to choose from, want to come to this little blight on the pretty Amalfi coast?"

"I guess we'd like to know that, too," Pine said. "To be frank, our coming here is sort of a shot in the dark."

Torello smiled crookedly, as if to say he could live with that lame explanation for now. "Well, if you should ever come up with a more complete answer, let me know. In the meantime, leave me the number where you're staying. I'll send over the names of those citrus growers later this afternoon, along with the letter of introduction."

Another deft move, Vlado thought, finding out right away where he and Pine were staying. But unless some local cop got lucky turning up one of their suspects—a doubtful proposition, at best—he figured this was the last they'd see of Signor Torello.

They ate a big lunch on the way back to the hotel, deciding to enjoy the afternoon while they could. They'd been on the move almost constantly for three days now, and the meal gave them a much needed chance to unwind, even if Vlado kept expecting to see Harkness at almost any moment, grinning from the next table.

As the waiter cleared away their dishes before bringing coffee, Pine leaned back in his chair, patting his stomach, and said, "It is true what they say. The Italians know how to live. Have your big meal in the middle of the day, then sleep it off. Is that how Bosnia was before the war?"

"Except for the food and the naps."

They laughed, enjoying the warmth and the smell of the sea, then returned to the hotel to find the information from Torello waiting as promised, copies for each tucked into their key slots.

"Efficient as a German," Pine said. "And on a Sunday."

"He'd very much like to know what we're really up to."

"I got that impression. Shit. What's this?" There was a pink phone message at the bottom of Pine's pile. "'Call ASAP. Urgent. Janet,'" he read aloud. "So much for a restful afternoon. You better come up. You can listen in. It's one of those places with an extension in the bathroom."

Janet Ecker answered in the middle of the first ring. She was at her desk on a Sunday, which was extraordinary enough. But her news was even bigger. "I've found the connection we were looking for," she announced.

"You mean the one between—"

"No need to say the names. Between the old one and the new one."

"You really think this kind of security is still necessary?"

"Probably pointless, especially considering what I've been up to all weekend."

"Which is?"

"Shaking every tree in the forest to see what might drop out. I've been in touch with all my old contacts in 'the community,' as you like to put it, so who knows how many alarms I've tripped along the way."

"But productive?"

"Not until an hour ago. I was beginning to feel like a teacher who'd walked into a classroom to find students cheating in the middle of an exam. Everybody was silent. Even scared. And I'm talking about people who are gossips by nature. They wouldn't even return my calls, and the few who did were no help. Then I got a telegram, of all things. In cipher. A code I still understand, fortunately. Directing me to an overnight-delivery service, where a package was waiting."

"Sent to a fake name, of course."

"Of course. Very cloak-and-dagger. Always part of the game with this one. But apparently the word had gone out: Say nothing to me or anyone at the tribunal."

"So what was it?"

"Copy of an old intercept, 1961, out of an NSA listening post in Zurich. Transmission from the Yugoslav Interior Ministry to Swiss banking authorities. Part of a Yugo search for looted federal assets via the State Bank of Croatia in April of '45. The meat of it was notes from a debriefing conducted by a military security officer at a coastal border post. He'd interrogated two repatriating Yugoslavs who'd come across the Adriatic. Pero Matek and Enver Petric. The officer questioned them for four hours and detained them overnight. Then he let them go. No charges. Curious, given the information they passed along."

"Which was?"

"Tales of gold they'd seen in Rome. Cratefuls. Plus all the dirt you'd care to dish on Father Draganovic. Names of fugitive war criminals who'd been spirited away, and so on."

"So why let them go?"

"Bribed, I'd guess. Either with money or privileged information."

"What makes you say that?"

"Common sense, for one thing. The name of the security officer, for another. An up-and-coming army lieutenant."

"Marko Andric," Vlado said.

"Exactly. He was twenty-two then. Spent the next thirty years working his way up the chain of command, which by the time Srebrenica fell left him in charge of a brigade in the Drina Corps. During all that time he requested permission to travel out-of-country at least six times. To follow up on whatever tips Matek and Petric might have given him, is my guess."

"He went to Italy?"

"We'll never know. Every request was denied. Not unusual, given his rank. They were always edgy about defectors. But he'd at least have had the clout to make sure Matek never left the country, either. Or Petric. Their names were probably on some sort of border-watch list. And when things might have started opening up in the years after Tito died, the war began, so Andric was still too busy to travel."

"Until now, when he drops out of sight the same day as Matek," Pine said. "After our friends Harkness and LeBlanc have arranged a joint operation to round them up."

"So maybe we really are looking for both of them," Vlado said.

"Then what would the so-called Popovic connection be?" Pine asked. Vlado found that he still flinched at the mention of the name. He braced for Pine to pass along news of the man's death, wondering how he'd explain it. But Ecker spoke first.

"Who knows?" she said. "Courier? Middleman? Or maybe just something out of Harkness's imagination to throw us off the trail. It seems to have worked with LeBlanc, anyway. Last I heard he was in Berlin, looking for him."

That was bad news, Vlado thought. And yet another point on which Harkness had apparently been telling the truth. Perhaps none of his warnings were bluffs.

"Now, if we only had better leads," Pine said.

"What *are* your leads?" Ecker asked.

"Lemon groves. That's about it. Matek and Petric may have worked in some, assuming they even lived here. All we've really got for proof is a label on the back of Vlado's photograph."

"Well, whatever you do, move fast. The way I've stirred things up, I have a feeling it's not going to be a very pleasant Monday around here."

CHAPTER TWENTY-THREE

Vlado and Pine were silent after hanging up. Pine came around the corner of the bathroom to find Vlado still seated on the edge of the tub. "I figured there was no sense mentioning Popovic was dead," Pine said delicately. "Not yet, anyway. There'd be too much explaining to do."

Vlado nodded, supposing he should feel grateful. He pondered what they'd just learned. Matek would likely find it easy to blend in here, having lived in Italy before. Andric would be a fish out of water. Everything about him—the way he dressed, the way he talked, per-haps even the food he ordered—should make him stand out, and thus be easier to find. If both were truly in town to retrieve two crates of gold, they'd need help, even if they knew where to look. Help from the docks, perhaps. Or a labor pool. Torello, the local cop, might know where to ask around, but that would involve telling him more than Pine wanted.

"Truck rentals," Vlado finally said. "That might be one place to start, if we really think one or both of them is here to haul buried treasure. Trucks and cheap labor, because it won't be a one-man job. Beyond that and the citrus groves, who knows?"

"Either way, you've got to figure it's a race. The news has been all over the papers about both of them, for anyone paying attention. Unless they've stayed in touch with each other." He looked toward Vlado with raised eyebrows. "Partners in crime, maybe?"

"You really think Matek's the sharing type?"

"No."

"Me neither."

Nor did Vlado believe that either Matek or Andric would necessarily pose the biggest threat. Harkness might be a third seeker of fortune in the formula, even if he was more interested in information than gold. A three-way race, then, between cutthroat competitors, each with his own brand of malice to answer for. If Vlado had his way, they'd bring Torello more fully into the picture, plus as many men as he could spare. Safety in numbers sounded like a good idea just now.

"Almost five," Pine said. "Might as well take that rest while I can. Maybe we can grab a light dinner later."

After their heavy lunch, Vlado didn't even want to think about food. What he needed more was a walk. Something to calm his worries. He wished he had another phone card, if only to check in briefly with Jasmina. He made a note to casually ask for a few more lire when Pine and he were out later.

"See you later, then," he said. "I'm going to have a look around the town."

"Tell Andric hello for me if you bump into him. Maybe he's at the hardware store, buying a shovel."

Andric and both of the others, Vlado thought. Strange how such a big place could seem so claustrophobic.

He exited the hotel harboring visions of a long, leisurely stroll, far into the hills and orchards above the town. But the first mile and the first few hundred feet of elevation reminded him of how weary he was. Too much strain, too much moving around. He'd slept in one strange bed after another, and faced too many strong and vivid revelations, their afterimages burned into his brain like a series of lurid photos. He, too, needed to lie down, despite his earlier nap in the car.

He returned to find a message from Pine right on the pillow, like a bedtime mint. Maybe later Pine would turn back his sheets for him, he thought, mildly irritated at the intrusion.

The message was simple and direct: "Vlado, call Robert Fordham." There was a number with a Rome area code. But his phone line was still blocked, irritating him further. No matter how much trust Vlado had earned, Pine was still being the loyal foot soldier about sticking to these silly security rules. Why, then, had Pine even bothered to leave him the message? Perhaps Fordham had called to offer another mea culpa. Or maybe he'd thought better of his confession, and wanted to recant. The whole business hit him wrong, so he strolled to Pine's door, knocking hard, even though he knew Pine was probably asleep.

"Just a minute," a faint voice answered. Pine poked his head out, hair in all directions, eyes bloodshot. "What time is it?"

"A little after six. I just got your message, but my phone's blocked, as you know, so I need to use yours."

"What message?"

"This one."

Pine frowned at the white slip of paper, examining the slanted handwriting in blue ink. It was written on hotel stationery.

"I didn't write that. Probably the front desk. Either way I guess you need my phone. Mind if I listen this time?"

"As long as it doesn't get too personal."

Vlado punched in the number, envying Pine the freedom of an open line. Perhaps he could coax a call home out of him later. A woman answered, saying something Vlado couldn't understand. Presumably it was Fordham's housekeeper, but when Vlado asked for him she rattled off something unintelligible. He tried the name he remembered.

"Maria?" he said, but that only produced another burst of babble, and when Vlado continued to flounder the woman hung up.

"That was weird," Pine shouted from the phone in the bathroom. "Almost sounded like an office. Maybe we can get someone at the desk to do it for us. They can at least translate long enough for us to find out what's going on."

They took the elevator, strolling up to the desk clerk.

"I need some help responding to the message you left," Vlado said.

"And your room number, sir?"

"Three-eleven."

The man turned, inspecting the key boxes. "I'm sorry, sir. You have no messages. Were you expecting a call?"

"No. This message." He held out the slip of paper from his pillow. The clerk eyed it curiously, knitting his brow. Vlado began to get an odd feeling. "It was delivered to my room."

"Not by anyone here, sir. There would have been a light flash-ing on your phone, and the message would be in your key box, or on the in-house voice mail. Perhaps a friend dropped by while you were out?"

Vlado and Pine exchanged worried glances.

"But it was on my pillow," Vlado said.

"Most unusual, sir. Just a moment." The clerk picked up a phone and made two quick calls, speaking only a few words each time, nodding briskly before hanging up.

"I'm sorry, sir, but neither the housekeeping staff nor the concierge has been in your room since you checked in. They'd be the only ones who could have delivered it. Unless you've entrusted someone with your key."

Vlado sighed, again exchanging glances with Pine.

"What do you think?" Pine said. What he thought was that Harkness must be in town. But if he said so, he might have to explain more than he wanted about the earlier run-ins. Telling Pine about Popovic was one thing. Telling him about the threats to his family was quite another. But Pine had apparently already reached the same conclusion from some other direction.

"Sounds like spook behavior to me. Harkness or LeBlanc, trying to shake you up. Unless LeBlanc really is in Berlin."

"Then what does the message mean?"

"Only one way to find out."

Pine turned back to the clerk, who was watching with interest. "Could you call this number for us? We tried from my room but couldn't get past the woman who answered. Neither of us speaks Italian. But it's this fellow, Fordham, who we're trying to reach."

"Certainly, sir. Let me see it again."

He dialed while they waited, muttering Fordham's name, just as Vlado had done earlier. "Uno momento," he said quickly, placing a hand over the receiver as he turned toward Vlado. "This Mr. Fordham. She wants to know if he is a patient."

"A patient?"

"Yes. This is a hospital you've called."

"I don't know. But he's not a doctor."

The clerk spoke some more, nodding, then picked up a pencil, taking a few notes. After a few moments he gently replaced the receiver and turned to them with an expression of grave concern. "I'm sorry," he said gently, "but your friend Mr. Fordham isn't taking any calls. He is in the critical-care unit just now." He paused, as if considering whether to continue. "I'm afraid they don't expect him to survive the night."

Vlado felt as if his stomach had dropped to his knees.

"Jesus!" Pine hissed behind him.

"Did she say why he was admitted?" Vlado said. "Was it his heart?"

"Some sort of seizure, apparently," the clerk said. "Of unknown origin. She said his illness was not yet diagnosed."

"That sounds like spook behavior, too," Pine said. "Of the worst possible kind."

CHAPTER TWENTY-FOUR

A wave of cold gray air rolled in overnight from the Bay of Naples. The false spring fled, and with it the sharp golden light that had scrubbed the town of its age and heaviness. The ocean had turned dark and choppy. The hills above the town had seemingly vanished, cloaked now by the drooping clouds. It was the sort of dreary winter morning, in other words, that made it difficult just to get out of bed.

Yet, even as Vlado and Pine were meeting for an early breakfast, Pero Matek was arriving refreshed and renewed, undaunted by the misty chill, at the entrance of the designated lookout post he'd scouted out the previous afternoon.

It was perfectly located, just across the street from a huge stone arch that would be the focus of his vigil. And because the chosen vantage point was a small and pleasant café, he wouldn't have to pass the time without warmth or sustenance. He sipped his first cup of coffee while scanning the surroundings. Besides the commanding view, the café also met his other needs—a rear exit, should he need one; suitably dim lighting, accentuated this morning by the prevailing gloom; and a calm and agreeable waitress, the sort who probably wouldn't mind letting an old man monopolize a single table as long as he tipped regularly and well, or even if he flirted just a bit.

The day before Matek had done a little shopping, buying some decent clothes, something more like what the locals wore. No more peasant garb; that look was gone forever. He felt a little embarrassed by the silly hat and these bulky sunglasses, especially on such a cloudy day. But cover was cover, and who knew whether the local police had been alerted, or perhaps even offered a photo.

Opening a newspaper, even as he glanced above the pages toward the massive arch, he fleetingly wondered what poor Azudin must be doing just now, the boy probably still in a panic after one of the mines had actually blown up as planned. At least he'd dutifully carried out his last orders. Although that would be the end of Azudin's career, of course. Just as well. The boy never could have stood up to all those country roughnecks. Now even the timid authorities of the Travnik municipality would probably feel emboldened to begin dismantling Matek's sprawling operation—after parceling out a percentage to their superiors, of course. He sighed. It had all been built with such patience and skill. Ah, well. Never too late to build something new, although this time his fortune would arrive ready-made.

He checked the time with the waitress, but only for the sake of precision, of keeping his bearings. It was far too soon to make any moves. He was here merely to watch and pass the time, playing out the idle hours and gathering information, while making sure no one beat him to the punch. Further action now might attract the attention of his competition. Best to let someone else move first. Then he would tend to the business of clearing the field for his final play.

His only other duty this morning was to recruit a young confederate, some lad with little to do and no schooling on his mind, and it wasn't long before he spotted a likely candidate lingering outside.

"Boy," he hissed, feeling proud that his accent had nearly returned to normal. "I've got something for a lad like you who might be willing to show a little initiative."

The child was probably around twelve. Old enough for the necessary stamina but probably still young enough to fear a tone of authority. He was wide-eyed, skinny, a little wary, too. Just the sort who'd appreciate an easy way to make a few thousand lire with a minimum of labor.

"How would you like to do a favor for me and make some money?" The boy backed away from the table just a shade. "Nothing to do with me, mind you." No sense having the boy think he was some sort of old fairy. "I just need someone to help me watch that old stone gate over there. The arch across the street. *Sì?*"

He held forward two 10,000-lira notes. More money than the boy would probably see for a month. The eyes lit up. Perfect.

"*Sì,*" the boy said eagerly.

"There's a man I'm waiting for," Matek said, lowering his voice so the boy would lean closer. "A man who will be going through that entrance, then leaving through it once he's done his business. You won't need to recognize him, because I'll be watching for him. But it might be hours before he comes. He might not come at all. But if he does, and when he exits, I'd like you to follow him. I'm old and can't do it myself, so I need a set of fresh legs like your own. He'll be from out of town, so he'll be going back to some pension or hotel. I just need to know which one, and which room. It would mean a lot to me." Matek unfolded five more 10,000-lira notes, holding on to them this time. "And these would be yours if you can find that out. Can you do that? Do you have the day to spend for a nice wage like this?"

The boy nodded solemnly, as if too stunned by his good turn of fortune to speak.

"Good," Matek said, smiling warmly. "That's very good. So when any man passes through that arch, you look my way. And when it's finally the right one, I'll nod and raise this newspaper in the air. Like this. You see?"

The boy nodded gravely once again.

"Very good then. And remember, this could take hours, even all day. You're okay with that, right?"

"*Sì*," the boy said, regaining his voice. And without further prompting he left the café, taking up a station just across the street in a Plexiglas bus shelter that would protect him from the rain and mist yet allow a full view in both directions. He took out his new money from time to time, scrutinizing it as if fearful it might have vanished, or transmuted to mere paper. But after a while he seemed convinced that there was nothing illusory about the day's windfall, and he settled down stoically to await the call to action.

Satisfied that he had chosen well, Matek settled back into his chair and resumed the guise of studying his newspaper, even reading a line or two. He might as well find some way to pass the time. But if there was one thing that an old man knew, it was patience. And after fifty-two years of waiting, what did one more day matter?

By early afternoon, Matek had removed his sunglasses, deciding that on a cloudy day they attracted more attention than they deflected. The ridiculous hat remained in place, if only because it seemed perfectly in keeping with what his local contemporaries wore. He had read six different newspapers cover to cover, and his young confederate across the way had seemed in danger of nodding off several times already. Matek was bored with his table, bored with the view, bored with the tired old arch that stared back at him with nothing but grayness. He was bored as well with the seemingly endless clatter issuing from the café's kitchen. But his waitress, though not as attractive as he would have liked, had been tolerant and polite. Only an older man would have been allowed to get away with this sort of camping out, he reflected, while ordering only a few coffees, a light lunch, and a bottle of mineral water. Or maybe it was his generous tips that had done the trick.

From time to time he had experienced fleeting bouts of panic. Perhaps he'd arrived too late. Maybe his quarry had come and gone. Or worse, perhaps the items he'd come for were gone altogether. Discovered and looted years ago, merely by chance. He'd certainly heard of worse luck. But such moments passed quickly. He'd planned too well and for too long to be upstaged even by ill fortune.

Then, looking up once again from his paper, as he weighed whether he could stomach yet another cup of coffee, he saw a face that banished all thoughts of failure. The man was across the street, walking slowly, headed straight for the arch. He, too, wore a hat, although his had not been as wisely chosen—no one in this town would be caught dead in it. In fact, to Matek's eye the man's entire appearance, from his clothes to his movements, screamed Balkan with a capital B, even if he doubted anyone from around here had a similarly discerning eye.

The boy, fortunately, was paying attention, and sprang to his feet the moment Matek gave the sign, nodding and raising the rolled-up paper as if preparing to scold a dog.

The man paused for a moment, then passed beneath the arch. He had gone gray at the temples, gray all over, in fact, and he seemed rounder toward the middle. Matek had seen enough newspaper photos to know what changes to expect. And the eyes, he knew, would be the same—the cool blue-gray that, so many years ago, had alerted him to the likelihood that this fellow was a hard bargainer, but a bargainer nonetheless.

But wait, Matek thought, setting down his paper, leaning forward across the table. Who was that lagging in the man's wake, floating to the rear as if on a long leash, if only the first man had the gumption to realize it? That was one of the pitfalls of being a general, Matek supposed. You grew accustomed to having others watch your back. Because it was clear this second fellow was paying attention, using too many of the old tricks to be anything other than a shadow, a man on the make, now pausing to light a cigarette, then simply waiting, just like the boy, with his eyes on the arch.

Or might it only be his imagination, because now the man was departing, well before his quarry had emerged. He was even heading in this direction, glancing toward the café, stopping outside at the rack of newspapers, and for the briefest moment he seemed to glance toward Matek, who retreated behind his paper, peeping above the edges to see that the man was again simply gazing at the newsstand, scanning the headlines. Was he local? Perhaps. Or British. That would be the better guess. Then the figure turned and headed back the way he had come, stopping occasionally to glance in a shop window, but inexorably heading out of sight.

A false alarm, it seemed, but one Matek could have done without.

It was another fifteen minutes before the first man emerged back through the arch, and the boy was off on his pursuit like a cat, as if he'd been born to the job. Matek smiled, briefly even considering a tip once the boy returned with the information.

But, no, he concluded. A bargain was a bargain. Besides, he'd soon have more pressing business to attend to.

CHAPTER TWENTY-FIVE

Vlado Petric and Calvin Pine worked fast on Monday, just as they'd hoped, but their labors produced little more than sore feet and empty stomachs. They hired an interpreter and roamed the suddenly chilly town from its docks to its foggy hillsides, checking pensions and truck-rental agencies, citrus growers and labor pools. But none of it turned up any sign of Matek or Andric, or even anyone with a Balkan name or connection.

Their visit to one of the lemon growers was typical—half an hour of waiting to see the boss, even though this was the slow season, a time for pruning and bookkeeping. At the first mention of employment records the man gave them a wary sidelong glance, as if sniffing a sting operation by labor regulators. He went so far as to hint at a possible bribe before being convinced they were truly who they said they were. At which point he lost interest altogether, assuring them that in the years following the war, workers had come and gone like fruit flies, too numerous and insignificant to count, much less keep any record of their names and wages. Payroll taxes? Those were for chumps, for men of little influence and less intelligence. Don't trouble me again, gentlemen, unless you have something serious to discuss.

"He reminded me of some of my father's clients back home," Pine remarked. "That's probably how he still thinks of his employees, as fruit flies."

But it was the perfect sort of supervisory attitude, Vlado figured, if you were a worker trying not to be noticed or traced. With employers like that, this would have been an easy place to lie low in the chaotic years following the war.

They returned to the hotel at dusk. Vlado was heading toward the elevator with his key when Pine groaned from behind him at the front desk. Vlado turned to see him holding another phone message.

"Janet again?"

"Worse. Here."

It was a fax on tribunal letterhead, and the message was as terse as a telegram.

```
Contact Chief Prosecutor Contreras at once at
the following number. Make no further contacts,
repeat, NONE, by phone, interview or otherwise
with regard to this case. Return passage booked.
Details to follow. Spratt.
```

Vlado checked the timeline across the top. The fax had arrived two hours ago.

"Then there's this one," Pine said, holding aloft a second sheet. "Came in a few minutes ago. Our itinerary. Ten a.m. flight out of Rome, meaning we'll have to leave around five in the morning if we're going to make it."

"They're recalling us?"

"Sure looks that way. Let's hope it's either the result of a hot tip or a change in strategy. Care to listen in?"

Vlado felt suddenly panic-stricken. To come all this way and feel they were so close to a breakthrough, only to be recalled, or perhaps redeployed, although his better judgment told him the former was likelier. For the moment his only solace was imagining Spratt's reaction, his ears spouting steam like those of a cartoon character.

"C'mon," Pine said. "Let's get it over with."

Vlado took up his appointed listening post on the edge of the tub. The only noise was the slow drip of the bathroom sink. A secretary answered and quickly patched them through, then Contreras came onto the line with the brusque tone of a news bulletin, without the slightest pleasantry or preamble. He was no longer playing the gracious and charming grandee, the welcoming cheerleader for justice in all nations. He was instead the imperious judge issuing a fiery proclamation from the bench.

"Are you aware, Mr. Pine, that between you and your partner's actions, as well as those of Janet Ecker, the American State Department has now lodged an official complaint with my office?" His voice had risen on the word *official*, as if that put their transgressions on a par with mass murder. "They say, and not without some justification, from what I've heard at my end, that you've been inquiring into matters and places that are completely out of bounds. And frankly I can't help but wonder what sort of freelance operation the three of you are running. Can you tell me that?"

"None, sir. We're just pursuing leads on the possible whereabouts of—"

"Pursuing leads? Do you refer to harassing an elderly former intelligence agent as merely pursuing leads? To the point where he has apparently suffered some sort of stroke? Or poking around old intelligence files, not even officially declassified, as merely pursuing leads?"

"We were harassing no one, sir. The man spoke to us of his own free will."

"The same man, I presume, who for years has been discredited as hopelessly unreliable. To the point that he became an embarrassment to his own government and was relieved of his duties. But nonetheless, he, too, filed an official complaint about your behavior, before his misfortune."

"Fordham? But he's . . . he spoke to us willingly."

"We received it straight from the American embassy in Rome this morning."

Pine said nothing in response. Janet Ecker had been right. Someone was pulling out all the stops, and it could only have been Harkness and those above him.

"Exactly what you're trying to accomplish, none of us are sure," Contreras continued. "But given the level of betrayal we seem to have experienced on this case to date, involving not just the escape of Andric but that of Matek as well, several of us have begun to question the motives of all of you. And bringing in the Bosnian on this, which I'm told was your idea, was our first mistake."

"My idea?"

"We were wrong to expect objectivity from a native. His personal connection to all this only made matters sloppier once things began to fall apart."

Vlado realized Contreras wasn't aware he was on the line, and he would have hung up then and there if it wouldn't have drawn attention to his presence.

"As for you and Miss Ecker," Contreras continued, "whatever grudges you may have against your old employers obviously have no place in your current work."

"But we—"

"Enough. This is not the proper forum for defending or explaining yourself. There will be ample time for that on your return. You're to leave Italy tomorrow, and in the meantime you're to make no further calls, conduct no further interviews, and pursue no further 'leads,' as you choose to call them. And you're expressly forbidden from any further contact with local law enforcement. There's nothing to be gained from disseminating our embarrassment any further. Clear on all counts?"

"Very clear."

"Report to me as soon as you arrive. Bring Spratt with you, as well as the Bosnian. He'll be discharged from employment and returned to Berlin. The sooner the better. Until tomorrow, then."

"Yes, sir."

Contreras hung up, the voice vanishing as instantly as a tornado that had moved on down the road.

So this was how it would end, Vlado mused as the line went dead. He raised the mute receiver like a hammer, then brought it down across the edge of the tub, cracking the porcelain as well as the receiver. Let the tribunal pay the damages, he thought savagely, his elbow aching with the shock of the blow. He gazed at the dripping sink, still tapping out the seconds, then he rose stiffly from his uncomfortable perch. The jolts and agonies of the past several days had been difficult, but they had at least led to the doorstep of discovery, or so it had seemed. Now he would be turned away before even knocking, and all he'd have for his trouble would be the humiliation of a peremptory dismissal. Sent home like a boy who had misbehaved at summer camp. He wondered vaguely what had become of all the grand promises of resettlement, of finding him a new job as an investigator, but none of that seemed relevant now. At least his family would be safe, although who even knew if that would hold true if LeBlanc or Harkness leaked word on the fate of Popovic.

"Sorry you had to hear that," Pine said, appearing at the bath-room door. "Pretty brutal."

Vlado nodded, too angry to speak.

"I'm sorry, Vlado. You've been treated terribly. And for what it's worth, using you *wasn't* my idea. Well, you know where it came from. But I guess somebody has already started rewriting the history."

"Yes. Funny how that keeps happening."

"If I—"

"Never mind," Vlado said. He was quivering, uncertain whether from his temper or from his anguish. "Just . . . never mind."

"Well," Pine said, at a loss. "I guess there's nothing left but to sit tight. We'll get some sleep and clear out as early as possible in the morning. Maybe later we can grab some dinner, if you feel up to it."

Vlado could think of no suitable reply, so he left, walking numbly to his room. After shutting the door he sat on the bed a few minutes. Then he rose to unlock the small refrigerator of the minibar, peering inside at the neat row of soft drinks, spirits, and beer. He selected a small bottle—Scotch, not at all his favorite, but it would do, and so would the rest of the little bottles, regardless of their contents. Once again, the tribunal could pay the damn tab. He would drink the place dry. Call out for room service.

But halfway through the first swallow he found he had no taste for it, and he poured the rest down the sink before changing his mind. He opened the window, then the shutters, gazing up into the dim haze of the hills, the contours of the land barely visible in the evening gloom. It was too cold to look for long, so he shut the win-dow, the room now raw with the dampness of the sea air. Then he lay back on the bed, shoes on. The red digital display of the clock on the bedside table said 5:37. The people in the streets were headed home to meals and quiet evenings. The end of the workday. And then he remembered Amira, and her invitation to call. Perhaps she had found the names, the ones from the Red Cross passports, if they'd ever even existed. Officially, it was now useless information, he supposed. But only if you were working for the tribunal. He'd just been as good as fired. So why obey orders when all promises have been broken? He sat up, reaching eagerly for the phone. He was still a policeman, still a curious son, eager to learn what he could. Without thinking he punched the number for an outside line, only to be connected to the night manager, who politely reminded him that his line was blocked.

Of course, he thought. Never trusted and never really considered anything but a utility, a lubricant for a rough and hasty coupling that had gone awry from the beginning. That angry thought was enough to get him out the door and down the stairs, his heart beating in the way that fingers drum a desktop in impatience and irritation. He ran the stairs, too impatient for the elevator, then burst through the lobby, barreling into the evening air as he threw on his overcoat. It took only five minutes to hunt down a *tabacchi*, where he used the lire he'd cadged from Pine the night before to buy a phone card. Then he found a nearby machine and dialed Amira's home number, pen and notebook at the ready.

She answered immediately, sounding as eager as Janet Ecker had yesterday. Happy, even. "I think I found what you were looking for," she said. "Two names. Both Italian, with birth dates matching the ones you gave me. Do you have something to write with?"

When she was finished he thanked her, told her he'd be in touch, then hung up, sorry to be so abrupt but wanting to preserve every possible second on the card. A block later he ducked into a café. When a waiter approached he reached for his wallet, calculating what he might be able to afford. But all he really wanted now, he realized, was time, so he waved the man away, then rummaged in his satchel until he found the photo.

"An Italian name," he said to himself in a low voice, scanning his father's face, then the woman's. "So who is this woman you're with, Signor Giuseppe DiFlorio? Your lover? Your wife? My stepmother, even? And is she still alive?"

He carried his satchel to the bar, marshaling the fragments of his meager Italian. "*Telefono libro?*" he asked uncertainly.

"*Sì,*" the barman answered, stepping a few feet away and reaching low for a thin, dog-eared volume, which he plopped onto the polished counter.

"*Grazie.*"

"*Prego.*"

There were eleven DiFlorios listed. If she'd remarried—presuming she'd even been his wife to begin with—then none of these would do the trick. But assuming she hadn't, and that she'd stayed, and that she was still alive—a weight of assumptions that suddenly seemed crushing—then she might be one of these eleven. He was that close, perhaps. So he scribbled every number and dropped the book back onto the bar, strolling past the baffled waiter back to the phone box outside, where he inserted his card and began punching in the first number.

But with his limited Italian, what would he say? Even if he were fluent, he wasn't sure he'd know how to proceed. "Hello. My father had the same last name as you and may have been your husband, can we talk?" Slow down, he told himself. Hang up and think this through.

Torello, he thought. He was the only hope. So he cradled the receiver and began walking toward the station, an investigator once again on the prowl.

CHAPTER TWENTY-SIX

In a small, gloomy pension a few miles across town, General Marko Andric decided that it was no use pretending he was a man of the world. He had been traveling for three days yet still couldn't shake his uneasiness over being in a foreign land. In a word, he was homesick. And to think of all the times in years past when he had tried so hard to come to this very place, only to fail to secure permission. It had taken help from one of the enemy to finally make it possible, but now that he was here he was spending most of his waking hours feeling awkward and uncomfortable.

To his mind, the only way to cover new ground was with an army, a consort at your fore and aft, tramping along in common cause. And his landscape of choice was rolling green hills, not these bare crags that tumbled straight into the sea.

The most jarring problem had been the language, an endless stream of bafflement that gave him headaches and made him feel like a child. The words here were like rubber balls, slippery and bouncing, moving so fast you could only grasp one or two at a time. By the time you had your pocket dictionary out, another twenty had bounded past.

The food, at least, was worthwhile, but even that was growing tiresome. What he'd really like now was a slab of meat, grilled to the bone, a substantial piece, not a mere slice or a few medallions like they always served you here. He pulled out a cigarette. Those, at least, were the same everywhere now. The American cowboy who ruled the world. After a few puffs he felt better, but he was worn out, sleepy. The strangeness of his journey had been giving him nightmares. Or that's what he chose to blame for the visions that had been visiting him lately.

The previous evening he had awakened in the dark believing that the dead were reaching out for him from the walls and floor, where they writhed like worms, their rotting fingertips outstretched, brushing against his bare arms and legs. Twisted faces loomed above him, cursing incomprehensibly. Speaking Italian, no doubt. He jolted to his senses, sitting upright and turning on the bedside lamp, comforted to find the walls bare and quiet. The ceiling was a blank. Children were shooting firecrackers outside in the street below. That must have caused it all, he told himself. But the taste in his mouth said otherwise. It was all too familiar. Lands, languages, and cuisine might change, but the chalky dust of Srebrenica still coated his tongue, as if his system were unable to expel it. Even now, in the wake of a late-afternoon rest, he could taste just a hint. So he set aside his cigarette and rose to rinse his mouth in the bathroom sink.

It was lonely, this way of living, and as he turned on the tap, swallowing, spitting, he wondered how long he'd have to endure it. His bare feet were chilly against the floor. Still cold and damp outside, he supposed, flipping back the shutter to see the clouds that had been settling on the town throughout the day. The daylight was nearly gone. Good. In a few hours, then, if all went as scheduled, everything would be over. Any moment he should have a visitor, someone who spoke his language, no less.

The thought was enough to get him moving, throwing on his clothes and allowing himself some excitement. Taught by experience and rigid training never to expect anything to go smoothly, he had taken a while to finally begin believing this might happen, that everything might really come off without a hitch. He'd been feeling that way a few hours now. Ever since he'd made his furtive reconnaissance, strolling past the place where the items were said to be stored. Thinking of the walk, he reached into his pocket. Finding nothing, he experienced a momentary panic. But at last there it was, rolled into a crease of the fabric. The old key. How amazing, he thought, that it still fit the lock. He had tried it, ever so briefly, turning it just enough to slide back the bolt without opening the door. Then he'd quickly relocked it. Too many visitors around at that hour to feel comfortable enough to do more. It would be more amazing yet if everything was still inside. But such things were possible, he knew, having seen it happen in his own land—secrets going to ground in one conflict, only to be resurrected in another.

For a while during his walk he'd thought that he'd seen his contact, his benefactor, so to speak, although it wasn't as if the man's services came free of charge. It had been the briefest of glances, an eerie sense of footfalls that seemed to match his own. But when he'd turned for a look he'd seen nothing but a small boy and a man gazing at a rack of newspapers.

The moment had unnerved him enough to give him second thoughts about continuing his walk. And what if someone recognized him, or started to ask questions? He'd been jittery that way since crossing the border, too nervous to even read a paper or turn on the news, for fear of seeing his own face. Better to lie low, now that the hour was approaching. So much planning, and it had all come down to a single evening.

But now, as if in answer to his thoughts, there was a knock at the door. The maid, perhaps? Or was it someone he was expecting?

"Yes?" he said, easing toward the door, reaching for the gun that bulged from a pocket in a jacket hanging by a brass hook.

"Marko? It's me."

So it really was him, then, speaking his own tongue, although with the slightest difference in tone and timbre from how he sounded on the phone. He'd swear that much of the man's accent was gone, too. Or maybe it was just nerves. But it was such a relief to hear words he could understand that he neglected to take the gun from the pocket. His guest was early, but any good general knew that even the most careful plans changed and shifted.

So he opened the door unarmed, his first and last mistake. Staring back at him was an entirely different face from the one he'd expected, although it, too, seemed oddly familiar. Who is this old man, he wondered, but before he could ask he found himself staring at the barrel of a gun, a thick ugly thing with something heavy jammed on the end. A silencer, he surmised. Not a good sign, even to someone so open to changes in plans.

"I know you, don't I?" he said, realizing as the words were out exactly who it was. "Oh my God. Yes. From the border."

The man nodded. He seemed to be wheezing, just a bit out of breath.

"Yes, now you remember," the old man said. "And you've come here to rob me blind. So I thought I might drop by for my key. So I'll have it now, if you don't mind. Just tell me where it is. And no reaching into drawers or pockets, please, unless you want our little chat to end prematurely."

The general was still trying to remember the man's name. Matek? Or was it Petric? He couldn't remember which of them had been the talker, the schemer, the one who'd ultimately come up with the plan that won his approval. But the man was now waving the gun in a very disagreeable manner, and General Andric felt his stomach going queasy, rolling on its side like a foundering ship. He wanted to burp, or worse, already tasting the chalkiness of the bile rising in his throat, flavored by the infernal dust. He licked his lips, a sticky sound.

"It's in my pants pocket," he answered, shamed by the quavering of his voice. His performance was dishonorable, and the general imagined his staff watching from the doorway, eyes downcast with disgrace as they witnessed his humiliation, the old warrior melting into a pile of jelly. It was this thought, finally, that rallied him, and with a sudden twisting lunge he reached for the hateful barrel, once again a soldier on the attack.

He died a soldier's death, shot full in the front with two thumping, whooshing impacts and a pair of great yellow flashes, throwing him clear to the window, where the rear of his head struck the sill with the loudest bang yet. Slumping to the floor, back pressed to the wall, he looked down to see his entrails wriggling free like a nest of wet snakes. It made an awful slurping noise, all the more surreal for its painlessness. He felt only a vast and empty cold down there. Then, pouring into his head, a great rush of heat and blackness, as if someone had torn open a door at the top of his spine. A nimble claw of a hand darted into his pants pocket, probing frantically, and the last thing the general heard was the voice of a gleeful old man, like some old troll in the woods. Or perhaps it was only a neighborly farmer from back home.

"There you are," the voice croaked. "Just as I left you."

CHAPTER TWENTY-SEVEN

Vlado was relieved to find Torello still at his desk. But the man's first question was the very one Vlado hadn't wanted to answer. "Where is your American colleague?"

"Mr. Pine is back at the hotel."

Torello seemed to consider the response with great deliberation. Normally that would be a bad sign, an indication that maybe Vlado was about to be shown the door, exposed as the rogue operative he'd become.

But Torello wasn't frowning, wasn't nervous or reaching for his phone. If anything, he seemed a trifle pleased.

"Tell me," he said at last, "you're not authorized to be here, are you? On your own like this."

Vlado decided to level with him. "We've been taken off the case. It seems we've become an irritant to U.S. authorities. So I'm not here as a representative of the tribunal. I'm now working for myself, mostly because my father was a colleague of the older suspect. Which I wasn't aware of until a few days ago, when the tribunal roped me into this job. So for me it's strictly personal."

Torello eyed him a moment. Now the question was whether he'd play along.

"A missing-persons case, then, is that how you'd characterize it? But no longer a war-crimes manhunt. In case my superiors ask later."

He said it with the beginnings of a smile. Vlado sensed a compatriot, even if he wasn't sure why.

"Exactly."

"It's nice that we agree. Coffee? You look like you could use some."

"Yes."

"And please," Torello said, pulling a cigarette pack from his jacket. "Feel free to smoke. This isn't America, you know."

"So you don't like Americans?"

"Far from it. I think Americans are wonderful. Especially their women, who seem to think Italian men are wonderful, as long as we're taken in limited doses." Torello's smile widened.

Yes, Vlado could just imagine him during the tourist season. The dark good looks that the rest of the world had come to expect of young Italian men. Slim and at ease, hair falling perfectly across the forehead, the impeccable English, and just enough sun in his face to suggest a man of action.

"But let's face it," Torello continued. "How often do people like you and me, from countries that generally remain on the sidelines, get the chance to do what we damn well please, especially when people from rather powerful embassies are demanding that we do otherwise? This fax, for instance, landed on my desk just this afternoon."

He handed it to Vlado. It was a message from the U.S. State Department urging police authorities to please check with embassy contacts in Rome before cooperating with any investigators claiming to be searching for suspects Marko Andric or Pero Matek, due to unspecified "diplomatic irregularities."

"They shout. We jump. And look at the two of us, speaking their language. But I will uphold the letter of this memo, of course." He held aloft the fax. "So if, for example, an official representative of the tribunal were to happen to telephone, looking for a missing colleague, I would of course have to refer him to these instructions, and say nothing. But a missing-persons case for a visiting policeman from Bosnia? That's another matter altogether."

Vlado let a moment pass, assessing the gravity of the leap he was about to make with Torello's help. He worried mostly about his family. He'd likely have a day, perhaps less, before being run to ground, either by Pine or by Harkness. He also worried on Pine's behalf, not wanting to ruin the man's career, although at one level he felt that Pine might actually approve. And if not? Likable or not, Pine and the tribunal had used him, and Vlado had earned his shot at rebellion.

"So, then," Torello said. "What brought you back in here, looking for help?"

"These names." He handed Torello the scribbled sheet of paper with the names DiFlorio and Barzini at the top, plus the eleven phone numbers below.

"DiFlorio was my father's name while he was here. Barzini was Matek. They probably arrived in the summer of '46, and stayed until '61. Then they went back to Yugoslavia. Why, I'm not sure, but my guess is that they had to leave in a hurry. Maybe some of the Ustasha people had finally found them. And they may have left something behind. Something Matek might have come back for." Vlado paused. This was the one piece of information he still felt uncomfortable about disclosing, but there seemed to be no other choice.

"They may have left behind two crates of gold bars, plus some documents that the United States, even today, might find embarrassing. Even damaging, for some people."

Torello leaned back in his chair, exuding an almost boyish pleasure as he steepled his hands in the air. *"Fantastico,"* he said in a low voice. "No wonder everyone is in such a, how would they say it, a tizzy. A lather. Perfect." Then his smile faded. "But those names. I'm afraid those alone won't do us much good."

"There was also this," Vlado said, and he placed the old photograph on Torello's desk, then explained why he'd copied the eleven phone numbers.

"I was going to try simply calling them—a wild shot, I know."

"A crapshoot, yes." Torello seemed to enjoy collecting scraps of American slang as much as Vlado.

"But, well, I don't speak Italian. Only a few words."

"I could make the calls for you, of course, but do we really want to start asking families all over town questions about this, getting them gossiping about who knows what? I don't think so. Checking records, that would be better." He looked at his watch. "I have a friend in the municipal authority who might be able to let us in after hours—marriage licenses, vital statistics, that kind of thing. But we can try here first. Police records. If your man Matek is as devious as his sheet from Interpol indicates, I can't imagine him being able to stay anywhere fifteen years without getting into some kind of scrape. Come on. Into the basement."

It took only twenty minutes. Torello thumbed open a few dusty ledgers, indexing arrests and incident reports from decades prior to

1970. The rest had been computerized. The first line to catch their attention was a smuggling case from 1953. The suspect was Piro Barzini. His date of birth matched the one on the Red Cross passport. The charges were dropped.

"But look," Torello said, thumbing to another page. "This one is better."

It was a 1961 citation, the report of an accidental death by drowning. There were two victims: Giuseppe DiFlorio and Piro Barzini.

"It seems they decided on the ultimate exit for their return home, one that would leave no expectation of return. Some sort of boating accident. With no bodies recovered, of course. And look. They both had wives."

So his father had married here. Even though Vlado had expected as much, the news went down like a ball of lead in his stomach. Torello was still staring into the book, oblivious to the effect of his words. But when Vlado remained silent the man turned, seeing right away what had happened.

"I'm sorry," he said. "This must be hard for you."

Vlado shook his head, cleared his throat. "What were their names?" he asked in a quiet voice.

Torello turned back to the ledger.

"Lia. And Gianna. Lia DiFlorio and Gianna Barzini. And if Lia is that woman in your picture, she probably still thinks of herself as your father's widow."

"If she's still alive."

"Let's see those phone numbers."

Lia DiFlorio was the seventh name on the list.

"Her address is the same as in the police report. Still no guarantee she's alive. Her children might have kept the listing in her name."

"Children. I hadn't even considered that."

"Would you like me to call?" Vlado swallowed hard. He nodded. "Come on, then. Back up to my office."

Torello pushed the numbers on the phone, then they waited. Just about everyone had cleared out of the station. There was no sound but the hum of the fax machine. The light of the desk lamp pooled around them as if they were characters on a small stage.

Vlado heard the line click, followed by a faint "*Sì?*"

"*Buona sera,*" Torello said. The rest was gibberish to Vlado, a rapid exchange that for all he knew was with a son or daughter, or someone else altogether. It was probably better not knowing what was being said. Just learn everything at once.

"*Sì, sì,*" Torello finally said emphatically, waving his free hand in the air. "*Prego. Ciao.*" Then he hung up. "It's her. And she will see us. Tonight."

Vlado nodded, not quite convinced it was happening.

"I think she's as curious as you, actually."

"What did you tell her? What did she say?"

"I told her I was a policeman, of course, and asked if her husband had been Giuseppe DiFlorio, the man reported drowned in 1961. She said yes. After that the rest wasn't so hard. I told her we had some new information about the events of those years, but mostly I wanted to ask her about one of her husband's friends from those times. Piro Barzini. She sort of scoffed, and said something about Barzini not being much of a friend. And I told her I was with a colleague of mine from Yugoslavia who might be able to offer her more information. She seemed to find that a little strange, as you might expect. She even sounded a little fearful, for whatever that's worth. But I wouldn't say she was alarmed. Then she invited us over, but asked us to give her a while to prepare. Meaning, I'm sure, that she needs time to cook for us. She's that type, I'm positive. It could be three a.m. and she would feel like she has to feed us."

"Just as well. I never ate lunch."

"Then she will love you like a son."

Torello reddened, having let the words go before realizing their import. But Vlado didn't mind. The moment had become so dreamlike that nothing would have jarred him. Well, almost nothing. He hesitated before asking the next question.

"Does she have children?"

"I didn't ask. She lives alone, for what it's worth. But I'd rather you be the one who asks that question."

"Did you tell her . . . anything else about me?"

"I'll leave that to you as well. As hard as this is for you, it's probably going to be worse for her, finding out that her husband lived, what, another twenty-two years? You'd better bring that photo with us. She may need some convincing. And we should leave now. It's a good half hour of driving. She's way up in the hills."

The sidewalks of the town were crowded with people heading for dinner or straggling home. As the car began to climb, the road narrowed, and after about ten minutes they eased into a forest, then an open field, the road twisting as it rose. Halfway up the hillside they pulled free of the dense bank of clouds that had squatted on the town all day. The stars were out, and as Vlado gazed through the windshield he thought: I am going to my father's old house. He wondered if this road had once been a daily route home from work. He turned to look back down the hill, but the town had disappeared, its lights a pale yellow smudge against the clouds.

He felt awkward from the moment they entered the door, the old woman nervous and fussing, flour on her hands, her apron still tied at the waist. The place smelled of spices and steam, a pot of pasta on the boil. But Vlado's senses were on full alert for other reasons. He felt shamefully like a bloodhound, an intruder. A spy scenting and searching for any sign of a past life, any remnant of a presence that had vanished thirty-seven years ago. That meant scanning the walls for pictures and looking for any sign of recognition in the woman's eyes. He remembered all too well the way Fordham had immediately noted his resemblance to his father. Perhaps she would detect it, too, although Fordham had held the advantage of knowing the name Petric, and what that might signify. She'd probably never heard that name in her life.

The woman watched Torello and him closely as they walked together into her living room, but the scrutiny was more in the manner of someone unaccustomed to visitors, of a wary soul assessing strangers who'd arrived after dark—and both of them policemen, no less.

She didn't speak English, so they agreed that Torello would handle the questions, translating for Vlado along the way. "I'll identify you as a Bosnian cop who has an interest in some of the events from her past," Torello had said on their way up the hill. "You can get more specific if you'd like."

It had been too dark to get a good look at the outside of the house. It was set back from the road in the crease of the hill. But in front of a stone outcrop to the left was a nearby grove of what looked like citrus trees. A welter of bushes and briars was on the right. Inside, the plaster walls were old and cracked but whitewashed clean. The glimpse of her kitchen as they strolled past revealed an ancient stove—reminiscent of the one at Aunt Melania's—with every burner in use.

As Torello and he settled onto the couch, Vlado saw a small framed photo in a far corner. Without thinking he crossed the room for a better look. Yes, he saw with a leap in his heart, it was Lia with his father. The photo had probably been taken within a year or so of the one in his satchel, but this one was from down on the beach. Round stones at their feet, clear waters behind them, with a steaming ferry visible in the distance. They wore the same look of deep contentment, or so he supposed. But it was the only photo in sight. No snaps of children, or babies, or anyone else. And no sign of Matek.

"*Scusi,*" Vlado said, employing his limited Italian when he realized that both Lia and Torello were staring at him, Torello somewhat uneasily. He returned to the couch, then Torello began speaking. Vlado quickly lost track of the conversation, but he did hear the name Piro Barzini and saw the woman frown. She said a few words in a low voice, then Torello turned to translate.

"I'm afraid this isn't going to be easy, and maybe not even productive. She seems very reluctant. She says her memory of those times is hazy. But I think it might be more of the case that the memories aren't very pleasant. At least as far as Barzini is concerned. The moment I mentioned he was really our focus, she seemed to clam up. But if you have any ideas—"

"Yes," Vlado said. "Perhaps if we showed her the photo. The one that I have."

"I'm not sure. Maybe it is too soon."

"But it will gives us some credibility."

"Or maybe it will just shock her. She's an old woman. Perhaps we should leave her in peace."

"I'm afraid it's too late for that. If she finds out somehow that Barzini is still alive—and let's face it, he'll end up in the papers, one way or another—do you think she'll be in peace then, wondering if her husband might have lived as well?"

Torello frowned. "Okay, then. Go ahead."

Vlado pulled the photo from his bag, knowing he was about to rob this woman of part of her history, a loss he knew acutely. He handed it facedown to Torello, who presented it to Lia DiFlorio. Her expression changed immediately, from stubborn skepticism to alarm.

She and Torello exchanged words in Italian, then she looked quickly at Vlado with wide eyes, a look of wonderment.

"She wants to know where you got it," Torello translated.

Then the woman spoke again, and this time Vlado understood every word.

"Where did that come from?" she asked. Her language was Serbo-Croatian, and somehow Vlado wasn't a bit surprised. Now it was Torello's turn to feel left out, but as he opened his mouth Vlado silenced him with an upraised hand.

"I'm Slovenian," she said, still facing Vlado. Slovenia, yet another ethnic fragment of Yugoslavia that had come loose in the recent upheaval, forming its own state to the north of Croatia and escaping virtually all of the fighting. But that hadn't been the case in the previous war, of course. "From near the border," she continued. "Not far from Trieste."

"So that is how you met . . ." Vlado stopped short, having nearly said "my father." "That is how you met Giuseppe DiFlorio. Because you spoke his language?"

She shook her head. Quite gravely, Vlado thought. She'd set her lips in a tight line. "No. When I met him he was known as Josip Iskric. He was a guard, and I was a prisoner. At the Jasenovac camp, during the war. You know of it?"

"Yes." Vlado swallowed hard, his throat gone dry. "I know of it. But you should tell me your story. Then I'll tell you mine. I think we have a few things in common."

"What's going on?" Torello asked. "She speaks your language?"

"Things are very complicated," Vlado replied tersely in English. "I hope you don't have any urgent appointments. We may be here awhile."

CHAPTER TWENTY-EIGHT

"We weren't at the camp long," she said. "Only about a month in all. We must have been some of the last arrivals. Just one busload from some of the fighting in the east. My family had been moving to another village with about twenty other people when the Home Defense Army picked us up. They didn't have the stomach to shoot us, and I don't think they knew what else to do with us. Things were falling apart so much by then, anyway. And by the time we got to Jasenovac everything was crazy there, too."

They were seated in Lia DiFlorio's dining room. As soon as Vlado had filled Torello in on the rough details of her disclosure, they'd agreed to take a short break, partly because she insisted that they have something to eat before another word was spoken. She needed fuel if she was going to talk about those days, she told them, and said they would need it, too.

Vlado doubted he'd have an appetite, but once they sat down before the platters piled with noodles and sauces, his stomach reminded him that he'd missed lunch. By the time Lia returned to her story, he'd finished the better part of the meal.

"They'd sent most of the women off to labor camps, in Germany and Austria," she said. "Slave labor in munitions factories. The ones who were still around knew all about it. But now the Partisans were coming. The Russians, too. The trains had stopped running north, and no one was going anywhere. So only the killing was left. They were going as fast as they could, especially with the men. They would take them out in the morning and shoot them, beat them, stab them, butcher them like pigs. Toss them in a hole or just throw them into the river. At night they burned the bodies in big piles. I'm sorry,

I know you are eating, but if you want to hear the story, I will have to tell it my way."

Vlado nodded, transfixed. He'd put down his fork and hadn't touched his food for several minutes. Torello, not understanding the language, watched blandly as he swallowed another bite of pasta.

"I could see some of it from the corner of the compound. Before, in our village, we'd always heard these things were happening, but I don't think any of us had really believed it. They'd taken some Slovenians earlier to Rab Island, a camp the Germans ran offshore. Nobody was sure what had happened to them, so this was all new to me, and I will never forget what it looked like. If I'd stayed there much longer, I'm not sure I ever would have recovered."

She seemed to retreat for a moment into her thoughts, and Vlado wondered what images were playing out in her head.

"She's telling me about life in the camp," he told Torello in English. "Her family was there the last month of the war." Torello nodded, still chewing.

"Some of the guards were pretty new, too," Lia continued. "They seemed almost as scared as us. Josip was one of them."

So here we go, Vlado thought, steeling himself for the worst while hoping for the best.

"He was in charge of the women in my group. About a hundred of us. He would march us out to the fields where we were helping with the planting. It was April, and some of the farmers had asked for hands. But every day we were watching the horizon, the roads to the west, to see if the armies might be coming. There were all sorts of rumors, so of course we were all hoping we'd be rescued."

"What were his duties?"

"Josip's?"

"Yes."

"Giving us orders, mostly. Keeping track of us. Most of the time it was nothing complicated. Just telling us to march. Halt. Keep moving. Count off. That kind of thing. But on the very first morning I saw him looking at me, and I could tell he thought I was pretty. And so I encouraged that, trying to look back at him the same way. Not because I thought he was any different from the rest of them—I would have killed him if I could have—but because I needed to feel like I was doing something to survive. Anything, even if it was just flirting with a guard. Because every morning they made him pick out three or four of us to be sent with a detachment to the river, and all of us knew what happened there. The ones who left never came back, and once the planting was finished we knew they wouldn't need *any* of us. So we tried to work as slowly as we could."

"He had to choose?" Vlado asked, gripping the edge of the table.

"Yes," she said. "He would do it quickly, without thinking too much. He'd pick some of the older ones, or the ones who were coughing, or sick. We all hated him for it, of course. He was the most powerful man in our lives. The moment he pointed his finger at you, you were dead. Our executioner. So I kept smiling at him, all that I could. Little smiles, so the other women wouldn't notice. For all I knew there were others doing the same. But so many of them were just skin and bones by then. I was nineteen, and healthy, and wanted to be the last one on his list. He would always pretend he hadn't noticed, but I knew he had. And then, later, of course, I forgave him everything. After what happened on the last day. When he helped us escape."

Vlado's heart leaped. He tightened his grip on the table, feeling that a dam was bursting. Steady, now. "He . . . he helped you escape?"

Even Torello seemed to sense something momentous in the air, because he had gently placed his fork on his plate and was watching them both intently.

"Yes. He and some of the other guards, the newer ones. It was a few weeks later, and we knew the Partisans were closer because you could hear the shooting, all day long now. The guns and the Russian artillery. Sometimes we'd see a plane, flying low, Russian markings on the wings. But the killing went on. They were almost in a frenzy about it by then. Finally one morning there was a riot. In the men's section. Everyone knew that freedom was so close but that the killing might come quicker, so some of the men rushed the guards, then the shooting started. The reaction on our side was immediate. Suddenly everyone was running, and all the guards were shooting. Except ours. It was strange. I think we had the only group that didn't fire. They shouted at us instead. 'Run!' they said. 'Toward the back! Run! We'll cut the wires.' And like idiots we listened, because for all we knew it was a trick. A way to shoot us in the back. But we ran, and they came with us, and cut the wires, and when we were through the opening they were still with us. There must have been six guards in all, and they seemed as desperate to get away as we were.

"Not everybody made it, of course. The other guards saw us and fired. There was some shooting back and forth and everybody running. I think only twenty of us got clear, maybe a few more. And only two of the guards. Josip and another. A guy named Dario who looked about fifteen. We'd all hated him, too. But now he was running like everybody else."

"What about the rest of your family?"

"They were killed." She said it without changing her tone, but her eyes were looking straight at Vlado. "My mother made it through the fence, but she was shot. I saw her on the ground behind me. I didn't look back again. My father must not have made it out. Later I heard that the Partisans arrived after another two days, but he must have been dead by then. I don't know if he died that morning or not, but I never saw him again. It was a miracle, really, that any of us lived."

"Where did you go?"

"We were walking for three days. Going north and, later, east. We wanted to get away from the fighting. Josip got rid of his uniform, his papers, but he kept his gun. By then we knew he wasn't going to hurt us, but I think he wondered if we might do something to him. After a few days there were just six of us left. The others had gone in other directions, trying to get back to their villages. Some were Slovenians, but most were Bosnians. Two weeks later we crossed the border into Italy. Half starved, but we made it. Some British soldiers picked us up and put us on trucks. A week later we were in a DP camp, in Fermo."

"Why didn't you go home?"

"There was nothing left to go back to. Our village had been burned and my family was dead. My brothers were off in the war—I didn't know where—and we hadn't heard from them for more than a year. I thought about going to Ljubljana, to look for an aunt, but I didn't know what the situation was there, and I was too afraid to travel alone. And by then I was with Josip. I know it sounds insane. Being with your guard. But he had freed us, too. And he'd looked out for me on the road. By the time we got to the DP camp we were traveling as husband and wife, not because I was in love with him, but because things went easier for you if you were married, part of a couple. If you were unattached, they might leave you in the camp forever. With a husband you were resettled sooner. And Josip was worried they'd find out he'd been working at the camp. As long as I was with him, no one would be suspicious. But it was because of Josip that I met Rudec, or Matek, as he was already calling himself. The one who later called himself Barzini."

"At Fermo?"

"Yes. He was from Josip's village, a little place in Herzegovina, and they saw each other in the mess hall. Josip told me Matek had been at Jasenovac earlier—he didn't want to tell me much about what he'd done—but that he had been transferred to Zagreb not long before my family arrived."

Of course, Vlado thought. How else would Matek have ended up in the convoy going north with all that gold? The clever opportunist had found the easiest way out once again.

And it was Matek who engineered their way out of Fermo, too, Lia told him, a clever way of keeping Iskric indebted to him, she believed. The first thing he did was get travel documents for all three of them, shedding his old name of Rudec in the process.

"He never said how he'd done it. He just showed up one morning at our barracks with all the papers and told us to make sure and attend a mass that Sunday to meet a Father Draganovic, who would take care of us."

After that, she said, things moved quickly.

"We went to Rome next. Josip wanted to go back to Yugoslavia, but Matek always had some plan, some scheme, and he always knew how to make Josip do as he said. And one morning Matek showed up with more papers for us. Passports from the Red Cross. He said we were moving here, to Castellammare. So now I was Lia DiFlorio. Before I had been Lea Breza. Lea with an *e*. Josip was now Giuseppe, and Matek was Piro Barzini. I didn't know what it was all about, of course. I just knew that by then I was in love with Josip and wanted to be where he was. So we came here, and for fifteen years we were happy, even though we were never able to have children. Or as happy as you could be, I guess, knowing that you still couldn't go home, or that at any time someone might find out who you really were. And there was always Matek, too, of course, who still had his plans and his schemes. Right up until the night when they left in a boat. He said they would be gone only a few hours. But they never came back."

"In 1961?" Vlado asked. Lia looked at him sharply, as if wondering how he knew the year. Very soon he'd have to tell his own story, and he wondered how to best break the news to this old woman with the shimmering eyes. He realized now that she'd probably never heard the name Enver Petric, that Matek and his father must have kept that identity a secret all along.

"Yes, 1961," she said warily. "On a clear night with a calm sea. The authorities concluded they'd drowned, but no one ever found their bodies. There was only the boat, which washed up later. But by then"—she shrugged, as if spent—"I had nowhere else to go, so I stayed. But I've always wondered if they really died. If they ever really went into the boat at all. And now I have a feeling I'm going to find out. And that the news isn't going to be very happy. Is that right?"

She gazed imploringly at Vlado, who wanted to spare her feelings yet knew he couldn't. He also had already given her an answer of sorts, because his eyes, too, were shimmering now. The woman had given him a tale of redemption that he hadn't thought was possible, but all he could offer in return was the knowledge of a betrayal. He took a deep breath, her eyes still on him. Then he began—slowly, deliberately.

"There are three things you should know first. One is that Pero Matek is still alive, and may well be here. Right down the mountain, in Castellammare di Stabia."

She took it without flinching, as if she'd expected no less.

"The second thing is that Josip Iskric lived until 1983. He reached Yugoslavia that year, probably after Matek gave him no choice but to return, and also to keep quiet about it. They crossed the Adriatic, and he became Enver Petric, and he settled near Sarajevo.

"The third thing . . ." Vlado paused, feeling short of breath, as if there was hardly enough air left in the room for the three of them. "The third thing is that I am Enver Petric's son, his only child."

Lia placed a hand on her heart, seeming to falter. But her eyes were again dry. She rose unsteadily from her chair, stepping toward Vlado, who realized that he had already stood to receive her. Placing her hands on his shoulders, she looked into his eyes, then slowly embraced him, tentatively at first, then tightly. Vlado hugged back, feeling an odd mix of emotions. She wasn't his mother, but she was something almost like it, the only thing close to a relative he had left from his father's side, except Aunt Melania. He felt her sob against him, a quiver that shook his breastbone, and he reacted as if that had been some sort of signal, finally letting go. A tight ball of heat seemed to melt in his chest, and his tears fell, released from the brimming pools in his eyes. Torello, still seated, wiped his mouth with a napkin and coughed, looking off toward the other end of the room. There was no sound now but Lia's light gasping, like a weary swimmer who had just come up for air.

After a few moments she released him, backing away unsteadily. Vlado slowly dropped his arms to his sides, his shirtfront damp. She dipped a napkin into a glass of water and dabbed at her splotchy face, then at his, her wrinkled hands moving tenderly, almost in a caress.

"How much longer did you say he lived?" she asked, her voice steady now.

"Until 1983. I was nineteen when he died, the same age as you when you went to the camps." She nodded. "I only found the picture a few days ago," he said, gesturing toward the black-and-white photo on the table. "My father had given it to his sister a long time ago, when I was a boy. My mother, as far as I know, never saw it. She died a few years ago. But I didn't really know who you were until now. This evening."

She nodded again, either too upset or stupefied to say a word.

Torello cleared his throat. "I would assume," he said in a low voice in English, "that the truth has come out about your father."

"Yes. And now I suppose we need to somehow start asking the meat of the questions. Not that I'm inclined to do it."

"Then we'll use that method they have in the American cop movies," he said softly. "Good cop, bad cop. I'll ask the intrusive stuff, the prying questions. She'll expect me to be that way, anyway. You can fill me in on what she's told you, then rest awhile. You look like you need it as much as she does."

"Okay," Vlado said, sitting back down, drained, yet also transported by a new lightness. He looked at Lia, who smiled, and he smiled back.

Bad cop or not, Torello handled it well, Vlado thought, if one could judge such things merely by tone or pacing. But it was also clear that Lia DiFlorio—or should he think of her as Lea Breza now, or even Lea Iskric?—said few words in response to most of his questions, and ten minutes later Torello told him they knew little more than when they'd arrived, especially with regard to any crates that Matek or Vlado's father might have brought with them to the town. They had traveled to Castellammare separately, she said, with Matek and Josip going a few days ahead of her, by truck. She had gone by train, a slow and halting journey that had taken days.

Neither Josip nor Pero—Vlado still couldn't think of them as DiFlorio and Barzini—had ever mentioned anything they'd brought from Rome, or any hiding place where they might have stashed valuables, and she knew of no place Matek might go if he were to return. Matek's wife, Gianna, had died years ago.

Did Vlado believe her? He wasn't sure. But he still felt, somehow, that she would help them, in her way, if she could.

After Torello brought Vlado up to speed on his last round of questions, everyone lapsed into an exhausted silence. The two men lit cigarettes, and Lia leaned over to pull one from Vlado's pack.

"I quit years ago, but tonight I can't help it," she said.

"So, where is my father's grave?" Vlado asked, figuring it might be worth a visit. Even knowing it was empty, it seemed a fitting memorial to the part of his father's life he'd never known.

"Not far down the hillside. I still go there to think about things. To talk to him about what I've been doing. It's very peaceful there. Or has been. But now . . ." She shrugged weakly, her voice trailing off. "If I'd had the money, I would have bought him a *cappella*, a big place I could really visit. But the money, there just wasn't enough."

"Excuse me," Torello said, perking up. "Did she say something about a *cappella*?"

"Yes," Vlado said. "It's some kind of grave?"

"A vault, in fact. A family burial chapel. Which would make it a perfect hiding place. Did she say that Matek—or Barzini—bought one?"

"No. She'd wanted to buy one for my father, but she couldn't afford one. All she could manage was just a plot and a headstone, and she didn't buy them until after Matek and my father went missing, so the timing is all wrong."

"Yes, you're right. I'm getting too tired." Torello frowned, the light gone out of his eyes.

"Was he asking about a *cappella*?" Lia said to Vlado, who was beginning to feel like an international mediator, all of this back-and-forth in two languages while the others spoke a third one between themselves.

"He thought if Matek had bought one for his family then he might have stored the crates there."

"But he did buy one," she said, with a sudden light in her eyes. "For his son."

Vlado slowly put his cigarette down on the edge of his dinner plate, wondering if he'd heard her correctly. "Matek had a son?"

"Yes. But he died very young. Influenza. So Matek went out and bought him a big *cappella*. Way too big for any infant, but that was Matek. He liked to make big gestures, to show off. It's in the same cemetery as Josip's grave. So, do you really think that—"

"I don't know," Vlado said. "I don't know if even Matek could actually do such a thing. Use his own boy's tomb as some kind of hiding place?"

Lia nodded firmly. "Yes. The Pero Matek I knew would do it." Vlado turned toward Torello to translate, but Lia stopped him. "No," she said, holding up a hand, which only served to pique Torello's interest. "I don't want them knowing. Not the local authorities. Please."

"What's she upset about?" Torello asked. "What's she saying?"

Vlado looked back at her, her eyes imploring, still moist, and he nodded slightly, as if to say "It's okay." Who knew why she was acting this way, but he'd go along with it for now. He owed her at least that much.

"She's worried about Matek," Vlado told Torello, trying to think fast. "She's worried he'll come up here. Try to hide here, or make her help him."

"Not likely," Torello said dismissively, "but I can have someone keep an eye on the place if it will make her feel better."

"Tell her, then."

Torello spoke, and Lia seemed to calm down, glancing toward Vlado with a return nod that said "Thank you." Then, switching back to their native tongue, she hurriedly told Vlado the directions to the cemetery. It was on the way back into town, she said, only a ten-minute drive, marked by a large stone arch at the entrance. But the better route—shorter, quicker, and more direct—was on foot, directly downhill through the trees on a narrow path that began just across the highway. Five minutes at the most.

She imparted the information without once using the word *cappella*, or any other obvious phrasing that might have alerted Torello. Then she told Vlado that Matek's spot was in the northeast corner, only a few rows from the headstone marking the empty grave for Vlado's father.

It was about then that Torello's pager went off, and he excused himself to phone his office from the car.

"I'll be right out," Vlado told him. "I think we're pretty much finished anyway."

But once Torello had gone Vlado placed both his hands on Lia's, grasping them as he rose to his feet. "I have to go," he said. "But I hope to be back."

She nodded. "Matek's *cappella* will be the only one without flowers," she said. "I don't think anyone has visited it since the boy's mother died. She wanted nothing to do with me after the men disappeared. I don't think her time with Pero was very happy. And remember, it will say 'Barzini.'"

They were at the doorstep now. He could see Torello at the wheel, talking on the phone with the dome light on. As Vlado turned to say good-bye, Lia placed a hand on his face, pressing it lightly, almost as if she were a medium, trying to detect some remnant of his father's soul or touch.

"I am tired," she said. "Talking about those times always wears me out. But this time, more than ever." Then, almost timidly, she asked, "Did you say that his name was Enver after he went back to Yugoslavia?"

"Yes. Enver Petric."

She smiled, lowering her gaze, dropping her hand to her side. "He was definitely not an Enver. Only a Josip. A Giuseppe, even. But Enver? He must have felt ashamed every time he said it."

"I wouldn't know," Vlado said, at a loss for words.

She looked up, reddening. "But maybe that changed when you were born. Having a son would have made being an Enver worth it, don't you think?"

"I hope so," he said, shrugging, smiling sheepishly.

"You're a father, yes?"

"Yes. My daughter is nine." And his smile broadened as he thought of Sonja, wondering what she'd make of all this.

"You wouldn't care what she called you. Any name she chose would seem right, wouldn't it?"

"Yes. It would."

"Good, then."

That seemed to give her a measure of peace, and she again placed a hand on his cheek, leaving it for a few seconds. Vlado felt the roughness of the wrinkled skin, but also the warmth. Out of the corner of his eye he saw Torello, now standing in the open doorway of the car, raising his eyebrows as if to ask "Well?"

"I should go," Vlado said.

"Let me know what you find," she said. "Promise me that. And when you do, then I may have something more to tell you."

It seemed to be all she wanted to say on the subject just now, so Vlado resisted the urge to ask for more. Then they said good-bye, and he and Torello climbed into the car for the long drive back down the hill, on the narrow road that disappeared into the clouds.

CHAPTER TWENTY-NINE

"That was my dispatcher," Torello said as Vlado got into the car. "There's been a murder at a pension in town. They think the victim is Andric. Healthy male in his fifties carrying three different passports. Face matches the photo from Interpol. Not much to see down below, though. Two shots at close range, large caliber, probably with a silencer."

So it was true, then, their whole theory about why Matek and Andric might both be drawn to the town. And now the younger and stronger competitor had fallen, leaving the way clear for Matek. Meaning Vlado had better get moving, even if he knew of only one place to look. He'd feel better having Torello with him, even if Lia had been insistent about not telling local police. He doubted she wanted him risking his neck.

But Torello apparently wasn't available anyway. "I'm heading there now," he said. "It's down near the port, not far from the office."

"It's probably best if I don't arrive at the scene with you," Vlado said, making it up as he went along. "Considering as how I'm not even supposed to be here. But you should alert Pine. Have your dispatcher call him at the hotel. Then I can find out through him, and meet you at the scene."

"Suit yourself. But I can't waste time dropping you at the hotel. I'll have to let you out on the way."

"Good enough."

A few minutes later they reached the outskirts of the town, sinking back into the clouds. In the bright blur of a streetlamp, Vlado saw a stone arch on the left, just as Lia had described it. "Drop me here. Just remember to tell Pine."

"Farther along would be better, a lot closer."

"Here is fine. I'll get a cab."

"Whatever you say." Torello sounded puzzled, perhaps a little miffed. The streets here were empty, and it was obvious that finding a cab would take a while. But he was in too much of a hurry to ask anything more, so he let Vlado out the door with a frown and nod, roaring away after a quick "See you there."

As the car's red taillights disappeared around a curve with a squeal of tires, Vlado walked quickly toward the arch, hoping he wasn't too late. The nearby shops were closed. The only sign of life was a small café, but even it was dimly lit, and the few customers had been chased indoors by the clammy weather.

No one was in sight as he entered, which Vlado took as a good sign. Scanning the ground quickly, he saw no tire marks. He doubted you'd be able to haul much out of here without a truck. Or maybe he was at the wrong place altogether. There were hundreds of likely hiding places, from ancient Roman catacombs to caves higher in the hills. Then there was always the possibility that Matek had simply dug his own hole, a place where no one but him would know to look. Although something about the rocky soil made that seem unlikely. Matek struck him as the type who'd cut a corner whenever possible. And what easier way to do so than stealing your son's tomb?

Just inside the cemetery walls was a small stone house, probably the caretaker's. But as Vlado approached the door he again confronted the language barrier. If the man didn't speak English, Vlado would only arouse suspicion, arriving with frantic gestures and no escort. No one seemed to be home anyway. The windows were dark, and the place was silent. Vlado checked his watch. It was just after nine. Too early to be home for the night if you lived in a cemetery. Vlado crept along quietly nonetheless, heading for what seemed to be a wooden maintenance shed just to the rear. It was surrounded by a high chain-link fence, padlocked at the front, but the fencing was old and loose enough that Vlado could pull back the gate just enough to squeeze inside.

Opening the door, he flicked his cigarette lighter. Two push mowers were parked cheek to jowl with a jumble of shovels, rakes, and hoes. On a rough wooden shelf were more tools. One was a long, heavy crowbar. Vlado took it. There were also two battered flashlights. He tried the first, finding the batteries were dead, but the second one worked. Slipping back outside, he paused to make sure the house was still quiet before continuing. No sound but a few passing cars out on the street. The northeast corner, Lia had said. Vlado oriented himself by facing downhill, toward the Bay of Naples, which was to the north. He angled off to the front and right, waiting about thirty yards before turning on the flashlight, his pants already wet from the dewy grass, the crowbar cold and heavy in his left hand.

He would have felt better with some backup, and for a moment he thought of heading back to the street, trying to reach Pine before Torello did. But it was probably already too late for that, and his curiosity was stronger. Besides, all was quiet. Anyone loading up crates or gold bars would be making one hell of a racket.

He made his way downhill past a long white aisle of tombstones toward the far side of the lot. There, off to his right and about a hundred yards from the entrance, was a wall of the *cappelle*, sloping downward like a miniature block of apartments, abutting a crease in the hill. Each was like a tiny chapel of granite or marble, with names and dates chiseled in slabs next to the door. The newer ones had smoked-glass doors, and as the flashlight winked past, he glimpsed bouquets of flowers and the greenery of plants. There were also flowers out front in brass vases. These were little temples of the dead, where the bereaved could step inside, sheltered from the noise and the elements.

Lia was right. There were flowers outside every *cappella* but one, which was about twenty yards down the row. Vlado swung the flashlight to see the name BARZINI engraved in stone. This one had a steel door, heavy-looking and rusty at the edges. The boy's name had been Carlo. The dates said 1951–1952. A year old at the most.

The lock looked substantial, hardly a surprise. But there was just enough room to poke the teeth of the crowbar between the door and the jamb, and five minutes of prying and grunting, the metal groaning, finally brought the door free with a metallic shriek and a loud snap, like a small gunshot.

Vlado checked behind him before entering, swinging the beam of the flashlight across the tombstones but seeing nothing. There was still only the noise of traffic, fainter from here, a few cars and trucks grinding their way up the rolling streets.

Pulling back the door, he shined the light through the opening, then stepped inside, amazed at the spaciousness. His footsteps resonated as if he'd entered a cave. No flowers in here, either. Nothing, in fact, but a damp smell like wet concrete. Somehow it all felt familiar, and Vlado remembered the *Fahrerbunker* from his last day on the job in Berlin. The thought made him a little weak in the knees, then a breeze outside began to shut the door behind him, and for a few panicky seconds he envisioned being locked inside. But with the lock sprung that was impossible, of course, and he chided himself, smiling, trying to relax. The door was so fouled by his jimmying that it merely tapped and bounced in the frame before finally coming to rest, a few inches ajar.

Resuming his inspection by flashlight, he saw granite ledges running lengthwise on both sides, presumably to be used as benches. The main attraction sat in the middle of the floor, a large stone tomb, about four feet high, three feet wide, and more than six feet long. Much too big for an infant. Big enough, in fact, for a large man. Or plenty of other things.

The lid was a slab of marble, the name engraved on top. Vlado ran his fingers beneath the overhanging edges. It looked heavy enough but didn't seem sealed in any way. He gave a test lift with one hand, but it didn't budge. Then he placed the flashlight on the ledge and grunted, pulling up with both hands, lifting the slab a few inches and sliding it over, just a fraction. It would be difficult but not impossible. Before getting started he took a final inventory, listening carefully for noises outside. Still quiet.

Lifting with all his might, he began swiveling one end of the slab slowly toward the ledge behind him. It began to ease free with a gritty, grinding sound, as warmer air from inside the tomb curled up around his fingers, an eerie tickling sensation. He hoped there wasn't a child's body inside, no matter what else he found.

He shuffled sideways a few feet, still holding one end, his shoes scuffing on the grit. Then he lowered the lid as gently as possible onto the ledge before stepping to the other end to repeat the trick, finishing with the lid balanced lengthwise on one of the bench ledges, nearly half of it overhanging precariously. With the flashlight resting low on the other side of the room, the inside of the tomb remained deep in shadow. Vlado was sweating and could feel the strain in his arms and shoulders. But now came the moment of truth.

He stepped to the other side, retrieving the flashlight, then pointed the beam inside. The sight was electrifying: two planked wooden boxes, nailed shut, with recessed metal handles folded down on two sides. The black stenciled lettering on top was in Vlado's language. STATE BANK OF CROATIA. There was no coffin. No body.

He felt for a moment like an exultant pirate. He wanted to shout, to pound someone on the back and roar with laughter. He hadn't felt this giddy in quite a while, but now it was more important than ever to remain quiet. The crates were nailed shut. He'd need the crowbar again, and he'd left it in the grass outside the door.

Pushing open the door he felt the fresh, wet air on his face. It was still quiet out here. Then the brightness of a flashlight beam exploded into his face, blinding him for a second, and before he could move another step he saw two dark silhouettes loom up suddenly from either side. A hand clamped across his right arm, and he heard a metallic click, letting him know his visitors were armed, followed by a voice, speaking in English.

"Nice of you to get us started." Harkness again. "And how convenient to find you literally at death's door, which is where you've been heading all along. Step back inside it, please. So I can conclude my business and get the hell out of here."

Vlado turned, and the other man swiveled the light. Vlado could now see that it was Matek, saying nothing. Even in the darkness something about him seemed different. Harkness held the gun. Before stepping through the door Vlado considered bolting—anything but going back in there at gunpoint. But the nudge of a barrel in his back convinced him otherwise. A strong smell emanated from Matek. Sweat and effort and worry. Blood, too. The man was breathing hard, a rasping that said he'd had a rough time.

"C'mon, now. Inside." Another shove with the barrel. "Keep your hands behind your back, where I can see them."

Back inside, their voices were now hollow, stony.

"If you would empty your pockets, slowly please, and carefully place the contents onto the floor. Particularly any firearms you might have."

Vlado had nothing with him but a pencil, a few scraps of paper, and some coins, but when this was all he produced, Harkness poked his own hand in to make sure.

"Nice of the tribunal to send you into the world so well prepared," he said. "I can't tell you how much it pains me to see you here, Vlado. Just as headstrong and meddlesome as advertised. But you've at least earned yourself a look, I suppose. Besides, I need your help."

"Sorry. It's not what I'm paid for."

"Fine. Then I'll shoot you. Your choice, family man. Just let me know when you've made up your mind."

Vlado had been telling himself for the past few seconds that Harkness wouldn't do him actual harm; that the man might be ruthless and manipulative but wasn't a killer. Now he knew otherwise, and should have all along. He looked again for an opening, any chance to kick or lunge, but Harkness was keeping himself cleverly beyond range, and seemed as alert as ever. Gun raised. Pointed right at him.

Matek, on the other hand, still hadn't opened his mouth, and Vlado now got a good look at him. His expression was glum, defeated, a countenance suggesting that this was anything but a willing partnership.

"Pero, why don't you lean in and pry the top loose on that first crate. Vlado, back away, and put your hands on your head. Move an inch and you'll have a very ugly hole in your chest. Faster, Pero, and no tricks. You've already seen where that leads."

As Matek bent over with a wheezing grunt, Vlado saw a dark, wet stain under his left armpit. Harkness saw Vlado looking.

"Don't worry about him. Tried to pull a knife on me, so I had to set him straight. Nothing fatal. He's still pouting about having to share."

That was a laugh. As if Harkness would really go through with such an arrangement. Vlado figured Matek would be killed the moment they got clear of here. He wondered if Matek realized that as well. Perhaps the old man was also hoping for an opening, a final chance. If so, then it would be two against one, if only for a moment.

Matek merely grunted in reply but seemed to recover some of his energy as he glared at Harkness, covetously eyeing the gun. Then he began working at the lid of the first box, using the crowbar Vlado had appropriated.

"Just pry it open on one side," Harkness ordered. "We're nailing it shut as soon as we've seen what's in there."

The wood snapped free, and even Matek couldn't keep from gasping, though he'd doubtless known what was inside. The flashlight beam glinted off neatly stacked gold bars that rose nearly to the brim, a dazzling color in this darkness.

"Just as advertised," Harkness said. Then he poked a hand inside, as if feeling for something that might be wedged at the sides. He came up empty. "All right. Shove that lid back on. We'll nail it in a minute. Next one, please."

Matek, still without a word, worked painstakingly at the second lid. Harkness was transfixed, and Vlado slowly began to lower his hands from behind his head. One inch. Then another. Then another. Harkness looked up quickly, swiveling the gun, the barrel coming to rest a few feet from his chest. The pitch of his voice rose by an octave. "Next time you do that, you're dead. No more testing."

The nails of the second crate screeched and groaned, and the lid hinged open. But the sight this time was a shock, even if Matek didn't act a bit surprised. The box was nearly empty. No more than a few rows of gold bars were stacked at the bottom.

"Jesus Christ, Pero, you profligate old bastard. What'd you do, spend fifteen years trying to corner the local market in *Limoncello*?" But Harkness sounded more amused than upset. He was more interested in a fat, dog-eared brown envelope wedged upright to one side.

He pulled out the envelope, the papers practically spilling from one end. It looked like a hundred or more pages. So there it was, Vlado thought, more fascinated than he had been by the gold. Somewhere in that pile, most likely, were the documents that had changed his father's life. That had, in their way, helped bring him into this world, he supposed. And now they might well usher him out.

"It's what you should have given us from the beginning, you welshing old thief." Harkness put down the flashlight a moment, still aiming the gun with his other hand. Then he pushed the envelope against his overcoat, folding it lengthwise in a one-handed motion before stuffing it into a wide pocket. "Now, gentlemen. Time for the real work. Pero, go and get the truck."

Unbelievably, Matek did just that, disappearing for several minutes before Vlado heard the roaring engine as the truck poked in through the cemetery gates and began crawling across the lot. Only his greed could have kept him going like this, Vlado thought. Almost any other man would have simply driven down the mountain and gotten out of there. Either Matek actually believed Harkness would split the take, or else he still held out hope of outsmarting the man, as if he held one last trick in reserve. Or perhaps it was simply the fatal hubris of a man who'd never yet been outfoxed.

Vlado, who'd waited in silence up until now, decided to get straight to the heart of the matter. "Tell me," he said to Harkness. "Are you going to kill me when we're done?"

"Just keep making yourself useful and stay quiet, Vlado. You know I'm not the sloppy type. But you want to know the real shame in this? I wouldn't even be here now if it weren't for you. Popovic was supposed to be here, doing the dirty work. But you went and spoiled that, didn't you. Then Matek slipped the leash and everything went to hell. Though it's funny how things have a way of working out. Here you are, handy for the heavy lifting, while Matek has already accommodated me by taking care of the worst of the chores."

"By killing Andric, you mean."

Harkness seemed momentarily taken aback. Then he recovered, forcing a smile. "So, they've found the body, then, and already made an ID. Impressive." His voice wasn't so smug now, and he glanced down at his watch. "Which branch of police?"

Nice to know there were a few things he hadn't found out about, such as Torello, for example. No sense telling him now. Vlado merely shrugged.

"Not the carabinieri, I hope, or they'll be here with armor. All the more reason to work quickly."

Matek had completed the drive up the grassy service road, coming up the lane of *cappelle* before stopping just short of the entrance. As he opened the door, Vlado could see the cemetery entrance, but the caretaker's hut was still dark and quiet.

"Get in here, Pero. There isn't much time." Harkness was all business now. No more joking. "Get a grip on that first crate now, both of you. Use both hands. Drop it and you're dead. Take a hand off before I say so and you're dead."

They bent into the tomb, gripping metal handles on either side of the box, then they groaned and heaved, pulling upward. Matek obviously was having the tougher time, and for a moment as they looked across the top of the crate their eyes locked, and something seemed to pass between them, if only a shared recognition of their misery. Anything else was unreadable, and the moment passed. They had the first crate nearly out, and as soon as it had cleared the top of the tomb they began scuffling toward the door. The handles were burning into Vlado's hands, but he didn't dare remove a hand now.

"Good. Keep it moving. Steady. Just push slowly through the door and watch your step."

They were back into the night air, a relief from the claustrophobia of the *cappella*. Still no noise but the hiss and grind of light traffic. Vlado darted a glance to either side, nearly losing his footing.

"Keep your mind on your work," Harkness barked. "You're not going anywhere without a bullet in the back. And don't think you can rouse the caretaker. He's having a fine time drinking down in the town, courtesy of the U.S. Treasury."

With another heave, they shoved the crate into the back of a small truck with a canvas cover. It was unmarked, not from any of the agencies Vlado and Pine had checked earlier in the day. They slid the crate back a few feet, then turned toward the *cappella*. Harkness was a good ten feet away. If Vlado was going to make a move, now was the time.

"All right, back inside. And to answer your earlier question, Vlado, no, I'm not going to shoot you. So breathe easy."

A ruse? Probably, but it had the desired effect, giving Vlado just enough hope to keep him from trying anything stupid, like running, or rushing Harkness. He and Matek between them could possibly overpower the man, but the one who made the first move would pay the price, and neither wanted to give his life for the other.

They loaded the second crate, then Matek shut the gate of the truck.

"Back inside again," Harkness said, following them into the *cappella*.

"Vlado, turn around and face the back wall, then slowly bring your hands down behind your back. Good. Pero, take this." Vlado heard Harkness pulling something from his coat, wishing all the while that he'd taken his chances outside. His moment of uncertainty had cost him. "Wire his hands together."

Matek worked slowly, the wire pinching into Vlado's wrists. He was making sure the fit was tight. So much for expecting help from the old man, or any sort of teamwork. Now it was too late for any move, and despairingly he realized he'd been tricked, just enough. His stomach sank toward his bowels, and he flashed on an image of Jasmina and Sonja, silhouetted in a brightly lit doorway, slowly waving good-bye.

"Now turn around slowly and step into the tomb," Harkness commanded. "C'mon now."

It was awkward doing it with his hands behind his back, but Vlado just managed.

"Pero, step away, and don't move. Vlado, get down on your knees."

"You said you weren't going to kill me." His voice was shaking. He hated himself for it, for doing as he was told, for asking these stupid and frightened questions. All those people trooping like lambs into the death camps. He'd have done exactly the same, fooled to the end, thinking he was helping his family.

"I say a lot of things I don't mean, Vlado. It's all part of diplomacy."

Here I am, Vlado thought, the pain and chill of the tomb's stone floor drilling into his knees. He'd helped Harkness keep things neat by lowering himself into a place where his blood would pool in the blackness and he would be sealed for eternity, a hermetic disposal with the witting assistance of the victim. So, as Harkness eased the gun forward, Vlado decided on a final move, no matter how futile.

"Pero, please step back," Harkness ordered.

His words were nearly drowned out by the roar of an engine. A flicker of headlights darted through the opening in the door.

"Pero, see what the hell it is," he said tersely. "If it's the goddamned caretaker, he's going in there with Vlado."

Matek pulled the door wide while Harkness glanced over his shoulder. Vlado inched forward on his knees, but Harkness swung the barrel back in his face, no more than a foot away. "Hold still!" he hissed. "Pero, who is it?"

"Two cars. Coming this way."

"Fuck!" Harkness glanced away again, and this time Vlado was close enough to lunge, trying awkwardly to strike like a snake, rising from his knees and bending at the waist while pressing his soles against the rear of the tomb for leverage. His head butted Harkness in the thighs, teeth against the wool of the overcoat, but the impact wasn't enough to knock him down. Harkness stumbled then turned, his face enraged, the black barrel again in place as he tilted his head slightly as if to aim. He squeezed the trigger with a blinding flash just as an arm fell on the gun from the side—Matek, seizing his moment. A dart of flame creased Vlado's left cheek, and he felt the sting of splintering marble against his forehead as the slug crackled and bounced through the echoing roar, as if someone had tossed a lightning bolt into the *cappella*. Harkness twisted the gun free from Matek's grip and shoved through the door, bursting into the cemetery like a horse from its stable, coattails flying.

"Fermare! Polizia!" a voice shouted on a loudspeaker. Vlado's ears were still ringing from the gunshot. Headlight beams were swinging wildly in their direction now, and he threw himself across the low wall of the tomb, then clambered awkwardly to his feet, his adrenaline on full throttle, though his hands were still bound painfully at his back. Out the door he noticed Matek off to one side in the shadows. Twenty yards to the left a dark shape bobbed among the tombstones, on the outer edges of the headlight beams.

"Fermare! Fermare!" the loudspeaker cried again, but Vlado had already ducked out of the blinding glare and was running after Harkness, head forward for balance with his arms behind him. He sensed dark figures somewhere to his left and rear, coming after them. The grass was slippery, and he nearly lost his balance, clipping a foot on the edge of a low-lying marker. Harkness was barely visible now, but Vlado could still see the gun in one hand. The man was in good shape, but being younger helped, and Harkness stumbled slightly as he, too, caught his foot on some low-lying stone. He must have heard Vlado huffing closer, because he glanced over his shoulder, his pale face flashing in the dimness. The voices of the police seemed to be receding. They must have been closing in on the truck, perhaps chasing down Matek or preoccupied by the *cappella*.

They were now on a rising slope, Vlado surging at an odd angle, barely keeping his balance but now within ten yards, driven forward by his anger. He saw Harkness pause, then turn, the gun out-stretched, so he swerved wildly, stumbling to the right as the muzzle flashed, accompanied by a boom echoing into the hills. He dove toward Harkness's ankles as he lost his balance completely, knowing that the next round would likely be from too close to miss. He felt the man's legs buckling beneath his chest as he collapsed, still lunging forward. They hit the wet ground hard, and Vlado felt his breath taken away. He scrambled up the body in an awkward crawl, hands still behind his back, Harkness groping for something, perhaps the gun. Vlado flinched at a second flash, but this one was much smaller, and he saw that Harkness had pulled out a cigarette lighter and was stretching it toward the edge of the old brown envelope, which lay just beyond him in the grass. The flame lit the scene with an amber glow, showing the whites of the man's eyes, rolled forward toward his target. The corner of the envelope was just catching fire as Vlado crawled toward it. Harkness squirmed beneath him, reaching far enough to grasp the envelope and flick it forward a foot. But the motion blew out the flame, and as the spinning envelope came to rest Vlado fell in a heap, his chest collapsing atop Harkness's head. The smoke from the envelope was musty in his nostrils.

"You goddamned fool!" Harkness's shout was muffled beneath Vlado's stomach, his enraged mouth moving against the buttons of his shirtfront as he thrashed like a buried animal trying to burrow back to the surface. Vlado rolled off, looking around quickly for the gun but not finding it.

"Vlado!" another voice shouted from behind. It was Pine, moving toward them from twenty yards away.

"Over here! I've got Harkness."

"I have a gun," Pine said. "So no sudden movements."

Vlado sat up slowly while Harkness remained prone, panting heavily and cursing beneath his breath. Pine knelt on the ground, picking something up.

"There," Pine said. "Now I really do have a gun. Must be his. Get up slowly, both of you. And if you think I won't shoot you, Harkness, think again."

"You're damned fools, both of you, if you think this is the right thing to do. You especially, Pine."

Pine ignored him. "You all right, Vlado? Is that blood on your face?"

"Just a graze. I'll be fine if you can get this wire off my wrists. Where's Matek?"

"He's here?"

"You didn't see him?"

"No. The cops are all in a lather back there over the crates. Your buddy Torello found them in the truck."

"Matek's wounded. He may not have gone far."

"You better go tell the others. I'll take care of this one. Here, turn around and let me get that wire. Harkness, don't move."

Harkness was still on the ground, spent. A policeman was running toward them through the tombstones, and Pine was happy to let him clip the wire off Vlado, who rubbed his wrists, his arms aching, then walked quickly toward the *cappella*. Vlado found two more policemen by the truck; one was Torello.

"We found a deed to the *cappella* in Andric's room," he said. "I figured we'd better hurry over. But I didn't think we'd find you here." There was a slight note of betrayal in his voice, but Vlado had bigger worries just now.

"Where is the other man?" he asked hurriedly.

"Your colleague, Mr. Pine?"

"The other suspect. Matek."

"I haven't seen anyone. Just you and that other American." He gestured toward Harkness, making his way across the cemetery with Pine and the policeman behind him. They were single file, striding as slowly and carefully as pallbearers.

Vlado checked inside the *cappella*, but found only another policeman poking around the tomb. Just outside the door he picked up Harkness's flashlight. It was still on, and he swung the beam in a wide arc into the distance. Nothing. All this, and Matek had again slipped away, a survivor for the ages. Vlado was sick with disappointment. He'd at least been able to save the documents, stuffing the envelope into a pocket of his overcoat. But where was Matek? He couldn't have gone far in the shape he was in, but if he'd reached the road, he could have hailed a cab.

Vlado moved past a row of graves, peering into the darkness but seeing only stone angels, marble vaults, and slabs of marble. Nothing living, and nothing stirring. Then the afterburn of his adrenaline brought him sagging atop one of the headstones. He turned off the flashlight, pondering his next move, wondering how late the trains ran.

One of the police cars restarted its engine. They were probably eager to spread the word about the gold. By dawn the whole place would be crazed, and it would be harder than ever to get anyone to look for Matek. But for now they could at least alert the train station and the taxi dispatchers. Vlado rose wearily to his feet in the dark. It would again become a slow, painstaking manhunt, one he probably wouldn't be allowed to join.

The police car began moving, and as it swerved the beam of its headlights swept past Vlado, illuminating the grounds before him like a searchlight. In that brief moment a single name leaped at him from the facing row of tombstones: DIFLORIO.

CHAPTER THIRTY

Vlado turned his flashlight back on to make sure it hadn't been his imagination, and there it was. Blood rushed to his fingertips as he stepped toward the stone. On the other side he found the dates, a perfect match. *Giuseppe*, the inscription began, and he roughly deciphered the rest as saying, *beloved husband of Lia*. Even though he knew that the grave beneath him was empty, Vlado was moved by the sight of the name. He crouched to place his fingers against the carved letters. Something of his father remained here—in this town, in these hills—no matter where his body reposed.

"So, tell me," Vlado whispered, this time half believing he'd get an answer. "Where has your old enemy gone?"

But the only response was the chatter of the scanner from the second Italian police car. Vlado looked over and saw two of the officers lighting cigarettes. One was already writing up the report, seated on the hood of the car. Vlado reached into a pocket for his own smokes, feeling his nerves begin to calm. But as he shifted his flashlight he saw something else—two red droplets on the grass, shining up at him from a few feet past the headstone. The hair stood up on his forearms, and he bent down to touch. The drops were warm. Shining his flashlight, he saw that the grass had been disturbed. There was a rough path of smudged footprints through the dew, leading toward the low stone wall on the opposite side.

He stepped in that direction, soon finding another scatter of red droplets, then another, until the smudged footprints reached a small opening in the wall, where a narrow path rose steeply uphill through the trees.

Only a five-minute walk, he remembered Lia saying, and as he began to climb, a patchwork of images and observations began to take shape with a sudden coherence—the old photo of Lia and his father, showing a ladder propped against a tree near a small ring of stones; Matek's careful brooding silence at the *cappella*; the emptiness of the second crate. Last, there was Lia DiFlorio, only an hour earlier, and the way she'd first reacted to the photo, then her adamant insistence that Torello not be told of the *cappella*. But come see her afterward, she'd said, and she would tell Vlado something more. With every step he took, the meaning seemed clearer, and Vlado quickened his pace even as he heard Pine's voice from behind him, well down the hill, plaintively calling, "Vlado! Vlado!" like a parent who has lost track of a wayward child. The sound soon faded, and within minutes there was only the night chirp of a few bugs, the snapping of twigs beneath his feet, a swish of branches overhead as he forded his way upward. The air was cooler here, the moisture clinging to the trees. Above the canopy, only starlight. He was again above the clouds.

The path reached the highway, and across the road was Lia's house, set against the hill. The lights were off. Vlado worked his way around to the left, where he'd earlier seen the citrus trees. He spotted another droplet of Matek's blood. Harkness had insisted he'd done the man no real damage, but Vlado wondered.

He moved slowly now, looking carefully for places where the dew and the grass were smudged or trampled. He passed the house well to the left of the chimney, then eased back into trees, picking up another path, this one fainter, but stained here and there by the telltale droplets. A minute or so later Vlado found himself in a grove of lemon trees, and he thought again of the photograph as the path emerged into a small clearing. With the view before him now, everything fell into place, even in the dim starlight. There was the same bluff as in the photo, the same ring of white stones. Before he had assumed the stones were for a campfire, but he had revised that assessment on his way up the hill, and now he saw with certainty that they formed the rim of an old well. Poking just above it now were the top few feet of a long wooden ladder—the same style as the one in the photo. Vlado paused, listening carefully, and heard a tiny scraping sound, like that of a mouse gnawing at a baseboard. It came from inside the well, which surely was dry, and had been for at least fifty years.

Vlado stepped carefully to the rim and peered down. Some twenty-five feet below, illuminated by a flashlight, was the gray head of Pero Matek. He was stooped like an old troll, hunched over his coveted possessions.

"Looking for the last of your nest egg?" Vlado shouted.

Matek lurched in surprise, then picked up the flashlight and shined it upward, momentarily blinding Vlado, who squinted but held his ground. For a moment the old man said nothing, then he began to chuckle, a tired wheezing laugh. "I was right," Matek said. "Just like your goddamned father. You never know when to let it go."

"Tell me, then. Was part of his share down there? Or were you the only one who knew about this place?"

"*His* share?" The wheezing laugh again. "His share was my agreement not to turn him in, plus the occasional handout. I got nervous leaving everything down in the *cappella*. Always having to visit it whenever I needed to make a withdrawal. Those old women with their flowers do a lot of gossiping. So I gradually moved half of it up here. And now there's enough for both of us. Here, I'll show you."

Matek bent over, then straightened up holding a gun, not gold. Vlado jerked his head back just as the shot echoed up the stone shaft like a blast of artillery. Now, where the hell had that come from? One of the police cars, probably. Stolen in all the confusion as the old man had slinked away in the shadows, one last trick in his bag. But the shot had missed, and Vlado now knew that he held a momentary advantage. Taking care to keep himself beyond the narrow cylinder of Matek's line of fire, he grabbed the top rung of the ladder, which was angled just out of harm's way. He gave a great tug, and by the time Matek realized what was happening Vlado had raised the ladder several feet. He heard the gun and flashlight clatter against the stones before feeling the ladder tug back. It felt as if he'd just hooked a huge fish on a large, unwieldy pole, and for a moment his grip wavered as Matek pulled back, gravity and leverage on his side. Then Vlado, no longer worried about the gun, stepped forward to brace his foot on the stone ledge, and pulled with all his might. There was a grunt, then a sharp cry of pain echoing from below, and Vlado nearly lost his balance as the ladder came free. Then he awkwardly raised it, one rung at a time, until the whole thing teetered awkwardly above him and he let it tumble harmlessly onto the grass.

He sagged back onto the wet ground, exhausted. Then he was startled by the sound of a voice, a woman's, coming from the darkness of the trees. "It's him, isn't it?" the voice said. "It's Pero, down in the well."

Vlado turned to see Lia DiFlorio standing in a long bathrobe at the edge of the path, her breath vaporing into the night. "Yes, it's him. But don't look down there. He has a gun."

"I know. I heard it. That's what brought me outside."

"Sorry to wake you."

"Oh, I was awake already. Far too stirred up to sleep tonight." She smiled just a bit, then the smile widened, and she broke into a satisfied laugh. "How nice to see him playing the fool for a change," she said. "Especially when there's been nothing down there to claim for years."

"Because you took it, didn't you," Vlado said, with just the slightest hint of scolding, to let her know she should have told him earlier. "I wouldn't have told Torello, you know. You're probably entitled, after all you went through."

"I'm sorry. But I was afraid. That gold paid for this house. Your father and I had barely been able to pay the rent before."

"Do you still have any?"

"Not much. But more than enough for me to live on. I don't spend it quickly. And Pero had already gone through a lot of it by the time they left. Which is one reason I never knew there was more than one place. I thought he'd put everything up here, until tonight."

"So, where is it now, the gold from the well? And when did you take it out?"

"In the house. Somewhere safe. I moved it about ten years ago. I was getting too old to keep climbing that ladder. Then, when you came and showed me that picture, I didn't know what to think. I was scared that you must have known about everything. But once you told me you were Josip's son, I wasn't so worried."

They were silent a moment, as if sorting out their thoughts. There was again the sound of digging from inside the well, and a band of light from the opening waggled back and forth, the old man again bending to the false promise of treasure. Matek obviously hadn't been able to hear their conversation.

"There's nothing there anymore," Vlado shouted, easing toward the rim. "Lia took all of it."

"Lia never knew it was down here," Matek grunted stubbornly, still digging.

"Josip told me," she said. "In a note he left me, the day the two of you disappeared."

With that, the digging stopped. No one said a word. Matek hadn't heard that voice in nearly forty years, and it had silenced him as surely as a ghost might have. Vlado sagged back on his haunches, trousers soaked by the dew. He took a cool, deep breath of the night air and looked back toward Lia, trying to read the look on her face, but there wasn't enough light.

Their silence was broken by voices and footsteps approaching along the path.

"Probably the police," Vlado said. "They must have heard the gunshot." Then he turned toward Lia, straining again to see her face. "Don't worry. I'll never tell. And him they won't believe. It's the only secret still worth keeping in this whole mess."

CHAPTER THIRTY-ONE

By late the next day, three nations and two local jurisdictions were fighting over custody of the gold bars found inside the Barzini *cappella*. Italy was first to lay claim, followed in quick succession by Croatia and the Federal Republic of Yugoslavia. Envoys from Rome, Zagreb, and Belgrade were en route, but they would have to contend first with the municipal officials of Castellammare di Stabia, who'd gotten the jump on everyone by moving the crate into the vault of a local bank. They'd done so over the strenuous protests of late-arriving officials from the Naples regional authority. By sundown even the *polizia di stato* were mulling a counterclaim, seeing as how nothing of value would even have been discovered if not for the independent actions of one of their officers, who, as they were emphatic in pointing out, had risked his life in the line of duty.

Italy's afternoon tabloids had already laid odds that the fight would go on for years, and with each hour another TV-crew van arrived down the Autostrada. Swiss officials, meanwhile, had begun quietly inquiring whether there was yet any reason they should be either embarrassed or indignant.

Lost somewhat in this hurly-burly was the fact that a major war-crimes suspect had been killed a few blocks away, and that another, more obscure figure, wanted on charges from actions a half century earlier, had been apprehended. And that an indignant American diplomat appeared to be in hot water.

And so it was, in the spate of interviews and interrogations and official paperwork that followed, that Vlado didn't see Pine until nearly noon of the next day, finally running into him in the hotel lobby, where they agreed to share a meal. Their flights back to The

Hague had been rescheduled. But the verdict on whether they were to be applauded or excoriated on their return apparently remained a work in progress, with Spratt and Contreras still monitoring prevailing winds from Washington, Paris, and London. Janet Ecker remained on administrative leave.

"Well," Pine said, as they seated themselves, "the early word is that Matek won't fight extradition."

"To Croatia?"

"Yes. He's convinced he can beat the rap. He's apparently already been on the phone to his attorneys and his Swiss bankers. Seems to think that if he can get a running start, there just might be enough sentiment in his favor to keep him free, especially with a trial in Zagreb. Who knows, maybe he's right."

"Maybe," Vlado said. "But he might be surprised. The Croatians may decide to make him an example. He offers the perfect chance for national atonement. And in the end, he wasn't even a good fascist, just a thief who stole from everyone, the Ustasha included."

"Which reminds me. The Croatians may want you to testify. If only to help establish provenance on some of the documents."

"The documents," Vlado said, shaking his head with a frown. "Now, if only I still had them."

It was the one aspect of the previous night Vlado was still glum about. He'd handed them over to Torello around midnight. Within an hour, outside forces intervened, and Torello regretfully informed him that the envelope and all its contents were being forwarded "upstairs," somehow having become part of the equation in the fight over the gold. Torello surmised that a swap was in the works: U.S. backing of an Italian claim in exchange for return of printed material, which, by all rights, was legally the property of the U.S. Army, never mind what the priests at San Girolamo would have once said about that argument.

"I never should have handed them over," Vlado said. "It's the same old story."

"I wouldn't be so sure," Pine said, and he slid a fresh manila envelope across the table.

"That's your set of copies. I've got one for myself. Torello slipped them to me around three in the morning, right after you'd gone back to the hotel. He was able to steal a few minutes at the copy machine just before sending the originals upstairs. I haven't had much time to look, but the little I've seen was interesting reading. Letterheads from Angleton, Colleton, the Vatican. Plenty of people to be embarrassed. And I did see your father's name once or twice about halfway through the pile, so I think you'll be pleased."

"What will you do with yours?"

"I've already done it. Faxed the entire load to Janet's apartment. She's got some time on her hands now, as well as a few axes to grind. She assures me that by the end of the week she'll have sent copies to three congressmen on the House Intelligence Committee, the attorney general's resident Nazi hunters, plus a fully annotated set to a friend of hers at the *New York Times*. So much for enduring secrecy, huh?"

Vlado felt like laughing out loud, like dancing on the tabletop. It had been a wrenching and emotional week, but this was the perfect finish. "So, what does this mean for Harkness? Criminal charges?"

"Doubtful," Pine said, smiling ruefully. "He's already gone back to the U.S. embassy in Rome. For all I know he's left the country altogether. Taking a few shots at you probably made it a little tricky. But he missed, fortunately for both of you. The only person he actually hurt was Matek. That was apparently the argument from the U.S. side, and, given his connections plus the fact that he didn't make off with a penny, it was enough. The police are keeping his name out of it, and the press only seems interested in the gold. If anybody's going to be able to make a stink, it's LeBlanc."

"Where's he?"

"Chasing false leads in Berlin, last I heard. Apparently he knew Harkness was up to something, but couldn't figure out what. Who knows whether he knew about all the stuff buried here. But you can bet he'd like to have a look at these papers, too."

"So Harkness gets off free, then?"

Pine shrugged. "His career will suffer. That's something, I guess. He'd hitched his wagon to Colleton's, and they'll both be watching the wheels come off during the next few weeks. But chances are he'll get a nice settlement. Probably a new life, somewhere warm."

"A lot better deal than Robert Fordham ever got."

Pine nodded grimly. "I called the hospital again this morning," he said. "They said he passed away a little after midnight. I'm trying to get Torello to ask for an autopsy. But even then they probably wouldn't find an injection mark. Too easy to hide if you know what you're doing." Pine lowered his voice. "One other thing you should know, for what it's worth. Torello told me Harkness was making some noise last night about you and Popovic in Berlin. Don't ask me how he knew, but I'd assume this won't be the last you'll hear of it. Sorry."

"It's okay," Vlado said. "I've decided to make a full report on all that."

"What do you mean?"

"A sworn statement to the police in Berlin. About what happened with Haris and his friend. What I did. Where the body is. They need to know."

"Why? Why are you doing this?"

"Because I need to."

"What, to confess? Then tell a priest."

"No. Someone from my family needed to come clean."

Pine grimaced, shaking his head. "So it's for your father, then. 'Bless me, for he has sinned, and so have I.' I guess some of the Catholicism really did rub off."

"No. It's for my own peace of mind. And because it's right. My father got his chance at redemption on the last day at Jasenovac, and he seized it. Lia DiFlorio is proof of that. For me there's no life to save, just a story to tell. And when I realized yesterday the way Harkness was using it against me, I knew I'd be under that kind of pressure for the rest of my life."

"Well, still not too late to change your mind, you know."

"It is, actually. I spoke this morning with a police lieutenant in Berlin."

For a moment Pine was speechless. Then he said, speaking slowly, "I'll do what I can for you, of course. I've got some contacts in German law enforcement. A few, anyway. And the tribunal certainly owes you and your family. Everything may yet work out."

"It already has," Vlado said, surer than ever that he was right.

Epilogue

Berlin wore gray for Vlado's homecoming. But for once he didn't mind as his plane descended through successive veils of cloud. Even the maddening flatness didn't seem to register as the jet circled low, searching the dimness of a winter afternoon for the landing strip at Tegel.

The authorities, by previous agreement, weren't waiting for him. So far the Berlin police had bent over backward not to seem jackbooted or Prussian. The lieutenant who'd telephoned Vlado in Italy had chatted with the bland, reasonable manner of a TV host arranging a panel on the euro as they'd discussed the likelihood of whether Vlado would remain a free man.

"It helps immensely that you came forward," the officer said in crisp English. "Given that you didn't actually participate in the homicide, and given as well the circumstances of the victim's past, most factors weigh in your favor. Though we'll of course have to verify your account with the two primary suspects."

No problems there. Haris and Huso had been only too happy to turn themselves over to international authorities in Sarajevo once the word went out, having spent the preceding days dodging undesirables from the Belgrade underworld.

Pine had done his part. He knew a German on the tribunal who was a friend of a friend of the chief inspector for homicide. Two phone calls later, everyone felt better, rebalancing a scale that might otherwise have tipped unfairly against an uprooted Bosnian.

So it was that Vlado received the welcome that he had missed five years earlier. Properly alerted this time, Jasmina unearthed a dress she hadn't worn since just before the war, to a wedding in '91. Sonja wore her one and only party dress, already a size too small, but that only made it more affecting for Vlado, who took it as a sign his little girl was growing up too fast.

They were waiting just outside the security entrance at his gate, and he emerged into a joyous implosion of Balkan shouts and grasping arms. They exchanged the usual phrases that can never stretch large enough to enfold such moments.

"It's so good to have you back."

"Good to be back."

"Did you catch them all, Daddy?"

"Yes, Sonja. I'm all finished with that now."

Then they drove home in a borrowed car—an Opel, not a Yugo—Sonja chattering as if someone had been winding her spring all morning. Were there really windmills in Holland? Had he eaten much spaghetti? Was there still an emperor with rows of centurions? She squealed with delight when Vlado gave her a small box of Vesuvian stones, which he'd discovered at an airport gift shop in the nick of time.

They burst into their apartment on a wave of cooking smells and the fragrance of cut flowers. The memory of his dreary arrival five years earlier vanished in the steam of roast lamb and warm dumplings, and as they ate their way through the celebratory feast the wine blossomed like a benediction in Vlado's weary head.

Yet, when it came time to tell the stories—the ones he knew he must tell of his father, of Lia, of old wars and old sorrows that inevitably gave way to new ones—he felt strangely claustrophobic. It all seemed lodged in his throat like some bite too immense to swallow. And for a moment he felt the crush of those earlier years—alone in a siege with too much to think about and no one to tell it to, his trapped words going stagnant.

Jasmina, seeming to read his thoughts, rose quickly from her chair. For a bizarre moment he thought she was going to slap him sharply on the back, as if he were choking. Instead she darted to a side table, an eagerness in her eyes.

"I meant to tell you," she said brightly, reaching for something. "This came for you this morning."

It was a small white envelope, stuffed plump as a great ravioli, the right side plastered with Italian stamps postmarked in Castellammare di Stabia. The handwriting was small and careful. He gently tore it open to find a short note:

> *Dear Vlado,*
>
> *There is much more for us to know about each other, and many memories to share about the man we both loved. Bring your wife and your daughter. My home was his, and now it is yours.*
>
> *Love,*
> *Lea*

She'd spelled her name the Slovenian way, he noticed, and she'd enclosed a stack of seven black-and-white snapshots. New prints from old negatives, it seemed, made just for them. They were shots of his father, young and smiling, some with Lea, some with others; but none, he saw with relief, with Matek.

Then, proudly, as if he'd just drawn a winning hand at poker, Vlado fanned the photos before him on the tablecloth. Eyes shining, he looked to Jasmina, then Sonja, both cocking their heads as if they had a thousand new questions.

"Sonja," he said. "Did you know that you had a . . ." What should he call her? "A stepgrandmother in Italy. On the seashore. She's been a secret, all these years, but someday we might visit her, all of us."

His audience was hooked, and Vlado was certain that now it would all come easily, even the darker chapters to be told later, on this thrilling night when he had at last come home.

ACKNOWLEDGMENTS

I owe a great deal to a great many for helping me complete this book.

Thanks to Tom Hundley, valued colleague and friend, for the germ of an idea that evolved into an important subplot, as well as for his hospitality to my family during our stay in Rome. Thanks as well to William Gowen, for sharing hours of vivid memories of his days as a U.S. Army counterintelligence officer in postwar Italy.

Greatly assisting my historical research were Ron Neitzke, former historian for the U.S. Department of State, and distinguished Croatian historian Jere Jareb, who directed me to a wealth of old memos, reports, and diplomatic cables on the subjects of looted Croatian gold and the escape of dictator Ante Pavelic, not to mention Dr. Jareb's harrowing personal memories of Croatia during the final days of World War II. Thanks also to authors John Loftus and Mark Aarons, whose book *Unholy Trinity* offered valuable perspective on the postwar ratline of Father Draganovic.

In preparing to write, and also during my work in Europe as a journalist, I had the pleasure and privilege of meeting in The Hague at various times with more than a dozen prosecutors and investigators for the International Criminal Tribunal for the former Yugoslavia. Perhaps nowhere on earth will you find a more tireless, selfless, and idealistic bunch. All accurate characterization of tribunal operations should be credited to their contributions, and the brief paragraph from a tribunal indictment glimpsed by Vlado Petric in the fourth chapter is excerpted from the "Jelisic and Cesic" indictment of July 1995. Any discrepancies or false notes concerning the tribunal—this is a work of fiction, after all—are my responsibility alone.

In Berlin, thanks to friend and journalist Anja Kolaschnik, for help in meeting Bosnian refugees in the city, and to Amir Kahvedzic and Boslijka Schedlich, for sharing their experiences and observations on the refugee life. In Sarajevo, Lejla Gotovusa, Emir Salihovic, and others offered valuable insights on the city's postwar state of mind.

For guiding me beyond the choppy seas of the first draft, profuse thanks to my agent and first line of defense, Jane Chelius; to brilliant colleague and friend Scott Shane; and to Soho Press editor Juris Jurjevics, who owed me nothing but helped anyway. Many thanks also to editors Jenny Minton in New York and Selina Walker in London, for deftly lighting the way to completion.

As always, I reserve my greatest thanks for my wife, Liz Bowie, for love, encouragement, and support.

ALSO BY DAN FESPERMAN

"Far more than just a murder mystery, Lie in the Dark *is a moody, at times dire evocation . . . of one honorable man's dogged attempts to find truth and reason within a most unreasonable, hellish landscape."*
—Dennis Lehane, author of *Prayers for Rain*

LIE IN THE DARK

Vlado Petric is a homicide investigator in war-battered Sarajevo, and he's suffering from malaise. His wife and daughter have been in Berlin for two years. He has little heat or food. It's been quiet at the bureau. Even the body he encounters in "sniper alley" on his way home from work one night seems little reason for pause, until he realizes it is the body of Esmir Vitas, chief of the interior ministry's special police, and that Vitas has been killed not by a sniper but by a bullet fired at close range. Inspector Petric's investigation eventually unearths "the transfer file," the heart of an international ring reaching back to World War II, and whose commodity "in value, stature, and scope" goes unfathomly beyond anything he could have imagined. Dan Fesperman, a journalist who has reported from a number of war zones, has written a masterful thriller that travels through the brutal and almost surreal mileau of the wartime black market.

Crime Fiction/0-375-70767-0